THE

BLACK

LEDGER

D.G. ALLEN

Copy Editor – Rachel Phillips

Cover art © Vivid Covers | www.VividCovers.com

If interested in learning more about *The Black Ledger*
or the author D.G. Allen, please visit my website:

donallenblackledger.com

Facebook: Don Allen

Twitter: TheDGAllen

Acknowledgements:

To my darling Sarah: You have worked tirelessly over the last ten years researching and compiling every facet of this novel and its production. I know you share the love of this project, and I can state unequivocally that without you, *The Black Ledger* would never be.

I would like to thank my family—Kelly, Dave, Lauren, Elise, Eric, Melanie, John, and Mindy—for listening to my rantings for the last forty years. You have never failed to support my passion for someday becoming a writer.

To my lifelong friend Dave: I love and miss you.

To John: Since high school, you have been my inspiration. Your superpower is courage in the face of adversity. I'm blessed to call you friend.

To Karen: It's easy to ascribe something to a miracle from God, but meeting you out of nowhere in a musical celebrating the life and times of Jesus, and then to have you support the efforts to revitalize this book, has truly been a miracle for me. Thank you.

D.G. ALLEN

The Black Ledger

is dedicated with love to

Lizzie Malcolm and Lucretia Lee

THE BLACK LEDGER

D.G. ALLEN

CHAPTER 1

Friday, July 3rd, 1981 — Evening

My very essence was drowning in sorrow, ravaged by guilt and tormented with the knowledge that I must suffer in silence and alone. It had been about eight hours since I discovered the news of the murders, but it felt like an eternity by the time I made it home that afternoon. I wasn't the same man that woke up that morning, and I knew it. Something inside me broke, and beneath the fabric of my own consciousness brewed a simmering caldron of anger that was near the boiling point.

Maybe I was delusional, but I finally understood what Ol' Man Wicks meant when he said the black ledger was a place that "promises everything but gives you nothing." To my mind, the ledger was no longer some evil myth or legend made up by crazy old men to scare new agents. I now believed it was a sinister force with an intelligence of its own that planned, plotted, and manipulated the lives of people for its unholy pleasure.

We were nothing more than actors, baited with promises and encouraged with hope to perform for the amusement of evil embodied in the despair around us. With the patience of Job, the black ledger contrived a wicked plot reminiscent of some twisted fairy tale in which we were seduced into participating. Complete with the evil mother who betrays her son, to the beautiful princess trapped in bondage, waiting to be freed by her knight in shining armor. *We played our parts perfectly,* I thought to myself as I opened the door and stepped inside my apartment.

"It's about time," my wife Jessica said with disgust. She barely threw me a glance, then stopped what she was doing and did a double take at the dark circles around my eyes and lack of color in my face. "Jesus, are you getting sick? Because the last thing we need around here is another cold with the baby just getting over the last one."

"No, no. I don't know. Maybe," I grumbled, trying to shut the door with my ledger book in one hand, briefcase in the other, while Rudy kept lunging at me from behind. "Stop it! Stop it, Rudy! Go lay down!" I shouted with anger at the rambunctious animal.

"He just misses you, Ron," she quipped as I finally managed to shut the door. I dropped my stuff on the floor and headed straight for the recliner without even pretending I was interested in the obligatory husband-wife kiss. A moment later, Jessica was hovering over me, hands on hips, while tapping a foot as if disgusted by something else.

"What now?" I asked in annoyance.

"Well, my mom's got the baby, and she's coming to pick me up in a few minutes. Did you cash your check?"

"Ah, no, shit, I completely forgot. I have it here," I said, digging in my back pocket and retrieving the check from my wallet.

"Goddamn it, Ronnie! Do I have to do everything around here?" she moaned while grabbing the check from my hand and disappearing into the bedroom. I closed my eyes, praying she'd be gone by the time I opened them, to no avail. A moment later, she popped out of the bedroom and marched into the front room. "Oh, and that's another thing. Are you in some kind of trouble at work or something?" she asked with folded arms.

2

"No. What ever gave you that idea?" I asked with a dry throat.

"Well, people from your job have been calling all day."

"Who?"

"Mr. Meadows called twice, and your manager, Roger Hamilton, called earlier in the day. Oh, and that sleazy agent you don't like called as well," she said as an afterthought.

"Teddy Lobranski called?"

"Yeah, their numbers are on the table. What's going on?" she asked.

"Probably has to do with a death claim we got earlier today," I said with a dismissive tone.

"So, why is everyone calling you?" she asked suspiciously.

"Because some people on my ledger were killed, and I needed help with the insurance claim. They're just being kind and returning my calls," I said with exasperation.

"Well, someone is grouchy today," she said before heading back into the bedroom. A short time later, her mother pulled up outside and beeped the horn. Jessie hurried past me then stopped by the door and turned with her patented anguished expression.

"Aren't you even coming out to the car to see your daughter?" she asked, baiting me for a reaction.

"Jessie, not that you care, but you should know I've had a really tough day. Do you think you could be civil for a change?" I asked without expression.

"It's always about you, isn't it, Ron? Not that you CARE, but we're going shopping and then over to my sister's house. So, we won't be back until late, if at all," she said, slamming the door behind her. I sat back in the recliner and closed my eyes at the pure joy of being alone. I was completely exhausted and didn't want to move a muscle. My clothes stank from smoke and sweat, and my mouth felt like a smoldering cigarette butt that had been snuffed out with coffee in an ashtray. The solace she left behind was almost heavenly, and, within moments, I closed my eyes and fell into a deep, dreamless sleep.

I woke up a couple of hours later and stumbled over Rudy trying to get into the kitchen for something to eat. The pickings were slim, but a couple of pieces of cheese and a few stale slices of bread toasted up and lathered with mayonnaise were enough for a feast. Rudy stood by patiently, figuring that I would make amends for pushing him away earlier and toss him a morsel of food. I willingly obliged and tossed him the last piece of cheese, then plopped down at the kitchen table with my sandwiches and a bottle of Coke, feeling as if the world had caved in around me.

As I munched away, I noticed the phone numbers Jessie had written down and pulled the list in front of me for a closer look. I figured both Hamilton and Meadows were checking in to see how I was doing, but I couldn't figure out why Teddy Lobranski would call. Curiosity got the better of me, so I reached over, picked up the phone, and dialed his number.

"Yeah?" was the response on the other end.

"Teddy?"

"Pickles, is this you?" he asked.

"Yeah, my wife said you called earlier."

"Yeah, man, I heard what happened on your ledger today. A couple of your clients got killed, aye?"

"Who told you?" I asked defensively at the idea that my business was already the subject of office gossip.

"It's cool, man. The big guy," he replied at my tone.

"Hamilton! What the fuck? Is he walking around telling everyone my business or what?"

"Hey, Pickles, come on. It ain't like that. I was in the office and overheard him talking with Irene about the murder and the size of the claim, that's all. Shit, man, a kid and all. Tough break, you know;" he said.

"Yeah, tough break," I said with a sigh at his fake concern. "So, what did you want, Teddy?"

"Well, hey, I was wondering, um, you remember what we talked about before, right?"

"Not really, Teddy," I said with exasperation.

"You know, man. These fucking niggers," he said with an emphatic tone, as if his derogatory words should jog my memory. "Shit, man, do I got to spell it out for you? You know this kind of claim can do a lot for you," he said. Suddenly, a loud banging came from the front door, and I told Teddy to hang on a minute.

"Who is it?" I shouted from the kitchen.

"It's your mother!" came the obnoxiously loud, slurred voice from the other side of the door.

"Jesus Christ, I don't fucking believe this," I lamented to myself as she banged on the door repeatedly. I took the phone away from my ear and pursed my lips in anger. *First, this son of a bitch wanting to scam a death claim, and now my mother banging on the door at the start of her Friday night crawl,* I thought to myself. "You know what, Teddy? There is no claim because I lapsed the insurance for nonpayment, so nobody's going to get fucking paid, get it?!" I shouted into the phone.

"Oh, fucking drag," he cried out.

"Yeah, fucking drag. I gotta go," I said, hanging up the phone and jogging to the front door. I pulled the door open so hard it slipped out of my hand and sailed into the wall, ricocheting hard into my shoulder. "What the hell do you want, Mom?!" I shouted in her face. She was so drunk she could barely stand, much less speak, but she managed to say her piece, nonetheless.

"I just came to tell you that your wife hates you and wants a divorce because you are a fucking assssss hoooleeee," she said, emphasizing and dragging out the word "asshole" as if it were stuck like peanut butter to the roof of her mouth.

"Well, if this don't just cap my fucking day," I said, grinning at her pathetic sight while wondering what in the world I did to deserve this.

"Well, you may think it's funny now, but we'll see how funny you think it is when you're working two jobs and paying child support to that whore while she's out screwing someone else. How's that going to feel, Ronnie? Huh? 'Cause that's what's going to happen," she continued.

"Are you finished?" I asked with civility.

"You're the one that's finished," she said, turning around and stumbling back into her apartment. My head was pounding so hard I could barely stand up. I shut the apartment door, then turned and flung my back against it, sliding down to the floor while cradling my head with tears streaming down my face. I had never felt so alone in my entire life. I couldn't tell anyone what happened, not my friends or my family—certainly not my wife or my mother. What a pathetic human being she had become. "We should have never moved into this fucking building," I mumbled to myself while struggling to my feet and making my way to the bathroom to splash some cold water on my face.

I leaned on the sink and stared at myself in the mirror. I was numb. My thoughts were racing a million miles per minute. I knew in my heart that I really didn't do anything wrong, yet I was to blame. It was my fault. It was worse than my fault because I could have done something, or should have done something, and now I was this focal point of anger, distrust, misery, and apathy.

After a few moments, I collected myself and lumbered back into the front room, collapsing into the recliner. I was too tired to sleep and just wanted to think. I needed to think. I needed to regroup and figure out what the hell I was doing. I was in such a fog, I actually felt detached from my body.

As if guided by instinct, I spotted the television remote and began clicking it robotically, changing channels without any thought as to what I was doing. Suddenly, I stopped clicking, mesmerized by a commercial for Mutual of Omaha's insurance company that put me into a trance-like state of mind. My head began swaying from side to side, my eyelids felt heavy, and soon the images on the television blurred to black. I was too exhausted to sleep, too drained to stay awake—caught somewhere in between. Memories like television episodes began playing in my subconscious. They were forcing me to relive the last two years of my life and face the hellish nightmare I was embroiled in, all for the sake of a temporary job.

Chapter 2

October 1979

I had absolutely no idea what I was getting myself into after accepting Mr. Hamilton's invitation for an interview. I can still remember hanging up the phone, sitting down on the kitchen chair, and staring at the floor, thinking I was nuts. I knew this job was only supposed to hold me over until I got accepted into the electrician's union, but this was crazy. I didn't know anything about insurance, and I certainly didn't want to take the time to learn about it knowing I was going to be starting electrician's school. The only type of insurance I was remotely aware existed was auto insurance because I couldn't afford any and was paranoid about getting into a car accident without it. I seriously began to reconsider this idea of becoming an insurance agent and was about to call Mr. Hamilton back to tell him I had changed my mind when a wonderful memory from my childhood popped into my head, reminding me of the great things insurance could do for people but not animals.

The soothing voice of Marlin Perkins, the narrator from Mutual of Omaha's *Wild Kingdom* television show, came back to me like it was yesterday. I loved that show and couldn't wait for it to come on every week, except that it aired on Sunday evenings, which was always a bummer since I had to go back to school the next day. Nonetheless, it was a great show with Marlin telling a story about all the different types of animals living in the wild, struggling to survive. As the host, he would narrate while his sidekick, Jim Fowler, would wrestle with alligators or rescue baby lions from starvation because a poacher killed their parents. Then, during the commercial breaks, Marlin would always pitch the benefits of having insurance from Mutual of Omaha. I loved it when he would compare the fate of abandoned lion cubs left hopelessly wandering the African plains to a child who loses his parents in some horrendous accident.

He always made you feel like the child would grow up happy and healthy because the kid's parents were smart enough to provide Mutual of Omaha insurance for their family. The lion cubs, on the other hand, were doomed, and it was too bad for them that "in the wild, lions couldn't buy insurance from Mutual of Omaha." The memory inspired me, and the more I thought about it, the more I wanted to do it—at least until the union called.

I told my wife Jessica that we had to scrape up some money for new clothes because the Mutual of Omaha agents were always dressed in suits and ties on the show. We couldn't afford a lot, so instead of buying a complete suit, I settled for a light blue blazer and a black pair of pants. I wasn't happy about a distant relative passing away a few months earlier, but the nice long-sleeved white dress shirt I bought for the occasion was exactly what I needed to complement the suit. My old trusty Beatles boots were pretty scuffed up, but nothing like a little good old-fashioned elbow grease wouldn't fix. The problem was the tie. On the rare occasions I wore one, it was usually of the clip-on variety, and that seemed out of place for an important business interview. Since I never had much use for one, I never learned how to tie a real knot. Without hesitation, I decided it was time to grow up and wear a real man's tie. So, with a certain amount of bravado, I led Jessica to the men's department and picked out a manly blue and black striped tie to complete my ensemble.

From the store, we went right over to my sister Judy's house, figuring that because her husband, Tony, was a cop and wore a tie every day, he would be the perfect instructor to lead me into the fellowship of tie-wearing businessmen around the world. However, we quickly realized it was a mistake to seek Tony's help when he began to regale us with a completely irrelevant story from his childhood that lasted twenty minutes. It seems that his father taught him to tie a necktie when he was nine years old using a story of a snake wandering around the woods and wrapping himself up in a knot. Though Tony was now in his thirties, every morning he had to repeat the snake story while tying his knot, or he couldn't do it. After listening to Tony repeat the story of the snake wrapping itself around the tree, down the hole, through the cave, and back out the other side for the fifth time, I gave up and just had him tie a knot that I could slip over my head and save for my appointment.

Not only was my stomach churning the morning of my interview, but also my palms were sweaty, my heart was beating double time, and I couldn't seem to swallow. Jess kept telling me I was getting worked up over nothing, but I couldn't help it. The expectations in my brain were all related to the images of Mutual of Omaha and the *Wild Kingdom* show. I had convinced myself that it was a privilege to be invited to join such a noble field. It didn't matter that I wasn't actually applying for a job at Mutual of Omaha because I just assumed that all insurance companies did basically the same thing. I somehow pictured smiling, grateful families seated on the other side of my big desk in a fashionable office thanking me for protecting their loved ones from an uncertain future. It wasn't until weeks after they hired me at Unified Insurance and I was plodding up and down the streets of the ghetto, banging on doors and demanding money from poor people, that I realized that all insurance companies were not alike.

Unified Insurance Company had several district offices scattered around the city and suburbs. Roger Hamilton's district was located in Berwyn, a suburb just west of Chicago. It took me about forty-five minutes to drive there from our apartment in Blue Island, which was south of the city. I knew his office was on the fifth floor of a bank building, but I didn't realize that the bank was the only multi-story building in the suburb. With a deep breath and a nervous stomach, I got out of my car and marched into the building like a man with a purpose, hoping that no one would notice that my immediate purpose was to keep from throwing up. While riding the elevator to the fifth floor, I kept my nerve, telling myself if I got the job, it wouldn't be that bad because I only had to do it until the electrician's union called.

I braced myself as the door opened, and I was immediately assaulted by a chorus of men's voices shouting, yelling, and cheering wildly as if a featured dancer in a strip club had just removed her top. The jarring noise knocked me off balance, and I fell back against the wall, thinking that a hoard of people was about to force their way onto the elevator at any moment. Then it just stopped, and I stood frozen trying to figure out what was going on. The elevator doors began to close, and I was just able to squeeze my foot between them and force them back open. Carefully, I stepped out into the hallway, turning my head in all directions, in hopes of figuring out where the deafening sound came from, when all of a sudden it roared up to greet me again. For a moment, the bedlam would subside, then regenerate itself to a fever pitch. Figuring I must have gotten off on the wrong floor while self-absorbed in my own pity, I quickly turned and scanned the floor directory for my location. No, this was the fifth floor, and there was the suite number for Unified Insurance Company: 501. "Holy shit," I muttered under my breath as the hall reverberated again with thumping hoots and hollers that seemed to grow in intensity.

As if choreographed to accompany the excitement, a percussion of clapping, banging, and foot stomping shook the hallway floors in unison with the cheers. As I took a few steps in the direction of the bedlam, a feeling of dread overtook me as I realized the noise was coming from behind the door of Suite 501, Unified Insurance Company. In that instant, all the warm and fuzzy feelings I had about Mutual of Omaha, or insurance in general, were totally obliterated.

I stood outside the glass door to the reception area and took a moment to collect myself. Peeking inside, I was surprised to see an empty waiting room that belied the sounds of the on again, off again jamboree pounding the walls. It made sense that the commotion was coming from behind a set of large wooden double doors to the right of the room as you entered. To the left was a single door, presumably leading to other offices, while straight ahead was a cut-out wall with a sliding glass window and small counter. I could just make out the top of a woman's gray hair bobbing up and down behind the window. I took a deep breath and opened the door when suddenly the cavalcade of sound went silent, as if my breaking the seal on the door had turned off a switch to a sound system. I paused for a moment, confused by the sudden discontinuance of noise that filled the air just moments before. In that moment, another door located a few feet down the hallway burst open with a billow of cigarette smoke. Chains of men streamed out the door, clamoring and laughing as they strolled down the hallway towards a restroom sign.

With a deep breath, I opened the glass door and stepped inside the reception area. Without warning, the heavy wooden doors to the right blew open, and several men raced past me, excusing themselves as they spun me around trying to get out the door I had just entered. Reeling from the stampede, I heard someone call my name and turned to find an exceptionally well-dressed man heading toward me.

"Ron Pickles?" he asked, at first pointing his finger then holding out his hand to greet me. Surprised, I just nodded and automatically extended my hand. "I'm Roger Hamilton. Thank you for taking time out of your day to come in and see us," he said with an excited grin while literally crushing my hand in his. I didn't know what to expect from Roger Hamilton, but I was immediately taken aback by his presence and stature. He was exactly what I pictured a Mutual of Omaha insurance agent to look like. At six feet tall, his build wasn't just proportioned—it was perfect. He had style and walked with a fluency of a man at ease with his position and confident in his ability. His skin was smooth and tanned to a honey brown that brought out a glimmer in his dark brown eyes. His sandy brown hair was longer than normal but flipped to the left and brushed back perfectly, covering his ears. His face was handsome and masculine with a pronounced jaw and strong cheekbones. A hint of crow's feet at the edges of his eyes betrayed the look of a younger man but added a touch of character to a face that was almost embarrassingly good looking. When he extended his hand to greet me, the cuff on his starched white shirt extended just past his jacket sleeve to display a sparkle of elegance from the diamond-studded cufflinks he wore. The dark pinstripe suit he was wearing looked crisp and fresh, and his shoes shined as if they had just been taken out of a box. His voice was sharp and sure of itself yet comforting, and I instantly felt at ease and welcomed to be there.

"Mrs. Bolger, do we have the application for Mr. Pickles ready?" he asked, turning towards the window while dropping my hand.

"Right here," said an older woman's voice from the other side as a stack of papers seemed to magically appear on the windowsill. Mr. Hamilton took the papers and shuffled through them, scanning each page to make sure everything he wanted was there. Agents started shuffling back into the office, and a couple of them excused themselves as they cut in front of me to ask Mr. Hamilton to sign off on paperwork they were holding. He commanded attention without speaking, and everyone stood silent while he attended to their issues. He dispatched the others with lightning speed before turning back to me and apologizing for the interruption.

"I'm sorry, Ron. Tuesdays and Thursdays are settlement days, and it gets kind of crazy around here. Come on in the agents' office and fill out this application," he said, leading me through the big wooden doors. I was anxious to see what kind of workplace produced all the enthusiasm that echoed throughout the hallway. I was more than a little disappointed to find a working environment that more resembled a bookie parlor than an insurance office. A unique combination of stale cigarette smoke, a burning coffee pot, and the lingering odor of two dozen men crammed into a room the size of a grade school class set the tone for my lowering expectations.

The agents did have their own desks but not quite the handsome setup I had imagined. The tiny metal desks were more akin to something you might find in a mail clerk's room circa 1950. They were placed together in groups of seven that divided the room into four distinct sections. Each group had three desks on one side, three on the other, and one on the end. They were pushed together nose to nose so that the agents faced each other while they worked. The desk positioned at the end of each group faced the other six in what appeared to be an uncomfortably close situation. The tops of the desks were littered with ashtrays, coffee cups, and an array of the agents' personal effects. I was intrigued by the wide variety of ancient hand-cranked adding machines scattered across the desks, and I wondered if anyone had ever heard of Texas Instruments. I noticed the door at the back of the room and figured it had to be the escape hatch I had seen the agents pour through out in the hallway.

We took about three steps into the office when Mr. Hamilton abruptly turned to the left and hurried over to the coffee station against the wall. I could see by the grimace on his face that he was perturbed with whoever took the last cup of coffee without removing the pot from the warmer. He flipped the warmer switch off and put the smoldering, caramel-crusted pot to the side of the table before directing me to a seat at one of the tiny desks. He placed the application on the desk and took a pen from his pocket emblazoned with the Unified logo and handed it to me. I thanked him for the pen and squeezed down behind the desk, banging my knee hard on a metal support.

"So, this was where all the noise was coming from," I said cheerfully, trying to conceal the throbbing pain in my knee.

"You probably heard board call," he said, pointing to the immense blackboard hanging off the wall in the front of the room. "Our agents call out their sales for the week, and we write them on the board. The more board calls you have, the louder the cheers you get from the other agents," he said, referring to the chalk line grid drawn on the board with names and numbers inserted in the squares.

"Why are there slashes instead of numbers next to some of the names?" I inquired, when a raspy voice called out from behind us.

"That's a blank. You don't ever want a blank on the board next to your name."

"...Oh, Ray," Mr. Hamilton said as we both turned around. "I want you to meet Ron Pickles. Ron, this is Ray Meadows. Mr. Meadows is one of our assistant district managers. The position you're applying for is on his staff," Mr. Hamilton said as Mr. Meadows extended his hand.

I thought shaking hands with Hamilton was bad, but this guy was torture. It was like ratcheting your hand back and forth in a sandpaper vice all the while forcing a smile to show how impressed you were with the agony he was inflicting. The thought crossed my mind that between my knee and my hand I incurred more pain in ten minutes trying to get a job with the insurance company than I did working for the last two years moving pinball machines.

"Nice to meet you," I said, pulling my hand away from his grip.

"Good to meet you, Ron," he said.

"I was just about to get Ron started on filling out his application. Do you think you can take over for me, Ray?"

"Sure, Roger, be glad to," Meadows replied.

"Great. When he's finished, come into my office so we can have a conversation," Mr. Hamilton said, and he quickly left the room.

It felt a little awkward being left alone with Mr. Meadows, and I was glad that some of the other agents began sauntering back into the room. Meadows appeared to be middle aged, maybe older, short, stocky, and strongly built, but not a particularly attractive black man. His face was round and tough looking; it was pocked badly with acne scars that ran together and aged his face. His eyes were dark and tired with a slightly bloodshot look to them. He was well dressed in a

15

dark sport coat and gray slacks, but I thought the white wingtip shoes were a bit over the top.

Before guiding me to a seat at the end desk, he asked me if I wanted a cup of coffee and looked relieved when I declined after glancing at the brown sludge in the bottom of the pot. I tried not to look at him while I was filling out the application, but I noticed that he had removed an ornate smoking pipe from his jacket pocket and laid it on the desk in front of him. Other than Sherlock Holmes, I had never seen such an elaborate Cavendish-type pipe. It had a black stem that curved downward into an ivory bowl carved in the shape of a winged Pegasus. I could tell that he smoked it a lot because the opening of the bowl was blistered brown and built up with residue from the burnt tobacco. He reached into his other pocket and withdrew a leather pouch and a strange little spoon-like tool that I had never seen before. He opened a desk drawer and took out a piece of paper, placed it on the desk in front of him, and methodically began to scrape and clean the inside edges of the pipe. Every couple of scrapes, he would turn the pipe over and gently hit it on the paper-covered desk in order to get the residue out of the pipe. About the same time, a tall black man strolled around to the desk that was facing mine and was about to sit down when he looked over at the coffee pot.

"Goddamn it, Meadows. Look at this shit!" he growled out in the deepest voice I had ever heard while pointing to the coffee pot.

"Yeah, I know, motherfuckers around here don't take care of shit," Meadows softly lamented without breaking the concentration he was giving to his pipe. Any remnants of my preconceived notions believing this career beyond reproach in terms of ultra professional behavior flew out the window almost as fast as the agents hurled obscenities about the office. Aggravated that Meadows wasn't going to do anything about the coffee pot, the big guy pulled the chair from beneath the desk facing mine and sat down. I didn't know if it was because of his large size or the little desks we were sitting at, but my initial impression of the layout was right, and I felt uncomfortably close sitting across from him.

"How you doing?" he asked more out of courtesy than concern.

"Fine, thanks. And yourself?" I asked.

"Alright," he drawled.

"Ron, this is Otis Wahl. Otis, Ron Pickles," Mr. Meadows said, introducing us to each other. Reluctantly, I held out my hand, figuring that a man of his size would definitely break whatever bones hadn't been pulverized by my first two handshakes. I don't know if he took pity or just didn't feel the need to impress me with a death grip, but I was pleasantly surprised to shake his hand and get mine back with the blood still circulating. Afterwards, he went about his work, and I proceeded to fill out the employment application in front of me.

Meadows had finished cleaning his pipe. Then, he stuffed it with tobacco from his pouch, leaned back, and lit it. Huge billows of smoke filled the air as he puffed away, oblivious to the cloud he was creating. I thought the sweet-smelling aroma generated by the pipe tobacco was a welcome change to the stale air re-circulating in the room, but Otis seemed annoyed.

"Damn, Meadows, blow that shit somewhere else," he said, waving his hands at a wayward puff of smoke that engulfed his desk.

"Sorry, Wahl," Meadows said unconvincingly as he reached down and pulled a three-inch-thick leather-bound accounting book from something that looked like a saddlebag sitting on the floor next to his desk. He placed the book on his desk and had just flipped it open when I finished the application.

"Wow, that's a big book," I sighed out loud, handing him the application.

"This might be your ledger," he said, letting the book close on itself.

"What's a ledger?" I asked.

"Roger will tell you all about that in his office. Let me see if he's ready for us," he said, taking my application with him as he left. Otis looked up from the work he was doing, glanced at the book Meadows left behind, reached down to the floor, and pulled up an identical-looking book that was easily twice the thickness of the one on the desk.

"See, that ain't shit," he said. "Now, this is a ledger book," he said proudly, letting the book drop to the desk with a loud thud.

"That's huge! How come yours is so much bigger than that one?" I asked, nodding in the direction of the book Meadows had left on the desk.

"Because I work this one, and nobody's worked that one for a while. That's the one you're going to get. Don't worry about it. They'll tell you all about that shit when you go in there," he said as Mr. Meadows came back into the room.

"Ron, come with me. Roger is ready to see you now." Mr. Meadows escorted me into Hamilton's richly decorated office and ushered me to a lone chair in front of his stately oak desk. I couldn't believe the contrast from his office to the agents'. Hamilton's desk was huge and sided up against the right wall facing the door as you entered so he could see outside the door of his office. Behind Hamilton's desk was a large oak cabinet with six double drawers and a hutch on top that took up most of the wall. The hutch was loaded with a vast array of awards and trophies complementing the walls of his office that sported plaques, certificates, and diplomas attesting to the accomplishments Mr. Hamilton had achieved during his career. To the left of the hutch, in the center of the office, were three windows extending from floor to ceiling, cut with such a narrow view that you had to strain your neck just to see the parking lot below. An oak bookcase covered the wall to the left and was neatly filled with an array of leather-bound books and encyclopedias. In front of the bookcase was a brown leather recliner with a gold reading lamp extending over the top of it from the rear. The wall attached to the entranceway facing his desk was beautifully decorated with seafaring paintings mounted in oak frames. Below the paintings was a brown leather couch sandwiched by two oak end tables and lamps designed like sailboats. Mr. Hamilton acknowledged me with a smile as I sat down in front of him but seemed intent on reviewing every answer I put down on the application. Meadows renewed his obsession with cleaning his pipe as he made himself comfortable on the couch set slightly behind me to the left.

"Wow! This is a heck of an office you have here," I said, half thinking that I should probably keep quiet.

"Thank you, Ron," Hamilton said, barely acknowledging my compliment while taking one last look at the back page of the application. Placing it upon his desk, he leaned back in his chair, put his hands behind his head, and studied me for a quick moment while taking a deep breath.

"How do you feel about making sales?" he asked in a tone that suggested he was genuinely interested in my response.

"I really don't know. I've never worked as a salesman, so it's kind of hard for me to say," I replied, trying to be as honest as I could. I heard Meadows muffle a snort, so I glanced back in time to see a small grin on his face, as if he were amused by my answer.

"Sure, you have. You just don't realize it," Hamilton said with a nod towards Meadows as if acknowledging their thoughts were the same. Then he leaned forward and quickly glanced down at my application before looking back at me. "You're married, right, Ron?"

"Yes, that's right."

"Did you ask your wife to marry you?" he asked rather coyly. I paused for a moment before answering, knowing that I was being set up but not quite sure how.

"Well, yeah, of course," I replied slowly, still not sure of the point he was trying to make.

"Then, you made a sale. Actually, you made a great sale if you think about it because you sold another person on the idea of spending the rest of their life with you," he said with a smugness I didn't like.

"I guess you could look at it that way," I said, thinking that my wife was pregnant when I asked her and probably didn't think she had much of a choice.

"Well, let me ask you something. Did you ever get a present for Christmas that you asked somebody to get you and actually received it?" he continued.

"Sure."

"Then you made a sale," he said with a smile. "Did you ever go to a party or an event of some kind and meet a perfect stranger who you ended up talking to and hanging out with for the rest of the evening?"

"Yeah, of course I have," I replied with a nod to imply that I had begun to understand his line of questioning.

"Well then, you sold a perfect stranger on the idea that you were a pretty good guy and someone they wanted to hang out with for the night, didn't you?" he asked somewhat rhetorically. "You see, Ron, most people don't realize it, but just about every interaction you make with another person can be considered a sale. When you go to your favorite restaurant for breakfast, it's because they sold you on their food or service or both. You go to the store to buy products you need at home, but what you don't think about is that the idea of buying those products was sold to you at some point. Whether it's coffee, toothpaste, or paper towels, you pick up that product because someone sold you on the idea," he stressed by tapping his desk with his finger. "Sometimes, it's your parents that sell you on the idea of buying things when you are just a little kid. Do you ever go to the store and buy a product just because your mom used it?"

"Sure, lots of times," I replied.

"That's because your mom was sold on the idea of the product and in turn sold you. Do you see what I'm getting at here?"

"Yeah, I do, but I have to admit that I never really thought about sales like that before."

"Most people don't, and that's a good thing for all of us, or everything we do would be negotiated to the point of making life miserable," he said with a chuckle. "You see, Ron, all a salesman does, and all we do here at Unified, is talk to people about ideas."

"Ideas? I'm not sure I understand."

"Well, you can't really buy insurance in terms of something you can put in your hands. It's not something you can look at or smell, like picking produce from the supermarket. Insurance is about ideas. It's about the idea of losing something in the future and compensating for that loss with a dollar amount. The job of the insurance salesman is to convince a prospect to buy insurance to protect their family in case of a loss. In order to do that, you have to sell yourself to people as someone they can trust to give you money now, knowing that they won't get anything tangible in return for years to come. Do you think you could do that?"

"Well, I'm sure it's a little more difficult than you make it sound, but yes, I do think I can do that," I said with a chuckle. Hamilton looked at me for a moment with a serious expression, and I could see in his eyes that he was not satisfied with my response or convinced that he had sold me on the job. After a second or two, a barely distinguishable smirk appeared on his face as if it had dawned on him exactly which buttons he needed to push to get me interested. With a long breath, he turned his attention to Mr. Meadows, who hadn't said a word the entire time.

"Mr. Meadows, would you do me a favor and show Mr. Pickles the ring you were awarded from the company?"

"Sure, Roger," Meadows said, hopping up from the couch. He still had his pipe in his hand, slipping it into his jacket pocket as he walked over and stuck out his right hand, displaying an enormous gold ring studded with diamonds on his pinky finger. As impressive as the ring was, I found myself drawn to the craggy condition of his hand. His fingers were thick like sausages with cuts and scars crisscrossing in every direction. Chips of dried skin looked like scales shedding from the underbelly of a lizard, and his knuckles looked like small doorknobs that had been dented with a hammer. I now knew why shaking his hand caused me so much grief, but I couldn't help but wonder what he did in a former life that could have caused such damage to his hands.

"Very nice," I said out of politeness, looking back at Hamilton.

"Take it off and let Ron hold it," Hamilton commanded. Meadows complied while struggling for a moment to bend the ring around his protruded knuckle, but he eventually navigated the ring off his finger and handed it to me. I never held a piece of gold in my hand before and couldn't believe how heavy it was. It made me feel bad that I couldn't afford to buy Jessica something like this when we got married. I studied the ring for a couple of moments, amazed at the host of diamonds aligned with a carving in the gold to form the initials "UI" for Unified Insurance, I assumed.

"I think you'll find eight or nine diamonds set in that ring. Am I right, Ray?" Hamilton asked Meadows.

"That's right, nine," Meadows confirmed.

"When Ray was an agent, he made Diamond Club nine years in a row. It's the highest honor you can receive from the company. I wanted to point it out to you because in order to achieve Diamond Club status, your income from sales alone, not including collections, has to exceed $30,000. Does that give you some indication of the kind of money Mr. Meadows has made as an agent?"

"Wow! Quite a bit," I said, handing his ring back much more impressed with Meadows than the moment before. Meadows returned to the couch and sat down while I turned my attention back toward Mr. Hamilton. "It sounds like you can make a lot of money selling insurance," I said, still reeling from the image of Meadows' ring.

"We wouldn't be here if you couldn't," Hamilton said smiling, knowing that he had begun to hook me into the job.

"Sounds kind of exciting, but I do have a question for you. What did you mean by collections?" I asked with more interest than I had displayed to this point.

"Well, most of the insurance we sell around here is life and fire that's paid on a weekly or monthly basis; every time somebody pays their bill, you then receive a percentage of that money. We call it 'ledger pay,' though most of the guys around here just call it their book pay. The bigger your black ledger grows, the more collections you make, the more you get paid," Hamilton said like a talk show host baiting a contestant into dreaming of the riches they could earn.

"You said that Mr. Meadows made $30,000 without collections. What did you mean by that?" I inquired.

"As an agent, you get paid in two ways: the collections that we just talked about and bringing in new business. New business is the key to becoming a successful insurance agent," he said, moving up his chair and leaning on his desk to get closer to me. He knew my interest was piqued by the money and used his hands to punctuate his points as he spoke.

"See, new business gets paid differently than existing business. Anytime you sell a new policy, you get paid with what we call a multiplier. For instance, if you go out and sell $1 of weekly premium life insurance, you get paid $25, or twenty-five times the amount you sell. That applies to weekly fire insurance as well. If you sell MDO, or monthly insurance, you get $7, or seven times the amount of every dollar you sell. Are you with me?" he asked.

"Yeah, $25 for the weekly and $7 for the monthly," I confirmed.

"Right, so if you talked to five people a day and sold them each a policy that costs $1 per week, you would make... Hold on a second. Let me make sure I'm right here," he said, taking a Texas

Instruments pocket calculator from his jacket pocket. He quickly punched in some numbers, then held the calculator out over the desk for me to see. "I thought so: $875 per week in sales money."

"Holy shit!" I blurted out in disbelief, staring at the numbers on the calculator. "I'm sorry," I said, instantly apologizing for cussing in front of them.

"Don't worry. I appreciate your enthusiasm. It reminds me of just starting in the business and being as excited as you are," Hamilton said.

"Wow! It's hard to believe because selling $5 a day doesn't sound that hard at all. I mean, from the ring on Mr. Meadows' finger and the trophies behind your desk, I can see that it's possible to make that kind of money," I said, overflowing with excitement.

"Well, I'm not finished," Hamilton continued. "That's just the sales part. You also get 20 percent of all the money you bring in the office, whether it's mailed here or you go to someone's house and collect it. So, if you sold $35 of weekly insurance, you would make an additional $7 in collection percentage, as well as the $875 you got for selling it."

"Mr. Hamilton, with all due respect, who cares about the $7?" I said with a laugh, already counting the buckets full of dollars I was going to make.

"Well, believe it or not, you do. You see, you get those $7 every week the new customers pay. Let me show you something," he said, punching up some more numbers on the keyboard. "If you sold $35 worth of premium every week for a year, you would have sold $1,820 worth of new business. That would be $45,000 in sales commissions in your pocket, but you only get that one time because that's the commission for selling the product. Do you follow me?"

"Yeah, I'm with you," I said.

"Okay, good. Now, the book, that $7 a week in collection money that you don't care about," he said with a chuckle, "the book would be paying you $365 per week just for collecting the premium that you sold during the year. So, if you continued to sell at a clip of $5 per day, next year you would get a $375 per week raise, and your pay would be $1,250 per week," he said, putting the calculator on his desk and pushing it under my nose to see.

"Wow! Do guys around here really make that kind of money?" I asked in disbelief, fixated on the calculator.

"Some do. I'm not going to lie and tell you that everyone in the office does, because they don't. Some people reach a level of income that they're satisfied with and kind of coast at that level. But be assured that if you work hard and talk to enough people, you will make a lot of money in this job. Now, does this sound like something you would like to do?" he asked with a confident smile, knowing that he'd sold me to the point where I would have jumped through a ring of fire for the opportunity to work there.

"Without a doubt," I said, wanting to hop out of my chair and dance a jig around the room. "Roger, I'm really thankful for the opportunity. I can't wait to get started. I can't wait to go home and tell my wife," I said, drunk with the thought of all the money I was going to be bringing home.

"We like your enthusiasm, but in all seriousness, I do have to ask you a question."

"Sure, anything," I said, eager to cooperate.

"Do you have any problems working with black people?" he asked in a tone that seemed to be apologetic for the question. I remember looking at him completely dumbfounded by the question. It came so far out of left field that there was no way I could imagine the implications of such a question. For some reason, I thought Hamilton was asking me if I would have a problem working with Mr. Meadows, who would be my immediate supervisor and the only person in the room of African descent. My initial reaction was to look over at Mr. Meadows, who for the most part seemed disengaged by the whole process, just sitting on the couch fiddling with his pipe. That changed, however, as the question seemed to intrigue him enough to put his pipe down and lean forward on the couch in anticipation of my answer. Meadows' eyes locked with mine as if daring me to say something other than what was expected. The intimidation worked, and instantly I blurted out, "Oh, absolutely not! I get along with everybody: black, white, green, yellow. No problems at all," I said with a twisted smile in hopes of defusing any hint of racism another answer might raise.

"Good, because we do service a lot of black neighborhoods, and I always want to be up front about it so that we don't have any problems later," Hamilton said almost as an afterthought. "I'm going to start you at $225 per week. Will that work for you until you pass the insurance exams and get your license?"

"Two hundred and twenty-five dollars per week," I repeated as coolly as I could, trying hard not to let on the fact that I had never made that kind of money in my life. My God, most of the jobs I had applied for paid minimum wage, which was $3.10 per hour. The best I had ever done was five bucks an hour moving pinball machines for my friend, and that was only two or three days per week. The rest of the time, I would drive my car around wealthy neighborhoods on garbage days in hopes of finding stuff I could sell at the flea market on Sunday. "Yes, I think I could make that work," I said, completely dismissing the black thing altogether.

"Good. You'll also be getting full medical insurance; I'll have Mrs. Bolger give you the forms to fill out when you leave. I'd like you to start next Monday at 9:00. Now, we don't punch time clocks around here, but believe me when I tell you that punctuality is a key to being a successful salesman. If we agree upon a time or you tell a client that you will be at their house at a certain time, I expect you to make every effort to be there," he said seriously.

"Yes, sir, I will do that," I said like a soldier accepting his orders. With a nod of his head, Hamilton signaled that our meeting was over. On cue, Meadows and I stood up while Hamilton pushed his chair away from his desk and came around to meet us.

"Welcome to Unified Insurance Company, Mr. Pickles," he said, extending his hand to shake. I gratefully shook his and Meadows' hands, accepting the pain they caused me, figuring it must have been some kind of ritual you had to endure in order to work at the company.

CHAPTER 3

June 1980 — 8 months later

Roger Hamilton was suave, good-looking, and very smart. Way too smart to admit that the job he had to offer would be better suited to an individual with either a background in urban warfare or, better still, an unstable personality prone to self-destruction. A quick reference to working with black people was his way of telling me the job I was about to take paid good money but at a price. He covered his ass. It wasn't his fault if I didn't fully understand the implication of his meaning.

Instead of asking me if I had a problem working with black people, Hamilton could have asked if I might have a problem working in the projects or walking up and down the streets of the ghetto with hundreds, sometimes thousands, of dollars of collection money in my pocket. Considering the fact that I have blonde hair, blue eyes, and look like I just stepped out of a Nazi youth camp poster, you might expect this revelation to cause me some concern.

He could have mentioned that the job entailed selling burial insurance and collecting money from people who derived most of their income from welfare, disability, or, in many cases, pimping, prostitution, or selling drugs. That, too, may have sent up a red flag and persuaded me to bolt out of his office with what might be considered undue haste. He knew he could never hire anyone if he explained in detail the risks associated with becoming a ledger agent. He conveniently left out the more unpleasant aspects and basically guilted you into the job, a job I hated but desperately needed until my application with the electrician's union was approved.

I had just pulled into the parking lot of Cabrini-Green, Chicago's most notorious housing project. I drove through the parking lot slowly, passing a half dozen or so beat-up cars and two that had been stripped down to their axles and left to decay. I headed towards the back, figuring the shade from the building might afford a little relief from the sun. I pulled up then backed against the mangled chain-link fence that lined the parking lot and turned off the engine. The spot gave me a good view of the building while offering protection from somebody sneaking up from behind the car.

I leaned forward and stuck my head over the steering wheel of my '74 Chevy Impala to get a better view of the nineteen-story behemoth in front of me. Like many of the high-rise housing projects in Chicago, this one was constructed of plain white brick from top to bottom that had weathered and faded over the years. It always astounded me that with all the architectural wonders a city like Chicago had to offer, the best they could do with housing projects was design little more than a big rectangular box. Frank Lloyd Wright could have scribbled with his toes and designed something more aesthetically pleasing.

I reached toward the console and grabbed my watered-down McDonald's Coke while scanning my surroundings for any sign of trouble. The condensation from the cup dripped on my shirt and pants as I slurped up the watered-down drink. In one motion, I returned the Coke to the cup holder and brushed the droplets of water from my clothes before they had a chance to soak in.

I glanced down at my watch and couldn't believe it was just 10:00 in the morning. "It's so fucking hot," I cursed under my breath. *What's July going to be like if it's like this in the middle of June?* I thought to myself. I was taking a chance with both the driver- and passenger-side windows rolled down, but the car was suffocating, and I thought the risk was worth the breeze until I realized that I was parked rather close to an overflowing dumpster. The heat of the day had brought to life an obscene mixture of garbage, urine, and bug spray that wafted in and out of my vehicle as if amused by the subtle agony it was causing me. The assault on my nasal cavity was punishing my senses and bringing forth vivid memories of the interview that landed me in the heart of the ghetto eight months earlier. I leaned back in my seat and took in the building, still questioning my sanity. I couldn't help but think how ironic it was; I managed to find the only job in the city encouraging a white guy to walk around the projects and sell black people on the idea of dying.

Otis Wahl was supposed to meet me at ten, and we were going to canvass this Cabrini-Green building together looking for sales. Though he sat across from me in the office, I had never worked with him in the field before. We agreed to work on his ledger, so there wasn't anything I could do until he got there. Besides, I didn't figure it was a good idea to go into my first project alone. I sighed, thinking I should just sit back, relax, and endure the heat and the stench because he was sure to be late. He was always late for our staff meetings, and I couldn't begin to count the number of times our staff manager, Mr. Meadows, had the "talk" with Otis about his punctuality.

What pissed me off was that I had told him at the office to show a little consideration and be there on time so I didn't become the next day's headline: "Asshole White Guy Who Didn't Belong at Cabrini-Green Found Dead." He just laughed as usual and with that choppy baritone voice bellowed out, "Pickles, you worry too much, like a bitch. Stop worrying and enjoy life, goddamn it." On that note, he departed the office and left me to wonder if he would even come close to meeting me on time.

I sat in the car, turning my head from side to side like a periscope on a submarine, looking for some kind of activity in or around the building. I looked up floor by floor, peering into the rusty mesh and looking for signs of life: kids playing, women hanging laundry, even gangbangers standing around outside. Any activity was good, or so

Meadows told me. My experience with the Jets had been limited to pulling into the parking lot of the Robert Taylor housing projects with Meadows just off the Dan Ryan Expressway. One time, we went to lunch, and I agreed to go with him to a project to make a collection. He was covering an open ledger and didn't want to go into the project alone. He pulled into the parking area and, without hesitation, pulled right out. "What are you doing? I thought we had a collection to make here," I asked, seemingly innocent enough.

"You got ten thousand motherfuckers living in that building, and you don't see one motherfucker outside. What do you think, boy? Everybody's on a picnic?" He went on to say that people in the Jets knew when it was safe to go out and when they had to stay in. If it was really quiet and you didn't see anyone outside walking around, you didn't need to be there. "Always go with your gut," he said. "If your gut tells you that something doesn't feel right, then leave the ledger. Go get some coffee and come back, or just go home and come back another day."

It was Meadows' idea for me to work with Otis. The office had a sales contest for a Bahamas cruise, and Meadows needed big production from the staff if he was going to make it. Otis had already made the trip and was leading the office in sales. I was about three-quarters of the way there and still had till the end of September, so I was in pretty good shape. It was the other guys on the staff that were killing Mr. Meadows, so he practically begged Otis to take me into the projects and canvass for sales.

At the office, Meadows said that even though Cabrini-Green had the reputation of being the most dangerous project in Chicago, the Robert Taylor Homes and Stateway Gardens were twice as bad. Otis told Meadows he was full of shit when he heard that, knowing Meadows didn't like to go into any projects and challenged him to come canvassing with us. Meadows grunted something about training a new guy and ran off before Otis could pin him down. Otis just shook his head and mumbled something about Meadows being a pussy and not knowing what the hell he was talking about. The fact that Otis didn't make a joke of it gave me pause and made me realize that Cabrini-Green was not to be taken lightly.

The Chicago housing projects were not like any other neighborhood, rich, poor, or someplace in between. The people who lived in the projects weren't there by choice; they were there because they had no choice. Over a thousand people could occupy the hundred-plus apartments, and all of them had two things in common: they were black, and they were poor. While cramming a bunch of poor black folks under one roof may have been someone's idea of a grand social experiment, it quickly turned to shit. About all it provided was a Third World experience for the downtrodden inhabitants of the world's richest nation.

To my delight, Otis and his big gold Olds Delta Eighty-Eight came charging into the parking lot and pulled up to my driver-side window. "Pickles, you ready to work?" he growled out the window.

"Let's do it," I replied. Quickly, I leaned over and rolled up the passenger-side window, took one last sip of my Coke, and reached in the back to grab my portfolio. Hopping out of the car, I rolled up the driver-side window and slammed the door shut. Otis had parked and was rummaging through his trunk for some applications. He shoved some papers in a black briefcase he was carrying, shut the trunk, and walked over to me.

An imposing figure at over six-foot-four, the nicely trimmed afro he sported easily added another three inches to his height. He had an athletic build and moved fluently for a man of his size. His face was narrow but proportionate to his body. The heavy black beard he grew helped hide the youthful appearance of his coffee-creamed complexion, as well as giving him something to stroke as he spoke to you. His disarming brown eyes were set back under a rounded brow that gave a soft appeal to his expressions and instantly put you at ease despite his physical stature.

He was always impeccably dressed, and today was no different, though I thought it would be. A starched, pressed white shirt laid the foundation, and a red and blue tie fastened by a diamond-studded gold clip set the theme for a perfectly fit three-piece pinstripe blue suit. His black Florsheim shoes were spit-polished, and the small tassels dangling on the top added a touch of style. A wedding band and gold watch completed the ensemble, and as he approached me, I realized that we did not communicate properly as to the dress code one wears into the Chicago housing projects. After all, I came outfitted in black pants and a short-sleeved white shirt with a blue tie. As a latent fan of the Beatles, I would search shoe stores high and low to find boots that resembled theirs when they landed in America in 1964, a challenge that I relished in 1980, knowing full well the boots I was wearing were some sixteen years out of style. I had no jewelry, and my gold-plated wedding band pinched, so I never wore that either. About the only accessory I had was a plastic pocket protector filled with pens and pencils stuffed in my shirt pocket. I thought it was kind of cool that our company gave these to the agents with the company logo stamped in big red letters across the top. Otis took one look at me, frowned, and shook his head.

"Man, take that shit outch your pocket," he said, half laughing with his deep bass voice while pointing at my pocket protector.

"But it keeps my shirt clean," I replied.

"What's it say?"

"You know goddamn well what it says: Unified Insurance Company," I shot back.

"It says, 'I'm a stupid motherfucker that needs to be relieved of my money.' That's what it says."

"Look at you!" I said in disbelief. "If I was going to rob somebody, I'd rob you, not me. You're dressed to the fucking nines and giving me shit about a pocket protector?"

Otis stared at me for a moment while pulling at his beard. The smile had left his face, and I could sense that a thought occurred to him, causing some concern. "You're right, I forgot you ain't done this before, and I know that Meadows didn't teach you shit about the projects," he said slowly and methodically, as if formulating a quick study guide for me as he spoke.

"Well, this is my second parking lot," I quipped.

"That ain't shit. Meadows don't know how to work the Jets. That's why he sent you with me. Now, listen up, Pickles, because I ain't fucking with you, you dig?" His tone turned serious, and I knew he was concerned that my lack of experience could be dangerous for us both.

"I hear you," I replied.

"Okay, listen up. You only got two groups of people that go into the projects that don't live there. The first group is cops, firemen, and paramedics… and none of them will go in without lots of backup. A motherfucker could be bleeding to death on the first floor, and a paramedic won't go in there without a half dozen pigs backing him up, you dig?" I just nodded my head in agreement, and he continued. "Okay, the second group is idiots like you and me that got to go in there to make a living either fixing something or selling something. We're the motherfuckers they prey on 'cause we don't belong in their building, and they want to teach us a lesson."

"What do you mean, 'teach us a lesson'?" I asked, somewhat confused.

"You know who runs these buildings?" Otis asked.

"Yeah, the Chicago Housing Authority," I answered calmly.

"No, fuck that shit," Otis snapped back in annoyance. "CHA don't run shit. The Black Rangers or the Black P. Stone Nation runs most of these buildings. If you ain't got their approval, they need to teach you a lesson so next time you show some respect."

"So, you're saying that we have to get permission from the Black Rangers before we go into the building?" I asked in disbelief.

"No, you can't ask for permission; you got to earn that shit."

"Man, I don't understand a fucking thing you're talking about," I said, shaking my head.

"You earn it by getting in there and getting some business. Once people know who you are and that you're cool, they'll speak up for you, and the gangs will leave you alone. The problem is that we got to go in there first and establish ourselves. That's why you can't be walking around with an advertisement on your shirt screaming that you're selling insurance. Now you dig?" Otis finished with a smile on his face as he was sure that I had begun to follow his line of thought, which for the most part I did.

"But one thing I still don't get. Why are you so dressed up?" I asked.

"Because I got a certain image to portray, for one thing," he said with a smile. "…And for another, you and I will look like a salt and pepper detective team. All the brothers know that white cops ain't got no style, so we should look perfect."

"I got style," I retorted.

"Okay styyyyle," Otis said sarcastically as he fingered the pocket protector in my shirt. "Now, put that shit back in the car, and let's get going before it gets too late and we can't go in there." I stared at Otis for a long moment, drew a sigh, and reluctantly opened the door. Removing a couple of pens, I threw the pocket protector on the front seat and shut the door. "Happy?"

"Nope, not yet. How much money you got on you?" he asked.

"I don't know… a couple of hundred in collections, I guess."

"You got a wallet?"

"Right here," I said, producing the wallet from my back pocket.

"Okay, what you do is put $50 in your pocket and keep the rest of the money folded up in your wallet. Take out your license and credit cards and leave them in the car."

"All right, I get the pocket protector thing, but now you're just fucking with me," I said.

"I'm trying to teach you something, goddamn it!" he said, raising his eyebrows. "A motherfucker robs you in there, he knows he's taking a chance on going to jail. He just as soon kills you as let you live so you can't tell who it was that robbed you. But you show that motherfucker a prize in that wallet, and he'll take off running, thinking he's hit the jackpot. That gives you a chance to run the hell out of there before he figures out that he ain't got shit and comes back to kill you." Exasperated at his logic, I just opened the car door and shoved my license and credit card under the front seat.

It was a decent walk from the parking lot to the entrance of the building, and Otis set the pace with his long legs, forcing me to double step in order to keep up. I craned my neck and dropped my jaw, trying to absorb the monstrosity we were about to enter. As uninspiring as the building was to look at, I couldn't imagine how depressing it must be to live there.

The big Jets like this one had two nineteen-story square columns on each end with apartments recessed in the middle, connected by horizontal concrete slabs of walkway. A vertical slab of concrete protruding from the middle of the building housed the sometimes-operating elevator system and separated the walkway. Without question, the most interesting aspect of the buildings was the walkway that joined the two columns of apartments together. Somebody thought it would be a good idea to create an outside view for the residents to enjoy as they strolled to their apartments. So, instead of enclosing the entire structure, they designed the walkway on the outside of the building.

My guess was that whoever designed these buildings must have thought that poor people would be "motivated to achieve" by experiencing the ever-changing Chicago climate from whatever floor they were lucky enough to live on. I imagined that the motivation was greatest on the upper floors of the building during the harshest winters. I couldn't help but wonder if the designers ever took a winter walk to the nineteenth floor to experience the thirty-mile-per-hour winds and sub-zero temperatures that routinely invaded Chicago during that time.

I did give the planners some credit, though. Even if it was an afterthought, someone must have realized that it might not be a good idea to leave the walkway completely exposed. It also occurred to someone that a banister might not keep an overzealous child from falling off the high rise. So, the solution was to install a thick steel mesh grate to the sides of the walkway from top to bottom. You could tell that it was strong stuff even from hundreds of feet away. It was the kind of mesh that city workers would sometimes throw over potholes on the street to prevent cars from falling in until they got a chance to fix them. Liquor stores in bad neighborhoods had the stuff bolted across their windows to protect them from being knocked out as patrons often consumed their beverages and tried to return their bottles through the store's windows. Of course, the steel rusted shortly after being installed, and, instead of designing a walkway for people to view the city, it took on the appearance of a structure meant to keep people locked in.

We passed an old lady pulling a grocery cart behind her and noticed a couple of teenage guys leaving the building and heading down the street. Otis pulled the large foyer door open and held it as I walked in the building. I had just seemed to adjust to the lingering odor outside but in no way was prepared for the stench of urine that hit me with my first breath inside.

"Holy shit!" I gagged out as the stink actually burned my nostrils.

"That shit will wake you," Otis said.

"What is the matter with these people? Pissing in their own hallway like this," I said, half realizing that Otis might be offended by the use of "these people." "You know what I mean," I said with an apologetic tone and shook my head.

"All the Jets are like this. Motherfuckers don't give a shit. Just piss wherever they are," he said without taking offense. Otis stepped in front of me and took the lead towards the elevators. I had been apprehensive before we entered the foyer, but once inside I was just plain scared. It was eerily reminiscent of the feeling I got as a kid entering my first haunted house, and I wondered how people could live in conditions like this on a day-to-day basis.

Even if you could learn to tolerate the smell, the inside was like a throwback to medieval times. The lighting was dim with an occasional low-watt bulb scattered throughout the hallway ceilings, covered by a filthy glass plate. Grungy gray concrete floors sucked the moisture from the air and lowered the temperature in the vestibule by ten to fifteen degrees from the outside, which was rapidly approaching ninety. It was like descending into a cave, and I felt goose bumps rising on my skin with the chill. The brick walls were just covered in graffiti—bleached out and painted over so many times, the colors had darkened and faded into each other to create a mural of confusion and despair. Discarded liquor bottles lined the corridors like miniature soldiers guarding a castle wall. As if dressed in tight-fitting uniforms, many of the bottles were still wrapped in the brown paper bags they were purchased in, a practice universally acclaimed as a "clever deception" by those who indulge in drink while walking the streets. Flies and other insects swarmed the half-eaten food morsels and other garbage that had been discarded, stepped on, kicked, and eventually trapped in every corner of the hallway.

The elevators were set back about twenty feet from the foyer entrance and designed to intersect with each floor's walkway, which led to the apartments. Designed to be tamper proof, they were built into a concrete bunker. The call button for the system was attached to the wall next to the elevator door and encased in a stainless steel plate that was bolted to the wall with heavy gauge metal carriage bolts.

Otis walked up, pushed the call button, and raised his eyebrows at the creaking and moaning emanating from the elevator shaft as the system responded. "Might as well start at the top," Otis mumbled as

if I might be curious as to his choice of floors. I just nodded my
approval, fearing the only words that would come out of my mouth
would be, "I want to go home!" The elevator took forever to arrive,
and by the time it reached us, the old lady with the cart we passed in
the parking lot came into the building and rode up with us. She got
off a couple of floors below us as we continued to the nineteenth.
Stepping out of the elevator, I had to admit it was a little nicer up
there than it was on the first floor. The graffiti still covered most of
the walls, but the smell was hardly noticeable, and the walkway
seemed cleaner. I followed Otis as we exited the enclosure housing
the elevator and onto the exposed walkway penned in with the steel
grate. I stopped for a moment and peered through the grate, amazed
at the view of the city, and momentarily forgot where I was till Otis,
who had walked a few feet in front of me, called out, "Pickles, you
ready?"

"Yeah, I guess so. Go ahead and knock on the door," I said,
catching up to him at the first apartment. We didn't get an answer on
the first couple of doors, which was no surprise as they could have
been empty apartments, or the residents could be out running
errands. The next few people answered through their door, telling us
to go away. It wasn't until we got to the end of the walkway that we
got our first hit.

"'Surance Man!" Otis bellowed out as he banged on the door
with his fist.

"Whach you want?" said the high-pitched female voice from the
other side of the door.

"We want to talk to you," Otis countered.

"Who y'all from?"

"Mr. Pickles and me are from Unified Insurance. We the 'surance
men in this area." I smiled to myself hearing Otis refer to us as the
"'surance men," though I knew he was perfectly capable of saying
"insurance." The first time Mr. Meadows brought me on the ledger,
he told me that from now on I would be known as the "'surance

man," and I might as well get used to it. We could hear the parade of locks up and down the other side of the door being unfastened until finally the door pulled open just enough for an eyeball to look us over.

"How you doing today, ma'am? Would this be an inconvenient time for me and Mr. Pickles to sit down and talk with you for a few moments? Here's my card," Otis said as he forced his hand through the crack in the door. We could see her studying the card and both of us sensed that she was unsure as to whether or not she should open the door.

"My name is Ron Pickles, and this is Otis Wahl," I spoke up. "Here, let me give you one of my cards as well. Can I ask you your name?" I questioned softly, repeating Otis' move and shoving my fist through the narrow opening to hand her my card.

"Mrs. Sophie Williams," she replied, now looking at my card. I stepped a little closer to the door and spoke to her in a tone you might use to praise a child for a good deed.

"You know something, Mrs. Williams? It's good to be careful, and you don't want to let just anybody come into your home. You see, Mr. Wahl is the agent in this area, and I just came with him today to make sure he is doing his job: letting everybody like you know about the great insurance products Unified has to help your family," I said. Otis took a step back and shook his head out of the sight of Mrs. Williams, as if dismayed by my transformation into a bullshit artist.

"I guess you can come in, buts I ain't got no money for no 'surance," she said, pulling the door open and walking away to let us enter by ourselves. I gave Otis a look of satisfaction then gestured for him to enter first. "Y'all go have a seat on the couch by my daughter, Chareese," she said, walking over to the kitchen sink. Otis walked in and took two steps to his left, attempting to follow Mrs. Williams' instructions, and then froze. I stepped in and turned my back to close the door, not noticing that Otis had stopped dead in his tracks. I spun back around and ran smack into Otis' back, pushing him forward a couple of feet.

The apartment was small, about what you'd expect from public housing. To the right of the entrance was the kitchen, and to the left was the living room. Against the rear of the living room wall and to the right of center was a closed bedroom door. A dark green Formica countertop divided the two rooms; it extended from the back wall to a few feet before the door we came in. There were storage cabinets under the kitchen side of the counter, while the countertop protruded over on the living room side, helping it double as a dining area. The two high-backed, black-and-gold-colored vinyl chairs pushed under the counter on the living room side had definitely seen better days, as shards of cotton stuffing could be seen erupting from the sides. The kitchen area was clean except for a couple of leftover breakfast dishes and some cut-out newspaper articles strewn about the counter. There were two metal dishware cabinets hung above the sink that were a dull white and looked as if they had been re-painted with flat latex wall paint. The stove and refrigerator stood against the right wall with a few inches separating the two. Mrs. Williams wisely used this space as a place to keep a broom, mop, and bucket out of direct view. The kitchen floor was a sheet of speckled vinyl that had yellowed and faded significantly from what you might guess was a creamy white at one time. Otis was blocking my view of the living room and hadn't said anything or moved a muscle in the moment I bumped into him. Mrs. Williams was clearing the dishes from the counter and putting them in the sink. I was about to ask Otis to get going when I noticed that he was fixated on the view in front of him. Instinctively, I took a step around his massive frame to see what had caught his attention and found myself bowled over by the sight.

"Chareese, turn that thing off and make some room for the 'surance men to sit down!" Mrs. Williams hollered over at her daughter when she saw the dumbfounded look on our faces, as if we had no place to go. The only furniture in the sparsely decorated living room was a worn and matted brown three-piece sectional sofa pushed up against the left side of the apartment with a glass coffee table in front of it. On top of the coffee table was a small television set tuned into a soap opera with the volume blaring. Behind the television, on the floor to the right, was an old oscillating fan pointed at the couch and rattling away with every turn of direction. Above the couch to the right was a picture of Jesus, and to the left was a picture of Martin Luther King Jr. Sitting back in the middle of the couch was a very pregnant and, with the exception of a pair of pink cotton panties pulled up to her belly, an extremely naked Chareese.

One more time, Mrs. Williams scolded her daughter for not moving to make room for Otis and me, adding that clothes were making her daughter uncomfortable in this hot weather. Slowly, Chareese raised herself to a sitting position and pushed the coffee table back with her feet as if opening a door to let us in. She leaned over and turned the volume down on the television but didn't move to either side of the couch. As a sign of courtesy, she picked up a towel that had fallen to the floor and fanned it out across her lap. However, she made no attempt to cover her swollen breasts that had comfortably plopped themselves upon her inflated stomach, which looked as if it might pop at any moment. She never once made eye contact with either of us and never took her eyes off the soap opera that had so captivated her attention.

"Go sit down," Mrs. Williams directed impatiently at our reluctance to advance any further into the living room. "Oh, don't mind Chareese," she said as if finally realizing that her daughter's nudity had become a barrier for us. "There ain't nothing you boys can do with her. She already been done to," she said as if we hadn't realized the obvious.

Hesitantly, Otis and I walked over to the couch. Otis paused and let me cross in front of him and sit to Chareese's left while he sat to the right. We both sat down and, in unison, leaned forward and focused our attention directly on Mrs. Williams across the green counter to avoid the slightest appearance of gawking at the enormous breasts that hung beside us.

"So, Mrs. Williams, it's a good thing we stopped by today with Chareese about to have a baby and all," I said with a smile.

"Why is that?" she asked.

"Well, for one thing, I know you would like to give the baby a good start in life, and for another, we have a special plan that covers the baby five days after he or she is born," I replied. Suddenly, I felt a tapping on my shoulder to get my attention. I knew it wasn't Otis who, out of the corner of my eye, was still gazing straight ahead. I briefly thought about ignoring Chareese, but I realized that Mrs. Williams had stopped doing the dishes and was leaning on the counter as if intently waiting to hear what Chareese had to say. I took a deep breath and slowly turned toward Chareese, trying desperately to keep my eyes focused directly on hers.

"Why does a five-day-old baby need insurance when he should live to be sixty or seventy years old?" Chareese asked, completely oblivious to the agony of awkwardness she was putting me through. It was a legitimate question, and one I had been asked several times before in my short career, but never by a sixteen- or seventeen-year-old pregnant girl with bare tits the size of pineapples less than a foot from my face. For a moment, I flashed back to one of my favorite childhood stories, Lewis Carroll's *Alice's Adventures in Wonderland*. Alice knew those doorknobs weren't supposed to talk, but in her dream they did, and they made sense. I knew that tits weren't supposed to talk, but as hard as I tried to focus on Chareese, all I could see were her tits. I felt like I was going crazy, like an actor hopelessly caught in a twisted scene from Theatre of the Absurd.

After a long moment, Otis finally came to my rescue. "It ain't like that, Chareese," he said with his gravelly voice, ignoring Chareese and speaking directly to Mrs. Williams. "Nobody thinks about nothing bad is going to happen to your baby, but you know how it is around here. You never know. But what Mr. Pickles is saying is that all parents want to look after their kids, and I'm quite sure you folks want to look after the baby. So, what we do is give you a plan. You know, God forbid something should happen, you can take care of business without going to the church or asking friends to help, you dig?"

For the first time, Otis glanced over at Chareese, who was nodding her head in agreement, satisfied that she understood. He then quickly turned back towards Mrs. Williams. He was very deliberate in his words, and there was a sense of seriousness in his voice, which I took as very professional and snapped me back in line. I followed Otis' lead and mustered all the willpower I could to forget about Chareese's breasts and focus on the reason we were there. "But this plan does do something else!" I added with a bit of excitement. "It's called an eighteen-year endowment. That means that when the baby gets to be eighteen years old, he gets all the money you paid to use for college or whatever."

"Like a savings plan?" Chareese added.

"That's right. Now, how much money do you ladies think you can put away every month for the baby till he reaches eighteen?" Otis asked impatiently. The mother and daughter looked at each with raised eyebrows as if both thought that it was a good idea and something they should consider, but neither answered Otis directly.

"I would love to have some 'surance on the baby!" Chareese exclaimed out of nowhere, as if it had been her idea all along to insure her child.

"I think it would be a good idea, especially in these damn projects. You never know what's going to happen," Mrs. Williams added.

"That's right," Otis said. "So, how much you want to put away every month?"

"I don't know, maybe $10," Mrs. Williams offered.

"I gotta get at least fifteen," Otis shot back sternly.

"Mama, we can do fifteen," Chareese said.

"Pickles, get out an application, and take some information from Chareese," Otis commanded before anyone spoke another word. Obediently, I retrieved an application and started asking the particulars without giving anyone a chance to make an objection. The sale had been made. We chatted a bit, and we had both mother and daughter sign up before giving our thanks and exiting the apartment. Quickly, we walked back to the elevator enclosure without so much as glancing in each other's direction. We didn't say a word to each other until after the elevator door closed and we knew no one could hear.

"Holy shit!" I yelled out in disbelief.

"Can you believe that shit?" Otis asked, just shaking his head while pushing the tenth-floor button. "What the fuck is the matter with that woman? Talking about her daughter already been done to. Put some clothes on, goddamn it," he said angrily.

"You sound pissed," I said, still grinning from ear to ear.

"I am pissed, goddamn it. That was bullshit. She can't tell her daughter to put a robe on for ten minutes while we talk to her? How many white people you think ever seen the inside of that woman's apartment?"

"I have no idea, but I wouldn't think many," I said.

"None. You were more than likely the first white man ever in the woman's house, and she ain't got the goddamn courtesy to put a cover on her daughter. …And you know what? That disrespects me," Otis said.

"You? Disrespects you? What about me? I'll be an old white cracker living on a farm somewhere still thinking about those huge black tits staring me in the eyes. That kind of shit can scar a man for life," I said with a straight face. For a moment I felt bad for Otis because I got the feeling that he was embarrassed as a black man for the idiotic behavior of Mrs. Williams and her daughter.

"I don't give a shit about you," he said, cracking a smile as if it had dawned on him that I hardly considered Mrs. Williams or her daughter representative of the whole black race.

"So, what are you saying? It would have been okay for her daughter to lay butt naked on the couch if you were there alone?"

"Nah, that's just ignorant bullshit. That woman's fucked up in the head. Normal people don't do that shit. You've been working the ledger for a while now. How many times you see something like that?"

"I can honestly say that before today, I have never sat on a couch next to a pregnant naked teenager, and I doubt seriously that it will ever happen to me again. But I got to admit, she had some amazing tits," I said, shaking my head. Otis finally started laughing. "Hey, Pickles, you won't see tits like that if you quit the ledger to become an electrician."

"True, but you got to admit that this job is a hell of a way to put food on the table," I said.

"Feed a lot of hungry motherfuckers with them things," he mumbled as we both started laughing uncontrollably.

"Ohhh shit," I sighed. "Why the tenth floor?" I asked, still chuckling about the bizarreness of our recent encounter.

"I had to put some distance between us and the crazy lady," Otis retorted.

"Well, just think—you get to collect her premium every month."

"Fuck that shit. She's going to learn how to mail her money in," he said as the elevator opened to the tenth floor. I was much more relaxed than when we started, and for a moment, I actually forgot we were walking around the most dangerous housing project in the country. Without paying attention, we walked past the first couple of doors we had an opportunity to knock on and found ourselves in the middle of the floor where Otis, still smiling, banged on the door and called out, "'Surance man."

The door opened wide, and reality blindsided the both of us as we were confronted by a soldier of the Black Rangers street gang. About as tall as Otis but easily a hundred pounds heavier, his frame filled the entranceway from top to bottom. He was shirtless but had two leather gun belts slung across his chest bandito style. The belts were loaded with ammunition and held a couple of chrome-plated .357 Magnums firmly against his side. The word "RANGERS" was emblazoned across his muscular chest with the gang's symbols carved below. In contrast to the war-making machine he advertised from the waist up, his bottom ensemble consisted of striped, gray dress pants and burgundy leather shoes. His complexion was dark, and his face was rigid and focused. The moment we saw him, we both knew we were in trouble.

The salt and pepper detective team that Otis had hoped people would mistake us for was not the look we needed in this situation. Any movement on our part misconstrued as an attempt to draw a weapon would have been our deaths. We were in a bad situation, and the last thing we could do was show fear because that would invite a swift beating or, as Otis liked to say, "teach us a lesson" for stumbling upon one of their safe houses. To my surprise, a look of indignation came over Otis' face as if he were in disbelief at what he saw. "Look at you, motherfucker!" he said, lashing out at the bandito while pointing a finger at the guns strapped to the bandito's chest. "You going to walk around with that shit, you need some 'surance, goddamn it! Pickles, can you believe this shit? Motherfucker walking around like that with no 'surance?" he said and looked over at me. I just shook my head as if stunned by the revelation. I wasn't acting, however. I *was* stunned. I had no idea where Otis was going with this. In the short period of time that I had sold insurance, I knew there were times when a good line of bullshit was important, and I knew that there were times that people would see through that line of bullshit. However, I couldn't imagine a situation where you would take a chance on pissing off a guy packing more firepower than Clint

Eastwood carried in all his *Dirty Harry* movies combined. I wasn't the only one, though, as the steely faced bandito seemed to be as dumbfounded at the tone and forcefulness of Otis' ranting as I was.

The three of us stood there looking at each other for what seemed like an eternity. In actuality, it had only been a moment or two when a muffled voice from inside wanted to know who was at the door. The bandito turned his head inside the apartment and kind of snorted out a reply, "Motherfuckers say I need some 'surance." He never turned back towards us; instead, he stepped aside, leaving the door half open and disappeared into the apartment. In the moment we were alone, Otis and I glanced at each other with raised eyebrows, knowing that our predicament wasn't over. We couldn't walk away, and we couldn't pretend it was a mistake that we knocked on their door and politely excuse ourselves. Though we didn't know it at the time, the next face we saw belonged to the third-highest-ranking member of the Black Rangers in Chicago.

Unlike the bandito who swung the apartment door open wide with a theatrical flair to let us get the full view of the weaponry he carried, this guy stayed behind the door and shielded most of his body while allowing us to see his face. Though his features were soft and pleasant, a jagged scar cut across his cheek, and his dark, piercing eyes told you that he was not a man to be taken lightly. While the bandito stood in front of us, expressionless like a statue, this guy studied us with a suspiciousness that actually felt intrusive. He was a serious man, and I got the feeling that he was a little more than annoyed by our presence. While holding the door with one hand, he looked back into the apartment and told the others it was cool.

"What y'all doing up here?" he asked, turning back towards us. He opened the door and took a step towards us, looking down both sides of the walkway. He had a muscular build that was complemented by a white muscle tee and the tight black slacks he was wearing. His arms and shoulders were covered with an array of menacing tattoos, but the standout was a round, blotchy scar at the top of his right shoulder. Obviously having a healed gunshot wound, he proudly had a tattoo artist etch a blue cursive "RANGERS" into the scar as a tribute to the sacrifice he made for the gang.

"Mr. Pickles and I are from Unified Insurance. I'm Otis Wahl. Mr. Pickles is working with me today, but this is my area," Otis said. The gangster nodded slightly, and his expression gave off a hint of recognition as he looked Otis square in the eyes.

"I've seen you. Yeah, I've seen you in some of the other buildings; you're Granny Jones' 'surance man," he said.

"No shit, bro. Granny Jones keeps me hopping," Otis said, laughing and slapping hands with the gangster.

"Damn straight," the gangster replied. Gangbangers watch everything and know everyone in their territories. I had no idea who Granny Jones was, but in all likelihood, she was of some kind of relation to this guy, which probably saved us a beating. Once he established that Otis was Granny Jones' insurance agent, we were no longer a threat, and his guard was dropped. "Come on in, man. It ain't cool to be rapping outside. I'm Ruppert," he said, shaking our hands as we passed through the door.

I had never been in a foreign country, but the feeling I got stepping into the apartment of the Black Rangers was almost surreal. Here I was, this white guy surrounded by gangsters in their sanctuary, with my only salvation being a client of Otis' whom I had never met named Granny Jones. It felt like I had just gotten off a plane in some hostile country and was welcomed by a dictator who could order my demise with a wave of his hand. There was no attempt to hide or even downplay the fact that these guys were openly engaged in some pretty serious illegal activity. They were so comfortable with their ability to operate, you would have never guessed that anything they did was wrong. Once Ruppert knew Otis and I weren't cops, he had no problem inviting us into the apartment.

From his point of view, there was nothing we could do to jeopardize their operation, and he knew it.

The sweet, musky aroma of marijuana lingered about the apartment, though it occasionally clashed with an assortment of cigarettes half lit or smoldering in the ashtrays of the gangsters as they went about their business. The layout was identical to Mrs. Williams' home nine floors above, right down to the green countertop splitting the kitchen from the living room. The difference, however, was that this was not a home—it was a hideout. There were no pictures on the walls of the living room and no dishes, pots, or pans in the kitchen. The stove was dirty and looked as if it hadn't been used in quite some time. There was garbage in the sink, and the green counter was awash in fast food wrappers and drink cups that looked as if they had accumulated over a couple of days. Two shadeless lamps rose above the trash on the counter and helped supplement the light from the circular fluorescent bulb mounted to the kitchen ceiling.

In the center of the living room were a couple of card tables that had been pushed together with folding chairs tucked under them. An overstuffed black couch was pushed up against the far wall. It was tattered and matted, with stuffing coming out of one side. Scrape marks along the bottom made it look as if it had been dragged out of an alley. A couple of fans chugged away on each side of the room, keeping the warm air circulating. Seated at the card tables were three gangsters, two on one side and one on the other, busy at work counting and separating money into piles as if they were allocating it to pay bills. The bandito was sitting on an old wooden chair, rocking back and forth in front of the living room windows that overlook the outside walkway. The dingy yellow curtains were drawn shut, but he kept a lookout by sliding his hand between them and peering out, alternating back and forth between the left and right. I was surprised that Ruppert let us in to see this, and I didn't feel at all comfortable that we were out of danger. He led us between the bandito and the card tables before he stopped and motioned for us to sit down on the couch.

He reached over between two of the guys sitting at the table and grabbed a half-opened pack of Kool cigarettes. He flipped them with his wrist a couple of times until some popped up, offering them to us before pulling one out of the pack with his lips. He tossed them back on the table and pulled one of the folding chairs over by us, flipped it backwards, and pulled it between his legs so he could lean over the back and talk to us.

He leaned to one side and dug deep into his pocket and pulled out a book of matches. He tore off a match and cupped it between his fingers, swiping at the matchbook until it ignited and lit his cigarette. He took a long drag and turned his head and exhaled as an act of courtesy, not blowing smoke in our faces.

"Y'all two crazy motherfuckers for coming up here," he said before taking another drag. "Nigga, you going to get this white boy killed walking around the Jets like this. There is some shit going down around here, and y'all better think about getting your ass out of dodge before y'all get caught up, you dig?" Ruppert said with a lecturing tone.

"No, man, we got no intention of hanging. We just came to see if we could get some new business and help out some of the folks in this building with their insurance. You know, like I did with Granny Jones, because there ain't too many people willing to come up here."

"I heard that," Ruppert acknowledged.

"So, we knock on a few doors and hand out our card so that people know someone is willing to take care of them if they have a need," Otis said. He spoke slowly, trying to convey to Ruppert that we were legitimately there to offer insurance to the people.

It was an important message because being poor in the black community wasn't shameful; everyone was poor. However, not having the money to bury a loved one properly was a disgrace. It meant relying on the church or relatives or, even worse, the government to come up with the money to bury a family member. Not being able to send someone off with a proper funeral was a real concern and one that Ruppert would understand as a good reason for us to be there. He nodded his approval and looked at me with a raised eyebrow and a devilish grin.

"What did you say your name was? Pickles? What the hell kind of name is Pickles? Like Mr. Potato head or something?"

"Ahh, yeah, Ron Pickles," I answered as a chorus of light laughter arose from the card tables.

"I'd have to change that, motherfucker," he said, laughing and shaking his head.

"No shit," Otis added.

"Well, the one good thing about it is that people remember who you are," I said jokingly.

"So, Mr. Pickles, what kind of 'in-surance' y'all sell?" he asked, articulating the term as if to let me know he could hold his own on any intellectual level he wanted.

"Just life and fire," I said.

"So, why did y'all tell Mosley over there he needed some insurance?" he asked, pointing to the bandito.

"So the motherfucker didn't shoot us," Otis piped up to everyone's delight. "But you know what? It wouldn't be a bad idea if you took out some insurance on these boys," he said. I cocked my head and looked at Otis in disbelief.

"What do you mean?" Ruppert asked.

"Y'all run a business up here," Otis said, ignoring the fact that the business consisted of gun running, drug selling, and money laundering. "One of your boys gets killed, it's going to cost you some money to replace him. It's called key man insurance. A key guy goes down, it hurts the whole organization, you dig?" My mouth must have dropped to the floor because Otis turned and gave me a look like I should get with the program and go along with him.

"Shit makes sense," Ruppert said. I looked around and noticed that everyone, including the bandito, had stopped what they were doing and begun listening intently to the conversation.

"Hey, Ruppert, you need to put a million fucking dollars on me to get your money's worth," one of the guys at the table said.

"Shit, your skinny ass ain't worth ten motherfuckin' cents," the guy sitting across from him countered.

"Hey, what about me?" the bandito spoke up. "Y'all know what I'm worth around here," he said.

"You ain't worth shit, Mosley. Fuck up my McDonald's order one more time, and I'll bury your sorry ass. Now, y'all shut the fuck up and let the man speak!" Ruppert's voice boomed across the room to what now had become quite intense laughter from the guys sitting at the card table. After a moment, everyone quieted down, and Otis resumed.

"Like I said, you, being the owner of the business, become the beneficiary. So, something happens to one of your guys, you get the money. You know, maybe help out the family or take care of putting them in the ground."

"Or take a fucking vacation," Ruppert added to everyone's amusement.

"You can do what you want with it, but at least you know you got something coming, you dig?"

"Yeah, I dig. What's that shit cost?"

"Pickles, write down everyone's age and look up the rates for $10,000 MDO on these guys." I looked at Otis incredulously as I opened my portfolio and flipped open my rate book. Everything Otis was proposing was illegal for us to do, and I couldn't tell if he was serious or just paying respect to Ruppert to get us out of there. You couldn't make just anyone a beneficiary; they had to have some insurable interest or experience a financial loss in the event the insured died. Otherwise, you could take out insurance on perfect strangers and hope they die just to get paid. Insurance companies frowned on that. The idea of key man insurance was correct, and Otis explained the idea to Ruppert properly. Businesses would insure a main guy or sometimes a host of important people in their company whose deaths would cause a financial loss to the business. The problem here was that Ruppert didn't really have a business; he had a gang. I was pretty sure that the piles of money being nicely sorted and stacked on the card tables had been derived from something other than the gang's legitimate business interests. I was also under the impression that this type of insurance required confirmation of a bank account, and I was sure that the cash-laden card tables wouldn't qualify. Then, there was the problem of the business' name; I had a hard time believing that Unified Insurance Company would issue a contract to a company named Black Rangers Inc. If all of that wasn't enough, there was the little matter of the key man's occupation.

Insurance companies were kind of concerned about the type of work performed by employees. Obviously, occupations such as skydiving, rock climbing, or any kind of circus acrobatics were higher risk, and the insurance companies charged accordingly. I wasn't sure, however, exactly what risk category "gangbanger" would be classified under, but I was positive that the life expectancy was lower than that of the general population and would need to be rated accordingly.

Now, taking all of that into consideration, I knew that we could not legally write key man insurance on these guys. I figured that Otis was trying to show them some respect by acknowledging their activities as businesslike. Ruppert might not have been as gracious and understanding towards us if we told him that Unified Insurance Company had a policy of denying coverage to gangsters, drug lords, or generally unsavory characters. I understood and agreed with Otis' approach, but I began to think that looking up rates might be going a bit too far.

MDO was an acronym for Monthly Debit Ordinary, a convoluted way of saying that the insurance was billed on a monthly basis instead of a weekly basis, which is what ledger companies really pushed their agents to sell. Weekly insurance was the most expensive insurance per thousand dollars you could buy, but it was also the cheapest to afford because you could actually buy increments as low as $100. It was a throwback to the Depression era. Money was so tight that people couldn't afford to buy any more than the exact amount it would cost to bury a body, which even then was a couple of hundred dollars. Companies such as Metropolitan and Prudential built their fortunes by hiring ledger, or "debit," agents to canvass communities and sell the policies they offered. Every week, they would go door to door and collect nickels and dimes from people to keep their insurance in force. The heyday for these companies and their agents was the nineteen thirties and forties. The advent of suburbia antiquated the idea of physically collecting premiums or just selling cheap burial insurance. People became more sophisticated and demanded insurance products that reflected the needs of their escalating lifestyles, effectively ending the era of the ledger agent. MDO was still expensive compared to the products offered by well-known companies but a lot better than the old-time weekly stuff and the only kind Otis would sell. He sold enough of it to put him at or near the top of the company's leader board every week.

I got up off the couch and went about the room, jotting down everyone's age and getting the correct spelling of their names. Otis and Ruppert had struck up a conversation and were joking amongst themselves as I returned to the couch. I quickly calculated the total premium and told Ruppert that it came to $120 per month for the four guys. Ruppert asked how much it would add to include himself, and I calculated the total cost to insure the five of them at $155 per month, a staggering sum of money by ledger standards. Though I tried hard not to think about it, the commission on a sale like this split between Otis and me would be more than $500 each. Ledger companies used a multiplier and a draw to pay commission to their agents. The multiplier for MDO was seven, so for every dollar of monthly premium you wrote, they would deposit $7 into your draw account. You could draw up to 15 percent of your account every week, so a sale like this would add $75 to my next six pay checks—money that I desperately needed.

"That's cool. Write that shit up," Ruppert said.

"I'd like to, but we got a problem," Otis replied, raising his eyebrows and shaking his head. *Finally, he's going to explain to Ruppert that he can't be everyone's beneficiary,* I thought to myself, trying to distance myself from the commission dollars rolling around in my head. I figured the only thing that appealed to Ruppert was the idea of getting paid if one of his guys got killed, and with their lifestyle it was more a question of "when" than "if" it would happen. We could still write them insurance, but I didn't think that Ruppert would foot the premium from the drug money if he weren't going to profit directly from someone's demise.

"The problem," Otis continued, "is that I got to be able to collect this shit, and we all know that you guys move the business from time to time. If that happens and I can't find you, the insurance is going to lapse. If it lapses, it ain't worth shit," he said.

"I hear you. What can we do?" Ruppert asked.

"Well, the first thing is we need you to pay at least three months up front, which will be $465. Then, when they issue the policies, I'm going to take them over to Granny Jones' place and leave them there. You'll get a receipt book for each policy, and I'll collect your money at her house."

"I'm hip. Count the man out $465," Ruppert commanded the guys at the table.

"Pickles, give me some applications. You go write up the guys at the table, and I'll take care of Mosley and Ruppert. Oh, by the way, leave the B section on the application blank. I'll take care of that later," he said. Without thinking, I looked down and saw that the B section on the application was the owner and beneficiary designation of the contract. Slowly, I lifted my eyes from the application and found Otis staring directly at me. It was then I realized that he never had any intention of writing key man insurance on the gang. He was just going to lie and make up some phony relationship between the gang members and make Ruppert the beneficiary. It was also a defining moment for me: Do I do the right thing and walk away, or do I fill out the application and go home $500 richer with a $77 board call for the Thursday meeting?

CHAPTER 4

We finished the paperwork on Ruppert and the gang, shook all their hands, and thanked them for the business as we exited the apartment. Otis and I looked at each other as if we couldn't believe what had just transpired and headed quickly toward the elevator. We both felt the intense need to exit the building as quickly as possible. It was entirely plausible that Ruppert could change his mind and come to the conclusion we had just relieved him of $465 for insurance he would find difficult at best to collect.

When we finally got to the cars, Otis insisted that I follow him to his favorite bar for lunch. He said that everything would be cool and that he'd explain how we were going to work out the policies at the tavern. I could actually feel the tension in my muscles begin to subside as I put the car in gear and followed Otis out of the parking lot. The tightness in my stomach was gone, and I couldn't believe the immense pleasure I was getting from taking several long, deep breaths as if I had just emerged from an underwater dive. I glanced in the rearview mirror at the building we left behind, praying the electrician's union would call so that I would never have to go back.

I really began to wonder how much more of this I could take. If it weren't for my wife and baby girl, I would have quit months ago, but I had to hang on to the job for them. I knew I had fallen into a money trap working for the insurance company and couldn't just quit. Where was I going to make four hundred-plus dollars per week with no real skills and just a high school education? It was crazy—I made over $500 today, and all I could think about was when the electrician's union would call and I could get out of this godforsaken place.

I began to wonder if I was putting too much faith into being accepted by the electrician's union, but my sister Judy kept telling me to hang in there because she knew I'd get called. I wanted to believe Judy about the union because I knew how Chicago worked and that it took time for things to happen, but I was really starting to get worried. In Chicago, you could never just apply to be a union electrician. You could send in an application—after all, the city and the unions needed to keep up appearances—but chances were pretty good that your application would be filed in some warehouse for ten years and eventually discarded as out of date. You had to know someone inside the union or connected to the city, someone who would put your name out for consideration. My "in" was Judy's old boyfriend, Bobby Cooker, an electrician and a union steward.

If it hadn't been for my sister, I don't know what I'd have done. She talked Bobby's ear off, asking him if there was anything he could do to help me get into the union. She told him how hard it was for me to get a decent job right out of high school, especially with a wife and baby to support. Bobby knew our family situation hadn't been the greatest and told Judy that he would see what he could do to help.

One day, Bobby sat me down and told me step by step what had to be done if I was to have any shot of getting into the union. "You have to go to the right places, meet the right people, and say the right things," he said. "It's almost like joining a club. There's a lot of benefits to being an electrician in the city, and the people in charge are very careful about who they let into the union to get those benefits."

The first thing he told me to do was fill out an application; this was the legitimate part of the process, except that I had specific instructions on what to do when I turned the application in at the Union Hall. Bobby told me to hand my application to the receptionist and deliberately say to her, "I was invited to the union smoker coming up in a few weeks." I did exactly what he said and handed the lady my application while articulating like a robot that I would be attending the union smoker. I stood there for a moment, thinking that she would give me a sign such as a nod or a wink acknowledging the secret code, but she just kind of smiled and jotted something down on the application before placing it in her out tray.

Bobby put himself on the line and let everyone in the union know that he vouched for me and wanted my application for an apprenticeship approved. Before that could happen, I had to attend a union function so the people who made those decisions had a chance to meet me. Bobby said I was lucky because a smoker was coming up, and the union boss told him to bring me along. I was excited but scared, knowing I had to impress everyone and convey how much I wanted to be an electrician. Bobby told me to relax and that I'd do just fine. He said that a smoker was nothing more than a boys' night out, complete with gambling devices, strippers, and as much alcohol as you could consume.

Bobby introduced me to everyone as his adopted brother. They all knew he was just joking, but the gesture implied that he would be offended if my name wasn't drawn for the next apprenticeship class since we had such a close relationship. The ploy seemed to work. Everyone seemed eager to meet me, shake my hand, and welcome me aboard.

When the evening was over, Bobby took me aside and told me that everyone was impressed and that I would be a lock to get accepted. I was super excited until he warned me that it might take six months to a year before I got the letter because I had just missed the deadline for the current year. When I told Judy that it might be a year before I got called, she freaked out. I knew she would. From that point forward, Judy made it her mission to find me a job that would hold me over until the union called. She had no idea what the black ledger was when she called in a favor and got me the interview at Unified Insurance Company, and I never had the heart to tell her.

In the moment I agreed to meet Otis for lunch, I was thinking we might be headed downtown or over to Little Italy on Taylor Street or Greektown on Halsted. It never dawned on me that his favorite establishment would be a couple of blocks away from the Cabrini projects, sandwiched between a vacant lot and a burned-out two-flat on the other side of his ledger. *Son of a bitch,* I thought to myself as he slowed down and waved for me to pull up next to him.

"This is it," he said, pointing to the dingy little brick building with no windows and a hand-painted wooden sign bolted across the top declaring that Joe's had the hottest wings in town. "Find some place to park, and I'll meet you at the door," he said before stomping on the gas and driving off. There was no parking lot, so we both had to fend for ourselves in trying to find an empty space between the rows of cars that lined each side of the residential street. I ended up parking half a block away and wasn't at all happy about backtracking on foot in the ninety-degree heat to eat at Joe's.

"You got to be shitting me. I thought we were going to go someplace decent for lunch," I asked as we met up at the door.

"Pickles, you got to try this place," he said as if he had discovered a local favorite nestled in the hills of Tuscany.

"I don't even like hot wings," I bemoaned.

"No, me neither, but they got the best fried buffalo in here that you will ever taste," he said with a proud smile.

"Fried buffalo? You mean like steak?" I asked.

"No, man, buffalo is fish. I'm telling you, you are going to love this shit, so shut the fuck up and give it a chance," he insisted. He pulled the heavy red door open, and a rush of cold air tickled my parched throat as I stepped inside to a fishy-smelling, noisy bar filled with black men who went completely silent as they turned toward me. I was temporarily blinded by the contrast of the white-hot sun outside and the dimly lit interior of the bar and didn't even realize that everyone in the room was staring at me. Otis stepped in behind me and started laughing at the expressions on everyone's faces.

"What the fuck, y'all never seen a cracker before?" he bellowed out as the whole place erupted in laughter and went back to their business. Slowly, my eyes began to adjust to the dim light, and I was amazed at the number of people crammed into the tiny place. I followed Otis as he made his way to the end of the bar, slapping hands and joking with some of the guys as he walked by. We found one empty stool at the end of the bar, which Otis helped himself to and pointed toward another leaning against the wall.

"Joe! Fry us up a buffalo!" he called out to the bartender while I fetched the other chair. "Pickles, what do you want to drink?"

"A Coke is fine with me," I said, still wrestling with the wayward stool to a position that would give me the appearance of sitting at the bar.

"Give me a Budweiser, and give Pickles here a Coke," he told the bartender. I hopped on the stool and looked down the bar at everyone as they picked at huge plates of greasy fried fish with their fingers. Sitting next to Otis was a nicely dressed older gentleman who was leaning forward with his elbows perched on the bar, holding his hands up like a surgeon waiting for a nurse to glove him. His eyes were focused straight ahead, and the determination scrolled across his face was intense. On the bar between his elbows was a plate of half-eaten fried fish. He caught my attention by scooping up a hunk of fish with the fingers of his right hand and shoving the whole thing in his mouth. Resting his elbow back on the bar, he seemed to roll the fish around in his mouth, cautiously chewing and swallowing some while using his tongue to pack some against his cheek like a squirrel. A moment later, ever so slightly, his lips would part, and several inch-long slivers of fish bone would strain from between his teeth. He would carefully remove the bones from his teeth with his left hand and gently deposit them on a napkin neatly positioned on the side of his plate before scooping up another hunk of fish and repeating the process.

Set back behind the bar was a full kitchen with a cook busily at work preparing food.

Joe, the bartender, tapped a beer into an icy mug for Otis and opened a can of Coke for me, setting the drinks in front of us and asking Otis if he wanted to pick out a fish.

"No, man, I'm cool. What about you, Pickles? You want to pick out a fish?"

"What do you mean, 'pick out a fish'?"

"Over there," he said, pointing to the end of the bar. I stood up from the chair and leaned over the bar to see where he was pointing. On the other side of the room, underneath the bar, was the biggest fish tank I had ever seen outside of the Shedd Aquarium downtown. It was propped up a couple of inches off the floor with two-by-fours and had to be at least six feet long and three feet high. It had all sorts of tubes and hoses hanging over the sides and running in different directions across the floor. The water on top was bubbling frantically, like a pot at high boil, occasionally splashing onto the floor. The glass was streaked with water spills that had crept down its sides and dried over and over again, leaving deposits of crud that obstructed most of my view, but a soft fluorescent light mounted under the bar cast just enough glow to make out the forms of a few dozen large fish packed into the tank.

"I never heard of a buffalo fish. What exactly is it?" I asked, sitting back in my chair.

"I'll get one," the bartender offered as he hurried off to get a fish before I could tell him that a verbal answer would have sufficed. Otis took a sip of his beer. I followed with a gulp of Coke as we waited for the bartender to retrieve the fish for our inspection.

"I take it you come here a lot?" I asked, returning the Coke to the bar.

"Whenever I need a break from the ledger, about every two hours," he joked while taking another sip of his beer.

"I hear you. I usually go up to the Lake Street Diner when I need to get away."

"That's Meadows' favorite place. He can drown himself in liver and onions over there," Otis said.

"Yeah, what is it with liver and onions? I never had liver and onions until I started working here, and every time we go to lunch, that's all he ever gets."

"He's got the whole goddamn office eating that shit," Otis quipped as the bartender returned holding a fat, silvery fish in both hands. We both leaned back in our chairs as he held the gasping fish up over the bar for our inspection, still dripping water.

"This is a buffalo!" he stated proudly.

"Okay, okay, that's cool. It kind of looks like a carp to me, but if you say it's a buffalo, then it's a buffalo," I said, motioning with both hands for him to take the fish away.

"That's what a buffalo is," he said.

"What, a carp?" I asked.

"That's right."

"Carp! You're not supposed to eat carp; they got some kind of garbage vein in them or something," I said with disgust.

"We cut that out. That's what James does over there," he said, nodding toward the fellow in the kitchen. "You'll see. Wait till you get a taste," he said and took the fish over to James for preparation.

"Carp? You took me to a place that serves carp for lunch?" I said in disbelief as I turned towards Otis.

"It's buffalo, goddamn it. Soul food. It's good for the soul. You need something that's good for the soul," Otis preached while taking another swig of beer.

"Soul food? I thought soul food was black-eyed peas, mustard greens, ham hocks, and shit like that."

"Goddamn it, Pickles! Soul food is whatever a black man says it is," Otis countered with a twinkle in his eye and a smile on his face.

"Really? Does that go for key man insurance as well?" I said, referring to the intriguing if not bizarre series of events that had transpired that morning. His expression changed instantly, and instead of sipping the beer, he chugged down the rest and put the empty mug on the bar.

"Fill me up, Joe," he called out before addressing me with a more serious tone. "I told you that I'd work that out."

"I know what you told me, but I'd like to know what the beneficiary designation is going to look like before I sign my name to the contract as one half of the writing agents. You know as well as I do that we can't submit a key man policy on a street gang."

He leaned against the bar and stroked his beard, then motioned with his head for me to move closer. He glanced around to make sure no one could overhear our conversation and spoke in a low, soft voice.

"Do you know who that motherfucker was?"

"You mean Ruppert?"

"Yeah, you ever hear of David Clarksdale?"

"No."

"Clarksdale founded the Black Rangers with Larry Drake; Ruppert is one of Clarksdale's cousins. These are some bad motherfuckers." We both paused as the bartender brought another beer for Otis.

"I know that," I said in a hushed tone as he left. "What I don't understand is why you went into all that shit about key man insurance."

"What you don't understand, goddamn it, is how close we came to getting the shit kicked out of us. That was his fucking crib we disturbed. You don't disturb a player's crib, you dig?" Otis arched his back up off the stool and took a deep breath before continuing. "He showed us some respect because I was Granny Jones' insurance agent."

"…And who is Granny Jones, anyway?"

"Granny Jones? Man… Granny Jones is like Mother Theresa in the projects."

"I don't follow you."

"She watches out for everybody, especially the little kids."

"Does she live in the projects?" I asked.

"Since they were built."

"No shit."

"Yeah, she does volunteer work out of the church, works with addicted mothers and shit. Probably raised half the kids growing up in the projects at one time or another."

"Wow! Ruppert sure seemed to respect her," I said.

"Even the Rangers won't fuck with Granny Jones, but I'm telling you, what saved our asses was treating him like a businessman and showing him respect," Otis said, tapping a finger on the bar as if to punctuate his point.

"Otis, I'm not stupid. I know all that. I've been on the ledger for eight months, and I know you got to do what you got to do. But we just took $465 from this guy and promised to write him up like a legitimate business, and we can't do that."

"Fuck that shit, Pickles. Ruppert just became everyone's cousin," Otis shot back. I looked at him for a long moment because I had figured that Otis was planning to make up a phony relationship the minute he told me not to fill in part two on the application.

"…And if one of his associates happens to get his head blown off, how is Ruppert going to prove he's their cousin? Don't you think he'll be just a little pissed off that he can't collect?" Otis looked at me as if I were insane, then cracked a smile and shook his head. "Damn, Pickles, you've been out here for eight months, and you still don't know what kind of insurance company you working for. Man… Unified Insurance Company is a substandard debit company. They don't give a shit who the beneficiary of a policy is as long as the premium is paid for two years. Don't you know that?"

"What do you mean, 'substandard'?" I asked, confused by a term that I had never heard before.

"That's the kind of insurance we write, substandard. You don't see Metropolitan or Prudential out here, do you? They're standard companies. They don't write the shit we do. How many times have you written up couples that are shacking together but not married?" he asked.

"Lots of times," I responded.

"What relationship do you put down on the application?"

"Meadows told me to put down 'common law.'"

"That's right, common law. Common law don't mean shit. There ain't no such thing as a common-law marriage. You're either legally married or you're not. Unified don't give a shit," he said. I looked at him for a moment then took a drink of my Coke. He made a point. I never thought about it before, but he was right, or I wanted him to be right because I desperately needed the commission we'd make from the sale, and I was looking for a way to justify whatever he had in mind.

"So, we're going to write them up as cousins. Do you have a problem with that?" he asked.

"…And if I said I had a problem, we'd go back and give Ruppert his money back?"

"No, fuck that shit. If you got a problem with it, then I keep the commission on the whole goddamn thing," Otis said with a grin.

"Yeah, I figured that's where we were going."

"Pickles, I'd never tell you to do anything crooked like those other cocksuckers in our office. I don't do that crooked bullshit, and I wouldn't tell you to do something to fuck yourself up, but you got to understand something," his tone turned serious.

"What's that?"

"You got to take care of yourself first, the people second, and fuck the company. They come third, you dig? You can't be walking around the goddamn projects like we did and not make any money.

That's bullshit. You can't piss off a guy like Ruppert when you're out here. If he wants to insure the whole goddamn gang, then fuck it, that's what we're going to do, you dig? This company doesn't write insurance outside the ghetto. They know what they're doing, and they're making money doing it, so fuck it; everybody's happy."

"I guess I just got an education," I said with a deep breath.

"Welcome to the black ledger," Otis said, lifting his glass for me to toast with my Coke. I tapped his glass with my can, not entirely comfortable with his logic, though I did agree that the company made certain allowances for beneficiaries. I took a swig of Coke and seemed to swallow my convictions with the sugary drink when something Otis had said popped into my head.

"What were you talking about with all that 'crooked shit' the other guys do?" I asked. Otis looked at me incredulously, as if I were the naivest person on the planet, then started shaking his head and laughing hysterically.

"Joe, where's that goddamn buffalo? Pickles is getting hungry!" he shouted across the bar, apparently dismissing my question out of hand.

"It's up now!" Joe shouted from the kitchen. "Y'all want to eat off the big platter or get your own plates?" he asked.

"I want my own. I don't know what kind of diseases this white boy has," Otis joked to the amusement of those sitting by us.

"That's nice; could you make me feel any more uncomfortable?" I softly lamented. "Seriously, what did you mean by 'crooked shit' those guys do?" I asked again with a harder tone. He looked down at his beer, then began stroking his beard as if contemplating how to answer. After a moment, he turned towards me and peered into my eyes. "Meadows is an asshole, but he truly doesn't want you to get mixed up in any bullshit in that office, you dig?"

"Yeah, Meadows is all right," I shrugged off.

"Shit, Pickles. You don't know half the shit that goes on in that office, and trust me, you don't want to. This shit stays between you and me, all right?" he demanded with a finger on my chest.

"Absolutely," I agreed.

"There is some seriously crooked shit going down in that office. Motherfuckers got deals with funeral homes, deals with whores, deals with drug dealers."

"You mean the stoner staff? I know they do all kinds of nasty shit."

"You don't know shit. Everyone in that office has his hand into someone else's pocket."

"Not Hamilton," I said in disbelief that our district manager was corrupt.

"I don't know about Hamilton. I think he just looks the other way when shit goes down because it's so hard to get motherfuckers to work the ghetto in the first place," he lamented.

"Well, don't worry about me. I'm not getting involved in any of that bullshit. Once the union calls, all you'll see from me is assholes and elbows as I run the fuck away from this job," I said laughing.

Just then, the bartender plopped down a thanksgiving-size platter on the bar with what I presumed was the once-gasping fish now deep fried to a crispy brown. I had to admit that it was an impressive presentation, though I wished they had removed the fish's head before serving. The fish was steaming hot, and the aroma was pleasant and inviting, unlike the rest of the place that just seemed to smell fishy. The fish was cradled upon the platter in a bed of greens and garnished with green onions and black olives. The bartender stepped back for a moment, as if admiring his work, and looked at both of us for approval. Otis and I instantly responded with an appreciative nod, and he continued his service by dealing us two smaller plates. He reached under the bar and came up with two squeezable red ketchup bottles and a stack of paper napkins that he placed between Otis and me.

"Ketchup?" I inquired.

"Naw, this one is barbecue sauce, and this one is wine vinegar," he said, placing the identically colored bottles on the bar.

"Got a fork back there?" I asked. Without saying a word, he glared at me with a snarled expression as if I had just committed some unholy sacrilege. Otis stroked his beard and just shook his head as if apologizing for bringing me into the place. The bartender nodded as if he understood, then he gave me a sullen look, turned around, and walked away. "What's the big deal with the fork?" I asked.

"Man, this is Chicago; there are some things you just don't do, like ketchup on hot dogs. You don't put ketchup on hot dogs. Somebody sees you putting ketchup on hot dogs, they'll think you're queer," Otis said.

"I don't put ketchup on my hot dogs. I asked for a fucking fork. What's the big deal?"

"Shit, Pickles. These people take pride in their buffalo. You insult them by asking for a fork, like saying the shit is too tough to eat."

"That ain't it at all," I tried to explain. "I just don't want all that grease running down my arms," I said.

"That ain't grease. That's juice, goddamn it. Don't you know the difference between grease and juice?"

"Actually, I do know the difference between grease and juice," I said sarcastically as I scooped up a handful of fried buffalo, head and all, dropping it onto my plate. Otis was impressed with my bold move and stared at me intently. With a look of cool indifference and not so much as a flinch, I borrowed the three-finger style from the guy sitting next to us and plucked a hunk of fish off my plate and slapped it down my throat. Otis was impressed and nodded his approval, then grabbed a hunk of the buffalo and slammed it down himself.

"So, whatch you think?" Otis demanded.

"You know, I'm not sure I'd go out of my way for it, but it's not half bad," I mumbled while trying to push the fish bones to the front of my mouth for removal.

"Joe, you hit the big time. This honky's going to spread the word to all his white folk to come by and get some buffalo!" Otis bellowed out across the bar. I just shook my head and stuffed another handful of fish in my mouth as the place blew up in laughter.

After lunch, I pulled onto the Dan Ryan Expressway and headed home for the south suburbs, still picking an occasional fish bone from between my teeth. The grease (or juice, as Otis liked to call it) from the buffalo left a coating in my mouth that half a pack of gum and two more Cokes couldn't seem to dissolve. My head was pounding from the events of that morning, and I was afraid my dreams that night would somehow tie a fish, a tit, and a black bandito into a twisted scene that was sure to scar me for life.

CHAPTER 5

Later That Afternoon

I sat in the car staring at the back of my apartment building, half thinking that I would rather be back working the projects with Otis instead of getting caught up in the mortal battle of supreme control between my wife and my mother. It dawned on me that I was beginning to dread coming home almost as much as I disliked going to work. I was glad to be home, but I was hot and tired and hardly in the mood to talk to anyone, much less my mother. Since my mom and little sister lived on the ground floor in the rear of the building directly across from ours, she always heard cars when they pulled up outside her window and parked.

Whenever Mom heard me come home, she would try to catch me in the hallway and strike up a conversation, pretending to be interested in the things that happened to me that day. However, her so-called interest was merely a ploy for dropping an innocent comment about something wrong with my wife Jessica. Her focus was Jessica. She constantly made snide little comments about the way she dressed, the way she took care of the baby, anything she could think of to get under my skin. Then, she would apologize for "bringing it up at all," but because she was my mother, she thought I should know. She was like a fly, tormenting me every time I tried to open my door, buzzing around my head one minute, then disappearing and pretending to be gone the next. Most of the time, I just wanted to tell her to mind her own business and leave us alone, but with her living right next door, I just listened to her ramblings and told her I'd look into whatever she was talking about. We should have never moved to the same city, let alone the same building, as my mom. Living next to her had become intolerable. I was pissed at myself for letting her talk us into it.

A few months back, we got caught in a bind. The owner of our previous apartment died, and his relatives sold the building. The new owners wanted both apartments for related living, which meant that Jessica and I had to move as soon as possible. Upon hearing the news, my mother was quick to inform us that the apartment next to hers was available and we should take it before someone else did. She talked our ears off about what a great place this was and how wonderful the landlord had treated her whenever something broke. Then, she extolled the benefits of living next door to each other, explaining how great it would be for Jessica to have a babysitter anytime she needed one. Between her and my little sister, Linda, someone would always be available so Jessie could get a break. She made it sound so good, even my older sister, Judy, bought into the idea, which of course made me think it was a win-win situation. Only briefly did Jessica and I discuss the negatives of living next door to Mom, who we both thought might be a pain at times but hardly worth abandoning the apartment over. The apartment was cute, and it was on the ground floor, which both Jessica and I thought was a real positive with the baby, so we took it.

We hadn't even unpacked the last box before my mom started to complain about the noise we were making, saying that the old lady living above us would tell the landlord. Then, she asked me not to park so close to the building because my parking spot butted up against her window, and we woke her up if we came home late. After that, she told us to keep the dog quiet because she could hear Rudy barking. It was something different all the time, but the straw that broke the proverbial camel's back was when she started telling Jessica what she was doing wrong with the baby.

Every day, she would knock on the door wanting to see the baby, only to make a disparaging remark on what Jessica could do better. She started commenting on little things, like the way Jessica held the baby, that she gave her the wrong food, or that she heard the baby crying for too long. At first, Jessica took it in stride, thinking that

Mom was truly looking out for the baby's wellbeing and just showing her concern. After a while, though, Jessica realized that Mom's whole purpose for intruding was to put her down. I don't think Jessica would take such offense if my mom were there to lend a hand or help with the baby in any way, but whenever Jess asked her for help, she refused. On the other hand, Mom was quick to enlist my services whenever she needed a hand with something, which, of course, brought Jessica to an immediate boil. I lost count of the number of times Jessica scolded me for attending to my mother's needs when she refused to watch the baby for even an hour so we could do the weekly shopping.

My mom was great at manipulation because she mixed just enough truth with her guilt-inflicting tone to make you think she really hoped things would get better. She couldn't understand why anyone would get upset; she only said those things because she cared so much. It was the little things that stayed with you and got under your skin, like the time she told me what a beautiful woman Jessica would be if she just wore a little makeup. I told her that I always thought Jessica's complexion was so smooth and soft, she never really needed makeup to highlight her looks, but the suggestion was planted. Another time, she told me how lucky Jessica was to have such lovely long, brown hair. Wasn't it a shame that she didn't brush it more often? Again, I defended my wife by explaining that I loved Jessica's brown hair and brown eyes just the way they were and wouldn't change a thing, but, like before, the suggestion was planted.

Then one day, I was in my mom's apartment helping her move a piece of furniture when out of nowhere she bemoaned, "Oh, Ronnie, I hope you make a lot of money with this insurance job because I feel so bad that Jessica has to wear the same old jogging pants and T-shirts every day." One more time, I explained to my mother that Jessica had lots of clothes to wear but that she still felt a little self-conscious about the weight she gained from having the baby and chose to cover up until she got her figure back. Mom would accept my explanation with a smile and compliment me for being so understanding. I walked away from her believing everything was fine, not having a clue that all I needed was a copy of *The Catcher in the Rye* to complete my brainwashed indoctrination as the next *Manchurian Candidate*.

It wasn't like I walked out of Mom's apartment into ours and demanded that Jessica comb her hair, wear makeup, and put on a short dress. Secretly, however, I did begin to wish for a little more sex appeal from my wife and wondered why she didn't want to fix herself up for me. Finally, after allowing the thought to fester for some time, I decided to tactfully suggest that she fix herself up a little. Bad move on my part. Mom never mentioned to me that she had been hinting to Jessica for months to improve her looks. I wasn't aware that part of my mother's daily affirmation to Jessica included an instructive lecture on how pretty she would look with a good makeover, better clothes, or a different hairstyle that might bring out her "hidden features." Jessica was not only prepared to answer any criticism, but she was also armed with an offensive reply that sounded as if it had been rehearsed for months.

"You son of a bitch! How dare you listen to that old hag talk about me?! What the hell do you expect? I clean your house, do your laundry, take care of the baby, walk the dog, and put up with that mean piece of shit next door all damn day! Do you come home and help? Hell no! The minute you walk in the door, you're over at her house like the perfect little mama's boy. Where do we go, Ron? Do we go to the show? Do we go out to dinner? No! We don't have the money to do those things, yet you expect me to be dressed like Donna fucking Reed when you come home. Don't you think I would like to get dressed up and go out once in a while? I have two outfits to my name. Maybe I should put them on to scrub the floor or feed the baby who eats like her mouth is on the other side of her head. Maybe you'd like me to clean up Rudy's diarrhea in high heels and nylons. And as far as makeup is concerned, forget it, pal. I don't believe in makeup; it's stupid. I want a husband that loves me for who I am, not for the kind of makeup I wear to fool you into thinking I'm someone I'm not!" She punctuated by slamming the bedroom door and forcing me to sleep on the couch that night. It was strange, but the more Jessica carried on, the more I wanted her to change her appearance. It was the power of suggestion. My mother managed to convince me that there must be something wrong with Jessica. Why else wouldn't she want to look her best for her husband? At the same time, Jess considered anything my mom said an insult and did exactly the opposite. Just thinking about it gave me an enormous headache as I slowly opened the car door.

Carefully, I stepped out of the car and shut the door as quietly as I could. Even though it was 4:30 in the afternoon, I tried to make as little noise as possible. I felt like a thief attempting to break into my own house, but there was no way I could deal with my mother today. To avoid her, I figured on skipping the front entrance to the apartment, which was actually located on the side, and walk all the way around the building to our back door that had its own entrance outside. With the stealth of a really bad cat burglar, I slinked around the building, confident that my plan worked like a charm. When I reached the back door, I looked both ways to make sure Mom wasn't creeping around outside someplace before pulling the screen door open and wedging my body between it and the back door. With my ledger book in one hand and my briefcase in the other, I managed to grip the doorknob on the back door and push it open a few inches before realizing something was blocking it on the other side. I knew Jessica was home because I could hear the washer and dryer chugging away in our tiny utility room into which the door opened. I called out to no avail, figuring that she was in the baby's room on the far side of the apartment, unable to hear me. My calls for help didn't go entirely unnoticed, however, as our loyal—though somewhat cross-eyed—dog, Rudy, excitedly popped his long nose through the crack in the door to greet me. The moment I saw that nose, I knew that my preconceived genius for avoiding my mother had just turned to shit.

Rudy was a beautiful brown-and-white purebred collie who was about as far removed from the stereotypical wonderdogs of Lassie fame that you could imagine. Against my wishes, Jessica insisted that we have a dog in our apartment for security to protect her and the baby. I tried to convince her that if we had to have a dog, we should get a small one that was easy to take care of and would fit easier into apartment life. Jessica would hear nothing of it, insisting on getting the dog she always wanted since she would be the one taking care of it.

Like everyone else in the country, she grew up loving Lassie and wanted a collie, so, undeterred by my initial criticism, she set off in search of a collie puppy to bring into the family. The problem was that we had a very limited budget, and purebred collies were very expensive. Undaunted by the lack of finances, she managed to find a breeder who was willing to sell her his last remaining puppy from a recent litter. Not knowing too much about dogs, neither of us were concerned with the fact that out of eight puppies, seven of them had been placed with families by the time they were eight weeks old at the full price of $300 each.

Rudy was fourteen weeks old, and the breeder was willing to let us have him for $75 if we signed an agreement not to use him for breeding. We were convinced that we had struck an awesome deal and that Rudy was meant to be part of our family. He told us that overbreeding by some unscrupulous breeders led to eye problems in collies and that we shouldn't be alarmed by the apparent cross-eyed condition of our little guy. However, I did become a little suspicious when the breeder handed us a bunch of prescriptions for the dog, explaining that sometimes collies had trouble with their stomachs and coats. "Not to worry, though," he said. "That stuff usually clears up after about six months."

Our vet just kind of snickered when we told him what the breeder said and informed us that we should take Rudy back immediately to be put down because he had multiple problems. I knew the moment he said, "regardless of the dog's condition," we were going to keep him because there was no way Jessica was going to take Rudy back to the breeder to be destroyed. So, a year later, Rudy was still banging into walls from his crossed eyes, throwing up if we gave him too much food, and getting terrible diarrhea if he ate anything other than the original puppy food the breeder gave us. Other than that, Rudy was an incredibly sweet dog that you couldn't help but love, despite knowing the issues he had to struggle through every day.

The problem with Rudy greeting me at the back door was that he had problems backing up. If he couldn't turn around and see where he was going, he wouldn't go. The utility room was like a walk-in closet right off the kitchen; it was tiny, and there wasn't a lot of room to get through when it was cleaned spotless. I got the door open far enough to see that Jessica had mounds of laundry piled on the floor. Rudy had wedged himself between the dirty laundry and the washer when he excitedly rushed to greet me and only now realized that he would have to back up to extricate himself from the position. He wasn't prepared to do that and instead struck the pose of a cat trapped in a tree, clinging for life on a tree branch.

I refused to give up and walk around to the front door, knowing that the consequences would result in a confrontation with my mother. Invigorated by the challenge, I began stabbing at the dirty laundry with my left foot while balancing on my right with the screen door bouncing off my butt, all the while holding the stuff I brought from the car. Sweat began pouring down my face as I cleared just enough room to get my foot under Rudy's chest. Slowly, I crouched down on my right leg and pushed at Rudy's upper body, sliding the huge collie back across the tile floor. I began to feel like a limbo dancer attempting to squirm under the lowest notch on the pole when my ledger book dislodged from under my arm and hit the ground with a thud. I twitched trying to grab it but got a cramp in my outstretched leg, forcing me to jump up reeling in pain.

"Shit! Goddamn it! Son of a bitch," I yelled out, dropping the briefcase while grabbing at my leg. Startled by the reaction, Rudy stood up and moved forward, sticking his nose back in the crack and reclaiming the precious inches I needed to get the door open. I backed up, hobbling around on my leg while letting the screen door slam shut. Suddenly, the back door opened, and Rudy nudged the screen door with his nose and bounced outside to greet me, trembling with excitement as if we hadn't seen each other in years.

"Okay, okay. That a boy. You're a good boy," I said, petting his head and rubbing his belly in an attempt to calm him down.

"What are you doing out here?" Jessica asked with a puzzled look. "What are you screaming and swearing at? Why didn't you come in the front door?" she asked in rapid succession while holding both doors open for me as I ushered Rudy back into the house, picked up my stuff, and squeezed by her.

"I was hoping to avoid my mother," I said, not realizing that I had just rubbed salt in an open wound.

"That must be nice. I wish I could avoid her," Jessica said as she closed the doors and followed behind me. I was exhausted yet relieved to be out of the heat and into our air-conditioned apartment. I crossed the kitchen, dropping the car keys on the table, and hobbled into the front room with Jessica in tow.

"You don't know how lucky you are. Do you have any idea how miserable it is to be stuck in this house all day with your mother banging on the door every fifteen minutes?" she complained as I collapsed on the couch in front of the television, still holding my briefcase and ledger book. She followed me to the couch, arms crossed and body twisted with attitude, venting about the ills perpetrated upon her during the day by my mother.

"That woman won't leave me alone. All she ever does is bitch about everything I do with the baby, but she won't lift a finger to help. If I ask her for help with something or to watch Jeannie for a minute, you know what she says? 'Oh no, I'm too busy. I can't. Oh no, I just can't. I have things I have to do,'" Jessica said while waving her arms, perfectly imitating my mother's stammering refusal to put herself out.

"I don't suppose you could give me a minute to relax," I interjected with a snotty tone when she paused for a breath.

"Sure, why not. You don't care. You don't care because you don't have to deal with her. You get to go off and collect money and do your little sales thing all day while I'm stuck in this house doing your laundry, changing your baby's shitty diaper, and waiting for your mother to bang on the door again," she said with disgust as she disappeared from my view back into the laundry room.

A few moments later, Jessica marched out of the kitchen, holding an overstuffed laundry basket in her arms on her way to the bedroom. "By the way, I thought you said you were going to bring McDonald's home for dinner," she quipped as she passed. I sat up on the couch, realizing there would be no peace until I brought home dinner, wondering to myself at what point in our marriage Jessica would learn to cook.

Exasperated, I got up and went into the baby's bedroom to check on our little girl, Jeannette. I figured she was napping because the door was shut, and Jess never shut the door if she was awake. I pushed the door open softly, as not to wake her, and peeked inside. She was fast asleep, safe and snug in her crib, and curled up like a little ball in pink pajamas. Her stuffed animals surrounded her like a military guard formation protecting their queen. I stared at her for a moment, thinking what a beautiful baby Jessica and I were able to make together while half wondering if we'd be together when she grew up. I tiptoed out of her room and quietly shut the door. Jessica was standing in the hallway waiting for me as if she had read my thoughts from the other room. She put her arms around me and buried her head into my chest. "I'm sorry. Sometimes I just have to let it out. You know what I mean?" she said, holding me tight. "I love you, Ronnie."

"I know, baby. I love you too," I said, returning her hug while guiding her into our bedroom.

CHAPTER 6

The Next Morning

The next morning, I got up feeling refreshed and ready to go. I took a shower, put on my best short-sleeved white shirt, and reveled in my newfound talent: shaping my favorite maroon tie with little blue dots into the perfect knot. Then, I carefully took the new dark blue suit I had bought for meeting days out of the closet and put it on, feeling like a million dollars. I wanted to look good for the board call today because I knew the sales Otis and I made were something special. After taking Rudy for a quick walk, I came back into the apartment, grabbed my briefcase and ledger book, kissed the girls goodbye, and jumped in the car for the trip to the office. Thursdays were settlement days, which meant we had to have our accounts in the window by 10:30 a.m. or Hamilton would ream our managers. I didn't want to give Meadows any more headaches than he already had, so I made it a point of getting to the office with plenty of time to get my paperwork finished.

I got off the elevator on the fifth floor and had just walked past the glass door to the reception area, opting to go in the back door of the agents' room, when Mr. Hamilton popped his head out and asked me to come into his office. Without question, I spun around and followed him. I wasn't the least bit worried about anything since I had a great board call, and most of my accounts were paid up to date. Of course, that was until I saw the uniformed police officers standing in his office. I slowed my step considerably and could feel a look of concern, if not dread, coming over my face as I stepped up to the officers while Mr. Hamilton took a position behind his desk.

"Mr. Pickles, this is Officer O'Brian and Officer Ancerwitz. They were wondering if they could ask you a few questions about T.J.?" Hamilton asked as if directing me to answer the officers directly.

"Well, sure, but I haven't seen T.J. since last Thursday. Is something wrong?" I asked. I was surprised by the question yet relieved that the officers weren't here because of something involving my family or me. T.J. was the only other white guy on our staff and had been on the job almost a year. He sat next to me in the office, and on occasion we would go out to lunch, but otherwise we didn't hang out together.

"His wife filed a missing persons report on him, and we're following up. That's all," Officer O'Brian said.

"Damn!" I said with surprise. "We were going to meet for lunch this week, but he didn't come in on Tuesday, so I thought he was sick or something, and I blew it off," I added.

"Mr. Meadows is your staff manager, correct?" Officer Ancerwitz asked while jotting notes on a pad.

"That's right."

"Do you and T.J. work together often?" he asked.

"No, actually, we never work together. A couple of us guys would just meet over at the Lake Street Diner on occasion for lunch before going out to the ledger to make collections."

"Did he ever confide in you?" O'Brian asked. I had to think about my answer for a second. Half the office knew that T.J. had been hanging out with the guys on the stoner staff, getting high and banging hookers two at a time on the ledger. Rumor was he'd been shacking up with some babe off and on since he started here, but I didn't want to be the one to tell that to the cops.

"No," I said after a long pause. "He never told me anything," I said with little conviction.

"Are you sure? Anything might be helpful," Ancerwitz asked again, picking up right away on the hesitancy in my voice.

"I wish I could help you, but I really don't know him that well," I said, trying to sound a little more confident.

"We appreciate your help, Mr. Pickles. Here's my card. If you hear anything or think of anything, give us a call," Ancerwitz said.

"I'll do that," I said, shoving the card in my shirt pocket. "Anything else?" I asked politely.

"No, that's about all. Thank you," O'Brian said, and I wasted no time leaving the room.

It was about 8:30 when I finally walked into the agents' room, and I was surprised to see that most of the guys on the other three staffs were already there chatting, talking on the phone, or hurriedly trying to get their paperwork together. The air was filled with a haze of smoke that choked me as I walked to my seat. It seemed like everyone was smoking and pushing the remains of their half-lit cigarettes into ashtrays that were already stoked to the rims with crushed-out butts. Mr. Meadows sat alone at the head of our staff, tucked behind his little metal desk, puffing away at his pipe. He had a ledger book open and was furiously flipping the pages of the book, pulling a full account.

The aroma of freshly brewed coffee somehow permeated through the seams of smoke-encrusted air, grabbing my attention as I walked into the office. I almost tripped over myself rushing to the table to get a cup while dropping my stuff on my desk as I passed. With as many as twenty-eight agents in the room at one time during settlement days, coffee was at a premium. We would all take turns making a pot, but invariably it would be gone before the last drop brewed out of the spout. One day, a couple of agents almost got into a fight when one of them decided to remove the pot during the brew process and insert his cup under the drip instead. Hamilton ended up devoting fifteen minutes of the meeting to educating us on the etiquette of proper coffee making. More than a few agents complained that the solution to the problem was another coffee machine. Hamilton contended that the only time there was a problem was on settlement days and another machine would be a waste of money. I think it was Otis that labeled him a "cheap motherfucker" after his lame explanation to the office.

I poured the steamy liquid into a Styrofoam cup, tore open a handful of sugar packets, and held them over the coffee, wiggling them back and forth between my fingers to get all the sugar out. Then, I carefully tapped the sides of an oversized canister, shaking out some dried creamer over the top. Cautiously, I stirred the floating creamer into the black abyss of hot java, anxiously awaiting the perfect beige color to emerge from my careful blending. I was dying for the first sip yet restrained myself, opting to garnish its full pleasure by enjoying it at my desk. Guardedly, I carried the cup across the room like a wild animal shielding his recently captured prey from others. I placed the cup on my desk and was just about to sit down when caught off guard by an intense gaze from Mr. Meadows.

"Is there something wrong?" I asked instinctively.

"Good morning, Ron!" he said forcefully.

"Good morning, Ray," I replied hesitantly.

"No! Good morning, Ron!" he shouted out as if I should have been aware of something that was bothering him.

"What!" I shouted back.

"You see me sitting here up to my ass in this book, and you can't ask me if I want a cup of coffee?" he barked out. I shook my head before giving him a long look of dismay.

"You know, Ray, you seen me pouring the damn cup and didn't say shit," I countered. "Do you want a cup of coffee?" I asked.

"Thank you, Ron," was his only response before returning his head to the book. I turned around just in time to see Ol' Man Wicks pour out the last drop into his cup and put the empty coffee pot on the table for someone else to refill. Not exactly racked with guilt, I placed my carefully prepared cup in front of my boss, then put my hand on the back of his thick neck and squeezed while whispering into his ear.

"You know something, Ray? I really don't give a shit, but I hope you like cream and sugar in your coffee," I said softly as I noticed a tiny smirk forming at the corner of his mouth.

"Thank you, Ron," he said, pleased with himself while I left to make a fresh pot. There wasn't a fresh water hookup in the office, so I had to go out the agents' back door into the hallway and stand at the water fountain, precariously tilting the coffee pot in different directions to get it filled. Vinnie Elder, one of the agents from the stoner staff, came up behind me and tapped me on the shoulder as I was filling it.

"Hey, Pickles, I seen Hamilton pull you in his office, man. What did they ask you?"

"Probably the same thing they asked you," I said, trying to ignore him.

"No, shit, man. I don't want to talk to them. I caught a little buzz this morning, so I've been hanging out in the toilet waiting for the cops to leave. They talked to Teddy, though, and he came down to the can and told me to stay there till they left, but I'm, like, fucking dying to know what's going on, man, you know? …Man, it's like they want to know what happened to T.J.," he said. "Did you tell them anything?" he asked, half slurring his words.

I finished filling the coffee pot and turned toward him. In his mid-twenties, Vinnie was about six foot tall with a nice build, a full head of curly, jet-black hair, and a pale complexion. His clothes were always on the shabby side. I could never remember seeing him in anything except brown corduroy pants and pullover shirts. Vinnie was one of those guys that everyone knows and usually does their utmost best to avoid. His life revolved around getting stoned, and he was firmly convinced that everyone else's should too. Other than turning his brown eyes to glass, getting high suited Vinnie. It brought out color in his cheeks and gave him somewhat of a personality.

"Vinnie, first of all, I don't know anything, and that's what I told the cops. If you know where T.J. is, you should go in there and say something. His wife just filed a missing persons report on him, for goodness' sake," I said.

"No, man, you don't get it. T.J. hates that bitch. That's why he doesn't want to go home," Vinnie said as if T.J. were in some mortal danger.

"Look, Vinnie," I said, trying hard not to laugh, "you and I both know that the only reason T.J. doesn't want to go home is because he's been boning some chick on the ledger and is stoned out of his mind. Eventually, he is going to have to go home. How much longer do you think Meadows and Hamilton are going to put up with this shit? They can't have cops coming in the office looking to drag T.J. home every week."

"I know, man, but his wife is such a bitch. He said he was going to take care of it. I talked to T.J. this morning, and he said he's coming in after the meeting to square up with everyone," Vinnie finally admitted.

"…And you don't want to tell the cops this?" I asked.

"Wow, man, I don't know. You think I should?" he asked hesitantly, looking into my eyes like an eight-year-old boy afraid to tell the teacher he stole her apple.

"Yeah, actually, I do. You might even be saving the dude's job if they think it's all a big misunderstanding and the wife just freaked out, you know?" I looked at Vinnie for a long moment, thinking to myself how ridiculous these two assholes were acting. "Come on, I'll go in the office with you. How does that sound?" I said, nudging him toward the reception area door.

"Yeah, all right, but Teddy told me to wait in the john, man. I don't want to piss him off, you know."

"Fuck Teddy. He doesn't know shit. Just go in there and be straight with these guys, all right?"

"All right, but you got to come with me. …Man, you know, give me some moral support, you know?"

"Okay, let's go. I got a lot of shit to do before the meeting, and I don't have time to fuck around all day," I said with a sigh while leading Vinnie into the reception office. I led Vinnie up to the open doorway of Hamilton's office, still holding onto the filled coffee pot, when Mr. Uhlen from Mr. Singh's staff jogged up to me, putting his thick hand on my shoulder and asking me for the pot.

"Everyone was wondering what happened to it," he said with a smile in a heavy Jewish/German accent.

"Sorry, Mr. Uhlen. Here it is all filled up for you. But do me a favor and make sure I get a cup," I said, handing him the pot before continuing into Hamilton's office with Vinnie behind me. Hamilton was still engaged in conversation with the officers who were standing in front of his desk. I quietly stood in the doorway with Vinnie behind me, waiting patiently for Roger to acknowledge us before speaking. He finally looked beyond the officers with an annoyed glance in my direction; that was my cue to interrupt.

"Excuse me, Roger. I'm sorry to bother you, but I was just talking to Vinnie here, and I think he might have some information about T.J.," I said with as much innocence as I could project in my voice. From the steely glare that shot past me and landed on Vinnie, I could see that Roger was not at all happy.

"Thank you, Ron. Vince, will you please step inside? Ron, please close the door behind you," he ordered in a tone that sounded like he didn't want me to witness the summary execution he was about to perform. Vinnie walked in the office, passing me with a grimace on his face like I had just sold him out, but I really didn't care. He was so high that he wouldn't remember what happened anyway. I just wanted to get back into the agents' room and pour that cup of coffee I wanted so badly.

I walked back to the reception area and fought my way through a line of agents standing at the window waiting for Mrs. Bolger to clear their accounts. I finally broke through into the agents' room and headed for the coffee pot when I felt like screaming at the top of my lungs; it was empty again. Taking a deep breath, I bit my lower lip. I was just about to grab the pot and start the process all over when Mr. Uhlen came over and held up a piping hot Styrofoam cup of the good stuff.

"I could have sold this for big money," he said with a twinkle in his eye, handing me the cup. The yellow short-sleeved shirt he was wearing exposed his massive arms as we made the exchange. I couldn't help but notice the blue identification number burned into his right forearm, a stark reminder of his captivity in a German concentration camp forty years earlier. I tried not to look at it, always feeling awkward, not quite knowing if I should say something or wondering if perhaps I was insulting him by ignoring it.

"Thank you, sir. You have no idea how much I've wanted this cup of coffee," I said with a smile and profound gratitude for his act of kindness.

"I'm just glad the coffee pot hadn't disappeared," he said with bugged eyes and a look of feigned astonishment before returning to his desk. A robust fellow in his early sixties, Mr. Uhlen had the best demeanor in the office. In stark contrast from Henry Weinstein and Mr. Guru, the other two Holocaust survivors on his staff, Mr. Uhlen had a personable glow about him that lit up a room. While the other two could be heard ranting and raving about ignorant clients or ills perpetrated upon them by the company, Mr. Uhlen seemed impervious to negative thoughts or ideas. I followed the stocky-built gentleman with an admiring smile as he walked back to his staff and took his seat next to Guru and Weinstein. Immediately, he fell into line with the others working the phones, filling out applications, and getting ready to turn in the accounts. I glanced up to the leader board where their names held three of the top four spots, only separated by Otis from my staff in the number two position. I just shook my head in amazement, looking at their numbers, before returning to our staff's group of desks where Meadows was still pulling the account.

"Damn. Is that T.J.'s book you're still working on?" I asked.

"Do you believe this fucking guy?" he said with disgust. "Roger called last night and told me to come in and pull all three accounts on his book."

"Just be glad T.J. didn't have the book. Do you think Roger's going to fire him?"

"I told him that I don't want him on my staff anymore, but I don't know what he's going to do," Meadows said.

"Let me get my summary in the window, and I'll help you call the account," I offered, opening up my briefcase and getting my paperwork in order.

"I would appreciate that, Ron, but don't you have a full account to pull?" he asked.

"Don't you look at the summaries?" I shot back. "My arrears are below 18 percent," I said proudly. I wanted Meadows to know that my accounts were up to date, so I slid the summary sheet in front of him so he could see that I was right. He looked at it for all of two seconds before sliding it back across to me.

"Your book is in good shape," he conceded. "I must be thinking about Terrell," he said as if that qualified for an apology. He let the ledger book close with a sigh, as if exasperated by the work, and began tapping his pipe on the desk.

"Well," I said with authority, "you can think about anyone else you want as long as it ain't me."

"Yeah, well, Terrell better get his ass in here soon, and that account better be pulled," he said, looking at his watch.

"Oh shit," I half muttered under my breath.

"What's wrong?" Meadows wondered.

"I forgot about these two cases I need to lapse, Brown and Peters. I talked to both of them on Monday and set up appointments to pick up their money tomorrow night. You know how it is. I hate to lapse them," I said, not realizing that Mr. Guru was listening intently to our conversation. He got up from his desk and walked over by us, standing right behind Otis' desk and facing me with a determined look on his face. Meadows stopped banging his pipe and looked at me with raised eyebrows as we both realized how unusual of an occurrence it was to get a visit from him.

Mr. Guru was a rare breed, a survivor of the Holocaust who extolled many more characteristics of his Nazi captors than the virtues of their Jewish victims. He was mean and nasty to the other agents, terse at best with his clients, and suspicious of everyone else. He didn't like black people and wouldn't hesitate to tell them so, a trait most of us found peculiar since we all made our living servicing black communities. Otis once told me that black people felt sorry for Mr. Guru because they knew he was a crazy old Jewish guy that Hitler missed, so they didn't pay him any attention. I didn't think he was demented, but he didn't look normal either. His dark blue eyes were lifeless, and though I'm sure he must have blinked at times, I never saw him. His face was tired and worn, heavy with wrinkles that drooped from his forehead like ripples of sand cascading down an ancient slope. His lips were the color of blood, peeled and cracked, painful to look at as they almost seemed to blister before your eyes. A crown of puffed white hair encircled his bald head, completing the look of a man on the brink of insanity or imitating Albert Einstein. His dress code was in total violation of the standards set forth by Hamilton's office policy, which insisted that agents wear a suit coat during the meetings. Mr. Guru wore a red-striped flannel shirt and beige baggy pants with brown loafers to work every day.

He seldom conversed with the other agents, preferring to mumble to himself when the situation required. When speaking to clients on the phone, he was fiery, bordering on abusive, demanding payment on an overdue policy in his old broken-English voice. "What is the matter with you? Are you stupid or what?" he would yell into the receiver. "How can I bury your kids if you don't send in your insurance money? Do you want to ask your neighbors for pennies to bury your child or dig the hole yourself when some drug dealer shoots him? Get off your ass right now, go down to the store, and make a money order and put it in the mail. Don't give me any of your bullshit. I am not listening," he would berate his clients on the phone.

Just as Mr. Guru was about to speak, Otis walked in and hovered over him like a giant, annoyed that he was being blocked from setting his things down on his desk. Otis looked at Meadows and me, copying our look of bewilderment, to which we both shrugged our shoulders at the same time, wondering what Guru was going to do. The old man looked at all three of us separately for a moment, then leaned forward towards me, placing his hands on Otis' desk to balance himself.

"IN ORDER TO LIVE... YOU HAVE TO EAT. IN ORDER TO EAT... YOU HAVE TO SHIT. IF YOU DO NOT SHIT... YOU DIE. THAT IS ALL!" he shouted in broken English to my face as everyone in the office stopped what they were doing to listen. He continued to lean on Otis' desk a moment longer than Otis was willing to tolerate, while everyone else returned to their business.

"Okay, Guru, you crazy motherfucker. Whatever it was, you made your point. Now, it's time for you to go back to your desk and take some pills," Otis growled out in his baritone voice. Guru looked up at him and scowled before quickly returning to his desk and burying his head in paperwork.

"What the fuck was that all about?" I whispered in Meadows' direction as Otis sat down.

"That's Guru's way of telling you not to hold those lapses," he said.

"Hold lapses?" Otis chimed in. "Shit, you're crazier than that old man if you do that, Pickles. You know better than that. Why do you want to pay for someone else's insurance?" he asked.

"I never said I was going to hold lapses. I said I hated to lapse these people because I made appointments to pick up their premiums tomorrow," I said with exasperation. "Trust me, I have no intention of paying someone else's insurance premium," I said, filling out a lapse log and listing the policies I had just mentioned.

Lapses were one of those little things that Hamilton conveniently left out of his sales pitch during my interview. As he was going on and on about all the money I could make by selling insurance and collecting the premiums, he neglected to mention that the company also took away money from you if a policy lapsed. The worst part was that it didn't matter if you wrote the policy in the first place or not. A weekly policy could be five years old, and the company would hit you for twenty-five times the dollar amount and deduct it from your commission draw if it lapsed. You could have sold your ass off that week; it wouldn't matter if you had the same amount in lapse. You could get it back if you reinstated the policy, which happened quite a bit, but sometimes people just couldn't afford it anymore or bought it from a different insurance company, and there was nothing you could do. One of the biggest reasons agents got fired was because they didn't lapse people on time and their accounts became short. It was mandatory to submit lapses whenever a policy fell out of the grace period, which was thirty days. If an agent held that lapse for an extra week because someone promised to pay and they didn't, he would have to put in the money from his own pocket to cover the shortage. There were times when I saw agents sign their entire paycheck over to the company in order to cover the shortages they incurred from holding lapses, something I swore I'd never do.

"So, did you guys do any good yesterday?" Meadows asked once Otis had settled down.

"We did alright. What did we get, Pickles, about $85 MDO between titty girl and Ruppert?" Otis asked casually.

"Damn, forty-two bucks a piece ain't too shabby," Meadows said with a smile.

"No, he meant $85 each," I corrected.

"No shit! Y'all wrote $170 worth of MDO yesterday?!" Meadows busted out with excitement.

"Damn, Meadows, why don't you just tell the whole fucking office now?" Otis scolded.

"Fuck you, Wahl; I need something to get excited about. I got this fucking white boy out here screwing every whore on the ledger, and I'm stuck in here pulling this asshole's account every week," Meadows said in a hushed voice.

"Hey, watch that 'white boy' shit," I scolded. Otis started laughing, and even Meadows cracked a smile before continuing. "Did you see the cops in Hamilton's office?" he asked Otis.

"No, man, what's going on?"

"T.J.'s old lady filed a missing persons report on his ass because he hasn't been home in the last two weeks," Meadows said.

"Oh man," Otis started cracking up. "Shit, that motherfucker is crazy," he said.

"No shit. This guy is killing me. I'm going to end up lapsing half this fucking book today because he ain't collected shit," Meadows said with disgust.

Just then, Terrell Love and Sean Meriwether strolled into the office and took their seats at our staff. I could see from the look on Meadows' face he was relieved they finally showed up. I liked Terrell, though he was timid and didn't exactly fit the image of an outgoing salesman. All the same, he was a really nice guy, about my age, who loved basketball. He used to brag about going to the West Side and playing ball with Isaiah Thomas and Mark Aguirre, a couple of big-time college players that played pick-up games in the hood. I never knew if he was telling the truth or not, but I could tell that it made him feel good if I seemed interested, so I acted impressed. He was really soft spoken and acted like he was going to get beaten if he said the wrong thing. Mr. Meadows probably wasn't the best choice to manage Terrell, as he lacked patience and wasn't accustomed to showing someone how to do things two or three times. Terrell would start to stutter and shake when Meadows yelled at him for making the same errors over and over again. Even Otis felt bad for Terrell and told Meadows to take it easy on the kid after a particularly brutal admonishment for doing something wrong.

I didn't really care for Meriwether, but I had only seen him on occasion when he bothered to show up at the office, so it wasn't too bad. Word around the office was that he was a pretty bad dude. He supposedly had a stable of girls working for him that he pimped out. He was also a major supplier of drugs for Teddy, Vinnie, and the other guys on the stoner staff. No one ever said if he belonged to one of the street gangs, and I figured it was best if I didn't know. You would have never thought he was involved in street shit by looking at him, but he had a really hard edge to his personality and took offense at the drop of a hat. He dressed very conservatively in gray and black suits with white shirts and black ties and kind of reminded me of a black version of Jack Webb from the old detective show *Dragnet*.

Sean and Otis had a mutual respect for each other, but occasionally he would test Otis, only to back down when Otis had had enough. He definitely had something going on with T.J., as the two of them would make several trips out into the hallway during settlement days to have a cigarette, knowing full well that they could smoke in the office. He didn't pay much attention to me except for the couple of times when we debated the contributions of Motown artists to those of the Beatles. He liked that I knew a little bit about Berry Gordy, the founder of Motown, and admitted that he was a fan of the Beatles, though he thought they were overrated. His favorite target was Mr. Meadows, and he took every opportunity he could to give Ray a hard time.

I felt bad for Ray because Meriwether thought nothing of humiliating him in front of the whole office. Ray was in a tough position because no other staff had ledgers servicing the projects, and anytime he found an agent willing to work them, he had to bend over backwards to keep them. Meriwether serviced the Stateway Gardens housing projects off the Dan Ryan Expressway. That's why he was able to come and go as he pleased. Even Hamilton looked the other way when it came to Meriwether, knowing the loss of business his district would incur if Sean quit the ledger.

I finished the last of my calculations, counted out the money I had collected since Tuesday, and was about to get up and turn in my summary when it strangely occurred to me that I was sitting all by myself on one side of the staff. Meriwether's desk was in the middle next to Otis', and Terrell's was on the other side of Meriwether's, closest to Mr. Meadows'.

"Hey, I don't want to accuse anybody of being racist or anything, but how come the white guy has to sit by himself?" I asked in the direction of all four black guys staring at me from across their desks. They all looked at each other for a moment with grins on their faces as they seemed to realize how ridiculous it was for four big men to be crammed together unnecessarily as they were.

"Oh, don't feel bad, Pickles," Otis grumbled. "Even if you were black, we wouldn't let you sit over here," he said to the amusement of the others.

"Pickles, you don't have to take that shit. Come sit over here with the white guys if you're tired of looking at the coloreds," Teddy called out from the stoner staff. Otis leaned back in his chair so he could get a better look at Teddy.

"Hey, Teddy, you better shut the fuck up, or I'm going to tell Meriwether here to cut your ass off," he said to a collective "oooohhh" from the other agents in the office. I got up laughing and went into the reception area to stand in line and deposit my account with Mrs. Bolger. I really didn't have to stand in line, as Mrs. Bolger would eventually get to your account if you handed it to her and sat down, but that would prevent me from gawking at Irene through the glass window as Mrs. Bolger balanced my book. Every agent in the office voted Irene the hottest chick any of us had ever seen.

There were times when a few of us would go to lunch and spend the entire time debating the reasons for someone as gorgeous as Irene to work there. Irene was definitely the first real sexual woman I ever saw outside of a magazine. She was the type of woman that made you want to go home and smack your wife for not having the sex appeal that drove you mad. Everything about Irene was sensual or desirable, and she knew it, she enhanced it, she encouraged it. Whether it was her long, black hair curling over her shoulders and bouncing with a shine as she walked or the ruby red lipstick that highlighted the lips of a seductress burning with passion, she had it.

No one ever had a chance to talk to her, as most of her time was spent in the office assisting Mrs. Bolger, who guarded her like a princess. You could hear a pin drop on the rare occasions when she ventured into the agents' room to hand someone a message. We speculated that she was of Mediterranean descent by her pale complexion and dark eyes that she shaded to perfection with whatever color outfit she chose to wear that day. She never wore jeans or pantsuits, only skirts with sweaters or low-cut dresses that showcased a good portion of cleavage from her luscious breasts. Her figure was a throwback to the days of Marilyn Monroe, when women relished curves and sex appeal to entice a man's imagination and create desire. She had fantastic legs, always made better with the addition of nylons and high heels. If there was a negative side to Irene, no one cared.

I hovered over the counter with faux interest in Mrs. Bolger's attention to my account while stealing every possible glimpse of the goddess sitting behind her. I was awoken from my trance by the steely grimace on Mrs. Bolger's face after she apparently told me twice that she was finished with my deposit. I just smiled and gathered up my receipts before returning to my desk, still drunk with the visions of Irene and me rolling around somewhere. Without any empathy for my amorous state of mind, Otis brought me back to earth by tossing the applications we wrote the day before in front of me. "Pickles, you want to check these out and sign the back before we turn them in, or do you have something on your mind?" he asked sarcastically. His tone snapped me back to reality and reminded me that we wrote a notorious leader of a dangerous street gang a whole bunch of life insurance the day before. I cleared my throat and looked up at him with a smile.

"…And miss a chance to have my body dredged up from the Chicago River on television when these policies don't pay off? What, are you fucking nuts? I can't miss that," I said before removing a pen from my shirt pocket and signing the back of each application.

"Shit, Pickles, that would never happen," he shot back.

"Oh no?"

"Naw, the worst they would do is strip you naked and ass rape you like a bitch," he said with a big grin as Meadows, Love, and Meriwether snickered.

"Sounds like the voice of experience," I said to the "ooohhhs" and "aaahhs" of the others as I slid the applications back to him and got up to head for the back door. On the way to the restroom, I saw Craig Branson coming towards me. Craig had only been there a couple of months, but we got along well, and I liked him a lot. We both got married and had kids before we should have and worked at something we didn't necessarily like in order to pay the bills. Craig confided in me that he was going to night school to become an accountant, and I in turn told him about the electrician's union. We never worked together on the ledger but met on occasion for lunch, and at least twice a week we found our way down to the Halsted Street arcade, where we passed a good deal of time waiting for appointments by playing a brand-new table-size video football game.

"Where have you been all morning?" I asked, walking up to him before noticing a huge shiner on his right eye. "Holy cow! Looks like the old lady finally had enough of your shit and decked you, huh?"

"You're close. Take a look at the size of this thing," he said, stopping and tilting his head upward for me to see his eye. The whole side of his face was puffed out and discolored with bruising that would leave him black and blue for weeks, but his eye was swollen completely shut and looked as if it needed a cut doctor.

"Jesus! What happened? It looks like you were in a car accident."

"I know, can you believe this?" he said. "I got home early yesterday and decided to do some work around the house, but it was so fucking hot outside, I just gave up and went inside to watch TV. Well, you know, my son, Tommy, was running around the house, and I started horsing around with him and wrestling and shit, and everything was cool. So, Bridget calls him into the kitchen for something, and I fall back on the floor and crash. When he's done with Mom, he comes running into the living room and jumps right on my face."

"Oh my God, you got to be shitting me," I said.

"No, man, it was awful. I screamed out at the top of my lungs and scared the shit out of him. Poor little guy will probably be scarred for life, but man, did he catch me good."

"How old is Tommy again?" I asked.

"He just turned five," Craig said. "I felt so bad for my little guy because he thought he killed me and wouldn't stop crying. My face felt like it got hit by a Mack Truck, and I'm holding on to him, trying to calm him down, because he's hysterical. You know, it hurt like a bitch, but it didn't start to swell up like this until this morning, so I took it easy getting in here, just sitting around with a bag of ice on it and trying to get the swelling to go down."

"It's a beautiful thing," I said unsympathetically.

"Yeah, I know," he said, realizing that it was time to move on to something else. "Did I miss anything around here?" he asked.

"Well, let's see... the cops were here this morning looking for T.J. because his wife filed a missing persons report on him. Vinnie was hanging out in the bathroom waiting for the cops to leave because he was stoned. Guru gave me the 'Don't eat, don't shit, or you die' speech, and Irene is wearing a summer dress that would strike a boner in a dead guy. Other than that, it's been pretty quiet," I said.

"Wow, Guru must like you," he said with a surprised look on his face while ignoring the other events.

"It was pretty weird," I said.

"Try being on the same staff with him," he replied.

"That's quite okay, dude. I'll catch you inside," I said, continuing on to the bathroom.

"Catch you after the meeting, Ronnie," he said, walking away. When I got back to the staff, I sat at the empty desk next to Meadows' and took the ledger book from him. He gave me a startled look before he realized that I was there to help him and repositioned the account sheet on his desk to make the work easier. I double-checked the account he was working on and started calling off the page numbers, date last paid, and premiums for him to enter on the sheet.

By 10:20 we were finished, and Ray took the account sheets up to the window to deposit. Looking up at the clock, I hurried up and called Jessica before Hamilton came in to start the meeting and asked her what I had been asking for the last eight months. "Did it come?" I asked with hopeful anticipation.

"No, I just checked. I'm sorry, not today," she said with disappointment in her voice.

"Okay," I sighed into the phone. "Maybe tomorrow," I replied before saying goodbye, a little more disheartened each time she told me the letter from the electrician's union didn't come in the mail. Hanging up the phone, I leaned back in my chair, trying to figure out why I hadn't received the news yet. The look on my face must have telegraphed my disappointment, as Craig came out of nowhere and tapped me on the shoulder.

"I saw you hang up the phone. No word yet, huh?"

"Not yet," I sighed. "I don't know what's going on here, Craig; I thought for sure I'd have heard something by now."

"These things take time, bud. You'll find out soon," he said, patting my shoulder on his way to drop off his accounts in the window. I smiled to myself, thinking about what a good guy Craig was, consoling me with half his face smashed. About ten minutes later, Mr. Hamilton stepped into the agents' room with his hand on the door, holding it open for Craig and Meadows and a couple of other agents to come away from the window and take their seats for the meeting. Simultaneously, all the agents in the room who weren't wearing their suit jackets stood up and put them on, straightening their ties and fixing their hair for the meeting. The low hum of voices making idle chitchat or talking on the phone came to a stop. Paperwork was cleared from desks, and a couple of agents rushed up to the coffee pot to see if they could squeeze another drop into their cups before the meeting started. Roger Hamilton was about to start the meeting, and like soldiers awaiting their commander for inspection, we fell in line with eager anticipation.

Roger Hamilton should have seriously considered a military career or gone into politics. He was such a natural leader that managing an insurance agency, especially a ledger agency, almost seemed beneath him. His style and swagger projected an air of confidence that he backed up with an in-depth knowledge of the insurance industry no one dared to challenge. If you asked him a question or had a problem, he knew the answer. He studied the arrears on everyone's account, knew how much lapse his district could expect each week, and knew to the rounded dollar how close each agent was to qualifying for the company trip to the Bahamas. He was confident, bordering on arrogant, but he treated every agent with respect, even those like Vinnie Elder who didn't deserve it. On meeting days, he never called you by your first name, insisting on addressing you formally as Mr. Pickles or Mr. Meadows or Mr. Wahl. The underlying suggestion was that you had stature or importance to the company and deserved respect. It was his rule that jackets had to be worn during the meetings and that desks must be cleared, though you never heard it come from him. If an agent came in without a jacket, he was offered the double extra-large hanging in the closet or excused from the meeting by his staff manager, an embarrassment no one suffered twice. The only exception to the rule was, of course, Mr. Guru, whom even Hamilton seemed leery of offending.

As soon as everyone was in the room, Mr. Hamilton shut the door and walked with purpose toward the front of the room, placing a file on the podium before stepping up to the blackboard. The honor of being called first was directly related to the leader board and the rank you held by sales for the year. Mr. Guru and Otis had been battling for the top spot most of the year, with Mr. Uhlen and Mr. Weinstein right behind them. I was eighth but the only agent with less than a year of experience to crack the top ten.

"Mr. Guru," he called out, holding a piece of chalk in his hand.

"Give me $6 weekly life, $0.40 weekly fire, and $10 MDO, Roger," Guru called out slowly with his heavy Yiddish accent as he strained to look at the amounts he jotted down on a note in front of him. The office erupted in hoots and hollers as we all stomped our feet or banged the desks in approval of Guru's board call. Guru remained tight-lipped and stoic with his arms folded across his chest as he took in the agents' approval. Hamilton waited a moment for the adulation to die down before calling for Otis.

"Mr. Wahl," Hamilton called out.

"Yes, Mr. Hamilton. Pickles and I got a split board call working together yesterday. It comes to $85 MDO each," he said with a matter-of-fact tone to a thunderous ovation from the office that dwarfed by comparison the one received by Guru. In a rare display, Mr. Hamilton put the chalk down on the blackboard ledge and walked over in front of our staff clapping his hands, motioning for the both of us to stand up. We looked at each other as if embarrassed by the recognition and stood for a moment to the continued applause from the other agents. When we sat down, Hamilton reached across the desks, shaking both our hands and congratulating us before continuing to take the rest of the board call. It was a good sales week for the office, all the better that Otis and I led the district with the highest amount. When Hamilton finished, he stepped up and gave the office an applause that was quickly copied by the staff managers that stood up and joined him.

"Thank you. I have to thank you, gentlemen, for an unbelievable week of sales. You have no idea how privileged I feel to be working with such an outstanding group of people," he said to another round of applause before moving back to the podium. "Before I start the meeting, I do want to take a moment to talk about the accomplishments of Mr. Wahl and Mr. Pickles for their outstanding sales this week. I hope the two of you won't mind me bringing this to the attention of the office, but Mr. Meadows informed me that you obtained this business by canvassing the Cabrini-Green projects yesterday. Is that right?" he asked in our general direction.

"That's right," Otis acknowledged softly.

"How long were you out there?" Hamilton asked.

"We started around ten because Otis was actually on time," I said to the amusement of the office. "I think we left around one or two."

"So, you knocked on doors for about four hours, and, if my math is correct, you each made $595 in commission. Is that right?"

"That's right," I agreed.

"Wow, not too shabby if you can make over $100 an hour doing it, wouldn't you say?" he asked.

"Not too shabby," Otis agreed.

"Thank you again, gentlemen," he said, satisfied that he made his point to the other agents, illustrating how a little hard work could pay off big in the insurance business. I was amused by the angle he played to the office now that I was able to see through his bullshit a little easier than when I first started. Actually, I was a little surprised he even mentioned Cabrini-Green, as the thought of entering the projects doesn't usually sit well with the other agents. He was careful not to ask us what kind of business we wrote, and he didn't ask us to share the details of the sale, like the fact that we wrote up a pregnant naked teenager and a bunch of gangbangers who could have just as easily killed us. That kind of information wouldn't have made the point. To hear him tell it, you got the impression that we conquered the heights of professionalism and serviced the needs of people just waiting to buy insurance from the first agent that knocked on their door.

After the meeting, a couple of agents came up to Otis and me, personally congratulating us, then wanting to know how we sold more than four times the average agent's board call for the week. We both figured it was probably better not to mention writing key man insurance on a Chicago street gang, but it was fun to gloat and throw out advice to others as if we knew all the secrets of making great sales.

After a quick bathroom break, I went back to my desk and started filling out a route card for the upcoming weekend. Sales were nice, but you had to collect your book or face lapses, which took money right out of your pocket. The weekends were for collections, and there were a lot of people I had to collect, none more important than Mrs. Brown or Mr. Peters, the two cases I had lapsed today. I was excited in a way because I had already called them both and was pretty sure I could pick up their money on Friday night, even though I wasn't thrilled about being on the ledger at that time. If I were able to collect them, I would have board call for next Tuesday and the rest of the week to concentrate on getting sales without being pressed. Terrell and I were the only ones left on the staff as Otis and Meriwether took off the second the meeting was over. Meadows was in Hamilton's office, attending a meeting with the other assistant district managers while a handful of agents, including Craig and Ol' Man Wicks from Mr. Singh's staff across from ours, remained.

I had just finished flipping through my ledger book and filling out the route card when, out of the corner of my eye, I saw T.J.

quietly sneak in the back door. T.J. staggered across the room, unable to keep his tall, lanky frame from banging into things, oblivious to the astonished gazes he received from the other agents. He was carrying a beat-up briefcase in one hand and a greasy brown bag in the other, looking absolutely terrible. I actually had to stare at him for a minute just to remember what he looked like the week before. It shouldn't have been too difficult since he was wearing the same gray polyester suit he was wearing when I saw him last. The only difference was that a week ago he wore a shirt and tie under the jacket, and today he appeared to be wearing nothing.

His young face was so red and puffy that it reminded me of a photograph I once saw in school of a woman who suffered a hundred bee stings to the head. His eyes were awash in bloodshot veins, and his neck was blistered like he just took a razor blade and shaved over a bunch of acne. His hands were shaking, and he showed all the signs of a man about to crash from a bad trip, a sight I remembered vividly from a friend who ended up committing suicide in high school after overdosing on smack.

I glanced across the office at Craig, who was mesmerized by the train wreck that had just walked in the room. Not wanting to alarm T.J., I stared at Craig intently until I got his attention, then motioned with my eyes for him to get someone while I stayed put. Craig calmly closed his book and strolled out the back door, as if going to the bathroom. I knew the second the door was closed that he would go in the reception door and bang on Hamilton's office.

"Hey, Ronnie, how you doing, man?" T.J. asked, almost falling into the chair beside me while dropping the greasy bag on the table and the briefcase at his side.

"The question is, how the hell are you doing?" I asked rhetorically.

"Everyone knows that I'm in the shitter, don't they?" he asked, barely able to keep his head from hitting the desk.

"I got to be honest with you, man, it's pretty fucked up," I replied, unable to take my eyes off a man who looked like he was in the final stage of a Dorian Gray picture.

"I fucked up, Pickles. Man, don't ever fuck with these guys. You have no idea who they are. I should have never let them talk me into this shit. I owe them money, and my book is a couple of thousand short," he said, talking a mile a minute while ripping the greasy bag of food open all over the desk. I watched for a moment as he stuck his head down and jammed half a hot dog and a handful of fries in his mouth all at the same time. His cheeks were stuffed with so much food that some of it came back out of his mouth and fell to the desk as he chewed. Terrell looked at me, horrified by the sight, and I just shook my head at him and lifted my hand slightly off the desk as if to tell him to be calm.

"Well, the first thing you'll have to do is get some rest and get off the shit so you can think with a clear head," I said sympathetically.

"Wow, man, can you tell that I'm fucked up?! Don't fuck with me, Pickles. Can you really tell that I'm fucked up?" he asked with an annoyed tone, abruptly pulling up his head out of the pile of food. I was surprised by his reaction and caught off guard by his reality, in which he obviously thought of himself as appearing completely straight. He stared at me with glazed-over eyes, demanding an answer. From years of experience dealing with a mother and father who drank themselves blind once a week, I knew better than to argue with him, but I was so sick of pacifying drunks that I couldn't do it.

"I don't know, T.J. You tell me," I said.

"What?"

"Look at yourself. Your head looks like it's going to explode, you're not wearing any clothes underneath your jacket, and you smell like shit. It doesn't take a fucking rocket scientist to see that there might be something wrong here," I said, trying to convince him that he needed help. I looked away when he turned his head back towards his food and scooped up another handful, which I presumed was heading for his mouth.

"RON, LOOK OUT!" I heard Terrell scream just in time to lean back out of the way as a barrage of french fries and hot dog parts came flying at my face.

"Motherfucker!" I shouted, jumping back out of my chair, realizing that I had been hit by shards of mustard and pickle relish streaking across my white shirt and tie. Instantly, Hamilton, Meadows, and the others came running into the office. Hamilton could see by the look on my face that I was pissed and ready to pounce on T.J.

"Okay, Ron, we got this," he said, grabbing T.J. under one arm while Mr. Singh grabbed him under the other, dragging him off into Hamilton's office.

"Son of a bitch," I bemoaned at the mess of food spattered all over the place. Meadows hurried up to me with a handkerchief and knocked a couple of the larger pieces of food hanging on me to the floor.

"Ron, why don't you go down to the bathroom and see if you can clean some of that stuff off you? Terrell, do me a favor and go ask Mrs. Bolger if she has something we can clean this mess up with," he said.

"Yeah, this is fucking bullshit," I said with disdain as I headed for the restroom, chalking up one more reason to be thankful I'd be leaving the insurance business soon. The damage wasn't that bad, and I figured that a good dry cleaning would fix up my shirt and tie. Wiping away pieces of relish, I was just thankful I had removed my jacket and hung it on the back of my chair. I walked back into the office just as Meadows finished picking up the last few fries off the floor.

"You okay?" he asked.

"Yeah, I guess," I said, looking over my desk, pleased with the job that Meadows had done cleaning.

"What brought all that on?" he asked.

"Nothing brought it on, Ray. The guy is stoned out of his mind," I said, picking up my stuff and heading for the door.

"Ron, you okay? You want to go get some lunch? Liver and onions? I'm buying," he said as I just shook my head and walked out the door. Ol' Man Wicks was already waiting for the elevator to arrive in his patented gray tweed suit when I walked up. Wicks may have been a small man in stature, only a couple of inches over five feet, but all the agents respected him as a man with great insight and ability to run his ledger. A darker-skinned black man with short-cropped hair, he sported a thin mustache that added a bit of seriousness to what otherwise might be a boyishly round face. He wore heavy-rimmed black bifocal glasses and, until you got to know him, seemed very unapproachable as a serious businessman. Mr. Wicks was a good guy, and I liked him. His ledger was next to mine, and on occasion we would bump into each other and bullshit about the crazy stuff that happened out there. He had worked at the company for over twenty years, alternating back and forth as an agent and a manager. At this point in his life, he was happy to be an agent and only put in a few days a week—just enough money to make his bills.

"You doing okay?" he asked after witnessing T.J.'s outburst.

"Yeah, I'm fine, but I do have this incredible urge to get some hot dogs," I said with a smile.

"I heard that," he said with a chuckle before turning serious. "…But that's what the ledger will do to you," he said.

"That's what smack will do to you, Mr. Wicks," I replied.

"Maybe, but it's the black ledger that makes you want to do that shit," he said calmly with a hint of Southern drawl betraying a voice honed on city sharpness. "The ledger gets all of us eventually. Just depends on how strong you are," he said with a sigh. I looked at him for a moment, realizing that he was trying to tell me something and not just making idle chitchat.

"What do you mean?" I asked.

"Man… the ledger has a life of its own. You should know that by now. Once you start working out there, it eats you up, consumes you, and spits you out. It takes away your soul, everything inside that makes you human, leaves you with nothing but emptiness. It feeds on you just like it does the people that live out there. You'll never be the same person you were before working the ledger because you'll never be able to get back what it takes from you. A lot of negative energy sucking the life out of people," he said.

"Then why are you still here?" I asked, finding a truth in his words that most people wouldn't understand without working the ledger.

"What else is an ol' nigga like me going to do?" he asked. "Ain't like I can pick up and go be a lawyer or something. But you, you're a different story. You need to get the hell out of this place before the same thing happens to you that happened to T.J.," he said.

"I don't do drugs," I said emphatically.

"You don't have to do drugs for the black ledger to fuck you over, son," he said as if amused by my lack of understanding. "The ledger isn't a place you go to collect money from po' niggas. The ledger is alive. It knows who you are and what you're thinking. Why, its whole purpose is to take away from you anything you think is important. What do you think it did to T.J.? It seduced him; it promised him everything and gave him nothing. It's true, it will destroy a weak mind faster than a strong one, but in the end, it gets us all. It always wins."

"You're a scary old man, you know that?" I asked, breaking his serious tone.

"Scary? Maybe so," he said laughing. "I just hope that someday you don't come up to me and say, 'Damn, Wicks, I wish you would have scared me the hell out of this business,'" he said, chuckling as we got on the elevator.

D.G. ALLEN

CHAPTER 7

It was Friday evening; the sun was going down as nighttime crept upon the city. I was sitting on the couch in my pajamas watching television, finding it difficult to get comfortable knowing I had to go collect at the worst possible time. For a moment, I flashed back to my first day on the job when Mr. Meadows explicitly said, "Never work the ledger on Friday or Saturday nights." It gnawed at me, but I had no choice. I had to get the credit back for lapsing Mrs. Brown and Mr. Peters' policies. At 8:00 p.m., I pushed myself off the couch and lumbered into the bedroom to get dressed, feeling like I was getting ready to report to prison.

"Do you really have to go?" Jessica asked with a sigh as I reluctantly headed for the front door.

"Trust me, it's not like I want to, babe, but I have to. If I don't revive these two cases I lapsed, we lose half the commission I made with Otis this week. You know how it works," I said, hugging her goodbye. "But I'm really glad I took the day off and spent it with you guys," I said, trying to make her feel better.

"I know, but it sucks that you have to leave now," she said. I kissed her and was about to walk out the door when Rudy came up to me, wagging his tail a mile a minute, thinking I was going to take him for a walk. I crouched down to pat his head while explaining to him that I had to go to work, and I said, "I wish you were a big, old, scary-looking German shepherd or something so I could take you with for protection."

"Hey, that's not a bad idea," Jessica said with an expression on her face that looked positively inspired. "You're always telling me that black people are afraid of dogs. Why don't you take Rudy with you tonight?"

"No, sweetie, you misunderstood me," I said, laughing at her interpretation of what I had told her in the past. "I said that black people always get the meanest dogs they can find for protection. They get shepherds, Dobermans, Rottweilers, pit bulls, and those kinds of dogs—the dogs everybody's afraid of, not just black people," I said emphatically. "I don't think collies qualify."

"Why not?" she said with outstretched hands, beseeching me to see her point. "What difference does it make, for God's sake? If someone sees you with a big dog, they don't know if it bites or not. For all they know, it's a specially trained dog to protect you. Besides, why are you putting down Lassie? Lassie was always beating the crap out of something or saving Timmy from falling in a hole," she tried to point out.

"Well, yeah, I guess you have a point, but Lassie wasn't cross-eyed and didn't get the shits if you looked at him wrong," I said, grinning from ear to ear.

"He is fine as long as I don't mess around with his food," Jessica shot back, holding back a smile.

"I don't know, Jess. I mean, for Christ's sake, he can't even back up by himself. I think it might be better to just get in and get out of there as quick as I can, you know?" I said, not convinced that this was a good idea.

"Listen, Ronnie, you've been telling me all day how you dread going out to the ledger at night, right?"

"Yeah."

"Well, then this is the answer. The bad guys don't know that Rudy is cross-eyed and scared of his own shadow. For all they know, he's the meanest dog in town. As a matter of fact, I'd bet they'd take one look at Rudy and walk the other way. Common sense would tell them, 'Hey, this must be a pretty bad dog.' Why else would a white guy bring it into the neighborhood if it wasn't for protection? Trust me, no one is going to come within fifty feet of you and that dog," she said with a certain conviction that frightened me because it actually seemed to make a lot of sense.

"Jessie, this could turn to shit really quickly," I said, expressing the misgivings I had about her plan. Any other time, I wouldn't have even considered taking the dog with me except for the fact that I hated to go out there at night.

"Ronnie, I'm right, and you know I'm right," she insisted. "I wouldn't mess with anybody walking around a bad neighborhood with a dog. I wouldn't care what kind of dog it is," she added.

"He does listen real well. It's those Central Park apartments that are the bad ones. That's where Mr. Peters lives," I said, more crawling onto the bandwagon than jumping. "I could walk him up to the apartment and have him sit by the door until I'm ready to go," I said, already planning a strategy.

"Trust me, what's the worst that could happen?" she said, convincing me that it was the smart thing to do.

"Okay, it's settled then. Get Rudy's chain. He's going to the black ledger with me," I said with a final pat to the dog's head. I didn't know if he understood a word I said, but the look on his face was beaming with excitement, as if he totally agreed that he should be going along to provide the protection I so desperately needed. We hit the road in good spirits, though the late-June heat wave was going to make it an extremely uncomfortable trip. Even with the windows down and air circulating around the car, I couldn't believe how hot it was outside and how doggy it smelled inside. Rudy didn't hesitate a moment to get some relief from the situation and promptly stuck his head out the back window to absorb the warm breeze, which set off a chain reaction of events that almost ended in a major collision with an oncoming vehicle.

Rudy was blissfully unaware that his beautiful brown-and-white coat of fur tended to shed on a constant basis. His exuberance and desire to hang out the window of the car immediately resulted in a poof of loose hair blowing off his body and into the circular jet stream inside the car. Within seconds, the swirling hair congealed into a furry floating mass that made its way to the front seat by me and stuck to my sweat-dampened face like an itchy wool sweater. Blinded momentarily by the swath of dog hair, I swerved the car into oncoming traffic and just barely pulled back into my lane before ending our journey in a fiery head-on crash.

I pulled over and stopped the car to regain my composure and pick the intertwined strands of hair from my eyes, nose, and mouth before continuing on our journey. I turned around and looked at Rudy, who, to my surprise, seemed completely unfazed by our near-death experience and anxious for me to start driving again. I was motivated by Rudy's fortitude and decided to take the event in stride, a small inconvenience for the valuable protection Rudy would afford.

It took about an hour to get into the city, as I made it a point to drive slow and steady, not wanting to upset Rudy's sensitive stomach or loosen any more hair from his body. I wasn't far from my territory when I decided to pull over again and close the windows. I figured we'd both die of heat exhaustion if the windows were rolled up tight, so I rolled the front windows up about three-quarters of the way, then crawled halfway over the bench seat to do the same in the back. Had I thought it through for a moment, I probably would have opted to get out of the car and physically open each door and adjust the windows instead of careening into the back seat like Superman coming in for a landing. I didn't think it would be a difficult task to accomplish because I didn't factor in Rudy's participation until I had already committed myself to balancing precariously over the seat, struggling to reach for the rear-window cranks on each side of the car.

Rudy was thoroughly worked up by my dramatic entrance into his realm and literally jumped at the opportunity to get some much-needed attention. Overjoyed at my close proximity and seemingly unaware of the rising temperature in the car, he inched up to my face and snuggled as close as he could, panting hard with excitement. I was already hanging over the front seat, perched on one hand, attempting to crank the stubborn window, and couldn't push him away. Frantically, I tugged and twirled the stubborn window handles on one side of the car, then the other, all the while being smothered by my dog and his atrocious doggy breath.

Once I finally managed to get the windows positioned properly, I pushed myself off the rear seat and slithered back into the front, exhausted yet grateful for air that didn't reek of stale Milk-Bones and regurgitated Puppy Chow. I couldn't be mad at Rudy; he was just being himself. So, once I caught my breath, I reached back and rubbed his head, thanking him for coming with me. Actually, he had been a perfectly well-behaved dog on the way here, and I was beginning to think how grateful I was that Jessica had talked me into bringing him. With the windows rolled up and Rudy sitting upright in the back seat, I glanced down at my route card to confirm that Mrs. Brown's house was on Monroe Street before driving away.

It was about 9:30 p.m., and the glow from the city's streetlights began to cast a yellow hue over the neighborhood while highlighting a path for cars to navigate the streets. The main streets bordering the residential neighborhoods were alive with activity and an energy level I had never seen during the day. Slowly, I cruised down the streets, amazed at the number of people walking about the neighborhood—and even more amazed at the contrast between those people.

It was *A Tale of Two Cities* on every block. On the one hand, you had folks gathered together on front porches, enjoying the summer evening. On the other hand, street dealers in white muscle T-shirts and dress pants brazenly stood by the curbs, waiting for people to pull up and buy their drugs. Pimped-out cars screeched down the streets blaring music while kids jumped and played in makeshift waterparks from gushing fire hydrants into those very streets. Prostitutes of all colors walked the streets in an array of outfits ranging from skintight elastic pants with skimpy halter tops to miniskirts and heels—all designed to attract the attention of drive-by shoppers. Businessmen driving luxury cars would hop off the expressway to flag down a prostitute or pull up to a dealer for a quick fix before going home to their wives and children. White kids from the suburbs cruised the area looking for drugs to bring back to their neighborhoods and sell at a profit. Even the Mexicans from the Pilsen neighborhood and the Puerto Ricans from Humboldt Park descended on the scene to make deals and buy drugs. Between the drug dealers, the prostitutes, the gangbanger wannabes, and the regular homeless people who pushed their life's possessions around the streets in shopping carts, the weekend ledger was awash in unsavory behavior.

Most disturbing was that, surrounded by this backdrop of soulless humanity, children were everywhere. I couldn't believe the number of kids roaming the streets, playing some kind of ball or jumping rope on the sidewalks. It was 9:30 at night, and there were so many kids running around that you would have thought school had just let out. I guessed that the late-June heat wave probably had a lot to do with the number of kids on the street, as, without question, the majority of them were cooling off in the open fire hydrants.

It seemed like every other corner had an open fire hydrant with jets of water streaming into the streets. Children were buzzing around the water like hornets whipped into a frenzy, trying to keep their balance while challenging the force of the water cannon. It was hardly considered a crime to open a fire hydrant and cool off in a gush of cool water on a hot summer day in the city of Chicago, but here the practice had a dual purpose. In addition to escaping the heat, the kids had devised an extraordinary way to gun down unsuspecting drivers with a stream of water diverted from the hydrants and aimed at passing cars. The kids took pieces of wood and jammed them under the torrents of water blasting out of the fire hydrant and diverted it high enough to swamp a passing car. Occasionally, an unsuspecting driver got blindsided and soaked by the deception, not realizing that the kids could direct the water through an open window. Mass celebration ensued upon making a direct hit that resulted in the poor driver being taunted and ridiculed by the children until he or she could drive away. The victim could be seen frantically attempting to roll up their windows, then stomping on the gas to avoid more humiliation.

Even though my car was in need of a good cleaning, I figured the last thing I needed to do was upset Rudy with an impromptu car wash. I had just turned northbound on Homan Avenue when I noticed another hydrant gushing onto the street up ahead. I couldn't tell what street the kids were abusing until I had committed myself to their obvious ambush, and, of course, it turned out to be Monroe Street, where I had to make a left-hand turn to get to Mrs. Brown's house.

As I approached the intersection, I could see the kids sizing up my car with eager anticipation in hopes of getting a point-blank shot of water to hit my windshield—or worse, to guide the water into my cracked windows. It was a four-corner stop, and there was one car behind me and two coming to a stop across from me. I carefully rolled up to the crosswalk and stopped the car. I knew full well that I was an unwilling participant in a match of wits with devious little minds that would stop at nothing to achieve their objective. The hydrant was on the right-hand corner across the street, spewing a full stream in my direction. I knew my tiny adversaries figured I would be forced to drive through the gushing water to avoid the path of the oncoming car as we began to cross the intersection at the same time. I could see by their faces how positively giddy they were at the thought of lifting the streaming water onto my windshield or into my car with their makeshift wooden rudder. In a move that took them off guard, I waited for the oncoming car to pass before cutting my wheel hard to the left and forcing the car behind it to stop in the middle of the intersection. That allowed me to creep around the corner onto Monroe Street and avoid the water. The look of disappointment on their faces was priceless as their expressions went blank and their mouths hung open at my cleverly designed maneuver that missed their impending trap. It was then that I heard someone screech, "LASSIE!" at the top of their lungs, followed by an onslaught of urchin voices screaming the famous name in my direction.

I immediately realized that I had misread their beleaguered expressions. Those weren't faces of children beaten in their own game of strategy—they were looks of astonishment witnessing a television character come to life. Before I knew what was happening, my car was swarmed with dripping-wet children knocking each other out of the way to get a better look at their hero. Kids were banging on both sides of the car begging for the dog's attention, some sticking their wet little hands in the window cracks trying to touch the fabled animal. Rudy seemed quite pleased with the attention of the children, eager to please all the onlookers and excited fans that were convinced he was the famous dog. I watched in horror as he scrambled from side to side in the back seat, pressing his nose against each window, eagerly allowing some of the lucky kids to grab a handful of fur as we crawled down the block. I flashed back to Jessica and her assurance that no one would come within fifty feet of me and the dog as kids flocked to my car, trampling over each other to the amused look of people standing up on their porches and pointing at the fiasco.

Instead of traveling incognito, slipping in and out of the black ledger like a shadow in the night, I was driving down the street like a float in a parade with a hundred kids stuck to my car. The only thing missing was a bull's-eye and a sign that read, "Dumb White Guy and Dog." I felt like banging my head on the steering wheel while cursing Jessica under my breath, knowing this was going to turn to shit.

Carefully, I sped up, not wanting to run over the little feet of Rudy's many fans. I prayed their short attention spans would kick in and they'd give up soon enough and return to their business of drowning passing motorists. Thankfully, it only took a few seconds to shake them off my car and continue down the block.

With a gigantic sigh of relief, I drove up the street and parked right across from Mrs. Brown's house. She and a very pretty young woman were standing on her porch with amused expressions on their faces, obviously intrigued at the Pied Piper effect I had on the children. Then, in a moment of both recognition and bewilderment, Mrs. Brown bellowed out, "Oh my God, it's my 'surance man!"

It took her a moment, as if unsure what to do next, but when she finally realized it was me, she grabbed the hand of the other woman and came down to the street to greet me. I was barely able to get out of my car before the two ladies were off the porch and next to it.

"Hi, Mrs. Brown. I'm sorry I'm so late," I said, attempting to ignore the spectacle I had just created down the block. Both women ignored me completely and stood gazing and pointing into the window to see what all the excitement was about. Rudy must have thought he had died and gone to heaven with all the attention he was receiving from the ladies about his remarkable resemblance to the famous canine.

"Take Lassie out and let us see him," Mrs. Brown insisted as I walked around to greet them.

"Well, okay. But, ah, well, he doesn't get around people much, and I, uh, don't want him to hurt you or anything," I said, mumbling and stuttering, trying to figure out some way to avoid letting Rudy out of the car.

"Oh, come on. Lassie ain't going to hurt nobody," she said as I maneuvered past them and opened the door. I barely got the door open before Rudy jumped out, stood on his hind legs, and buried his head in Mrs. Brown's oversized bosom. *Traitor,* I thought to myself as he acted like Mrs. Brown was his long-lost family member. "Look at this, Sandra," she called out to the pretty girl who had followed her off the porch.

"He's beautiful, Martha," the young lady said, moving closer to pet the dog.

"Sandra, this is Mr. Pickles, my 'surance man I told you 'bout coming to see me tonight," she said.

"Hi, I'm Sandra Wesley," she said, extending her hand towards me.

"Ron Pickles," I said, awkwardly shaking her hand while trying to hold Rudy back from mauling Mrs. Brown.

"I think you might be my mother's insurance man," Sandra said with a smile of recognition. "She told me that her insurance agent was a white guy with a funny last name," she said, trying not to giggle.

"It's all right; you can laugh. I don't mind being called a white guy," I joked while admiring her lovely smile and sparkling brown eyes that were filled with life. I liked her instantly and could tell that she still looked at the world with wonder and amazement through a young girl's heart.

"I don't have a Wesley on my book. Is that your married name?"

"Divorced, but I kept the name. My mom is Othra Buckley," she said.

"I keep telling you to get rid of that ol' Wesley name. It ain't been anything but bad luck for you, Sandra. Get your old name back," Mrs. Brown interjected.

"Yes, Martha, I know," Sandra said to Mrs. Brown with an appeasing tone.

"So, you're Mrs. Buckley's daughter from over on the next block? I remember her talking about you. You got three kids, right?"

"Yeah, that's right. I've missed you the last couple of times you picked up at my mom's house, and I keep forgetting to remind her, but I do want to get some insurance for me and the kids," she said.

"Do you live around here?" I asked, hoping that she lived on my ledger so I didn't have to split the case with another agent.

"Right here next to Mrs. Brown," she said.

"No way! I've been coming to Mrs. Brown's house since I started, and I never seen you around here," I said with disbelief.

"The kids keep me busy, but I'm around," she said.

"Are you going to be around tomorrow?" I asked.

"Whatever's good for you?"

"I have to come back tomorrow, but I collect in the morning, so I wouldn't be able to spend much time with you until the afternoon," I said, hoping that she could see me.

"That would work out great because I promised to take my kids to the park in the morning, so the afternoon would be fantastic," she said with an energy in her voice that sounded as if she really wanted me to stop by. I knew we were talking about insurance, but for the briefest of moments, I wished we weren't. Her spirit was so warm and inviting that it captured something inside of me I hadn't felt before.

"Sounds good. Let me get your phone number, and I'll stop somewhere to call and make sure you're home," I said, reaching for a pen.

"You can get me at Mrs. Brown's house," she said, deflecting the question by kneeling down and kneading Rudy's coat with both hands as she praised him as the most beautiful dog she had ever seen. I knew she was embarrassed at not having a phone, and telling me I could reach her at Mrs. Brown's house was sort of a code. I was angry with myself for asking the question. "What did you say his name was?" she asked, still stroking his head.

"It's Rudy," I said.

"Rudy, that's different," she replied.

"Well, what do you expect from a guy named Pickles?" I asked as she got up and looked at me with an amused expression.

"Well, I'm not sure what I can expect from a guy named Mr. Pickles, but I have to go in and check on my babies right now, so I definitely expect to see you tomorrow afternoon," she said with a smile. I was taken aback for a moment and felt myself skip a breath when our eyes locked before she turned to leave. "I'll talk to you later, Martha," she said, walking away.

"I'll see you tomorrow, Sandra," I happily called out to her, allowing Mrs. Brown to fuss over Rudy as my eyes followed her into the house. Caught off guard, I quickly turned away, feeling flushed when Sandra looked back for a moment and caught me staring at her. "I better put him back in the car so we can go in and take care of your business," I said with a sigh while shaking off the effects of something I wasn't sure I understood.

"Okay, well, it's good to meet you, Mr. Rudy," Mrs. Brown said, oblivious to my reaction to Sandra. Then, I carefully turned him around by the collar and guided him back into the car. I rolled the back window down a couple of inches before closing the door and walking around the car to do the same with the other windows. I followed Mrs. Brown onto her porch and into her apartment. She held the door as I walked into her living room, where the receipt book from Unified was sitting on the coffee table. I sat down and made myself comfortable while picking up the book and flipping the calendar pages to the current date. She walked into the dining room a few feet away and took her gigantic black purse off the table, then came back over to the couch and sat beside me, fumbling around inside it.

"Well, I'm glad you were able to see me today because your insurance is pretty far back," I said, looking at the last time I marked the book several weeks before.

"Don't be too glad. I can only give you two weeks today, but you come back next week, and I'll get you the rest," she said as I looked pathetically upon the $17 she untangled from her purse and placed on the table.

"Wow, I don't think I can do that," I said with exasperation, thinking that I was risking my life coming out here at night to pick up seventeen bucks. "I really need to get eight weeks here, or your policy is going to be running in arrears, and it's going to lapse," I said, looking at her with concern.

"Don't you ever collapse my 'surance. You know that I may be late, but I's always pays my 'surance, Mr. Pickles," she said while sliding the money towards me.

"I know, Mrs. Brown, but I really don't have anything to do with it. If the policies fall out of the grace period, they automatically lapse," I said.

"Don't be talking that stuff to me," she shot back. "Ray Meadows was my 'surance man for ten years, and he told me all about how agents could hold someone's 'surance or collapse it," she said with authority. I shook my head and almost started laughing in disbelief as I thought about Meadows' "do as I say, not as I do" style of management.

"I wasn't worried about you paying, Mrs. Brown, but I got to get more than two weeks from you tonight. You're almost two months behind. Even Meadows wouldn't hold your insurance that long," I said, calling her bluff. I could see Ray holding her insurance for a week or two, but I doubted seriously that he would have gone beyond that, and, from the look on Mrs. Brown's face, I was right.

"How much more?" she asked in a depressed tone.

"Let's see. You pay $8.45 per week, so I need to get $67.60 to get you caught up," I said with a sigh.

"Damn, Mr. Pickles! This is your fault I'm so far behind! You got to come and see me when I got this damn money," she vented at me with a disgusted look on her face.

"I'm sorry, Mrs. Brown. You're right—it is my fault. I missed you two weeks in a row, and I apologize. Why do you think I held your insurance? I knew you'd take care of it when you could. I wasn't worried about you," I said, trying to take all the blame for her inability to pay the premium. This was another part of the job Hamilton neglected to tell me about. Instead of getting the most insurance for their money, people on the ledger got the least, but they did get a benefit other insurance companies don't provide. They got a personal account manager, or bill collector, who coaxes, prods, and badgers them into paying their insurance each week or month as the cases called.

I felt bad for Mrs. Brown because I knew she always had good intentions about paying her insurance. It wasn't that money was tight—it was scarce. Mrs. Brown was in her mid-fifties, and she had little, if any, education. The best she could hope for was back-breaking minimum-wage jobs to carry her through and hopefully be enough to survive. Her only salvation, if you could call it that, was time. She made a life for herself by working two, sometimes three, jobs. She would work sixty or seventy hours a week doing laundry, sewing, and cleaning other people's houses. I knew this because she told me the reason I couldn't see her on Saturday was that she pulled a double shift working the laundry room at a North Side hospital. I sat there on her couch, looking at a woman who was doing the absolute best she could to keep her life together but kept coming up short. I never even tried to make her a "mail pay" client, knowing that she would send in a few dollars here and there, ending up so far behind that her insurance would lapse. I knew this was the reason it was so important for me to come here tonight; if I had waited, the money would be gone.

It wasn't like she considered the insurance a luxury; she struggled to pay the insurance because she believed in her heart that her family needed it. The $8.45 weekly premium that Mrs. Brown was paying provided $1,000 of burial insurance on each of her grown kids, as well as a half dozen grandchildren. Just enough to get them in the ground without asking for help. She once said to me, "Mr. Pickles, sometimes trying to pay this 'surance is like getting run over by a car while waiting for a bus. I know we gots to be put in the ground someday, but Lord Almighty, it's a struggle when you ain't making but a couple dollars an hour." I could see by the distress on her face that she was struggling to figure out how to come up with more money. I hated this part of the job. I hated prodding people for money I knew they couldn't afford. "Okay, Mrs. Brown. What is the absolute most you could give me tonight if you promise to see me again next week and get caught up?"

"All I got is $40 until next Tuesday," she said, shaking her head.

"Can you give me the forty and still get by?"

"I think so."

"Let's see. $42.25 will get us paid up for five weeks," I said, doing the math on the back of my route card.

"I'll stick in the $2.25 if you give me the forty, and you can pay me back next week. How does that sound?"

"I can do that," she said with a little more pride in her voice than she had a moment before. "How much more do I need?" she asked.

"You got $17, so all you need is $23," I said. After a moment of hesitation, she scrambled through her purse again and came up with exactly $23 in singles to add to the $17 already on the table.

"Mr. Pickles, you don't keep me up to date, and I'm going get me a new 'surance man," she said with feigned anger.

"I swear, Mrs. Brown, you're going to be seeing a lot more of me because I sure can't let you get another 'surance man," I said with a raised eyebrow. I checked off five weeks of payments in her book and held it up for her to see before signing it and putting it back on the table. "I really appreciate you seeing me tonight, and I promise you that I won't let you get this far back again," I said as we both got up and walked over to the door. She opened the door and held it for me as I walked outside.

"You better not, or I'm going call that ol' nigga Meadows up and tell him I want me a new 'surance agent," she said, laughing as I walked away.

"Don't you do me like that, Mrs. Brown," I hollered back at her.

"Watch yourself, Mr. Pickles," she said as she closed the door. *Words to live by,* I thought on my way to the car.

In the time it took to sort out a payment plan with Mrs. Brown, a quiet metamorphosis had taken place in the neighborhood. I stopped in my tracks as if my senses had set off an alarm. I looked around, trying to figure out what was different. I quickly realized the porches were empty and the sounds of children playing in the streets had evaporated into an eerie silence that blanketed the area. Everyone was gone. It was reminiscent of the time Meadows and I pulled into the parking lot of a project that looked as if it had been deserted for years. The people knew when to get off the streets. I picked up my pace and was unnerved by the click of my own heels hitting the pavement as the echo bounced off the street and sounded like footsteps following me to the car. Rudy was a welcome sight standing up in the back, wagging his tail with his head hanging over the front seat as I opened the door and sat down. I started the car, closed my eyes, and leaned back, taking a deep breath as Rudy nuzzled his head against my cheek and gave me a big sloppy dog kiss before returning to his favorite position: curled up in the back seat. With the smell of musky dog beginning to stick to my skin, I quickly decided to put the car in gear and pull away in order to get some fresh air circulating.

Central Park Avenue was just a few blocks away and a busy thoroughfare for traffic. It only took me a few moments to get there, and I was able to squeeze the car into an open parking spot in front of Mr. Peters' entrance, which made me feel good knowing we wouldn't be exposed to a long walk on the street.

I had never met Mr. Peters in person and had only spoken to him on the phone earlier in the week when he called me from his job. Ever since I began working the ledger, he had been leaving his money and his receipt book with another client of mine, Mrs. Hendricks, who lived in the building next door. She moved out the month before and told me I had to make other arrangements to get Mr. Peters' money. Since he didn't have a phone and was never home during the day, I tacked up a note on his door, hoping he would call me. He had left several messages at the office but never a return phone number. He finally got ahold of me on Monday, and we agreed that after I got him caught up tonight, he would begin to mail his money to the office.

I never liked going in the red brick apartment buildings across from Garfield Park during the day, much less at night, mostly because of the entrance. The six-flat units were built side by side and butted right up against the sidewalk just a few feet away from the street. They lacked a courtyard or entranceway of their own where you might have some vision as to what was going on around you. The doors didn't lock, and the lights in the hallways and stairwells were usually burned out, so there was no way of telling from the outside if people were hanging out in the vestibule. Mr. Peters' apartment was readily accessible to the criminal element roaming the streets. Bums and homeless people slept in the hallways at night, and prostitutes serviced their johns inside the vestibules on a regular basis. Teenagers wanting a place to smoke weed came and went as they pleased, and the street dealers used the blacked-out entranceways to hide from the police when stings were conducted.

This is what I had in mind when Jessica convinced me to bring Rudy. Ol' Man Wicks was right when he referred to the black ledger as alive, like someone's always watching you and looking for weaknesses they can exploit. I was hoping Rudy would be seen, not necessarily by children who wanted an autographed paw print, but by people who might be inclined to do me harm if the opportunity presented itself. Jessica was on target in one sense; regardless of the breed, no one is going to look at a powerfully built animal by your side and disregard the dog as harmless.

Rudy was anxious to get out of the car and could hardly contain himself as I snapped his blue leash to the collar around his neck. I made him sit while I reached into the front seat and grabbed my route card, then shut the door and walked him up to the building. The look on his face seemed serious; it was almost like he knew there was a job to do and was ready to get started. There was something about having him by my side that really calmed me down and made me feel secure. I took pride in believing that just his presence would be enough to deter anything from happening.

As we approached the doorway, I looked up and thought how wonderful these apartments must have looked when they were built and how awful they had become. The original doors were gone, and the ornamental glass inlay highlighting the arched entrance had long since been removed. Pieces of rectangular plywood were cut to fill in the framework that had once held the glass above the transom. The plywood was painted dark brown but had chipped and weathered badly, making it look like a board-up service was used to conceal a crime scene. The replacement door was made of metal and painted dark brown as well. It was crooked and battered with dings and dents from people kicking it open all the time. Its hinges were separating from the frame, and the heavy door drooped out of alignment, making it impossible to close properly. There was a small square window at the top center of the door with the glass knocked out, and I could see the black abyss awaiting me in the hallway. I had to stick my fingers in the empty hole where the doorknob should have been to get a grasp. I tugged hard at the heavy door, opening it as far as I could to allow the light from the streetlamps outside to illuminate the foyer before entering.

A stale odor of heavy varnish, mixed with human stink and charged by the heat of the day, greeted me as I stuck my head in to look around. I studied the hallway carefully to get my bearings and make sure no one else was there before guiding Rudy inside and letting the door close behind me. The stairs leading to the upper floors were a few feet ahead to the right. I made a mental note to keep away from the brass mailboxes built into the wall on the left as one of the slots had been pried open and hung down, just waiting to cut an unsuspecting passerby.

My first step into the building should have forewarned me to turn and leave, as I managed to land on a small piece of dislodged tile and skated across the hall until I was brought to a knee in front of the stairs. With the door slamming shut behind me, the hall went black with just a small trickle of light filtering in from the holes in the door. Rudy had little choice but to follow me as my first reaction was to yank his leash for balance until I cascaded to a stop. He wasn't happy when I leaned on his back for support and gingerly rose to my feet. I praised the dog for his understanding and tried to explain how sorry I was for pulling him down with me. I thought my good-natured encouragement would do the trick and he would understand that everything was okay so we could move on, but he seemed to have a problem. About the same time, I heard men's voices approaching from outside, and I figured it might be a good time to get up the stairs to the safety of Mr. Peters' apartment. Rudy had it figured differently. For some reason, he decided it was not in his best interest to go any further than he had already come. I immediately recognized his cat-stuck-in-a-tree posture as he hovered close to the floor with outstretched nails gripping at the tile, and I started to panic. "Oh shit, Rudy, not now!" I shouted in as hushed a tone as possible. "Come on, be a good boy, let's go, please, please!" I begged the dog as the voices grew louder and more menacing with every passing second.

I stood there for a second, staring at him in the near darkness, unable to comprehend his fear of climbing. It was then that I realized Rudy's reluctance appeared to be related to the stairs. He had never gone up stairs before. As the cajoling outside got louder, I started freaking out and pulling on the dog's neck to get him up the damn things. The stagnant air in the hallway conducted the heat, and sweat beads began to run down my face as I tugged in vain to get Rudy to move. In desperation, I took his front two paws and placed them as far up the steps as possible, then moved behind him and pushed on his butt, hoping that he would get the idea to climb the stairs. It was then that the door to the building flung open, casting a spotlight on Rudy and me from the glow outside. I turned quickly to see who came in when my grip on the dog slipped and I fell to my knees, straddling the dog from behind on all fours. I have no idea what the expression on my face looked like as I grabbed for the banister to pull my prone body off the rear end of my trembling dog, but I do know that I was horrified at the ridiculous circumstance the dog had created. I scrambled to my feet and immediately assumed a defensive posture, dripping in sweat, just barely able to make out what appeared to be astonished looks on the three black men's faces that had come in the door. It didn't immediately occur to me what thoughts might be going through their minds by the puzzled looks on their faces.

"What the fuck you doing to that dog?!" a voice shouted at me.

"Um, nothing. He gets afraid sometimes," I tried to explain.

"You see that!" said another who was pointing at us, grabbing his stomach, and leaning against the wall in a fit of laughter.

"I know it looks bad, but…"

"Motherfucker!" one of them screamed in disbelief before bending to his knees and howling.

"No, man, that shit is wrong," another bellowed at the top of his lungs before hunching over and laughing.

"Why the fuck you got to bring Lassie to the ghetto to ass fuck him?" screamed another as all three burst into hysterics. I waited for them to calm down a moment and regain their composure, figuring that once they heard my explanation, they would totally understand my predicament.

"You don't understand—he doesn't like stairs," I pleaded with a tone that alternated between anger and embarrassment as the three bombarded me with rapid-fire quips.

"Bet he don't like getting ass raped either!"

"Fuck no! Look at his face!"

"Lassie be like, 'Timmy, help!'"

"No, no, no, motherfucker be like, 'Help me, niggas! Help me, niggas! This white boy be crazy!'"

"What the fuck you tell your wife? Be back in a while, honey. I'm going to go fuck—I mean walk—the dog."

"Shit!"

"That shit is fucked up!"

"He doesn't like to back up," I said with a stutter, hoping to calm them down.

"Not with you waiting to fuck him," one lamented as all three almost started hyperventilating and nearly fell to the ground in uproarious laughter. I just stood there shaking my head while looking at Rudy clinging to the steps as if he were about to fall off a twenty-story building.

"Oh man, I can't fucking take this shit," one of the guys said, bent over as if in pain from the excruciating spasms of laughter. He stood up, turned around, and lumbered out the door, snorting and cajoling at the sight he had just witnessed.

"Shit, man, I seriously don't know what the fuck you're doing with that dog, but you need to find a better place to take your girlfriend," another slurred with amusement as he followed the first guy out. The last guy just waved his hand at me and joined the others, slamming the door shut as he exited the building. Once outside, they broke into uproarious laughter again as they debated the wisdom of a white man straddling the ass end of poor Lassie on a Friday night in the heart of the ghetto.

Just then, the thought occurred to me that being robbed or beaten might have been preferable to the amount of ridicule, sarcasm, and mockery I had just endured. In addition, it dawned on me that, unlike being robbed, which would have been quickly forgotten, this event would be told over and over until it became the basis of folklore. For the rest of my life, I would be known as "the white guy who ass raped Lassie in the ghetto."

Realizing the hopelessness of the situation, I figured it would be better to move forward, so I wrapped my arms around the seventy-five-pound collie's chest, just behind his front legs, and picked him up for the arduous climb to the third-floor apartment. With Rudy's hind legs dangling, I began the climb. I was happy that the second and third floors each had a low-wattage bulb screwed into the ceiling, offering a dim, but welcome, change to the near blackout on the first floor. Rudy seemed quite content to let me struggle with his dead weight as we walked up the stairs, bouncing his hind legs off each step like a kangaroo. By the time I got up to the apartment, I was drenched in sweat and gagging on dog hair as I dumped Rudy on the floor and knocked on Mr. Peters' door. The door cracked open until the security chain pulled tight, and one old eye looked us up and down.

"You the 'surance man?" he said skeptically.

"Yes, sir, I'm Ron Pickles," I said, fumbling in my pocket to hand him a card.

"Whatch you doing with that dog? I ain't never seen no 'surance man with no dog before."

"Well, you know, sir, with it being so late and all, I thought he might offer some protection," I said humbly.

"A collie? You brought a goddamn collie into the ghetto for protection? What dumbass told you to do that?"

"That was my wife," I said, seething with sarcasm. Mr. Peters gave me a blank stare, not quite sure how to answer.

"Shit, them boys would eat that dog up and spit him out," he said as if disgusted by the whole thing. "Y'all wait right there," he grumbled while taking my card as he closed the door. A few moments later, the door cracked open, and a skinny black arm popped out holding the receipt book. Mr. Peters didn't seem pleased with either Rudy or me and opted to perform the entire financial transaction in the hallway.

As soon as Mr. Peters closed the door, I looked down at the pathetic excuse for an animal I owned, realizing that I would now have to carry his sorry ass all the way back down the stairs. I reached down and grabbed Rudy under the front of his chest and lifted him as high as I could, then quickly plopped him back to the floor. It dawned on me that his hanging hind legs were going to be an impediment that could easily cause me to trip. Though my state of mind was definitely unhinged, I knew that falling down the stairs would have literally sent me off the edge, resulting in an insanity that would have ended poorly for both the dog and me. So, using better judgment, I heaved the seventy-five-pound beast up into my arms and cradled him like a baby. Rudy misinterpreted my actions and was convinced that I was attempting to demonstrate the great love and affection he knew I felt for him. So, he promptly licked my face and rested his head on my shoulder to show how grateful he was for our love. I never hated an animal more in my life.

So, as I navigated the three flights of stairs downward, sweating profusely, stinking to high heaven, humiliated beyond belief, and choking on dog hair, I felt it necessary to vent my dissatisfaction with his behavior.

"You are without a doubt the most useless piece of shit dog to ever inhabit the planet Earth," I whispered in a low, angry tone through clenched teeth. "You're like Baby fucking Huey, you know that? You should be ashamed of yourself. You fail so horribly, miserably, at being a dog. Actually, you're not a dog! You can't even be considered in the same breath as a dog! Do you know what you are? You are a piece of shit—a nasty piece of shit. You know what kind? That crumbly yellow dog shit that gets stuck in the cracks of your shoe and is impossible to get out. That's you! Jesus Christ! I can't fucking believe this," I muttered over and over while Rudy just laid quietly in my arms, taking in my hushed words with the love he knew I was offering.

CHAPTER 8

I woke up at 7:00 a.m. the next morning feeling better than I could remember. Jessica waited up last night to tell me that Bobby Cooker called and said the letter was sent, my application had been approved, and I was going to electrician's school in September. I couldn't believe it. For the first time in my life, everything seemed to be falling into place. Even the ledger seemed more inviting, and I eagerly jumped out of bed to get the day started. I was more determined than ever to make all the collections I could and ask everyone I met to buy some insurance. I needed money so I could quit the insurance job and concentrate on the six months of classroom studies that would begin in September. Jessica and I had already figured out a plan that would get us through until I actually started my apprenticeship and began to make some money. When I started school, her mom was going to watch the baby during the day so Jessica could get a job. I was going to go back to delivering pinball machines on the weekends so I could concentrate on homework during the week. We knew it would be tight, but we also knew that after my four-year apprenticeship, I would be making union scale, and our money problems would be over.

After a shower and a quick bowl of cereal, I quietly snuck into the bedroom and gave Jessica a kiss goodbye before doing the same with little Jeannette. I had taken Rudy out earlier and already forgotten about our exploits the night before when I noticed him standing by the front door with a serious expression on his face, fully expecting to accompany me back to work. I looked down at him with folded arms, a raised eyebrow, and an uncompromising smirk on my face. He looked me square in the eye, or at least as square as his crossed eyes would allow, then lowered his head and slowly walked over by the couch where he heaved a big sigh before laying down, resigning himself to the fact that his ledger days were over.

I always took Western Avenue down to the ledger on Saturday mornings instead of the expressway because the street was wide open with very little traffic. It was about a forty-five-minute drive with all the stoplights, but the extra time helped me concentrate on the collections I needed to make and focus my mindset on working the ledger. It was going to be another hot day, but the morning air felt great swirling around the car with all the windows open.

As if instructed to personally enhance my mood and add to my jubilance, the radio station played "Help" and "Hello, Goodbye" by the Beatles that morning. The ride to my territory went by way too fast, and, before I knew it, I had crossed the Eisenhower Expressway and was forced to contain my exuberance and put on my game face. You could never just haphazardly approach the black ledger.

The change in complexion from Friday night to Saturday morning was astounding, and the aftermath of the night's activities was plainly evident. I turned west on Madison Street to find two smashed cars that had collided sometime during the night, with a tow truck just now clearing them from the area. I spotted two crews of men from board-up companies measuring and cutting plywood on the sidewalks in front of businesses. Behind them were gaping holes in the storefronts where windows had been knocked out the night before. The city streets were void of people, with the exception of an occasional drunk sprawled out on a bus bench or a homeless person huddled under a cardboard box in the entrance of a store.

After a few months of working the ledger, I amused myself by trying to distinguish and catalog the different classes of homeless people that made a living out of being homeless. The lowest class was the cardboard people. Everyone despised them because their sole purpose in life seemed to revolve around begging for enough money to buy booze and drink themselves to death. They were actually the most harmless, as 90 percent of their day was spent in a drunken stupor, covered up like a turtle under their cardboard.

The next class consisted of the newly homeless—people who

couldn't make it in society but didn't really understand how to survive on the streets. They were the most dangerous because they hadn't killed enough brain cells yet to prevent them from formulating ideas. Meadows told me about a guy in this category who went around stealing stop signs and took them to the recycling plant as scrap metal. Eventually, the usually discreet scrapyard attendants turned him in to the police. Then, there were the burnouts. These were the people who got ahold of some really bad stuff and physically destroyed their minds. They were easy to spot because they would be standing around one minute and kicking at invisible objects and talking to themselves the next.

Without question, the "shopping cart" people were the highest class of the homeless set. These people were the entrepreneurs of the street—pillars of hope in a world of despair that embraced the streets as an opportunity to live life on their terms. Like rungs on a ladder, each additional shopping cart attached to their train represented symbols of status, demonstrating the heights they had climbed to achieve street-savvy independence. While one shopping cart loaded with shit showed that you had promise, two or more shopping carts strung together with bits and pieces of salvaged garbage and sorted neatly into the baskets meant you had arrived.

My Saturday morning collections always started the same way: climbing up the creaky back stairs to the second floor of Lanni Tisdale's apartment. After knocking on the door, I would wait patiently as her five-year-old boy, Max, would struggle to open the door and let me in. Then, her nine-year-old daughter, Takesha, would go into the bedroom and tell her mother that the 'surance man was there. I would sit down on the couch with Max, and the two of us would watch the Saturday morning cartoons for a moment until Takesha came back and said it was okay to go into the bedroom and see her mom.

In a strange sort of way, Lanni Tisdale reminded me of my mother when I was growing up, and her kids, Takesha and Max, a version of my sister Judy and me. Lanni was a single mom who worked as a bank teller during the week and provided all the support for her children. She was an attractive woman, with an angelic face and dark complexion, and though she wasn't fat by any means, she carried heavy bones on her six-foot frame that could seem intimidating. Like my mother, she seemed obligated to reward herself for the sacrifices she endured raising her children by hitting the town and drinking herself blind every Friday night. Takesha would take care of Max, feeding him dinner and getting them both off to bed at a decent hour with strict instructions to stay inside the apartment and not to open the door for anyone.

With Takesha leading the way, I was escorted to the bedside of Lanni, who was semi-conscious and sprawled out across her bed, still fully clothed in the party dress she had worn the night before. It was my guess that she had just made it into the house a few moments before I arrived. She had one leg pulled up to her side and the other hanging over the bed with a black pump dangling off her foot, still attached by a strap to her ankle. Her short dress had bunched up around her hips, exposing a garter clinging to the black nylons she was wearing and giving me a more intimate view of my client than I would have preferred.

"Good morning, Lanni," I said cheerfully, pretending to ignore her hungover, half-naked condition. Lanni didn't say a word as she struggled to raise her arm and point a finger to the end of the bed as an indication for Takesha to get her purse. Without opening her eyes or lifting her head off the mattress, Lanni would fumble around the purse for some money and the receipt book, then hand it to Takesha to give to me. I would mark the book and make changes before giving it all back to Takesha and saying goodbye to everyone. The whole process never took more than a few minutes, and I was on my way to the next stop.

When I first started working the ledger, it was strange knocking on the same person's door each week. I felt like a rent collector beating down people's doors and harassing them for money. After a while, though, I began to realize that people expected the 'surance man to come by every week, and once I felt welcomed, it was like visiting an old friend or relative. Almost every client's house I walked into on Saturday morning offered me coffee, biscuits, or bacon, and more than a few people would invite me back during the week to have supper with them. Since Mr. Meadows had been on the ledger for ten years before me, everyone would ask how he was doing, and we would laugh and joke about his shortcomings and especially his affection for liver and onions, which everyone seemed to know about.

All in all, the morning went pretty smoothly, and I made just about all the collections on my route card. It was about 12:30 when I decided to break for lunch, figuring that I only had one more collection to make before stopping by Sandra's to see if she wanted to buy some insurance. I was thrilled to see Craig Branson's car in the parking lot of the Lake Street Diner when I got there, so I quickly parked the car and rushed inside to tell him my news.

"I'm going to get it, dude!" I called out with a raised fist in the air when I spotted him having a coffee and reading a paper in a booth as I walked into the restaurant.

"No shit, you got the letter?" he yelled back.

"The letter will be here in the next couple of days. My buddy called last night and told Jessica that one of the honchos from the union said I was approved."

"Ronnie, that's fucking great news, dude!" he said with genuine enthusiasm while holding up his hand for a high five.

"Damn, Craig, you have no idea how I've been sweating this thing out. Man, I don't know what I would have done if this didn't go through," I said, shaking my head as I tucked in and sat down across from him at the booth. "Did you eat yet?"

"Yeah, I was just getting ready to leave."

"Hey, your face looks a little better. Now it just looks like your wife slapped you around a bit instead of your kid stomping on your skull," I observed.

"Yeah, I don't feel quite so abused today," he laughed.

"You want some coffee, honey?" a waitress called out from the other side of the counter.

"I'll have a Coke," I yelled back.

"Wow, man, that's fantastic about the union. I know how important this is for you," Craig said.

"No shit, the only reason I even took this job was to hold me over so I could go to school," I said.

"So, when do you think you'll start?" he asked.

"I won't know exactly till I get the letter, but I'm pretty sure the class starts in September."

"Wow, that's great! Except that you're so close to qualifying for the Bahamas cruise, and now you're going to miss it," he said.

"Yeah, I know. That would have been pretty cool, but it's a small price to pay when you think about it," I replied.

"No doubt."

"It's so weird, Craig, you know, this has been the best week I've ever had. I sold a shitload of insurance with Otis, I came out here last night and picked up enough money to reinstate the policies I lapsed on Thursday, and I met a girl who walks up to me on the street and tells me she wants to buy some insurance. I'm going to see her this afternoon. On top of all that, I get the news from Bobby about the union. I'm on a crazy fucking roll," I said with amazement as the waitress pushed a Coke in front of me.

"Are you going to order something?" she asked.

"Yeah, but YOU don't laugh," I said, pointing a finger at Craig. "Give me the liver and onions," I said.

"What is it with you guys and the liver and fucking onions?" he asked in disbelief as she walked away.

"It's that fucking Meadows. Liver and onions, liver and onions—that's all he ever talks about. Every client I see asks me about

Meadows and if he's still eating liver and onions. I go to bed at night dreaming of fucking liver and onions. He's brainwashed me or something!" I said in an exceedingly loud voice.

"Okay, okay, calm down," Craig said, looking around the restaurant at the attention my small tirade had garnished from the other patrons.

"I can't help it. I'm so pumped right now," I said, doing a drum roll on the table. Craig snorted his approval, then took a sip of coffee before looking me in the eye with a curious expression.

"Hey, not to change the subject or rain on your parade or anything, but I was wondering if Hamilton said anything to you about T.J.?"

"Meadows said he was fired," I shrugged. "Hamilton never said anything. Besides, what is he supposed to say? 'Hey, Ron, hope this makes you feel better. I fired T.J. because he threw a hot dog at you,'" I joked. Craig just rolled his eyes in agreement.

"You're right about that, but all the same, I think he got himself involved with a really bad element and is paying the price," he said as trying to make a point.

"You think more than whores and drugs?" I asked with a shrug.

"Come on, Ronnie, you know what I'm talking about."

"Not really," I snickered.

"The scams, you know?"

"A little clarity, please. Which scams do you speak of, pray tell?" I asked with a smile and open arm gesture while Craig shook his head and chuckled at my antics.

"Yeah, I know there's a million ways to steal on this job, but the one that gets me is this bullshit with the funeral homes," he said.

"Oh, those," I said with a sigh. "You think T.J. is doing that stuff?" I asked with a more somber tone.

"I don't know, but I overheard Guru and Mr. Uhlen talking about the police showing up and saying there might be more to this than a missing persons report. That's why I wondered if you heard anything."

"I haven't heard shit, but I know T.J. was hanging out with those guys on the stoner staff, and I wouldn't doubt for a second that there's more going on than we've been told." He looked at me as if he wanted to say something else and then just shook his head as if exasperated by the whole ordeal.

"Ah, fuck those guys," he finally said.

"Exactly, who cares? You and I will be out of here soon enough," I reasoned.

"Yeah, I know, it's all bullshit. Sorry I brought it up," he said with a dismissive tone. "Hey, what are you doing later on?" he chimed up.

"I told you, I got to see that chick I met last night about some new business," I replied.

"Oh, that's right. I was going to ask if you wanted to go downtown and play some video football," he said with a bit of disappointment. Then, as if hit by a thunderbolt, his expression instantly changed to one of astonishment. "Holy shit, dude! I can't believe you came out here on a Friday night!"

"Yeah, I know," I said dismissively. "Trust me, it was the first and last time I'll ever work the ledger on a Friday night."

"So, how did you meet this girl?" he asked.

"Well, it's kind of weird. The whole thing actually started with Jessica."

"You didn't take her out here with you?" he asked incredulously.

"Not Jessica, the dog."

"You took your dog to the ledger?"

"Yeah, I know. Bad idea. But Jessie was worried about me going out so late and convinced me to take our dog Rudy with for protection."

"Wait a minute, isn't Rudy your retarded collie dog?"

"Not retarded, crossed eyed," I said.

"You took a retarded, cross-eyed collie to the black ledger for protection," he uttered while breaking out in a fit of laughter. I stared at him expressionless for a few moments until he calmed down.

"Do you want to hear the fucking story or not?" I asked, still not sure I wanted to accept the humor of my dog's failed exploits.

"Yeah, I'm sorry, go ahead," he said, squeezing his lips together to keep from laughing.

"Anyway, this really cute chick is standing with my client on her porch when I pull up, and they both come running down to see the 'retarded, cross-eyed' collie in the back of the car," I said, accentuating the point for Craig's amusement.

"She was super hot, huh?" he asked with a newfound interest in my story.

"In a way, but not like you're thinking. It was weird," I said, hesitantly trying to explain the hypnotizing effect she had on me. "She wasn't Playboy material or anything, but don't get me wrong, she was really cute."

"…I know, for a black chick, right?" he cut me off.

"No, man, not for a black chick. I hate when people say, 'Yeah, she's okay for a black chick.' That's such bullshit."

"Hey, I didn't mean anything by it," he said.

"You're missing my whole point here, so let me finish the story," I said with a note of defensiveness in my voice.

"Go ahead."

"I don't even know how to explain it to you," I said, taking a deep breath while looking around the room.

"Hey, man, I'm sorry. I didn't mean to put her down or anything," Craig said, misinterpreting my hesitation as a sign of displeasure over his remark.

"No, it's cool. I know you didn't mean anything by it. I'm just trying to figure out how to explain this chick to you so you don't think I'm nuts," I said.

"Come on, now you've piqued my curiosity."

"Okay. She's a tiny little thing, maybe five-three, five-four, with a really cute figure, especially considering the fact that she has kids. Her hair is about shoulder length, straightened and parted down the middle, but the thing I remember most is that she had the most amazing eyes I've ever seen."

"Now you're scaring me," Craig piped up with an expression of concern.

"What are you talking about?"

"It's one thing to tell me how hot the chick is and that she has a great ass and you'd love to bang the shit out of her, but you're thinking about crossing the line when you start talking about what great eyes some broad has."

"What line? You asked me what the girl looks like, and I'm trying to tell you that she's something kind of special, and you got me crossing a fucking line! Are you crazy?" I asked with a bewildered tone.

"Liver and onions," the waitress said while dropping the plate on the table and walking away.

"Ronnie, I'm just telling you to be careful. I got some chicks on my ledger that are smoking hot and come on to me every time I collect from them. I think that's what got T.J. into so much trouble. It's so fucking easy to get laid out here it isn't funny. And you know what's worse? No consequences."

"I don't follow you."

"Other than assholes like T.J. who drug themselves into comas and don't come home for weeks at a time, there is no way your wife will ever find out you're fucking around on her. Unless, of course, you bring her home a dose of the clap or something," he said as an afterthought.

"Trust me, Craig, I got two more months in this shit hole, and I'm out of here. The last thing I'd ever do is fuck around on the ledger. Besides, I don't think Jessica is real fond of crab meat," I said with a grin.

"Oooohhh, Pickles, you're a sick fuck. Now that thought's going to be floating around in my head the rest of the day," he said with a feigned look of disgust on his face.

"I'm a sick fuck! Which one of us justified screwing around on the ledger because they won't get caught?" I asked with a raised eyebrow.

"I never justified it; I was merely trying to tell you to watch out for the girl with the amazing eyes."

"I appreciate the concern," I said flippantly. "Hey, you want some liver and onions to go with your crabs?" I offered with a smile, pushing the plate of food in his direction.

"Oh man, I can't sit here and watch you eat that shit," Craig said as he gathered up his newspaper and stood up to leave.

"You're a pussy. A real man would suck it up and have a plate," I teased him.

"Oh yeah, well, a real man doesn't give a shit what a chick's eyes look like either," he said, smacking me on the back of the head with his paper as he headed for the door. "Let's get together next week for a game."

"Sounds good. Catch you later," I said, staring down at the massive amount of liver hanging off the side of the plate, still wondering what on earth possessed me to order such a thing.

After lunch, I got into my car and drove over to the poorest part of my ledger on Madison Street, amazed at the diversity I encountered from block to block by driving down the street. It occurred to me that Madison Street represented architectural development in Chicago like a human timeline. Beginning at Michigan Avenue, driving west on Madison, you are surrounded by man-made wonders that force you to peer hundreds of feet into the air, breathlessly trying to glimpse the tops of mammoth steel and glass structures that make up the Chicago skyline.

A few moments later, you're looking over blocks of vacant parking lots waiting to fill up with anxious fans attending hockey or basketball games at the Chicago Stadium. A couple more miles and you pass one of the most beautiful botanical gardens in the country in the Garfield Park Conservatory. As if a tribute to the everlasting significance of the human spirit, the street deposits you at the birthplace of Ernest Hemingway when it closes its run of Chicago and kisses the suburb of Oak Park.

Sandwiched about halfway between Michigan Avenue and Hemingway's birthplace, on a street that could literally bring you from rags to riches, was a strip known as Madison Row. Naturally, Madison Row encompassed the length of my ledger and consisted of boarded-up businesses and dilapidated storefronts that looked like a picture postcard of the Warsaw Ghetto after Germany invaded Poland. A closer look above those businesses and you find two- and three-room apartments in such a sad state of repair it would take an upgrade to call them squalor. Lost in the extremes of a street that reflected the best and worst a city like Chicago had to offer lived people like my clients: Winnie Hawkins and her husband, Willie.

Winnie Hawkins lived, or I should say existed, with her drunken husband, Willie, in one of the infamous two-room flats above the only thriving business on Madison Row, Mooches Liquors. Though few people outside the ledger would recognize it as such, the neighborhood liquor store—with its array of indigent characters strutting around the establishment like vultures scavenging for food—was a known safe haven of the community. In addition to the usual assortment of hard liquor, cheap wine, and cold beer, the store would stock a small supply of groceries for neighborhood consumption. It was commonplace for moms to send their kids to the store for a gallon of milk and a loaf of bread, as well as a pack of cigarettes with a signed note. It was also a place to pay the utility bills and pick up light bulbs if you paid a few extra cents on your bill each month.

I parked in front of the store and boldly instructed one of the more intelligent-looking transients to keep an eye on my car while I took care of some business, handing him a couple of dollars for his trouble. It was always a good move to say something to the guys standing around so they knew you were watching and weren't afraid to engage them. One of the relatively few advantages of being a white man working in the ghetto was the doubt it could raise among onlookers as to whether or not you were an undercover cop of some kind.

The doorway to Winnie's apartment was in front of the building, a few feet away from the liquor store's heavily fortified window. It was inevitable that a bum had to reposition himself away from the door so I could ring the bell to get buzzed into the apartment. Once inside, I closed the door tightly behind me before climbing the narrow staircase up to her floor.

"That you, Mr. Pickles?" Winnie called out from above.

"It's me, Winnie. I'm coming up," I called out to her, trying to breathe through my mouth and avoid the stale mix of bug juice and fermented liquor permeating the old wooden stairs on a warm day. At the top of the stairwell, Winnie was eagerly waiting for me with a smile while holding the door open for me to walk in.

"How you doing, Winnie?" I asked, squeezing past her.

"Oh, you know me, Mr. Pickles. I got some aches and pains, but you sure won't hear me complain about them. The good Lord sure does look out for me and Willie, and I ain't got no good reason to complain," the tired-looking lady said as I looked around the sparsely furnished apartment she and Willie called home. I walked into the dimly lit front room where a beat-up mattress with a number of pee stains was propped up against the wall by the front windows overlooking Madison Street. The apartment was so small, the mattress had to be leaned against the wall when not being used.

Willie was lounging back watching television on a black leather recliner with a long rip down the side and a book under one corner where a leg should have been. I immediately noticed two mason jars on the old hardwood floor next to his chair. One was filled with ice water, and the other was a spit jar for his chewing tobacco that had dark streaks of drool running down the side where he missed the opening. He was watching the Cubs baseball on a small black-and-white television that was precariously balanced on a TV dinner tray with a bent leg.

"How you doing, Willie?" I asked, reluctantly reaching out to shake his hand, knowing that it had to be ripe with the brown spit from the jar. I wasn't disappointed as I withdrew my hand to find a brown spattering of tobacco stain smudged across my palm, as if a grasshopper had just shit in my hand.

"I's be doing a whole lot better if you could spare a couple of dollars for me to run down and gets a bottle of beer to watch this game with," he said with a glimmer of hope in his eyes.

"Willie! What's the matter with you? Badgering Mr. Pickles for money to get you liquored up," Winnie hollered at him from the other room before suffering a coughing spell that came from deep within her lungs.

"Y'all be quiet, woman. Nobody axed you nothing for you to be sticking your nose in anyone's business," Willie responded, ignoring the obvious distress his wife was going through.

"Mr. Pickles, you come in here and let that ol' fool be by himself," Winnie wheezed as I stood there staring at my hand while taking in their exchange. Following her command, I walked back into the other room where she was standing at an old wooden table, busily counting out the exact change she needed for her insurance.

"Did you see a doctor about that cough? It sounds pretty bad," I asked.

"You pay no mind to me. It's just my allergies. Now, y'all sit yourself right down there and have a cool drink," she said, pointing to a sparkling clean mason jar filled with ice water she had fixed for me. It looked so inviting that I felt obligated to take a sip and reached for the jar, only to pull my hand back as fast as I could when a rather large cockroach crawled across the table and seemed to take offense at me moving the glass. Winnie didn't notice as I slowly pushed myself back from the table and studied every inch of my surroundings, afraid to blink in case one of the little buggers targeted me. Though roaches could be found in almost every home on the ledger, they seemed to flourish unabated in Winnie's house, and I was sure that Jessica would find little comfort in me bringing home roaches almost as much as giving her a dose of the crabs.

Fighting through the hacking and coughing that left Winnie gasping for each breath, she managed to count out the money for her insurance and walked over to the wall where she had nailed up the receipt book.

"Looky what's I did, Mr. Pickles," she said, proudly pointing to the book on the wall.

"Winnie! You found your receipt book," I said with a big grin.

"I's sure did. Now you won't have to be writing me all them paper receipts. You know I's lose them two minutes after you leave the house," she laughed.

"I swear, Winnie, I haven't marked up your book since I started as your agent," I chuckled. She removed the book from the hook and handed it to me before sitting down across the table. I flipped it open to the last time I recorded a payment when I only noticed one policy number on the inside cover where the policy numbers were listed.

"Is there something wrong?" Winnie asked as I studied the book for a moment.

"I'm not sure. It's been so long since I looked at this book. You have more than one policy with us, don't you?"

"No sir, I's only got the one on me," she said.

"What about Willie?"

"Willie don't believe in no 'surance," she said.

"Who's the beneficiary on your policy?"

"You mean who gets the money if I's pass?"

"Yes."

"Willie," she said, nodding in his direction.

I paused for a moment and looked down at her book, trying not to reveal the disdain that came over me for the man sitting in the other room. I had talked to Winnie enough since starting the job to know that she provided all the support for the two of them sewing hems on dresses at a dry cleaner. I also knew from the occasional bruising around her face and eyes that all she could count on from Willie was a beating if she didn't provide him with drinking money every week. But until today, I never realized that the $17 I picked up every two weeks was for the sole purpose of providing money for Willie in the event of Winnie's death. It bothered me.

"Well, what would happen if Willie passes before you do?" I tried to ask as pleasantly as I could.

"I knows what you talkin' 'bout, Mr. Pickles, but Willie don't believe in no 'surance."

"That's right!" Willie shouted from the other room. "We ain't spending no more goddamn money on 'surance. I done told that to you, woman," he continued.

"Nobody is asking you to buy any more insurance, Willie. I just wanted to make sure there wasn't a policy here I was missing," I said to diffuse the situation before it erupted into something.

"That's all right, then," he said with a meek and apologetic voice while reaching for his spit jar. "Winnie, come clean this chew jar and bring me some more ice for my water," he hollered towards Winnie in a demanding tone that was clearly for my benefit. I felt bad, but I was resigned to the fact that I couldn't do anything to change the situation. With a deep breath I went about recording her payment and made a beeline for the door.

"It's always good to see you, Mr. Pickles," Winnie said with a smile as I passed her on my way down the stairs. I turned around and stopped, looking back at her worn face still smiling as she watched to make sure that I made it safely down the stairs. For the briefest of moments, I wondered why such an angel was forced to live a life of such indignity.

"Call me if you need anything, anything at all, okay?" I said, knowing that she wouldn't.

"Oh, Mr. Pickles, don't you worry about me or Willie. The Lord provides for us just fine," she said as I waved my hand at her and exited the building.

CHAPTER 9

The despair I felt at Winnie and Willie's situation began to subside when I turned the corner onto Monroe Street and rolled up in front of Sandra's house. I must have passed the old white stone four-flat with the big concrete porch a hundred times since working the ledger, but today it seemed as if I were looking at the building for the first time. Unlike the cookie-cutter homes found in the suburbs, the homes built in the old upscale neighborhoods of the city were designed to be unique and everlasting, with a distinct flavor all to themselves.

Three large windows with rounded stone sills stood out from under the shadows of the stone porch in a building that looked as if it had been relocated from a Scottish hillside. The entire facade on the turn-of-the-century home was pieced together with large blocks of quarried limestone that had discolored somewhat over the years but still had a glistening luster in the midday sun. A half dozen stone stairs offset to the right took you up onto a concrete porch that was, in essence, the first floor. A cut limestone wall encircled the porch like a castle moat with slabs of three-inch stone capping the wall like dominos placed end to end.

I grabbed my portfolio, got out of the car, and walked up to the steps of the massive porch with a queasy feeling as butterflies swirled around my stomach as if I were going on a first date. It was a ridiculous feeling, and I consciously tried to rationalize the fact that I was just going to see a prospective client and nothing more. I was married with a child of my own, and this girl was nothing more than a sale. I forced myself to get a grip by concentrating on the fact that I was here to conduct business and remembering that I was going to be an apprentice electrician in two months.

I climbed onto the porch and instinctively stopped just short of the door as if I had forgotten something. Looking around like a lost puppy, it dawned on me that I had never asked Sandra for her apartment number. To make matters worse, I had completely forgotten to call Mrs. Brown and tell her what time Sandra could expect me. Then, I remembered that Mrs. Brown probably wasn't home anyway. I went to leave, turning to face Mrs. Brown's, wondering if I should try anyway. My mind went blank. I turned back and hesitated again as a feeling of apprehension came over me when suddenly a voice admonished me from the open window overlooking the porch.

"Ron, are you going to stand out there all day or come inside?" Sandra's voice called out.

"Oh, there you are!" I exclaimed with surprise while squirming under my skin, figuring she had probably been watching my dance of indecision the whole time. I pushed open the heavy glass entrance door and quickly headed for the first door on the left, which I guessed was Sandra's. I turned the knob and gently pushed her door open to find her sitting on the arm of a couch with a highchair pulled up, carefully spoon-feeding her baby. The front windows overlooking the porch were part of a small breakfast nook with an arched ceiling and a built-in window seat. Sandra had given the little room a smart, practical look by placing a loveseat along one wall and a television along the other. The television was turned on to the Cubs game with the sound barely audible. A warm breeze from the open windows enticed a lovely set of soft white drapes to perform a graceful ballet while Sandra attended to her child.

"Hi, Sandra. I'm sorry, I probably looked like an idiot standing outside, but I forgot to ask you what apartment you lived in last night," I said, stuttering for words.

"Yeah, you looked a little confused out there," she said while gently trying to entice the wiggly baby to eat another spoonful.

"Wow! I didn't know you had a tiny one," I said, walking over.

"I got three. This is my little guy, Lee. He's a problem eater," she said, gently using the spoon to remove some strained turkey and

152

carrots that the baby had shifted to his eyebrows.

"I have that problem with my little girl. I hope she grows out of it," I said as an afterthought, watching Sandra struggle with the baby who found wearing his food much more pleasurable than eating it. "He just hasn't figured out where his mouth is yet," I said.

"No, but he's found every other part of his body," she said with a smile.

"How old is he?"

"We just had his first birthday party last week," she said.

"One down and about seventy-three to go, according to the latest statistics," I said while she toweled off the baby.

"I think you've had enough, young man. It's time for a nap so I can have a nice visit with Ron the insurance man," she said, looking up at me with a smile and that same twinkle in her eye that had warmed me the night before. "Sit down, make yourself comfortable, and watch the game while I put Lee to bed," she said, lifting the baby from the chair as I held it steady. I barely hit the couch before she bounced back into the room, tucked her legs beneath her, and sat down beside me. Her petite form looked good in a tight-fitting, red, short-sleeved V-neck that showed just a hint of cleavage and a stylish pair of blue jeans that fit her like a glove. Her hair was pulled back into a ponytail, exposing an expressive face that was bright and cheery, seeming to smile all the time. But it was the life in her eyes that captivated my imagination and made me tingle with delight to be around her, as they seemed to marvel at everything they saw.

"Wow, those children about run me ragged," she said with a deep breath as she leaned back and took a well-deserved moment for herself.

"I had no idea you had three kids," I said with mixed emotions as it struck me that Sandra was indeed a special girl, but a girl who had fallen into the same cycle of having kids and depending on welfare for support like so many others.

"Lee, who you just met, Lucy, who is six, and Liz, who is three," she said, counting on her fingers. "The other two are over at their grandma's house. We stopped by Mom's after the park this morning. I told her you were coming over, and she agreed to watch Lucy and Liz so we could have a few minutes to talk about the insurance. I may use you as an excuse to have Mom watch the kids more often," she extorted.

"It's okay with me, but remember, your mom is a client of mine. My silence may cost you," I said.

"Well, forget that. I'm going to have to get me a new insurance man already," she said, shaking her head.

"No, no, no, before you can get a new one, you have to have an old one," I said with a smile.

"Well, yeah, I guess you're right about that," she conceded.

"…And on that point, we should talk about getting you and the kids some insurance," I said, resigning myself to the business at hand, still trying to quell a desire I felt inside.

"Yeah, I really want to get some insurance on me and the kids with all the garbage that goes on around here," she said seriously.

"It sounds like you've been thinking about it then?"

"Yeah, especially since my divorce and the neighborhood and all. If something happens to me, the kids won't have anything, you know."

"It's a tough place to live, isn't it?" I asked with sensitivity, looking into her eyes and instinctively knowing the answer.

"There are some really nice people around here, and I love my neighbors, like Mrs. Brown and all, but sometimes you can just feel when things aren't right and bad stuff happens. These boys walk around the streets with guns and drugs, and they don't care who they shoot as long as they get their money, you know. I never let my kids go out on the street by themselves. You know last night when you came over and had all those kids hanging off your car? That was ridiculous. Where are those kids' parents? Don't they see what we see?" she asked rhetorically.

"Trust me, I was thinking the same thing. Last night was pretty crazy," I said with a sigh. She looked at me for a moment, then dropped her eyes before bringing them back to mine with a different, almost resigned expression on her face.

"It's not like that in the white neighborhoods, is it?" she asked, catching me totally off guard. In all the time I worked the ledger, no one ever compared a black neighborhood to a white neighborhood. The question made me uncomfortable, and, for the first time, I looked away from her eyes and the hypnotic pleasure they provided. I was embarrassed at what to say next because she knew the answer. She just wanted to hear it from me.

"Well, Sandra, we have some bad neighborhoods too. It's not like black folks have them all to themselves," I said with all honesty. A quick nod with a feigned smile told me she wouldn't accept my deflected answer. She looked for honesty, and appeasing her with a canned answer was an insult. From that point forward, I knew she was someone to take seriously.

"That may be true, but the white friends I have don't worry about walking down the streets of their neighborhood, afraid they might get shot," she said.

"I don't know, Sandra. I just kinda think it's the world we live in. I mean, you can get shot anywhere—not just in black neighborhoods."

"Well, let me ask you this, Mr. Pickles," she said very formally. "Which street would you rather let your kids play on: mine or yours?" I didn't even think about the question because we both knew the answer, but her expression and her tone had another effect on me. This was the first girl I had ever met other than my sister Judy that expressed a passion, desire, or concern about something with real value. Her words weren't flippant or meaningless; she chose them carefully and knew what she wanted to say. She wasn't hiding from the fact that she was black, nor was she blaming others for her problems. She embraced her color and her ancestry by challenging her surroundings and asking the fundamental question: Why did she have to be afraid to let her kids play outside? "You know the answer," she finally said with a bit of arrogance that I understood.

"Well, all that may be true, but white people do have some problems that black people don't have," I said with a sly smile.

"Really, what's that?"

"White trash."

"White trash?" she asked with an expression of surprise.

"Yeah, white trash," I repeated. "You know, rather large, trampy white women with flannel shirts tied up into halter tops, short shorts, and no shoes."

"I know what white trash is, but I don't know…"

"What don't you know?" I asked with a frown.

"Well, I hate to break this to you, but we do have some white trash living around here," she said with a smile.

"No shit! Then that's the problem with the neighborhood, Sandra. If you got rid of the white trash, this place would clean up in no time," I said as we both started laughing. "Hey, but in all seriousness, where do these people live?" I asked.

"Well, it's not like a group of people or anything, but you will see an occasional white woman living with a black guy out here," she said.

"Isn't that kind of racist?" I asked with a raised eyebrow.

"What do you mean? I'm not a racist," she said indignantly.

"Well, how can you just assume a white woman living out here is white trash?"

"I don't know. I just figured they weren't born and raised around here, so they must have chose to come here. Who in the heck would choose to live in the ghetto? If that isn't trashy, I don't know what is," she lamented. We smiled at each other, fully enjoying the clever parrying that had turned from serious to silly in a matter of moments.

"Naw, no, no, that doesn't count," I said with a dismissive drawl.

"Why not?"

"Because they're not true white trash."

"What do you mean?"

"They're more like Amazon women."

"They're not that bad," she insisted with a smirk.

"Sandra, I've seen the occasional white woman out here, and the one thing I can't figure out is why black guys are interested in them," I said.

"So, you're saying black men can't get decent-looking white women?"

"That all depends on your idea of decent looking because the only white women I've ever seen around here weigh about 250 pounds and have beards," I shot back.

"Oh, that is so mean!" she snorted, covering her hand with her mouth. "I don't know if I want a mean insurance man."

"All right, I'll stop being mean to the big, nasty white women if we…"

"Oh, oh, oh, just a second," she said, jumping off the couch as if distracted by something. "Excuse me for just a second, Ron. Dave Kingman is coming to bat, and I got to watch for a second," she said, turning up the volume on the Cubs game. We watched for a few moments as the Cubs slugger took three big swings and struck out, to Sandra's chagrin. She then turned the volume down, then sat back on the couch as if nothing had happened.

"God, I thought something caught fire there for a second the way you jumped off the couch," I said as she slumped back, dejected.

"I love Dave Kingman, but I hate when he strikes out," she said, shaking her head. "Do you like the Cubs?" she asked with a sigh.

"Well, yeah, I do, actually, though I'm not sure if I do as much as you," I said, still amazed at how quickly she reacted to the game.

"You have no idea… I've loved these guys since I was a little girl," she said with her eyes glowing.

"Really?"

"Yeah, my dad and I watched almost every game together. I was fourteen in '69 when they almost won it all, and all my girlfriends thought I was strange because I wouldn't come out and play when there was a game on," she said.

"That's nothing. I was ten years old in '69, and I got into a fist fight with this girl who told me she knew more about the Cubs than I did," I said, shaking my head in disbelief at a memory I hadn't thought of in ages.

"What started the fight?"

"Oh, I don't know exactly. It was something dumb. I think about the names of the players or something. My grandma used to babysit for me, and she told me the girl must have liked me a lot, or she wouldn't have bothered," I said, almost blushing.

"Smart grandma," Sandra added.

"Wait a second," I said, looking off to the side as the memory came back to me. "Now I remember. She said that she watched more games than I did and knew more about the team, but she could only come up with the first three players in the lineup, so I knew she was lying."

"You mean Kessinger, Beckert, and Williams," she said.

"Don't tell me you…"

"Wait, wait, wait!" she pleaded. "Ernie Banks, Ron Santo, Jim Hickman, Randy Hundley, and… wait, don't tell me… um, Don Young, or one of the utility guys, like Adolfo Phillips or Paul Popovich," she said, beaming with pride. I just stared at her with my mouth open like a ten-year-old boy, shocked out of my senses that she could possibly know the whole line up of the '69 Cubs. "Do you want the starting rotation?" she asked matter-of-factly.

"No, no, no, you've passed the test. I'm a believer," I said, holding up my hands as if surrendering. "From what I've learned about you today, you're the last girl I want to have a fist fight with," I joked as we both started laughing. "Have you ever gone to a game?" I asked as a strong burst of warm air momentarily blew one of the dancing drapes over my shoulder.

"No, that's something I'd really love to do someday," she said, closing her eyes and taking a deep breath as the warm breeze gently washed over her face. She opened her eyes, and a slight smile crept across her soft lips while a hint of melancholy dimmed the glow of her expressive eyes.

"Is there something wrong?"

"No, not at all. It's just that the breeze gives me goose bumps sometimes," she said, folding her arms in front of her body as if caught by a chill.

"Are you cold? Let me shut the window." I was about to get up when she stopped me.

"No, I want it open," she said, shaking off the chill.

"Maybe you're getting sick or something, 'cause it's like eighty-five degrees outside," I said, trying to rationalize her reaction.

"No, it's not that. It's silly, actually. It's just that the breeze reminded me of something," she said as if her mind had momentarily drifted to another place or time.

"What? If it's not too personal, I mean."

"It's nothing, really. Just listening to your story and all reminded me of something I did when I was a little girl. Sometimes, on a warm summer day, I would drag a big, old blanket by the television or cuddle up with it on the couch and watch the game. Talking about the Cubs and feeling that breeze brought it back to me. I guess it reminds me of being a little girl, when I didn't have so much to think about. I guess it's kind of like my way of going to a Cubs game. I can't even imagine how exciting it would be to actually go to a game in person," she said with a long sigh. "Have you ever gone?" she asked. I looked at her for a long moment, captivated by her beauty and mesmerized by her passion and love for something that seemed so far out of her reach.

"Yeah, my mom actually took me to a game the following year when I was eleven," I said with a bit of embarrassment for having an opportunity that she didn't.

"Did you love it?"

"It was pretty amazing. Kind of like experiencing *The Wizard of Oz* firsthand. You know the part when everything goes from black and white to color? That's Wrigley Field."

"It must have been fantastic," she said, arching her back and leaning forward, eagerly wanting me to continue.

"I don't know, I guess when you're a kid it's different because everything is so new to you."

"Tell me about it," she pleaded with eyes begging to hear more. I hesitated at first, not wanting to boast or brag about something she didn't get a chance to do, but her desire to hear my experience was so genuine, I felt as if she truly wanted me to share the story with her.

"Well, we lived on the South Side, so we took the Rock Island train downtown, then jumped on the L-train over to the ballpark. I never took a train before, so that was a huge deal all by itself."

"I love trains," she giggled.

"When you go in the park, they take your ticket, and you walk inside to this big hallway that circles all around the field, but you don't see anything 'cause it's totally enclosed. It's where the bathrooms and food stands and stuff are located, you know?"

"Uh huh."

"Well, as you walk around, every hundred feet or so there is a ramp and tunnel that leads out into the stadium. So, my mom drags me halfway around the stadium looking for the right ramp to go up and get our seats. Finally, she finds the tunnel, and we start walking up the ramp to the stands," I paused for a moment as a rush of emotions filled my head. Sandra nodded as if she understood. "I can remember it like it was yesterday. You wouldn't believe how this amazing ballpark slowly emerges from the shadows of the tunnel with each step you take. It's almost unreal. I can remember almost being blinded by this bright green grass in the middle of this huge stadium. It was too much for my eyes to handle. It literally took my breath away. In a million years, I could have never pictured anything so beautiful. But it isn't just the sight of the ballpark for the first time. It was everything: the smell of the hot dogs, the crowd, and the vendors shouting at the top of their lungs, hawking everything from peanuts to pennant flags."

"It sounds wonderful," she said, absorbing every word.

"But you know what really freaked me out?" I asked, pointing a finger at her.

"No, what?"

"The ball players."

"Why is that?"

"Well, you know how on television everyone looks so small?"

"Yeah."

"I had no idea that these guys were giants. I mean, they are *huge!*"

"Really?"

"Oh, Sandra, you have no idea!" I said with excitement. "I used to love Don Kessinger, but when I saw him on that field for the first time, he literally scared the shit out of me."

"Why?" she bellowed.

"He was huge! He was like the biggest guy I ever saw in my life, you know? All these guys are just enormous, and when they run out onto the field, it's like the whole thing shrinks up because they're so big," I said as Sandra just stared at me with amazement.

We talked about baseball for at least an hour before realizing time was running out and that Sandra had to retrieve her other two children from Grandma's before it got too late. Insurance fell off the radar and seemed to be the last thing either of us wanted to talk about, so I asked point-blank what she wanted to do, and, for the first time ever, I told a prospective client the truth about Unified Insurance Company.

"Sandra, it's a substandard company that sells shit for the most part, but if you could afford a little more money and were willing to pay it by the month instead of by the week, you could get something halfway decent," I said.

"I want something good, Ron," she said with a trusting expression.

"Normally, I don't think twice about asking people some of this stuff, but after getting to know you a little here, it feels kind of weird."

"Why, what do you have to ask me?"

"Well, I know you're divorced, and with the kids, I imagine..."

"You mean the aid checks?" she asked, reading my thoughts.

"Well, yeah, in order for me to figure out something you can afford, I kind of got to know what you have to work with," I said, struggling with the topic. I had gained so much respect and admiration for Sandra in the short time we talked that it felt wrong asking her about welfare. She was way too smart and passionate about life, let alone beautiful, to be trapped in a system that rewarded you for having kids so you could live the rest of your life in poverty.

"Yes, I do get some money and stamps for the kids, but don't worry. I'm getting support money from my ex, and I do hair on the side under the table. As a matter of fact, I'm saving up to go to beautician's school," she said proudly.

"Wow, that's great!" I said, congratulating her on the effort.

"So, how much insurance do you think I need to get?" she asked.

"In all honesty, at least $15,000 on you with term riders on the kids," I said, figuring that she could never afford the premium but not wanting to tell her something that wasn't true.

"Would that be really good for me and my kids?"

"I think it would be good," I said seriously.

"How much would the fifteen thousand cost me?" she asked.

"That's a good question. I don't know. Let me look it up. How old are you again?"

"Twenty-five," she replied as I opened my portfolio and scanned the MDO rate card. I took the calculator from my pocket and multiplied the rate times fifteen, then added the kids on as riders.

"Thirty-four bucks a month would give you a $15,000 whole life policy with a $5,000 term rider on the kids until they reach twenty-one."

"What happens when they reach twenty-one?"

"Then they come off the insurance, but they have the option of buying five times that amount without insurability, you know, if they're sick or something, so it's really a pretty good deal."

"But my mom got each of us kids our own policies when we were young," she questioned. "Last year, she let me cash it in so I could buy new stuff for the baby. It was pretty cool," she said. "I'd like to be able to do something like that for my kids."

"Let me ask you something: How much cash did you get from that policy?"

"About $400."

"How long was she paying it for?"

"I don't know. Since we were kids, I think."

"The difference between what your mom did for you and what we're going to do for your kids is about $4,000," I said to a look of astonishment.

"Four thousand? Are you serious?" she asked.

"Look for yourself," I said, holding up the rate card and pointing at the cash values of the policy in fifteen years. "See, if you multiply this amount by fifteen, you get $4,275 on the fifteenth anniversary of the contract. But, unlike your mom's policy, you'll have the option of keeping it, borrowing against it, or cashing it in."

"That's what I want! That's what I want for my kids. How do we get it started?"

"Do you have $34?" I asked. Without question, she hopped off the couch and skipped into the other room to retrieve her purse. I was proud of her while, at the same time, ashamed of myself for thinking a girl of her character would be satisfied with sitting at home having babies and collecting welfare. I studied her carefully as she walked back to the couch, counting out money. I was sure whatever had happened in her past was behind her, and, from the sound of it, she was taking life by the horns and charging straight ahead. We laughed and joked while I filled out her application, talking about all the great things we wanted to do and see, with a baseball game being first on her list. Before leaving, I wanted to share my exuberance of going to school and becoming an electrician with her, but I thought better of it. I didn't want to tell her that someone else would take my place and be her insurance man.

CHAPTER 10

July 1980

The long, oppressive heat spell that began in the second week of June was still blasting away in the second week of July as I sat in traffic on my way home from another Friday collection. I was in a near panic almost every day because the letter from the electrician's union hadn't arrived, and Bobby Cooker was still in Hawaii. It had been almost four weeks since he talked to Jessica and assured her to watch out for the mail because the letter was coming. I cursed myself for not calling him after he talked to her, but I had no idea he was going on vacation for a month.

Except for Rudy, the house was empty when I got home. Jessica had taken the baby to an afternoon birthday party at one of the cousins' houses and told me she was going to stay for a while and visit. I scrambled in the door with feigned gratitude towards Rudy's absolute jubilance at my arrival while desperately trying to push him out of the way as I made it inside. I was barely able to make it into the bathroom without pissing myself, then ran back to the kitchen, grabbed the mailbox key, and bolted out into the hallway to check the mail. Frantically, I shuffled through the mail only to fall despondent when I came to the last envelope without finding something from the electrician's union. On cue, my mother's door opened across the hall, and she poked her head out to see if it was me she had heard. I hadn't seen much of my mom since she started a full-time job as a payroll clerk a few weeks back, and it was nice to see her for a change. "Oh, Ronnie, I'm glad you're home. Do you think you can come over and help me move the cedar chest so that I can clean behind it?" I instinctively knew the sound of Johnny Mathis records playing in the background meant she had almost finished her Friday ritual of cleaning the house and was getting ready to down a six-pack of beer.

"Yeah, sure, Mom. Just give me a minute to change my clothes, and I'll come right over," I said as the phone in my apartment started ringing. "Let me get that. I'll be over in a few minutes." I closed the door and trotted into the kitchen to pick up the phone. "Hello?"

"Hey, Ronnie, it's me," said my sister Judy.

"Hey, sis, what's up?"

"Just wanted to check in and see if you heard anything from the union yet?" she asked.

"No, I just got in the door and checked the mail. Still nothing. I don't get it, ya know?"

"I know. I wish I could get ahold of Bobby," she said with a sigh of concern.

"Do you know when he gets back from vacation?" I asked.

"This weekend. I think Sunday night. You should call him Monday morning and see if there's a problem," she said.

"Definitely. This has been stressing me out every day since he told us to look out for the letter."

"Don't worry, it'll be fine. I'm sure it just takes time for the paperwork to go out once the decisions are made. You know how city hall works," she joked. "What are you guys doing tonight?"

"Oh, Jessica and the baby went to one of her cousins' houses for a birthday party, and I just got recruited by Mom to lug the cedar chest from one side of the house to the other while she cleans," I said.

"Is she drinking?"

"Judy, it's Friday night, and the Johnny Mathis records are already in full swing."

"You need to get going," she laughed.

"I know, time is of the essence," I chuckled.

"Okay, call me if you hear anything."

"I will. Bye-bye," I said, hanging up the phone, thinking how much I loved my sister.

Judy was eleven years older and meant more to me than my own mother. For all practical purposes, she actually took on the role of both mother and father to my younger sister and me. It was strange in a way because Judy was only our half-sister, though we both felt closer to her than either of our full-blooded parents. Our mother managed to have three children with two different men (neither of which she cared about) over a span of nineteen years, spending most of her time in a drunken stupor. By the time Judy was nine, her father had had enough of Mom and filed for divorce. He promptly wed another woman and pretty much left Judy and Mom to fend for themselves. Mom discovered right away that her newly found freedom fit the late-fifties lounge scene like a glove. The burden of parenting a nine-year-old daughter didn't bother her as long as she could pawn off Judy on relatives while she tramped around from bar to bar.

At first, the relatives were overjoyed to have Judy, and she was relieved to have a night off from Mom. However, as the nights grew into weekends and eventually weeks, the relatives willing to burden themselves for the sake of Mom's indulgence became shorter and shorter. Mom was running out of options and became desperate for a place to warehouse her daughter. After a day of celebrating Judy's eleventh birthday at Auntie Gwen and Uncle Bud's house, her eyes welled with tears when Mom drove off waving and blowing kisses while promising to pick her up at the end of the summer. After three months, Judy was thrilled to be going home with Mom, only to be disillusioned by the bulge in mom's stomach and the presence of her new stepfather, Jack. Her job as surrogate mother began a few months later when I was born and mainly consisted of keeping me out of the path of frying pans, beer bottles, and an array of readily available objects that could be hurled at my father by our mother.

By the time I was four and Judy hit the ripe old age of fifteen, our family had settled into a weekly routine in which Mom and Dad worked all week and drank all weekend. Even as a toddler, I can remember the excitement of Friday nights as Judy and I would wait to see if Mom and Dad came home with groceries or met after work and pounded down their paychecks in a weekend binge. If they didn't come home, Judy would bundle me up and take me to a friend's house or to an all-night laundromat for the weekend.

She knew that both Mom and Dad were mean drunks and found considerable pleasure in plastering each other with an array of leftover food, household cleaners, or kitchen utensils. Having participated in the routine on more than one occasion, Judy decided it was safer for us to be with a stranger or walk the streets than get caught up in the middle of Mom and Dad's weekend housewares demonstration.

On Sunday morning, we would return home to find them both passed out half naked on the floor with garbage thrown all over the apartment. Mom spent Sunday afternoons cleaning the walls and mopping the floors in preparation for the week to come while Dad sat on the couch in his boxer shorts, drinking beer and watching television. This went on for a year or so until Mom caught Dad cheating on her with a waitress at their favorite lounge. After that, we didn't see Dad for a couple of years. Then one day, he popped in unexpectedly and sat around in his underwear for a couple of weeks, then left again. Nine months later, our younger sister, Linda, was born. I was eight years old, while Judy was nineteen going on twenty. Mom settled down with the birth of Linda and limited her drinking to Friday nights, when she would pull out the Johnny Mathis records and reminisce about the good old days while drinking herself blind.

I strolled about the kitchen for a couple of minutes, rummaging through the cabinets and refrigerator to find something to eat. I was disappointed at the available offerings and settled upon the usual cheese slices before heading to the bedroom to change my clothes and mentally prepare to move that stupid cedar chest.

That old cedar chest reminded me of the conversation I had with Sandra about Mom taking me to the baseball game. Though most of my life with Mom was a struggle, I had to admit there were times when she tried her best to give us something special. She was far from perfect, but, in her way, she did her best to make a life for us kids. I sat on the bed and laced up my gym shoes, smiling as I thought about all the crazy things my mother attempted to do for us.

I remembered going through my scientific phase when I was twelve or thirteen, convinced that my future plans lay somewhere between digging for dinosaurs and commanding a starship. I was most intrigued by the latter. To that end, I thought it would be a good idea to build an ultra-powerful radio in order to converse with aliens from another planet. My mom had just finished reading a book by Erich von Däniken called *Chariots of the Gods*. The book convinced her of the possibility that the human race had not only been visited by aliens, but also, more likely than not, humans were the offspring of such beings (and this was while she was sober). It only seemed prudent that contacting such beings would be of great interest to the human race, so she wholeheartedly endorsed my quest to build the most powerful radio in the world. The experiment began with a small radio kit for aspiring geniuses from the local hobby store. It took me several hours of winding what seemed like hundreds of feet of copper wire around a plastic spool before the instructions said that I had constructed a primitive electrical conductor. By attaching the conductor to a pre-built transistor and speaker included in the kit, I was able to hear the faint sounds of a local radio station's top ten countdown. Both my mom and I were excited to hear sound but quickly realized I had not yet achieved the necessary skills needed to build a communication network suitable for conversing with space aliens. She therefore decided it would be better to forgo the building process and head directly to the radio store and purchase the proper radio needed to communicate with the far-reaching galaxies.

I could still picture the helpful expression on the clerk's face when my mother, with a serious tone, asked to see the most powerful radio transmitter available. He seemed jubilant in his haste to

produce a twenty-three-channel CB radio from under the counter
with a picture of an 18-wheel truck running down the highway. My
mom glanced at the box for a moment and then looked up at the clerk
like he was an imbecile who didn't know the first thing about
communicating with aliens. "My son doesn't want a CB radio," she
said with disgust. "He wants to be able to transmit into space." The
clerk's expression changed from one of a helping associate to that of
a person carefully considering the degree of insanity the person in
front of him possessed.

"We have ham radios, ma'am, but you'll need a license," he said,
cautiously gauging her response to make sure she didn't get violent.

"Don't you have anything we can use to send messages into
space?" she said.

"I'm afraid not," the stoic clerk replied as his eyes darted from
side to side as if wondering when the *Candid Camera* crew was
going to come bursting into the store. Mom turned to me and put her
hands up in frustration, saying there was nothing she could do, when
she spotted a metal detector hanging on the wall, and her face
seemed to explode with inspiration.

"Hey, Ronnie! What about looking for buried treasure? We could
be rich, rich, rich with that thing!" she said, leading me over to the
device as the store clerk carefully followed us with his eyes. I looked
at the picture on the box with some kid holding out a handful of lost
pirate gold with a big smile on his face and totally forgot about
communicating with aliens. I began to lose myself in the idea of
finding lost riches. Yes, it was perfect. With this highly sophisticated
tool of science, I could send beams of electromagnetic energy deep
into the earth's surface in search of pirate gold. There was no limit to
the amount of wealth I could unearth or mysteries I could solve with
a tool such as this.

Of course, it didn't occur to either of us at the time that few
pirates sailed the high seas of Lake Michigan or traveled up the
closest body of water to our house: the man-made river called the

Calumet Sag Canal. None of that mattered. We had changed our pursuits from contacting aliens to the much more profitable occupation of securing booty. My mom gave me $25 for my birthday to add to the money I had saved from other gifts, and we walked out of the radio store with a $100 metal detector. For the next month, I hit everybody's yard within a two-block radius of our house, digging up any hunk of metal, discarded pull tab, or bottle cap I could find, while leaving divots the size of mole holes to the delight of our neighbors. I started laughing to myself and figured I'd best stop reminiscing and get over to her apartment before the witching hour began, somewhere between the fourth and fifth beer.

I had it figured just about right as Mom welcomed me into the house, dressed in her Friday attire, which consisted of an oversized button-down white blouse tied into a knot on one side with tight knit shorts and dirty white canvas sneakers without laces. A rag was tied around her head to keep her flaming dyed-red hair out of her eyes as she went about cleaning the house. She was wearing one of those "I've had two beers and feel happy" smiles on her cigarette-aged face, and I knew that one or two more would electrify her tiny five-foot, 105-pound frame into the nasty lush we all knew so well. She darted around the apartment like a fly in a fishbowl, removing stuff from the top of the cedar chest so I could move it, all the while fussing about the house cleaning she needed to do.

"Where's Linda?" I asked at the absence of my little sister.

"She's ruined my whole day. I spent half the morning getting her ready to spend the night at her girlfriend's house," she said, coming to a stop long enough to wipe her forehead and down a swig of beer before taking more stuff off the chest. When everything was finally cleared off the top, I looked down at the pathetic box with disdain, knowing that once again I had to deal with my hated nemesis. It had become my lot in life to serve as the beast of burden to a family relic that should have been chopped into kindling years ago. While a cedar chest in many families is looked upon as a sacred family artifact in

171

which a treasure trove of memories and heirlooms is stored, my mom's more resembled a small tomb recently unearthed in an attempt to exhume some unholy wretch. While priceless artifacts have been known to survive wars, insurrections, and a multitude of abuses hurled upon them by thieves, pillagers, and looters, I submit that few objects could have survived the careless mistreatment and disregard perpetrated upon my mother's cedar chest.

Purchased by my grandmother some seventy-five years before, the chest remained in pristine condition until the first day ownership was transferred to my mother. My mom was shocked when Grandma bestowed the prized family heirloom to her care and accepted the gift without hesitation, demanding my father carry the wooden box out to the car. Unknown to Grandma was the fact that Mom took the chest knowing full well she and Dad intended on moving us out of our second-floor apartment that evening to avoid a pesky landlord who seemed perturbed by their inability to pay rent. At Mom's insistence (to vocal opposition from Dad), she demanded he lug the heavy chest up to the apartment that afternoon as a precaution against theft, though she knew it was coming back down that night. As a way of passing time until they considered it safe to move our belongings, Mom and Dad had a few drinks to calm their nerves. In addition to relieving anxiety about skipping out on the rent, the alcohol actually induced them into a state of false bravado, which helped them feel justified in screwing the landlord. As nighttime came and other inebriated friends arrived to assist in the stealth operation, a loud and boisterous party broke out in our apartment while an empty pick-up truck with the engine running sat at the bottom of the stairs. It didn't take long for the landlord to arrive with police in tow, advising Mom and Dad to vacate the premises or spend the night in jail.

The indignity of such a prospect weighed heavily on the swollen brains of my parents, which led to the fastest removal of furniture from a second-floor apartment in recorded history. With a long flight of stairs becoming an obstacle and slowing up the moving process,

Dad began to employ the known effects of gravity to assist in the operation and started flinging items over the banister. When it came to the cedar chest, even Dad realized that this maneuver was likely to cause an excessive amount of damage that Mom wouldn't tolerate, so it would have to be carried down the stairs. However, seeing no reason to exert any more energy than needed, he and a friend flipped the chest upside down and let it slide down the two flights of stairs to the bottom. It wasn't until Mom and Dad sobered up the next afternoon and surveyed the remnants of the move that they realized a trip to the linen store would be necessary to find a suitable doily large enough to hide the grooves and scratches cut in the top of Grandma's cherished chest. From that day forward, the chest was beaten, whipped, peed upon, and, on several occasions, used as a weapon.

The problem with moving the cedar chest was that it had to be done in pieces, beginning with the lid, which had been unhinged in some previous battle. Then, I had to pick up one side of the heavy chest and kick the rear leg out of the way with my foot. Another casualty, the rear leg broke off some years back, but when perfectly aligned with its still intact counterpart attached to the underside, it managed to keep the chest level. Once the pieces of the chest were removed, I could concentrate on the difficult part: dragging the loaded chest out of the way so my mother could vacuum or mop the floor. The weight of the chest was unbelievable, and I was always amazed at how much crap she was able to fit into the four-foot chest, musing to myself how this was perfect training for her to become a homeless cart pusher someday.

I managed to move it out far enough away from the wall for her to clean, and then I wrestled the chest back into position before spending the next fifteen minutes trying to get the splintered leg to match up correctly underneath it. In the meantime, Mom had downed one more can of beer and was working on another. I could literally see the transformation in her personality as she became less talkative and her happy smile turned sour. Her appearance changed as well. The rag she had tied to her head had come undone, and a long strand of matted red hair snaked out across her forehead and over one eye, giving her the look of a gypsy from a B-rated horror flick. Her steps became decidedly horizontal in attempts to navigate from one place to another as she lost the ability to travel in a straight line. Knowing the end result of this metamorphosis, I fought hard to finish my task before she turned on me.

I struggled mightily to get the leg aligned and chest balanced before retrieving the lid and setting it carefully atop the beat-up crate when I noticed something I hadn't before. There was an unopened letter pushed halfway down along the side of the chest that looked out of place mixed up in the heap of wrinkled papers and bent-up pictures. As an afterthought, I tugged the letter loose from the grip of junk piled against it and stared at it for a long moment before gasping a breath and falling to one knee. The letter was addressed to "Mr. Ronald Pickles." It was from the United Electrical Union Workers Local Chapter.

I swallowed hard, not being able to comprehend what I was looking at or even coming close to understanding why my mother would hide the letter so precious to me inside her cedar chest. I tore into the letter, which was dated Wednesday, June 18th, 1980. I thought back for a moment, trying to remember the exact day Bobby called Jessica; it was the Friday night I took the dog with me to the ledger. I jumped up and ran over to my mother's calendar that was hanging on the wall in the kitchen. I ripped the calendar from the wall and frantically flipped the pages looking for June when all I had to do was calmly go back one month. When I finally found June, I scanned across the daily brackets like a blind man reading braille looking for dates. Bobby called on Friday the 20th, two days after the letter was sent. I quickly read through the letter, stopping at the mandatory requirement part and re-reading it again. In big, bold type, the instructions read that "YOU MUST RESPOND TO THIS

NOTIFICATION WITHIN 10 DAYS OF RECEIPT OR YOUR ACCEPTANCE WILL BE WITHDRAWN." My tongue was so dry I couldn't swallow as I looked back at the calendar to see that I was fourteen days beyond the ten-day requirement. I couldn't believe it. I missed it? Was it over? Was the opportunity I had been praying for every day for the last nine months gone? I stood there feeling like a child who had just had his bike stolen by the neighborhood bullies, watching hopelessly as they furiously peddled down the street.

I was dumbfounded and aimlessly walked back to the front room where Mom was sitting on the floor, thoroughly wasted, chugging another can of beer, and fumbling for a record to play. "What is this?" I asked, holding out the letter for her to see. Her head bobbed from side to side with casual indifference as she glanced at the letter then shrugged her shoulders slightly, as if it didn't concern her. "WHY, MOM?" I demanded.

She looked up at me unapologetically with a feigned look of surprise, as if she didn't have a clue as to what I was talking about.

"Why what?" she asked, annoyed that I had broken her reflective mood.

"Mom, this is my letter—the letter from the union. I found it in the cedar chest. Why did you do this?" I asked, skipping a breath as if the air had been taken from me. "Mom, this was my future! What's it doing in your cedar chest?"

"You don't want that job," she slurred. "You don't want to be a ditch digger like your old man."

"A ditch digger? Jesus, Mom! I'm talking about becoming an electrician. Do you know what that means?" I shouted down at her with my hands outstretched, begging for an answer that made sense. I knew she couldn't be reasoned with in this condition, but for the life of me, I couldn't understand what she was talking about.

"I know you, Ronnie," she slurred. "You love being the big shot at that insurance company. All you ever talk about is how you made hundreds of dollars selling this or hundreds of dollars selling that. You don't want to be a ditch digger like your old man."

"Are you out of your mind?" I asked rhetorically as I began to pace about the room. "You don't have the faintest idea what I do at the insurance company," I said, coming to a stop and hovering over her with disdain. "I service black people in the projects, Mom! I collect money from people who ain't got no money. Goddamn it!" I screamed down at her in disbelief that this was happening to me. "I risk my neck every time I go out that door. You don't have a clue as to what I do. I'm like a walking fucking target just waiting for someone to take a shot at me. YOU STUPID FUCKING BITCH!" I burst out in anger. "I'd stand in line to be a fucking ditch digger if I could!" I shouted with tears streaming down my face.

"Bullshit!" she screamed back. "You're starting to make some money. You're going to win a trip to the Bahamas. You dress up in nice clothes to go to work every day, and you take off whenever you want. Why would you want to come home all smelly and dirty to your little wife?" she asked, seething with hatred and jealousy. "Do you think she'd appreciate you sticking those dirty fingers all over her? Do you think that little bitch would put up with that?" she snarled with contempt.

"My God, you're a filthy woman with a filthy mind," I shot back, wiping the tears from my face and shaking my head at what I had just heard.

"GET OUT OF MY HOUSE!" she screamed while hurling an empty beer can in my direction. I looked at her stunned and disillusioned. I couldn't believe the venom that was flowing from her lips. I couldn't believe this was my mother. She poisoned every relationship she ever had, and now she took something from me, her own son, because she was jealous of my wife. I took several steps towards the door, chewing furiously on my bottom lip, desperately holding back an amount of rage I had never felt towards that woman before.

"You're wrong here, Mom," I snarled out in a gravelly voice before turning one last time and staring her down. "You didn't have the right to do this to me. This is something I wanted, and you knew it. I'll never forgive you for this," I said before walking out of the apartment and slamming the door shut as she continued to spew obscenities in my direction. Without hesitation, I ran back into my apartment and called Judy, praying she might have a solution.

"Oh, Ronnie, I don't believe she did that to you, that bitch!" she bemoaned when I told her what had just transpired. "You actually found the letter in the cedar chest?"

"I swear to God, Judy. I'm holding the letter in my hand right now," I said. "I don't know what to do. Bobby is going to be so pissed."

"But it's not your fault," she reasoned.

"I should have gone down to the hall. He told me to look for the letter, and when it didn't come, I should have gone down to the fucking hall," I said frantically.

"Ronnie, calm down. It's only two weeks late. I'll bet Bobby can talk to someone and save this thing for you. After all, people go on vacation, and things get lost in the mail all the time. I'm sure they want people to respond as fast as possible, but I'm just as sure that they make allowances. Think about it. They make you go through all this stuff to get accepted then won't let you in because you don't get a letter?"

"Do you really think so?" I asked with a faint whisper of hope.

"I can't promise anything, but I sure wouldn't write it off just yet. Bobby gets home this weekend. I'll call him first thing on Monday morning, and we'll see what we can figure out," she said before hanging up. I slumped down at the kitchen table and buried my head in my arms, exhausted, confused, and utterly drained.

Jessica came home about an hour later, upset to find me passed out fast asleep at the table. "Damn it, Ronnie, you could have come over to my sister's house and helped me with the baby," she said, startling me awake as she stampeded into the house with the crabby baby in her arms.

"Did you guys have a good time?" I asked, still groggy from the nap as she disappeared into the baby's room.

"Jeannie had a great time. It would be nice if her father could be there once in a while to see his daughter do things for the first time," she said sarcastically.

"You need to see something," I said, pushing myself away from the kitchen table and meeting her halfway into the front room.

"Is this what I think it is?" she asked, taking the letter from my hand.

"Read it, and read it carefully," I told her with a tone she recognized as serious. Her expression changed to one of concern as she unfolded the letter and read the contents, scrutinizing each word. I saw her eyes dart around the paper as I figured mine had done when I first saw it. "Notice anything?"

"Ronnie, I don't understand. Why is this thing dated over a month ago? According to this, we missed the deadline. How is that possible?"

"Sit down. We need to talk." She sat there like a zombie as I related the entire episode from finding the letter in the cedar chest to my conversation with Judy. When I finished the story, I looked into her eyes, desperate for some comforting thoughts or at least some reassurance that no matter what happened we would get through this thing together. In return, I got a steely look and a rigid expression that caught me off guard.

"That's your mother for you," she said arrogantly with outstretched hands.

"I know. I can't believe she did this," I said in agreement.

"I don't know why you're so surprised she screwed you over," she said, implying that everything was my fault.

"Jessica, we both know…"

"I've been telling you that woman is a bitch since we got married!" she yelled out while jumping off the couch and pointing a finger in the direction of my mother's apartment. "Do you know what she asked me before I left for the party today?"

"No, what?"

"She asked me if our washer or dryer was broke. Do you know why?"

"No, but what's that got to do with anything?" I lamented.

"Because the bitch had the nerve to ask me if I had been wearing the same clothes all week. That's why! What fucking business is it of hers what I wear? I told you we should have moved out of this apartment the day we moved in, but 'Oh no, give it a chance,' you kept saying. I've been telling you for months that she's an evil, conniving bitch that wants nothing more than to see us break up," she said, seething with anger. "But all you ever say is, 'It'll get better,' 'Just ignore her,' 'Give it a chance.' Well, now, we gave it a chance, and see what it got you? Your mommy over there just fucked you out of the job of your life. Maybe now you'll see how I feel," she said, finishing her tirade by walking off into the bathroom and slamming the door.

I leaned back on the couch dejected. My eyes hurt with pressure from inside, like someone was prying them loose from their sockets with a crowbar. I rubbed them swollen for relief and found myself squinting in even more discomfort as I irritated them to the point of being sensitive to the light, and they began to water. I felt terribly alone and caught in the middle of something I didn't understand. My mother's actions were despicable and inexcusable but not totally out of character, as throughout our lives she had managed to sabotage one thing or another with a justification that only made sense to her. Jessica, on the other hand, disturbed me; I needed some comfort and some understanding, not another browbeating, telling me what I deserved because my mother was a bitch. My only salvation that night seemed to be Rudy, who ambled over to the couch and put his head on my lap as if to say he understood. The rest of the weekend was a blur, except for Sunday, when Mom called to apologize for Friday night, dismissing her diatribe as the ranting of a drunk.

She insisted the letter came to her by accident since the mailman was always mixing up the mail, and she put it in the cedar chest for safekeeping and simply forgot about it.

She bolstered her case by telling me her new job was killing her and that she was so tired when she came home at night, she couldn't even think straight. I listened to her justification and rambling apology until I had enough, then dismissed her without reason and hung up the phone. I didn't know what to believe, and at this point I really didn't care. In that moment, all I could think was how I would have given up the baseball game, the metal detector, and the handful of other nice things she did in my life if she had only given me the letter.

I got in the office a little after 9:00 a.m. Monday morning, saying hello to Mrs. Bolger and Irene as I passed their window without stopping. I was thrilled to find the agents' room empty as I headed for the nearest phone. I sat down, pulled a phone close, and dialed Judy as fast as I could. "Yes, I just got off the phone with Bobby, so keep your fingers crossed," Judy cautioned. "He said he was going to make some phone calls and get back to me."

"Oh man, Judy... how did he sound, honestly?" I asked timidly, picking up on her tone.

"I'll admit he wasn't happy, Ronnie, but I told him what happened, and he said he'd see what he could do. Do you have his number?" she asked me.

"Yeah, I know it by heart."

"Why don't you give him a call and let him know how bad you feel. He's a good guy with a great big heart. He likes that kind of stuff."

"My God, I do feel bad, Judy. I don't know what I'm going to do if this thing doesn't work out."

"I know, Ronnie. This is just unbelievable. Give him a call and let me know what he says," she said.

"Okay, bye." Without hanging up the receiver, I just pushed extension buttons until I got a dial tone and dialed Bobby's number. About the same time, Mr. Hamilton came into the office and poured a cup of coffee.

"Good morning, Mr. Pickles," he said, greeting me before stepping up to the blackboard and erasing the board call numbers from last week.

"Good morning, Roger," I said, covering the phone with the palm of my hand as I heard Bobby pick up.

"Hello, hello, anybody there?" Bobby's muffled voice came out of the phone.

"Sorry about that, Bob. It's me, Ron," I said in a soft voice, not wanting Hamilton to hear my conversation.

"Ronnie, Ronnie, what in the hell were you thinking?" he questioned, shouting into the phone. "Why in the fuck do you think I called you guys and told you to look out for the letter? Didn't Jessica tell you that I got a call from my buddy saying you were approved?"

"Yeah, Bob, she did, and I looked for that letter every day. I had no idea that my mom had it," I whispered, at a loss for words.

"For Christ's sake, speak up, will you? I can barely hear a word you're saying."

"I'm at the office, and it's kind of hard to talk. I said I didn't know my mom had the letter."

"Fuck the letter, Ron! The letter didn't mean shit! When you didn't get it, you should have gone right down to the union and asked about it. It's been four fucking weeks, kid! What were you thinking? They got nothing better to do than wait around for you to show up? The whole reason they called me was to give me the heads up and make sure you got your ass down there and registered. Ronnie, listen, they only fill 150 seats in the class each year. First 150 guys to register win. They give the heads up to the guys they would like to see in the union. You were one of those guys," he insisted. "This way nobody can accuse them of picking favorites."

"Bobby, Bobby, I didn't know that. I thought I had to have the letter," I said, wishing he had made that clear to Jessica when he spoke to her.

"Yeah, well… I called my buddy this morning, and he said you're pretty much fucked. He can't even get your name on a first-alternate list in case somebody quits or dies. There's like fifty guys ahead of you, and the list has already been posted," he said with resignation.

"Shit!" I screamed into the phone, causing Hamilton to turn back and look at me with raised eyebrows.

"Sorry, Roger. Something at home," I said, addressing his concern. He nodded his head and smiled before returning to his task.

"I'm sorry, kid, but that's where it stands. My buddy said he'd get you on next year's list if you're still interested." I heard his words, but the tone in his voice told me he was done.

"Bobby, I'm sorry, man. I can't tell you how sorry I am for this. I know you put your name on the line for me, and, no matter what, I really appreciate it," I said as sincerely as I could.

"Tough break, kid. Who knows? Maybe this will work out for the best. Keep in touch, okay?"

"Yeah, right. I'll see you around," I said, swallowing hard as I hung up the phone in a daze. I had no idea how long Hamilton had been standing beside me until he cleared his throat.

"Oh, Roger, I'm sorry, I… ah, didn't see you there."

"Is everything all right at home?" he asked earnestly.

"Yeah, yes, yes. Everything is fine. Thank you for asking. I got something to take care of, that's all," I said, just wanting him to go away and leave me alone. I got up from my chair and walked over to the coffee pot with my thoughts racing in a million directions, and the last person I wanted to share anything with was Hamilton.

"Okay, well, if there is something I can help you with, don't hesitate to ask."

"Thanks, Roger. I appreciate it, but everything's cool," I said.

"Okay, well, let me know," he offered one last time before disappearing into his office. I poured a cup of coffee and returned to my desk, wavering somewhere between shock and disillusionment at the turn of events that altered my life that weekend. I sat down and lost myself in a host of thoughts, trying to make sense of it all. I felt like the recipient of a voodoo doll curse with all the people in my life sticking needles in their personal versions of me at the same time.

My mother, whom I never counted on for anything, managed to make herself the focal point of this disaster by stabbing me squarely in the back, regardless of her intent. Jessica's obsessive condemnation of my mother was driving me insane, and even though Bobby Cooker worked to help me get this opportunity, I couldn't help but feel even he let me down to some degree. Ultimately and correctly, I came to the conclusion that I had no one to blame but myself. I should have called Bobby instead of just hearing it from Jessica, which was my fault. After a while, I resigned myself to the fact that it really didn't matter who was or wasn't to blame. Any way you cut it, I wasn't going to be an electrician.

That afternoon, I went home and explained the situation to Jessica. I made the mistake of venting a lot of my frustration towards my mother, to the absolute joy of my wife. I watched as she began fluttering around the apartment like a butterfly in a lily field, dusting, cleaning, and rearranging knick-knacks while taking in every disparaging word I spoke. It was like my venting fueled her energy. I began to see a direct correlation between what she perceived as my anger with my mother and her general happiness.

Later that day, we put the baby in the stroller, leashed up the dog, and walked over to the park. Jessica took advantage of the opportunity by continuously barraging me with her hatred of my mother without restraint. Along the way, I pushed the stroller and played with the baby, preferring to tune Jessica out until she turned her attention to me. "You know, the more I think about it, the more I'm really glad this happened, Ronnie. This is a good lesson for you," she said, finally baiting me into the conversation.

"Me?"

"Yep, now you get to see what I've been talking about this entire time," she said with a smirk while nodding her head.

"What are you talking about, Jess? How in the hell is this good for anyone? Are you saying that you're happy I won't become an electrician? 'Cause if you are, you're crazier than my mother," I said in disbelief.

"I'm not happy about it. I'm just glad that you finally get a chance to see how she really operates. She plays people, especially you. You always let her get away with it, but now she's gone too far, and you finally see it. It's like that crap she tried to feed you yesterday about forgetting the letter; does she think we're stupid?"

"I don't know, Jessie. Why didn't she just throw it out if that was the case?" I asked, honestly looking for an answer—but not excusing my mom.

"What is it with you? The woman destroys our life, and you're defending her!" she shot back with disgust.

"Stop right there," I demanded. "I'm not defending her. What she did was wrong, but I'm just saying that you'd have to know my mom to know that maybe, just maybe, she stuck it in the cedar chest as a way of safekeeping and forgot about it," I said.

"Really, and what about that stuff she said about me? Are you going to make up excuses for her about those too?"

"Jessica, I'm not making up excuses for her!"

"I'm asking you a question."

"What stuff are you talking about?"

"Like sticking your dirty fingers inside me?" I stopped pushing the stroller to turn and look at her. Jessica knew I didn't say anything about sticking dirty fingers inside of her, and the exaggeration angered me to no end.

"She didn't say that, Jessie!"

"Well, that's what she meant, and you know it. You're supposed to be my husband, and I would expect my husband to be furious if anyone said something so disgusting about his wife!" she exclaimed. I shook my head and bit my lower lip while pushing the stroller ahead of her at a quickened pace. I couldn't do this. I didn't have the emotional strength to argue with her, agree with her, or even patronize her with something that would appease her. At that moment, I just wished there was some way I could take the baby and get away from both my mother and Jessica. "So, what do you think she meant?" Jessica called out from behind when I didn't answer.

I stopped in my tracks and turned to face her. "I don't fucking know, and I don't fucking care, Jessie!" I shouted at her.

"That's the problem. You need to care!" she shouted back.

"She was drunk," I said, exhausted at the badgering.

"That's always your mom's excuse, Ron. She was drunk. She's always drunk! You can accept that if you want. Maybe it will make things easier for you when you spend the rest of your life working for the insurance company."

"I don't follow you," I said, shaking my head.

"Well, won't you feel better selling insurance to niggers the rest of your life knowing that your mother was drunk when she fucked you out of the best opportunity you ever had?" she said so contemptuously, it rivaled anything my mother had said. My face tightened with anger as I turned the stroller around and headed back for the apartment. I couldn't believe what she said or the way she said it. "I thought we were going to the park?" Jessica asked at the abruptness of my actions.

I turned towards her with a scornful look. "Don't you ever use that word again to describe the people I work with. It's ugly, and it makes you ugly when you say it," I said with a disdain for my wife I had never felt before. Jessica knew the expression on my face was serious and that she had crossed a line with me in her attempt to ridicule my mother.

"It's not like you never said it," she said, dropping her eyes in an attempt to redeem herself.

"I don't say it anymore. And if you knew those people the way I do, you wouldn't either."

"Well, I'm sorry I said it, but your mother just makes me so mad I can't even think right," she said with a long sigh. We walked home in silence.

CHAPTER 11

August 1980

"Ron, your wife is on line two," Mrs. Bolger called out from behind the glass.

"Thanks, I got it," I said before picking up the phone and explaining to Jessica that Meadows hadn't arrived and I was going to be later than I had originally thought.

"Well, what am I supposed to do for food?" she complained.

"Find something to cook," I said.

"Great, you get to eat out, and I have to stay home and cook crap," she said, laying the usual guilt trip at my feet.

"Okay, listen, I'm going to be out a while, but when I'm done, I'll call and bring you something home for dinner, all right?" I said, trying to appease her.

"I want chicken," she said sharply.

"Fine, I'll stop and get you Kentucky Fried on the way home. Bye," I hung up the phone, half wishing she'd choke on a chicken bone.

As a matter of civility, Jessica and I had put the electrician debacle behind us, but a lot of resentment remained, and I was angry. More than just mad or upset, I was coming to the conclusion that our relationship was terribly one-sided, hinging entirely on my contribution as opposed to a joint effort.

I had to get her chicken tonight because I ate out and she didn't. I had to go grocery shopping with her because she didn't know what I wanted. I had to bring her home a Coke from McDonald's every day because it tasted better than the Coke in the cans. I began to realize that she didn't contribute to our marriage; she took from it. It was always my fault that she couldn't do something. She wouldn't cook because I would never tell her when I was coming home. She couldn't get a job and help out because, according to her, "I don't want a wife that's gone all day." I was tired of her selfishness, and I was tired of her constantly blaming other people for our problems.

If losing the job I had dreamed about for a year wasn't bad enough, I had to contend with a wife who was obsessed with blaming my mother for all our woes. Not once since learning of the lost opportunity with the union did Jessica offer a word of comfort or encouragement. Not once did she ask me how I felt or what we should do next. My mother became her entire focus, and Jessica was determined to drive a permanent stake through the heart of my relationship with her. It bothered me because I was more upset with my mother than Jessica could ever imagine, but I didn't hate her. She was my mother, and I could never hate her. Jessica couldn't understand that. She wanted me to despise my mom as much as she did.

For the first time since getting married, I began to see Jessica in a different light.

She wasn't that shy girl who looked at the world differently. She wasn't that cute little thing marching to the beat of her own drum without a care as to what others thought. She was a loner with no ambitions who didn't want friends because "they were a bother." She didn't read and had little interest in current events, which made conversation between us practically non-existent. She once told me that she had married me to get out of the house and away from her parents. At the time, I thought she was kidding, but now I wasn't so sure.

When I was seventeen and we started dating, I thought she was beautiful, and the blue jeans and flannel shirts she wore seemed to fit her sexy body like a glove. It didn't matter to me that most people looked at her like a cute fourteen-year-old girl. I knew that she was a twenty-one-year-old woman, and I yearned for her experience. I didn't pay any attention to the old panties with the ripped crotch she was wearing the first time we had sex, as losing my virginity was paramount on my mind. Four years later, I had to agree with my mother: The old, baggy jogging pants and stained T-shirt day after day grew tiresome. The old, ripped panties remained in her drawer.

I began to wonder if I had married Jessica because I loved her or because at seventeen I loved having sex with her. After the first couple of months of handholding and some passionate kissing, we finally did it in the back of my mother's station wagon. From that point forward, we did it all the time—every day, everywhere we could. I was addicted to the sex and found myself not being able to go without it. Jessica was a willing participant who never refused my advances. I could have it anytime and anywhere I wanted under any conditions, and it hooked me. When we got married, she told me it was her duty as my wife to have sex with me. At first, I thought I had died and gone to heaven. What else could a man wish for? But after a while, I realized that it wasn't passionate, loving sex she was offering me but instead a place to relieve myself so I wouldn't be tempted to look elsewhere.

The Thursday meeting had been over for two hours, and my head was throbbing from sitting in the office all day with nothing to eat. Meadows had insisted that Otis and I wait for him to get back from processing a death claim that morning so he could treat us to lunch for leading the office in sales the previous month. We both would have been happy with a handshake and a twenty-dollar bill, but Meadows insisted on lunch. Otis was adamant about getting something from Meadows, convinced that if it were not for his MDO sales, Meadows would have been sitting in the office by himself while we were all enjoying ourselves in the Bahamas. He took it as a personal affront that Meadows didn't show more appreciation for his efforts and hounded Ray daily for the well-deserved lunch.

Feeling the effects of several cups of coffee, I found it necessary to make almost as many trips to the bathroom. When I returned to the office, Otis had disappeared, leaving stuff scattered across his desk. My headache was killing me, and sitting alone in the office staring at the four walls seemed to increase the pain exponentially. I wasn't even aware that Irene the seductress had quietly sauntered into the room to drop messages upon the agents' desks.

Even her bulging breasts and short black skirt couldn't distract me enough to relieve the pounding as she reached over my shoulder and placed my mail and newly issued policies on my desk.

"Are you okay?" she asked, probably confused that my eyes didn't pop out of my head or I didn't start babbling like an idiot to impress her like the other guys did when she walked into the room.

"Yeah, I'm fine. Thanks for the mail. Hey, Irene, did you hear anything from Meadows?"

"No, is he supposed to call you?"

"He's supposed to be here. Otis and I were supposed to meet him here for lunch," I said.

"Are you sure? I know Mr. Hamilton excused Mr. Meadows from the meeting today because he had to take care of a death claim," she responded.

"I know about that; he told me and Otis to wait here. I don't know where Otis disappeared to either."

"I saw Otis down in the bank lobby. He was probably cashing his check. I'm sure he'll be right back up," she said, walking away from me.

I was in no mood to sort through the stack of mail pays and new policies that Irene had dropped in front of me. The company's policy was to have the agents process and record the mail pays immediately, but I just couldn't look at numbers with the way my head felt. Without opening them, I shoved the envelopes into my desk and quickly fanned through the policies to see who got issued. I stopped about halfway through the stack and went back a couple of policies as it slowly registered in my food-starved brain that the policy I had been waiting for had finally arrived.

I was ecstatic to find Sandra's policy issued exactly the way we applied for it and ready to be delivered. Ever since we met, I tried to think up excuses to go back and see her but backed out each time.

The new policy was like a free pass, and I couldn't wait. In that moment, a surge of energy renewed my spirit as an adrenaline rush wiped away my headache. Looking up at the clock, I couldn't wait to finish lunch and get out of there. I didn't want to be at the office, and I certainly didn't want to go home. I wanted to go see Sandra.

Without hesitation, I got up and walked over to the secretary's window, asking Mrs. Bolger if I could get one of the nice vinyl policy jackets she kept locked up behind the window. The old paper envelopes in the office made the insurance policies look like a last will and testament instead of an investment in the future. I wanted Sandra to have something nice.

"What color do you want?" she growled in a smoker's voice that was slowly slipping beyond baritone.

"What do you got?"

"Green or blue."

"Blue sounds good," I said. Mrs. Bolger went to retrieve the jacket, and I opened Sandra's policy, studying it for a few moments to make sure everything was spelled correctly.

"One dollar, please," she came back and demanded. I dug around in my pockets, looking for some money, and finally came up with enough change to make a dollar, handing it through the window to Mrs. Bolger. It was bad enough having only one coffee pot for twenty-plus agents, but making us pay a dollar to give our clients a nice policy jacket was just ridiculous, especially since the office got them free by leading the company in sales. When questioned about the dollar policy, Hamilton contended that the supply was limited and he didn't want agents to waste them, figuring a small charge would encourage discretion. The longer I worked at Unified, the more I began to agree with Otis—Hamilton was a "cheap motherfucker." I went back to my desk, sat down, and folded the new policy, fitting it perfectly into the new jacket.

A few moments later, Meadows came barreling into the office like the proverbial bull in a china shop, heaving his leather satchel onto a desk.

"Where the hell have you been? I thought we were going to lunch," I said.

"Oh man, I gotta shit!" he grunted in pain. His swollen, pock-marked face looked as if it were going to explode at any moment.

"Thanks for sharing," I called out as he raced for the agents' door. Otis walked in a second later.

"Did Meadows make it, or did he shit in his pants?" Otis said with a grin as he took his seat in front of me.

"Let's put it this way: I wouldn't want to ride in the same car with him today," I said with Otis smiling from ear to ear.

"Fuck that shit. I didn't want to ride in the same elevator as him," he quipped. "Motherfucker almost killed me coming up here—stanked up the whole goddamn thing. It's no wonder with all the shit he eats. Shit would kill most people!" he exclaimed.

"I wonder if this means we don't get lunch," I said.

"I don't give a shit if he's got to wear a goddamn diaper. That cheap motherfucker ain't getting out of buying us lunch. We earned that shit," Otis stated as he picked up the phone and started dialing.

What I loved about Otis was that he approached the world differently, and though he didn't know it, his presence always lifted my spirits. He seemed to take life in stride, picking out what he wanted, discarding anything that annoyed him like trash, while artfully commenting on everyone else along the way. He could never be the leading man in a movie because you couldn't depend on him to be there from one moment to the next, but all the same, you relished the thought of him by your side if you had to march into battle. About ten minutes later, Meadows came sauntering back into the office like a man with a great weight lifted off his shoulders.

"Feeling better, Ray?" I asked as he approached our desks.

"You have no idea," he said, propping up his bag and removing a ledger book, some papers, and, of course, his pipe-smoking kit before sliding the satchel beneath the desk.

"Are we still going to eat?" I asked, wanting to get out of there.

"Damn, Ron, give me a minute to sit down and get my stuff turned in," he said with a frown. Otis was hunched over his desk, holding the phone tight to one ear and covering the other with his free hand. Meadows, noticing that Otis was occupied, leaned toward me and whispered in my direction. "Damn near killed Wahl coming up in the elevator," he said, nodding in Otis' direction with a devilish grin on his face.

"Yeah, I know. Otis was quick to point out his brush with death when he came in," I sighed. "How long before we go eat, Ray? I've been here all morning, and I'm starving, and I'd like to get out to the ledger and deliver this policy," I said with an attitude.

"Jesus, Ron. Why don't you get a fucking candy bar or something to hold you over?" he said with the same frown he was wearing the moment before. "Who gets the nice policy jacket?" he asked, noticing it on my desk.

"Remember that $34 MDO case I wrote last month?" I asked to a blank expression on his face. "You do remember last month, don't you? Otis and I led the staff in sales. We made the Bahamas trip—helped you make the Bahamas trip—and you were so grateful that you promised to take us to lunch," I said, dripping with sarcasm.

"When did you turn into a smartass? You weren't a smartass when you first started here. I should have never let you work with Wahl; he turned you into a smartass. Let me see that policy. What was the name again?" he asked, reaching over and taking the policy from my hand.

"Sandra Wesley," I said.

"I know her. That's Buckley's daughter," he said, nodding his head.

"Yeah, you remembered."

"The Buckley's are good people. Wow! Fifteen thousand whole life. That's good," he said, pulling the policy halfway out of the jacket and examining the declaration page before wrapping it back up and handing it to me. I was just about to push my chair away from my desk and stand up, saying, "Thanks, can we go?" when he cut me off in mid-sentence.

"I knew Sandra when she was just a teenager—before she married that asshole," he said, sparking my immediate attention and bringing me back into my seat.

"Really? What do you know about her husband?" I asked.

"Nothing really, except that he's got kids with a couple of different women besides Sandra and that he treated her like shit," he said while moving some papers to the side of his desk. As an afterthought, he fingered through a couple of papers he had just moved, then retrieved one he deemed of no importance and placed it on the desk in front of him.

"How do you mean?" I asked with concern.

"I know he used to knock her around quite a bit. She was always packing up her kid and moving back home," he said with a sigh while reaching around the side of his desk and pulling a wastebasket next to him on the floor.

"Are you sure we're talking about the same girl? Sandra has three kids."

"She might now, but when I was working your book, she only had the one," he said. I watched as he carefully laid his pipe upon the paper he had placed on the desk. Like a surgeon preparing a medical tray full of instruments, he methodically placed the cleaning tool next to the pipe and then put the leather tobacco pouch next to it. Once he was satisfied that everything was lined up properly for the operation, he began scraping the debris from the inside of the pipe and emptying the contents in the wastebasket. I didn't interrupt his ritual because I wanted to learn more without seeming too anxious for information. It took a couple of moments, but my patience paid off. "That guy she married was bad news," he finally said.

"Well, she said she's divorced now," I said.

"That's good. I remember she used to be a pretty little thing," he said, looking up while still scraping away. "What does she look like now?"

"Ah, she's still a pretty little thing," I said, trying to seem indifferent. "I like her a lot. She seems really nice."

"Maybe she's grown up then," Meadows commented.

"What do you mean?"

"She used to give her mom fits when she was a teenager. A nice girl, but the attitude, whew boy, I tell you, she used to get up in her mom's face a lot."

"Imagine that, a smartass teenager, huh?" I asked rhetorically.

"Well, this was ten years ago," he chuckled. "Couldn't tell her a thing—knew it all," he said, shaking his head. "She was always a pretty smart kid, though; I'm not surprised that she bought a good insurance policy. You were smart to give her MDO instead of weekly," he said as if contemplating the transaction like a science. "Some other agent may have sold her weekly. She would have dropped that in a second," he concluded with a scholarly tone.

"This company ought to burn that fucking weekly rate book," Otis said, butting into our conversation as he hung up the phone. "I don't know why you even sell that weekly shit, Meadows."

"Because there are some people who pay weekly better than monthly, and it's none of your fucking business what I sell, Mr. Wahl," Meadows countered with eyebrows raised and eyes bulging at Otis.

"Yeah, well, you do a disservice to your people selling them that weekly shit," Otis replied.

"Fuck you, Wahl. The people I write stay insured because they can afford what I give them. When I was an agent, I never had half the fucking lapses you have."

"That's because you never wrote half the fucking business I do," Otis fired back. "Speaking of which, when are we going to get our fucking lunch? Pickles over there is wasting away to nothing. Look at his sorry ass. The boy needs some food," he said, pointing a finger in my direction.

"Gentlemen! Gentlemen!" Hamilton called out as he rushed into the room. "I have guests in my office," he said, admonishing all three of us like children.

"Sorry, Roger," Meadows said.

"My bad," Otis followed. Hamilton looked at me as if anticipating a response.

"I haven't said shit; all I want to do is get some food!" I said, holding up my hands in surrender.

"Can we please watch the language and act like professionals, gentlemen?" Hamilton admonished before leaving the room.

"See what you started?" Meadows grumbled like a scolded child while dropping his cleaning tool to the desk and pointing a finger at Otis.

"Fuck you, and get that nasty-ass finger out my face," Otis replied in a quieter voice.

"What is it with you guys?" I asked, annoyed at the bickering. "You argue like an old married couple," I said, getting both of their attention.

"It ain't none of your goddamn business, Pickles," Otis shot back, taking offense at my remark. "Besides, it ain't me. It's him. Motherfucker knows I'm right. That weekly shit sucks. If it wasn't for my MDO sales, motherfucker wouldn't be going on no trip. Ain't that right, Meadows?"

"He's right. He's always right. I know that. Can't have a discussion with Wahl. He's always right," Meadows said mockingly while putting his head down and resuming his obsession with pipe cleaning.

"'Bout goddamn time you realized it," Otis said smugly. "I don't know why you got to go pointing them nasty-ass fingers at me and shit," Otis continued, half smiling and trying to goad Meadows some more. "Pickles, did he ever tell you why them hands of his are so fucked up?"

"I hadn't noticed," I said dismissively, not wanting to embarrass Ray.

"You never noticed his hands? Shit, motherfucker, you blind? Goddamn things look like they went through a meat grinder. You ever tell Pickles what you did as a kid?" he asked Meadows.

"Nope," Meadows replied stoically. I looked over at Ray, who didn't seem the least bit interested in talking about his hands, which made me all the more curious.

"Motherfucker used to set pins for white folks in a bowling alley. Show Pickles your hands," Otis commanded with a hint of empathy in his voice. Meadows seemed perturbed at the intrusion and gave Otis a look of displeasure as he stuck the pipe in his mouth and placed the cleaning tool back on the desk. Like an act of deliverance, he purposely held up both hands for me to examine. Of course, I lied when Otis asked me if I had ever noticed Meadows' hands. He was right. You would have to be blind to miss them. They were so grotesque, you felt compelled to stare at them like some human deformity at a freak show.

I knew something must have happened to his hands the first time I met him. They were lumpy and horribly scarred, with dead skin constantly peeling away from his fingers. They reminded me of an old leather baseball glove I had when I was a kid. I left it outside one winter, and it got waterlogged. When it came time to play baseball, I found the mitt laying in the yard where I had left it the year before. It was swollen with water and smelled really bad, so I propped it up on some rocks and let it sit in the hot sun, where it promptly dry-rotted and began to shed its outer skin. Meadows' hands looked just like that dry-rotted glove. I never had the nerve to ask him before, but Otis gave me the opening, so I took it.

"So, what happened to your hands when you were a kid?" He took the pipe out of his mouth, leaned back in his chair, and stared out ahead as if trying to recollect the memory.

"Oh shit," he sighed. "I guess I was maybe twelve or thirteen when I started setting pins," he said while lifting his arms behind his head for a good stretch. His pauses were killing me; I couldn't resist but to ask more questions.

"What are all the bumps from?"

"Those?" he said, putting his hands on display once again. "The doctor says those are calcium deposits. You get those when your bones break or fracture and don't set properly," he said while opening and closing his fingers as if demonstrating that they still worked.

"Jesus, your hands are covered with those things. How many times did you break your bones?" I asked. He looked at Otis, and the two of them smiled at each other as if amused by the question. Otis seemed captivated, which intrigued me even more.

"Well, I didn't set out to break them. I had some help," he said as if amused.

"You guys are losing me here. I don't understand," I said, shifting my head back and forth between the two of them.

"Just be quiet and listen to the man, damn it," Otis instructed. Meadows seemed to appreciate Otis' reprimand, as if acknowledging that his story was something of importance.

"Well, you know when you go bowling nowadays how a machine sets the pins from above the alley so they line up perfectly each time?"

"Yeah, of course I do," I replied as he reached over and took the pipe and tobacco bag off his desk. He placed the bag on his lap, holding it steady with the same hand he was holding the pipe with, then unzipped the pouch and dug his pipe into it like a shovel, scooping out the tobacco inside. Satisfied that he had the bowl stuffed with the right amount, he zipped up the pouch, then tossed it on the desk.

"Well, before the machines, you had to set the pins by hand," he said while clenching the pipe between his teeth. "You know, the pins you knock down?"

"Yeah, I know what bowling pins are," I said, giving Otis a quick look. "It just never occurred to me that somebody had to set them back up by hand."

"That's how Meadows' hands got fucked up. He was a pinsetter," Otis added.

"Oh, I see. What, did you drop pins on your hands or something?" I asked.

"Yeah, something like that," he said with kind of a sarcastic tone. I watched as he lit a match and put it to the bowl, puffing hard on the mouthpiece while blowing billows of smoke in the air before looking at me with piercing eyes through the smoke. "In the old days, bowling alleys looked the same as they do today."

"With the exception of black people," Otis quipped.

"Black people weren't allowed to bowl?" I asked incredulously.

"You going to let me tell the story, Wahl, or do you want to tell it?" Meadows asked rhetorically. Otis just shrugged while Ray continued. "There wasn't a lot of bowling alleys in black areas, and most of the time black folks didn't have the money to go bowling anyways. Women didn't bowl that much either. It was mostly a guy's thing."

"A white guy's thing," I joked.

"Yeah, pretty much," he agreed. "See, the reason they hired kids back then was because you had to be small enough to squeeze into a small cubbyhole above the alley where the pins are set up."

"A cubbyhole?"

"Like a catwalk. We'd called it the pits," he said, illustrating with his hand how you hovered over the pins. "That was the pits. You would sit there and wait for the pins to be knocked down, then jump off the catwalk and clear them to the back of the lane by hand into a hole at the end of the alley so you could fill the hopper."

"What's a hopper?" I asked, wanting to know everything. Meadows nodded his head as if realizing I didn't understand.

"The hopper was this big mechanical contraption that would tilt towards you so that you could fill it with the next set of pins from the ones you just scraped into the hole. It was below the catwalk, just above the floor where the bowling pins stand," he said, looking for a sign that I was beginning to understand. He realized immediately that I wasn't and scratched his head as if thinking of something to say.

"You ever see a guy fill up a pop machine with bottles?" Otis spoke up.

"That's it exactly," Meadows continued.

"Sure, all the time," I said.

"Well, the hopper looked a little like that, except bigger. It had slots for the pins, and our job was to fill up the slots, then push the hopper back in place and jump back up on the catwalk and wait for the drop," he said with confidence that I understood the procedure.

"The drop?"

"That's right, the drop. You listen for the drop. See, when you're bowling, you hear things differently. What you hear in a bowling alley is the sound of everything traveling away from you," he said, motioning away from his body with his hand. "People's voices, the balls rolling down the lanes, even the crash when the ball hits the pins—it's all traveling away from you. Do you understand?"

"Well, I never thought about it, but yeah, I guess," I said, unsure of what he was getting at.

"That's not what you hear in the pits," he mused. "You don't hear things the same way. Sound comes at you in the pits, and it gets louder and louder as it gets closer and closer. So, you hear all these voices and laughter coming at you and then nothing. Total silence. Everyone shuts up as a courtesy to the bowler, but you can't see the bowler from the catwalk, so you have to wait for the bowler to drop the ball in the alley and listen as that bowling ball starts to pick up speed and head toward you. When you're sitting on that catwalk, you can feel the vibration of that ball rumbling down the lane like a freight train barreling down upon you. The vibration gets stronger and stronger, and the rumble gets louder and louder till BAM! The ball hits those pins like a lightning bolt tearing into a tree limb!" he shouted out, practically knocking me off my chair, much to the amusement of Otis.

"I think you just made Pickles shit his pants," Otis snickered.

"Jesus Christ! I think he did too," I couldn't help but laugh. "So, the pace of the game depended on how fast the pinsetters cleared the old pins and set up the new ones," I assumed.

"That's right. The faster we could keep up with the bowlers, the more they tipped us. That's how we made our money," he explained.

"You probably wouldn't get tips if you were slow," I said with a harmless laugh.

"Shit, boy, you wouldn't have fingers if you were slow!" he scolded. I was immediately taken aback by his change in demeanor and sat silently, watching as his outburst threw him into a coughing jag that lasted several moments. He was finally able to bring up some phlegm, then swallowed it back down before continuing. "It was different back then," he said as his expression darkened. "A nigga couldn't be slow setting them pins, or you'd goddamn know you'd hear a drop when you didn't want too," he said as a matter of fact.

"You mean they would deliberately throw the ball at you?" I asked with astonishment.

"Nigga be dodging bowling balls all night if you didn't clear them alleys fast enough." My mouth dropped open as he put a finger to his mouth and removed a piece of tobacco that had made its way to his lips. "Man, that was something," he said with a blank expression as if he had gone to a different place. "Every ball them boys tossed down the alley would scare the hell out of you. Shit...

you don't know what pain is till you feel a bowling ball crash a bunch of pins into your hands," he said, taking another drag from his pipe. "It wouldn't just get you once. It get you maybe twenty times. 'Move your ass, nigga!' them white boys would be yelling out after they got you a good one."

"Holy shit! That's unreal," I said under my breath, captivated by his story.

"My momma would make me spend half the night soaking my hands in salts to get the swelling down so I could go to school and back to work the next day. We needed that job. Yes sir, you had to learn. If you were fast and kept up with the game, you'd get some nice tips. But boy... if you weren't hustling, they'd get that nigga. Those were the rules. Funny thing is, though, you get your hands smashed between them bowling pins a few times, and you'd be surprised how fast you start to move," he lamented while examining his hands again.

"From the looks of those hands, nigga never did get too fast, now did he?" Otis snorted.

"Fuck you, Wahl," Meadows fired back.

"Jesus, Ray, that's fucking awful. Did you ever call the police or anything?" I asked, immediately realizing the idiocy of the question before I had finished asking it.

"Yeah, Meadows, how come you didn't call the NAACP or Doctor King and put a stop to that shit?" Otis quipped before the last syllable left my mouth.

"Stupid question, okay, I get it," I said, leaning back in my chair and taking a long look at Meadows.

"Damn, all this bullshitting has made me hungry. Let's go eat." Meadows pushed himself away from the desk and quickly headed out the door. Otis and I looked at each other sympathetically as we got up from our chairs, knowing that Meadows had churned up some emotions he would have rather forgotten. The picture Meadows described of a twelve-year-old black boy scrambling to avoid the impact of a bowling ball launched by a group of white bowlers ramming into bowling pins stunned me. The cruelty was incomprehensible.

CHAPTER 12

Later That Day

The sky was heavy with rain clouds that afternoon, and a cool drizzle was a welcome relief to the summer heat. After lunch, I hurried out of the restaurant and dashed over to my car, fumbling for my keys as I dodged the raindrops. I quickly opened the door and slid into the car, eyeing Sandra's policy on the front seat. I hesitated for a moment, trying to decide what to do. I really wanted to see her, but I was having second thoughts. Rush hour had just begun, and traffic was already snarled in the rain. I was getting tired, and I hated to drive all the way back into the city without knowing if she'd be there. "Damn, I wish she had a phone," I mumbled to myself as I started the car. I leaned forward, closed my eyes, and pressed my head against the steering wheel, trying to decide what to do. I felt like a man trapped between two worlds and belonging to neither. I lost myself in the irony of the week's events; I couldn't believe that I actually felt better about going to the ledger than I did about going home. Before I knew it, I was heading towards Sandra's house.

The door opened, and I immediately knew I had made the right decision from the smile on Sandra's face. She looked fantastic, dressed in a short jean skirt with thick white knee-high socks scrunched down to her ankles, just above her blue tennis shoes. She had on a soft white sweater with short sleeves, trimmed with lace and a rounded neckline. A little gold necklace with a locket in the shape of a heart laid upon her neck and enhanced the supple look of her creamy brown skin. Her hair was straightened and parted down the middle, just as it was the first time we met. She looked perfect in every way.

"This is a surprise!" she said, beaming while welcoming me into the apartment. A hint of perfume tickled my nose as I passed by her, and I had to restrain myself from turning back to get more.

"I'm sorry to just barge in on you like this, but your policy came in today, and I was driving by, so I thought I'd take a chance," I said, ignoring the fact that I drove twenty miles out of my way through pouring rain to take that chance. "Did I catch you at a bad time?"

"No, I just walked in the door a few minutes ago myself. Is it still raining outside?"

"Just a little drizzle, not too bad," I replied.

"They say a big storm is coming," she said.

"What do they know? Weathermen in Chicago—they're all a little flakey by the laky. Are you sure this isn't a bad time? I can come back if you're busy..."

"Ron, don't be silly. Come on in and have a seat over by the window," she said, guiding me to the loveseat while going about picking up some toys and things the kids had left scattered throughout the house. I casually glanced around the place, noticing things I hadn't on my first visit. There were white-lace doilies under the lamps in the living room, pastel-colored throw rugs across the hardwood floor, figurines on the tables, and decorative pillows on the chairs. I was intrigued by the little extras she put into the tiny apartment that touched up the rooms and gave them a woman's feel.

"Hey, it's way too quiet in here. Where are the kids?" I asked while sitting down.

"Well, Lee is at Grandma's, and Lucy and Liz are driving my sister crazy at her house. They split the duty when I have class. Remember, I told you I was going to beautician's school," she said, disappearing into another room.

"I didn't know that you started already. That's fantastic," I called out.

"Thanks," she said as she came back into the room. "I started two weeks ago. I really feel like I'm going to accomplish something." She sat down beside me like a lady, making sure her legs were together and her skirt was tucked under her as she came to rest on the couch. She squared her shoulders quite properly and folded her hands in her lap, ready to receive the information I had for her.

"I'm proud of you," I said with all sincerity. "It's so hard to go back to school these days, it's unreal," I said, half thinking about my situation.

"Tell me about it. They should have one whole class in high school dedicated to teaching kids how miserable they'll be if they want to try and squeeze school back into their lives once they're out in the real world."

"Well, most people aren't as lucky as you," I said.

"How's that?"

"Having the three kids is rough. I have one, and I know how hard it is for me. You're really lucky to have a family that helps you out," I said, thinking about the troubles I had with my own.

"My family has been so supportive. It's been great. You know my mom and dad, right?"

"Uh huh."

"They can be kind of stuffy sometimes, but they've just been thrilled that I'm doing something with my life. They never wanted me to get married in the first place," she said, shrugging her shoulders as if acknowledging that they were right.

"Why is that?"

"My ex-husband."

"I take it they didn't like him, then."

"It's the same old story," she sighed. "I thought I was in love, got married, got pregnant. Twice. Then, I got into fights with my husband and got divorced. I was pretty bullheaded when I was younger. They tried to tell me, but I didn't want to listen to them," she said, unknowingly confirming what Meadows had told me earlier in the day.

"That doesn't really account for the baby," I teased.

"This is true. Lee was the result of an experiment," she said with reservation.

"I see. So tell me, Doctor Wesley, what was the outcome of this experiment?"

"The outcome was a success, but, unfortunately, the experiment failed," she said with a nod.

"I think I tried that experiment with my wife, and it failed for us too," I grinned. "I will admit, however, that it produced an outcome that I love very much today," I said as we both shook our heads in agreement. "So, you guys decided to get divorced?" I asked.

"I did. I wanted it. I think I needed it," she said reflectively. "I think I've really grown up over the last few years with the kids and all, and I just want something better for myself and for them. I'm tired of not being able to afford a phone or a car or anything. I really don't want my résumé to say, 'welfare recipient' the rest of my life," she said with determination.

"You sound like a woman with a purpose."

"I'm just tired of other people telling me what to do. It's like for the first time in my life, I'm doing something for me instead of someone else. Do you know what I mean?" she asked.

"I know exactly what you mean. It's like your whole life you do what's expected of you instead of what you want," I replied.

"Exactly, and I'm tired of it. I want to be selfish for a change and just do something for me," she said with a slight hesitation in her voice. "But don't get me wrong. I love my kids more than anything in the world, so this is kind of like for all of us, you know?"

"I know what you're saying, and I totally agree with you. How can you make your kid's life better if you don't make your own life better?"

"Ron, it may sound crazy to you, but just knowing that I'm going to have a skill I can make money with is so cool," she said with an excitement in her voice that brought back a flood of emotions from the events of the weekend.

"Trust me, Sandra, I know. I just blew a chance to do exactly what you're talking about," I said with a sigh while dropping my eyes.

"Sounds like you're upset. What happened?" she asked with concern. I looked up at her for a moment, wanting to tell her my story but hesitated.

"It's just that, well…"

"What is it, Ron?"

"Jeez, I don't know. It's such a long story, Sandra. I wouldn't even know where to begin. I don't want to bore you with it."

"You're not going to bore me with something that's important to you. I'd really like to know," she said, patting my leg.

"Well, I feel bad because I didn't tell you this last month, but I got accepted into electrician's school this fall."

"That's wonderful. Why wouldn't you want to tell me something like that?" she asked.

"Well, it meant that I would be starting school in September, and I would have to quit the insurance job," I said sheepishly. "I didn't want to tell you after we just got to know each other, and I was talking about how I'd come and pick up the insurance money every month."

"You don't have to be my insurance man for us to be friends. I was going to buy insurance from somebody somewhere. It just happened to be you," she said without concern. "What's important for you is that you go to school and learn a trade. That's what's important," she said.

"You're right, I know," I said softly, looking away from her briefly and wishing someone else had felt that way. "Well, it doesn't really matter now, anyway," I sighed.

"So, tell me what happened," she said, crossing her legs and leaning back on the couch.

"I don't know. The more I think about it, the more stupid it gets," I said, beginning to recount the entire saga from attending the electrician's union smoker with Bobby Cooker to the weekend discovery of the letter in my mother's cedar chest. I even broke down and told her about the problems I'd been having with Jessica and my mom, ending with the observation that the only one who seemed to care was my dog Rudy.

"That was the whole reason I took this insurance job in the first place," I said, summing up the situation. "To get me by financially until I could go to school. Actually, Sandra, if you want to know the whole truth, I hated this job up until about four weeks ago. Until I met you, that is," I said shyly.

"That's so sweet," she said with a smile. "My God, you poor guy. What a week this must have been for you," she said sympathetically. "You're absolutely certain that there is no way you can get into the school this year?"

"Nope, they already posted the names of the alternates. This shit is so political. I had my chance, and I blew it," I said with a sigh.

"You didn't blow it—the people around you let you down, starting with your wife," she said, looking at me for a long moment while shaking her head as if she couldn't believe what she had heard.

"You mean my mother," I said like a robot parroting my wife's programming.

"No, I mean your wife, Jessica. You're out here working every day trying to support your family doing a job you don't want to do. Do you tell your wife that you work in the ghetto? Does she know how dangerous it is out here for you?"

"She knows. It was her idea to bring the dog out for protection," I grumbled.

"Wait a minute," Sandra said, sitting upright. "Are we talking about that cute little Lassie dog with the funny eyes?"

"Uh huh."

"Is that girl crazy? She could have got you killed. You're lucky one of these boys out here didn't bang you on the head and steal that thing," she said with a look of disbelief.

"Yeah, I never thought of it that way, I guess," I mused as Sandra sat there dismayed.

"See, that would be the difference between me and her. If I was your wife, you could bet your ass that you would have been down at the school the next week asking why you didn't get your letter."

"Why do you say that?"

"Because it wouldn't matter to me what your mom did. You ain't married to your mom; you're married to me. I will say that common sense should have told both of you that your friend was giving you the heads up when he called," she said, criticizing me truthfully with a strong voice. "What your mother did was wrong, but it sounds like she may be a little crazy."

"More than a little," I joked.

"I don't even know how you can laugh about this thing. Boy… you got me so riled up, I feel like going down to that old school and kicking somebody's booty," she said with a huff.

"Well, you may not believe this, but just being able to talk to somebody else about it really helps. Actually, you're the only one I've told about this or the way I feel. I didn't realize it until now, but I really needed to talk about it." She looked at me as if pleased to know that I had shared something personal with her.

"I feel so bad for you, I don't know what to say," she said, pursing her lips and shaking her head. "But I do think you're a strong enough guy to come through this thing alright," she said with a reassuring tone. "You need to take a little time and think about what you want to do. Even if you have to wait till next year, it's only one year. Who knows? By then, your life might completely change, and you'll find something else you want to do."

"You're right. I've been thinking about it a lot, and I know deep inside that it's not the end of the world, but I have to admit, it really feels good to hear it come from someone else," I said humbly. Sandra smiled and took a deep breath, slapping her legs before jumping off the couch.

"Are you hungry? Can I get you something to drink? I just made a big pitcher of grape Kool-Aid for the kids, and I have lots of ice," she said, going around the corner to the kitchen.

"Oh, thanks, but I'm not hungry. I just had lunch with my manager, and I'm still pretty stuffed, but a glass of Kool Aid sounds great!"

"Alrighty then, one glass of Kool-Aid for Mr. Pickles, coming right up. Hey, isn't your manager that little ol' ugly black man that used to be my mom's insurance man?" she asked from the kitchen.

"That's not nice," I called back.

"Oh my gosh, that must have sounded awful. I'm so sorry!" she cried out with laughter. "I didn't mean it in a bad way."

"It must have been the 'old ugly' part that confused me," I joked as she walked back to the couch and carefully sat down with two glasses of Kool-Aid. "But now you've scared me," I said with a grimace.

"Why is that?"

"I can just imagine how you describe me to other people. 'So, this whiny little white guy comes over to my house and cries about his life,'" I said with a smirk while accepting the glass and carefully taking a sip.

"You have nothing to worry about," she stated emphatically.

"Oh no?"

"No, I didn't know you were this whiny when I talked about you last week."

"You're so sweet," I chuckled.

"Nope, as a matter of fact, I was just telling my girlfriends about you the other day."

"Well, if you were talking about me to your girlfriends, that sounds promising," I said with a nod.

"Oh yeah, we talk about you guys a lot," she said, playing along.

"Really? What do you mean, 'us guys'?"

"Insurance men. It's true—each one of my girlfriends has some old, nasty insurance man coming over to their house," she said with a giggle.

"…And this is why I have nothing to worry about?" I questioned.

"My one friend has some old Jewish man that comes by and swears at her all the time. She thinks he's nuts."

"You're joking, right?" I laughed out loud.

"No, I'm not. I was at her house once when he stopped by to get her money. He was the rudest, nastiest little guy I've ever met," she said incredulously.

"Wait a minute. I think that might be Mr. Guru!" I blurted out. "About this big," I said, raising my hand a few feet off the floor. "Looks like Albert Einstein?" I asked.

"THAT'S THE GUY!" she bellowed. "He's insane!"

"Absolutely, totally nuts," I confirmed. "That's me in a few years if I keep this job, by the way," I joked.

"I don't think so, Ron. He's like 105 years old," she lamented.

"Thirty-two next week," I replied with a straight face as we both started laughing.

"Good Lord, that is just too funny," she said, shaking her head.

"He is an exception to the rule. Trust me, most of the insurance guys I work with aren't as bad as him," I said.

"Really? Well, my other girlfriend lives on the South Side, and she says her insurance man is the oldest, blackest man she's ever seen. She calls him Kunta Kinte," she said, laughing harder than before. I started laughing along with her until my jaw began to hurt and tried to regroup.

"Just out of curiosity, do you girls ever have anything nice to say?" I said.

"Just wait a minute and let me finish," she said, taking control of the conversation.

"Okay, go ahead."

"Well, you should have heard them cackle like a bunch of hens when I told them about you."

"I can't wait for this," I said skeptically.

"I told them that you were my mom and dad's insurance man, as well as Mrs. Brown's, and how highly they all thought of you. Then, I told them how funny you looked driving down the middle of the street with all those kids hanging off your car and how you brought this big, old, fluffy dog with you everywhere. I told them how we sat on the couch and talked about all the things we had in common, like baseball, and how you made sure that I got the best insurance policy you could give me. And then... you should have seen the jealousy written across their faces when I told them that you were just the cutest little blond-haired, blue-eyed insurance man I ever saw," she said in a sultry tone while drawing up a smile and biting on her lower lip.

Her smile captivated me, and the sparkle in her wonderfully expressive eyes warmed me all over. I knew she was teasing me, but with more than a hint of truth. She studied my face for a reaction and seemed happy that I hadn't missed the meaning of her words. My eyes locked with hers, and for a moment, it seemed as if the world had come to a stop. The rush of emotion was so intense, it caught us both off guard, and we turned away at the same time, flushed with a feeling that something had passed between us. It was an awkward moment. A nervous laughter gripped the two of us as we both took sips of Kool-Aid at the same time while looking at each other over the glasses. I swallowed hard and put the glass on the floor beside me.

"Well then, I think the only thing left to do now is to discuss your insurance policy," I said, bursting out in laughter before finishing my sentence. Sandra joined me, covering her hand with her mouth.

"Dear Lord, dear Lord... wait until my girlfriends hear about this," she hooted.

CHAPTER 13

September 1980

The month of September didn't exactly get off to an auspicious start, at least not for Otis, who got smacked in the head and robbed in the same project we had canvassed three months earlier in June. His advice to me was sound. His attackers demanded his wallet and found the $100 prize he had stashed away for just such an occurrence, then bolted from the scene. He escaped with a nasty cut on his head and a bruised ego. That, by his own admission, was a small price to pay.

Otis had pretty much put the incident behind him and was already joking that if the robbers had been smart and robbed his car instead, they would have gotten all his collection money from the weekend. Then, one Tuesday afternoon about two weeks after the robbery, Otis and I were doing paperwork in the office when he took a phone call, hung up, and stared at me with a glazed-over look. I knew it was serious because he didn't make a move to stroke his famous beard that always seemed to spark an amusing anecdote or obscene observation.

"What's up?" I asked with concern.

"You know who that was?" he asked, nodding towards the phone.

"Who?"

"Ruppert."

"Ruppert? Black Rangers dude from the projects?" I asked, hesitantly realizing the look on his face answered my question. I closed the ledger book and placed my pen on the desk. I leaned forward and looked around to make sure none of the other agents in the room could hear our conversation. "What did he want?" I half whispered. Otis mimicked my actions, looking around the room and leaned forward as well.

"He wants us to meet him," he said, holding up a piece of scratch paper with a hastily written address across the top.

"Bullshit! Meet us or you?" I said forcefully in a hushed voice, determined not to let Otis drag me into something.

"I'm not shitting you, Ron. He told me to bring Mr. Pickles along because he had something to show both of us," he said convincingly.

"Trust me, that guy has nothing I want to see."

"Pickles!"

"Come on, Otis, man… I just won the fucking trip to the Bahamas! I don't want to go out there and see this guy," I cried back.

"You won the fucking trip to the Bahamas because of this guy," he shot back. "Besides, what other choice do we have? We don't go see this motherfucker, he's going to get pissed off."

"What if he's already pissed off?" I said, shrugging my shoulders.

"What the fuck, you think he's going to call the office and ask for an appointment to kill us?" Otis asked rhetorically.

"How the fuck should I know how gangbangers go about killing people?" I snapped. He rolled his eyes and snorted, which meant I was being an asshole. "Alright, alright, Jesus Christ. What do you think he wants?" I asked with a little more conviction. Otis leaned into his desk and finally began to stroke his beard.

"I think it might have something to do with the robbery," he said seriously.

"I don't follow you."

"That project was his building."

"So?"

"Maybe he's pissed because his boys didn't get enough money," he said with raised eyebrows.

"You think Ruppert had you set up?" I questioned as if he were insane.

215

"They let me off pretty easy, Pickles. One dude punched my head so I wouldn't start no shit, but that's it. Maybe Ruppert is pissed off that they didn't get more money," he repeated.

"That doesn't make sense. Why would Ruppert want to steal from his own insurance man?" I asked, leaning back in my chair, confused by Otis' logic as usual.

"Ruppert knows that shit's insured; he knows I wouldn't lose anything," he whispered in his choppy baritone voice.

"If that's true, why is he calling you here? And for God's sake, what would he want to show both of us?"

"I think he wants us to pay him some tribute," he said.

"Tribute! We aren't gangsters! You act like this guy is fucking Don Corleone. Besides, if what you're saying is true, how much more could he want?"

"Probably five hundred," Otis said seriously.

"Five hundred bucks!"

"That's the price you got to pay for doing business in the man's building," he said.

"You're dead serious about this, aren't you?" I asked, seeing the fear in Otis' face.

"You can't fuck around with these guys, Pickles. They don't think the same way we do. You know that."

"Alright, look, let's say you're right. Can't we meet him in a restaurant or something? You know, like Michael Corleone did in *The Godfather*, so we feel safe?"

"This ain't no movie, Pickles. You see the lump on my head?" he said, twisting for me to see.

"Exactly, that's my point. You just got your ass kicked out there, and now you want to drag me back with you to pay these fuckers for the privilege. Isn't that ridiculous?" I lamented to a pair of eyes that were all too aware of what happened. We looked at each other for a moment, then turned away and shuffled some papers, pretending that either of us could concentrate on something else besides Ruppert. I was sick to my stomach. I could barely afford to pay my rent, much less come up with $250 for a payoff to a gangster. Dealing with gangsters in real life was a whole lot different than what was portrayed in the movies. Otis was right about that. The one thing all gangsters had in common, whether black or white, from the boroughs of New York City or the projects of Chicago: they were businessmen whose business was all about earning respect on the street and making money.

"You know I don't have that kind of money to just throw at this guy," I lamented with disgust.

"I didn't ask you," Otis replied indignantly.

"I'm saying this isn't fair. We only made $500 each in commission," I pointed out. "Remember, you make three times the amount of money I do. Two hundred and fifty bucks is a fortune for me."

"Pickles, I ain't asking you for a goddamn thing," he said in an angry voice.

"Fuck you, Otis. We're friends, aren't we? We're in this together. I'm not going to leave you hanging. You know that," I said with frustration.

"I ain't worried about it," he said with a shrug.

"Look, all I'm asking is if you can cover this today. I'll make payments back to you. Is that cool?"

"It ain't shit," Otis replied with a crooked grin as if that had been the plan all along. I knew it made him feel better that I was taking some of the responsibility and also helped solidify a friendship that had been growing since we worked together. "Come on, wrap up your shit. I told him we'd be out there in an hour," he commanded.

"An hour! You never said that!"

"I didn't want you to act like a little pussy and run away," he said with a smile.

"You're an asshole," I drawled.

Before leaving the building, Otis stopped at the bank and withdrew $500, of which I agreed to pay half in installments to appease Ruppert for the slight.

We decided to take his car and jumped on the expressway without much conversation. About halfway there, Otis reached into his jacket pocket and took out a handful of "while you were out" notes and handed them to me. "Here, find that address again. It's mixed up in this shit," he barked at me.

"What's the matter? Don't you know where this is?" I asked.

"Should be across the street from my ledger, north of Lake Street, but there ain't nothing there," he said with a tight face, as if straining to remember.

"Nothing? What do you mean, 'nothing'?"

"Shit, Pickles, nothing means goddamn nothing!" he said angrily. I didn't pursue the issue, knowing that our combined stress levels were already on overload.

We got off the expressway and snaked our way around the area until we reached the outskirts of Otis' ledger. After a couple of turns, Otis came to a stop sign and motioned with his head down the intersecting street. "That's where we got to go," he said softly. I could see why he was upset when we turned down the block. It wasn't even a residential street. On the left side was a massive, old brick foundry building that seemed to go on forever. The right side mostly consisted of vacant lots where homes or apartments once stood but had been bulldozed and cleared. All that was left was a dumping ground for discarded furniture and old, beat-up appliances in their place. In the middle of the block stood two brick apartment buildings that even from a distance appeared to be gutted by fire.

"That's got to be Ruppert," Otis said, pointing to a black Lincoln Town Car parked in front of the first building with two men leaning against it smoking cigarettes. Otis and I stopped talking as we pulled up behind their car, having no idea what to expect. As soon as we parked, Ruppert walked over to greet us while the other guy climbed into the driver's seat of the Lincoln. For the middle of the day, Ruppert looked out of place dressed in tight pants and a double-knit shirt, as if he had just walked off the dance floor of some late-night disco.

"How y'all doing?" he asked graciously, extending his hand first to Otis and then to me as I walked around the car to meet him.

"How are you doing, Ruppert?" I asked solemnly, grabbing his hand. Ruppert seemed to sense our apprehension right away and immediately tried to calm our concerns.

"Man, I appreciate y'all coming out on such short notice, but I got some business I got to take care of, you dig?"

"It's cool," Otis replied.

"I got something for you around back," he said, pointing to the remnants of what used to be an apartment building. I looked up at the dilapidated ruins, apparently gutted by fire and abandoned some time ago, wondering why gangsters couldn't ever pick a safe house that didn't reek of death and destruction. "Follow me," he said, assuming we wouldn't disobey his command.

Otis and I gave each other anxious looks before dutifully getting in line behind Ruppert, feeling a little like condemned men being led to the gallows. He took us to the back of the building around a corner and down some stairs into a dark and dingy basement. The only light came in from the basement windows, which were surprisingly still intact. Sitting at an old wooden table with a murderous look on his face was our gun-toting bandito friend from the projects, Mosley. One of his .357 Magnums was lying on the table with his hands inches from the handle, as if daring one of the two young men sitting on the other side to make a move. The two kept their heads focused on the floor and didn't budge an inch when the three of us entered the room. The bandito's expression was grim, and the ferociousness in which he was eyeballing them scared the hell out of me.

One of them was wearing an army jacket and a neatly trimmed Afro. The other had a really dark, almost pitch-black complexion with thick features and dirty, matted hair cropped close to his head. Both looked as if they had endured a beating, but this guy's face was cut up, and he had crunchy, dried blood chunks congealed around both nostrils. I couldn't see the look on Otis' face, but he must have been horrified when Ruppert announced that these were the two men who had robbed him. Neither Otis nor I could speak as Ruppert commanded them to stand up. Apparently, it was these two, and not us, who had incurred the wrath of Ruppert.

"You got something for my insurance man?" Ruppert said with a demanding tone.

"SPEAK UP, MOTHERFUCKERS!" the bandito shouted out immediately.

"Yeah, we fucked up, man," the guy with the army jacket responded in a stuttering voice.

"Did I punch out your fucking vocal cords?" the bandito questioned the other guy.

"No, man, we fucked up," he said without moving a muscle.

"Hey, man. We're really sorry about the other day. We didn't know you were with Ruppert, you know," Army jacket said, not daring to raise his eyes from the floor.

"WHAT ABOUT YOU?" the bandito shouted with ferocity while smashing his fist to the table and directing his displeasure at the scummier-looking guy. I had no idea what was going through the mind of the dirty-haired dude, but I knew what was about to go into my underwear if the bandito even looked in my direction.

"We're sorry, man. We fucked up," the bad-hair guy said in a barely audible voice. Both Otis and I glanced in Ruppert's direction at the same time. He ignored me and stared directly at Otis with an expression that seemed to be asking if he was satisfied with the forced apologies. Otis remained stoic and just slightly nodded his approval to Ruppert, who then seemed anxious to conclude the whole affair.

"Alright, then. What y'all got for my man?" Ruppert demanded as the first guy quickly reached into the pocket of his jacket and retrieved Otis' wallet.

"It's all there," he said, handing it over.

"I appreciate it," Otis choked out.

"Alright," Ruppert said as his expression turned mean in a hurry. He marched up and hovered over them and glared down, as if daring them to make a move. "I ain't got time for all this bullshit. You motherfuckers better check with me before you pull shit in my city, or next time it will be your motherfuckin' asses, y'all dig?" Ruppert said, jabbing a finger into the chest of the dirty-haired guy. The two men just stood there with their heads down, nodding in agreement, as Ruppert turned and left with us in tow. Neither Otis nor I could form words at that point, so we just quietly followed him back outside and around to the front, when suddenly he stopped. He turned towards us with a much calmer demeanor, directing his words at Otis. "I'm sorry to have to drag you guys out here to see that bullshit, but I got to show by example," he said to two people who hadn't caught a breath in nearly a minute.

"Hey, man, you know, ah, thanks for taking care of me and getting my wallet back," Otis growled, struggling for something to say.

"Nobody fucks with my shit or my people," he said, grabbing Otis' hand. "You know how it works," he said with a steely look before releasing his grip and extending his hand towards me.

"Mr. Pickles, you seem a little whiter for some reason," he joked.

"I got to get more sun," I quipped. He laughed then headed for his car and drove away. Otis and I stood frozen as we watched the car roll down the block.

"You want some beer?" Otis asked out of the corner of his mouth.

"I want some toilet paper," I said as we both broke out in laughter and headed for the car.

D.G. ALLEN

CHAPTER 14

The following Saturday, I stopped by Sandra's apartment anxious to see her. Since delivering her policy back in August, I had become a regular fixture at the house. I tried to stop by at least once a week to see how things were going, help her hang a picture, or just chat about life in general. I knew she loved to see me, and even her kids began to look forward to my visits—especially because I always brought some kind of treat or surprise, which her six-year-old daughter, Lucy, seemed to cherish.

We both knew there was something special about our relationship and that one day it might grow into something very special. We also knew our situations were so complex that we couldn't just throw caution to the wind and do whatever we pleased. I was married with a little girl, working a job I despised, while she was divorced with three kids, trying to learn a skill and get a job for the first time in her life. We never even talked about the black and white issue and all the outside garbage that it would bring into our lives. For now, we were both content with our developing friendship, careful not to let emotions get the best of us and cross lines we shouldn't.

Sandra's little apartment was always abuzz with activity on Saturday afternoons, and this day was no different. Two of her girlfriends from beautician's school were just walking out the door when I showed up. Sandra introduced me as "just my insurance man" with a wink in my direction as I came in and they went out. I turned to the left, thinking I would go over to my usual spot on the loveseat when I realized that today everyone was congregated on the right side of the tiny living room.

Her younger children, Lee and Liz, were spread out on the floor, calmly calculating the correct positioning of their toys. Behind them, a clock radio was sitting atop a table, playing a great mix of top ten and oldies tunes. Lucy was sitting on a kitchen chair, propped up on a couple of phone books smack dab in the middle of the living room.

"What are you doing to Lucy?" I asked, studying the top of her head. The poor girl had selected strands of hair pulled away from her scalp and tied up with an array of pink felt strips.

"Oh, she's volunteering—against her will, of course—helping me with some hairstyling homework," Sandra said while removing the stylist apron that covered the jeans and short-sleeved shirt she was wearing.

"She looks a little like a displaced Munchkin from *The Wizard of Oz*," I said, teasing the little girl.

"Mom, can I be done now?" Lucy moaned.

"Just a few more minutes, baby, and I'll start to take those out," Sandra said.

"Can they have these?" I asked Sandra, holding up three boxes of animal cookies.

"I guess, but you have to stop bringing these guys stuff. They're getting spoiled," she said with a commanding tone for the kids' benefit. I gently dropped two of the boxes by the kids on the floor and put one on the lap of a frowning Lucy.

"Will that make it better?" I asked Lucy. She just nodded her approval and tore into the cookies.

"Hey, can you hand me that jar on the table?" Sandra asked while pointing to it.

"Sure. What do you do with this?" I asked.

"It's a moisturizing cream; black girls use it to make their hair shiny. Ain't that right, young lady?" she directed towards Lucy, who was busy chewing off the head of an elephant animal cracker.

"When you finish with that cracker, I'm going to show Mr. Pickles how we put this in your hair."

"Mr. Pickles is a funny name," Lucy giggled with crumbs flying out of her mouth.

"Lucy, every time I come over, you laugh at my name. Why is that?" I teased her.

"Because pickles are something you eat," she could barely say through her laughter.

"Okay, enough with the crackers," Sandra said, looking down at the mess Lucy was making.

"Hey... watch the cracker talk. I'm sensitive," I said, trying to be funny.

"Well, Mr. Sensitive, do me a favor and run into the kitchen and wet a rag so I can wipe this young lady's face," Sandra commanded while ignoring my humor.

"Gosh, I could stay home and get this kind of abuse," I quipped, then dutifully headed into the kitchen and retrieved the rag. As Sandra was toweling off Lucy's face, I noticed the little urchin giving me a funny look. "What do you find so interesting?" I asked her.

"Momma, how come you don't pluck Mr. Pickles?" she asked while chewing the last of her cookie.

"What! What did she say?" I asked, almost falling backwards. Sandra stopped what she was doing, put her hands on her hips, and looked at me with a raised eyebrow. "She said pluck, Ron—pluck with a P," she said, articulating the letter.

"Oh... pluck!"

"You didn't really think she..."

"How am I supposed to know what she said? She's got a mouth full of cookie crumbs, for crying out loud," I tried to defend myself.

Sandra just grinned. "Lucy saw me pluck the eyebrows of one of the girls who just left. Didn't you, young lady? Oh my, you're getting heavy," she said with a grunt while helping Lucy off the chair.

"Okay, you can play with your brother and sister now," she said, patting Lucy on the head before looking at me. "Ron, do me a favor. Go sit by the window for a second," she said, ushering me along while following behind. With a serious expression, she sat down beside me, looking into my face but missing my eyes.

"Is there something wrong?" I asked hesitantly.

"Lean back," she said, ignoring my question while pushing my shoulder back against the couch. She leaned closer, licked her thumb, and slid it across my eyebrow with wide-open eyes and a sly smile creeping across her face.

"Would you mind if I plucked you?" she asked in a sultry voice that sounded like it was mocking my initial reaction. For a moment, I got lost in all the possibilities before coming to my senses.

"Pluck what?" I finally asked.

"Your eyebrows, silly," she said, backing off with a girlish giggle.

"Why would you want to pluck my eyebrows?" I asked incredulously.

"Because they're growing wild," she said. "Hey, Lucy, come over here and tell Momma what you think," she called out. Lucy came running over and crawled up on the other side of me, mimicking her mother by staring at the top of my head.

"You need to be plucked," the little girl snickered before jumping off the couch and running away.

"See? Two women's opinions," Sandra concurred.

"She's six. What does she know? Besides, she's on your payroll. You guys are giving me a complex," I said, attempting to lean forward before being pushed back down by Sandra. "I don't understand why I need to be plucked. I'm very fond of everything I have, and I'd prefer to leave it just the way it is, thank you," I said.

"They're growing wild, Ron. Your wife should be ashamed of herself," she said with a tone of disgust.

"What's she got to do with it?" I asked in a confused voice.

"Every self-respecting woman knows you can't let your man run around with messed-up eyebrows. Another woman sees your eyebrows growing like weeds, and they automatically know that you're not being taken care of at home."

"Really?"

"Yes, I'm serious. So, ah… can I pluck them?" she asked again, sounding a bit like a depraved scientist.

"Well, I don't know, Sandra. I've never been *plucked* before," I said, finding it difficult to say the word.

"Oh, come on. It will be fun." She jumped off the couch and ran into the bathroom. A moment later, she came back with a small manicure case and the jar of cream she had used on Lucy's head and placed them on the couch.

"Hey, wait a minute! You said that cream was supposed to make black girls' hair pretty," I said with concern.

"Oh, don't worry. It's multi-purpose," she said, jumping off the couch and bouncing into the living room. A moment later, she came back with a metal tray loaded with styling tools. At first, she set everything up directly in front of me before shaking her head with a change of mind and moving the tray out of the way.

"Why did you move it so far away?" I asked innocently.

"Just in case you twitch or something. I don't want you to kick it," she said.

"Whoa, whoa, whoa!" I said, waking up in a hurry. "Hold on a second. What would make me twitch enough to knock over a tray?" I asked in a panic. "I'm going to twitch? Is this going to hurt?"

"No, silly. Girls do this every day. Stop worrying," she dismissed.

"But…"

"Will you calm down? It'll take two seconds, and you'll be done. Stop acting like such a baby," she scolded before I had a chance to act like a baby. Lucy wandered back into the room and took her front-row seat beside me with a big grin on her face.

"You two had this planned all along," I grumbled to the little girl who just smiled at me.

"Okay, I want you to lean back and tilt your head up so I can get the best light from the window," Sandra commanded as I tried to follow her directions. "Good," she said while climbing up on my lap and straddling my left leg like she was riding a horse.

"What are you doing?" I asked, instinctively putting my hands on her waist to help her balance as she leaned over my head with long tweezers, ready to pluck her first hair.

"I need a good spot," she replied, seemingly unaware that her shirt had ridden up over her midriff and I was now holding her bare waist in my hands. Even though I couldn't see, I knew that little Lucy was carefully watching the procedure, which made it hard to feel romantic in any way. However, I had to admit that it was giving me considerable pleasure to hold Sandra on my lap, and I began to think I might like this whole plucking thing—until she yanked the first follicle from my forehead.

"JESUS CHRIST! That hurt!" I yelled at the top of my lungs to the immense delight of Lucy, who clapped her approval. "Your kid's got a sadistic side, you know that?" I complained to Sandra while grabbing at my eyebrows to see if I had any left.

"Whew boy, that was a big one," Sandra said, holding the turnip-shaped root from my head for me to examine. Suddenly, Sandra stopped what she was doing and perked up as if she had heard something. "Lucy, run over real quick and turn up the radio. I love that song," she said as I strained to hear what I thought sounded like a Paul McCartney tune. Lucy turned up the sound, and I immediately recognized the piano chords from Paul's song "Maybe I'm Amazed," which brought a smile to my otherwise pained face. Lucy, not wanting to miss a moment of the action, or my reaction to pain, resumed her seat in front of me. For the next few minutes, I endured the agony of the plucking, the pleasure of holding Sandra's waist, and the inspirational music from one-quarter of my favorite band. All this under the watchful eyes of her six-year-old daughter, who seemed terribly disappointed that I didn't act like a bigger baby throughout the ordeal.

When it was finally over and the last wayward nub had been removed from the top of my eye socket, Sandra reached over to the jar of cream and dabbed a touch on her fingertip to massage it into my plucked, swollen brows. The gentle caress of her fingers stroking my forehead did wonders for the sting, and within moments I had completely recovered from my first plucking.

CHAPTER 15

October 1980

The first Thursday morning in October, Teddy Lobranski walked into the agents' office, closed the door, and announced that a special guest had arrived to see Mr. Pickles. He then opened the door and paraded Willie Hawkins, the tobacco-chewing, drunken husband of Winnie Hawkins from Madison Street, to my desk. Willie looked like a refuge from a Salvation Army post. He was rail thin and dressed in the remnants of a suit that looked as if it had just been peeled off the skeletal remains of a corpse circa 1920. His jacket was dirty and tattered, while a stained white shirt hung out of his trousers and appeared to be unraveling by the moment. Both of his shoes, which resembled turn-of-the-century logger boots, were missing chunks of leather, exposing his sockless, gnarled toes underneath. He stank of stale wine and body odor and looked as if he hadn't bathed in quite some time.

Teddy's flamboyant introduction of Willie into the office had the goal of embarrassing me in front of the other agents. It worked like a charm. I could feel everyone's eyes staring at the wretch of a human that had lumbered into the room. Some were taking pity, some were amused at Teddy's stunt, but most were salivating like vultures. They knew that 99 percent of the time a visitor to the office meant a death claim, which all the agents looked upon as an easy sale—or, in some cases, a financial bonanza.

Quickly, I jumped out of my seat and escorted him all the way out into the hallway while giving Teddy a look that made him drop his eyes and return to his desk.

"Yes sir, Mr. Pickles, I's lost Winnie last night," Willie lamented while removing her insurance policy from inside his jacket pocket and holding it up for me to see.

"Last night? Willie, I'm so sorry…" I started to say before he cut me off.

"Yes sir, Mr. Pickles. I's sure does need this 'surance money," he said, fanning out the policy in case I had missed it the first time.

"Okay, Willie, I can see that you are really upset here, so let's see how fast we can fill out the claim form and get you on your way."

"Yes sir, Mr. Pickles, I's sure does need this money bad now thats I's lost my Winnie," he said.

"Okay, why don't you have a seat in here, and I'll go get the forms to fill out so we can get this thing taken care of for you," I said, escorting him to the front office and steering him to a seat while I continued back into the agents' room. I quickly walked over to the supply cabinet against the back wall and had begun searching for the right forms when I felt someone breathing over my shoulder.

"Oh, it's you," I said, taking one look at Teddy and turning away. "You're a fucking asshole," I said with disgust. Though Tom Minka was the official manager of the stoner staff, everyone knew it was Teddy Lobranski they looked to for leadership and advice. Teddy was in his mid-twenties, about six feet tall, bony faced, with thinning blond hair. He was always impeccably dressed and carried himself like a man with a purpose. You only had to know him for a short period of time to know that his sophisticated look was a front for a man who never missed an opportunity to enrich or entertain himself at the expense of others.

"Oh, come on, Pickles. That was classic," he said, grinning from ear to ear.

"Bullshit, Teddy. That was wrong, and you know it," I shot back.

"Alright, fuck that. I'm sorry, man. I just couldn't resist. But listen up, dude. Do you want some help handling this guy?" he asked in a hushed voice, looking around the room like a weasel to make sure no one else could hear.

"I got this one," I said, fumbling for the forms, trying to ignore him.

"Who died?" he asked.

"His wife."

"That's too bad," Teddy said, not caring whatsoever.

"Yeah, she was a nice lady," I said with a solemn tone.

"You know how to do this, right?" he asked.

"I've done claims before," I replied.

"No, man, come on. Pickles, come on, man. You know how to handle this guy, right?" he said forcefully.

"I told you, I've done claims before," I said with annoyance. He looked at me for a moment, then bit on his lip, trying to figure out how to approach me.

"Look, you've got some place to assign the policy, right? You know, some place cool? You know what I mean?" he asked, looking for some kind of affirmation about the scam he was proposing. I finally stopped what I was doing and turned to make eye contact with him so he'd stop pestering me.

"I don't do that shit, Teddy," I said with conviction.

"What shit? Come on, man, I can help you with this!" he pleaded.

"I'm not interested. I'll get him to buy some insurance on himself, but that's all."

"How big is the claim?" he asked point-blank.

"Teddy, it doesn't matter." I hesitated, not really wanting to tell him. "...It's five thousand, alright?"

"Five thousand! Shit, Ronnie, don't be a fool," he said. "You know what that drunken piece of shit is going to do with $5,000?"

"I really don't care, Teddy. He's the beneficiary. It's his money," I shot back.

"Ronnie, I got a guy on my ledger that can help us out."

"Not interested, Teddy!"

"Come on, man, don't be a dick. Just listen to what I have to say," he said, inching closer and pretending to help search out the right forms. "This guy I know owns a funeral home on my ledger. We can trust him. We assign the policy to him, he picks up the body, gives it a decent burial, and kicks back a hunk of change to the good guys in suits. You dig?"

"What does Willie get?"

"Fuck Willie! Willie will think he's hit the fucking jackpot. We'll buy him a couple of cases of Mad Dog 20/20 and give him five hundred bucks. He'll be thrilled to death. I mean, Pickles, did you get a good look at that guy? You don't want to give that fucking piece of shit five grand. You'd be nuts!" he said louder than he wanted, glancing around to make sure he hadn't attracted anyone's attention.

"Sorry, Teddy, just can't do it," I said as Meadows came up from behind, startling both of us.

"Ron, don't listen to this punk motherfucker," he said angrily in Teddy's face.

"Fuck you, Ray. This is none of your business," Teddy slammed back.

"He's on my staff. That makes it my business, punk. You guys do whatever the hell you want on your own staff, but you leave my guys alone, you dig?" he said, backing Teddy down.

"Fuck, Pickles, you don't know what you're missing, man. This nigger doesn't give a shit about you," Teddy muttered out of the side of his mouth. Meadows immediately grabbed him by the collar and banged him hard into the open cabinet, spilling forms all over the floor.

"You ever call me that again, boy, and I'll put your head through this goddamn wall," he shouted two inches away from Teddy's face. The bent look on Teddy was priceless, almost confirming a change of shorts would be in the offering. Instantly, Hamilton's voice rang out across the room as Meadows loosened his grip on Teddy's throat.

"Gentlemen, I'd like to see you both in my office this minute," he called out from the doorway.

"I'm sorry, man. I shouldn't have said that, Ray," Teddy apologized as Meadows released him and turned towards an office filled with stunned expressions.

"Hey, Ray, this is just between us, right?" Teddy asked in a trembling voice while putting a hand on Meadows' shoulder.

"Get your hand off me, boy," Meadows said with a scowl. "I told you, Teddy, I don't give a shit what you guys do on your staff, but you leave my guys alone."

"Cool, man. I hear you, Ray. So, are we cool, then?" he asked, holding out his hand.

"Yeah, we're cool," Meadows said with a fierce expression, ignoring Teddy's extended hand. "Go in and tell Roger I'll be in his office in a minute," he commanded as Teddy nodded in obedience and headed for Hamilton's office. Ray turned towards me and stared hard into my eyes.

"You know those guys are bad news, right?" he asked me with fatherly concern.

"Don't worry, Ray. I know what I'm doing," I said.

"It's one thing to assign your client some insurance, but you don't want to get mixed up in that other shit," he said.

"It's cool, Ray. I'm not into that," I assured him.

"Alright," he said with a deep sigh. "You want some help with the client?" he asked.

"No, I'm good, thanks. Now, get in there and come up with a good excuse why you had to kick Teddy's ass," I said with a smile, nudging him along in front of me.

"Is there something wrong, Mr. Pickles?" Willie asked when I got back to him. "I's heard all that noise in there," he continued.

"Oh, no, that was nothing, Willie. A couple of agents were discussing the proper way to stock the supply cabinet and accidentally bumped into it. I do need to talk to you about this insurance settlement and see how you want to handle it," I said while holding out an intimidating array of forms in front of him.

"I's need my money. That's the one thing I's know for sure," he said.

"Yeah, I got that part, Willie, but we got to take care of a couple of things before I can get you that money, okay?"

"Whatever we got to do," he said.

"Well, first of all, did you make the burial arrangements for Winnie yet?"

"Her sister is doing all of that," he said.

"I didn't even know she had a sister," I said with surprise. "How do you want to pay for the burial?" I asked.

"Her sister is taking care of all that."

"I understand she is handling the arrangements, Willie, but don't we need to take some money out of this policy and give it to the funeral home so Winnie gets put away nice?" I suggested. In a heartbeat, his expression changed from a man looking for sympathy to a man filled with contempt at the slightest notion that Winnie's insurance money was going anywhere besides his pocket.

"Not with this money! This money is mine!" he insisted. "Her sister is going to take care of all the other stuff," he said with an aggravated tone. I looked directly into his bloodshot eyes and knew he was lying.

"Okay," I finally said with a sigh. "You got the policy right here, but I didn't see the death certificate. Were you able to get that already?"

"What death certificate?"

"The piece of paper that says Winnie died."

"Damn, Mr. Pickles. I ain't got no paper that said she died, but I know she did," he insisted.

"I'm sure she died, Willie. I'm not suggesting that she didn't, but one of the rules is that you have to give the company some proof so that bums don't walk in off the street and claim their wives died when, in fact, they hadn't," I said, knowing the inference would go right over his head.

"I ain't got one," he said.

"Well, that's a problem," I said with a deep breath. "I could help you, but, unfortunately, you're not my client."

"You was Winnie's 'surance man. That makes you my 'surance man," he said angrily.

"Yeah, but Winnie's no longer with us, so I ain't nobody's 'surance man. Unless, well… never mind," I said, waiting for him to question me.

"Unless what?"

"Well, if we wrote you up an insurance policy, then I would become your insurance man," I said.

"I don't want no damn 'surance. I just wants my money!" he shouted.

"I know. Forget about it. It was stupid. I know you don't mind waiting six months for the money," I said, knowing just what buttons to push.

"Six months! What the hell kind of bullshit is that… Why I got to wait six months to gets my money?" he demanded to know.

"You don't have to wait six months if you stay a customer and let me get you some insurance," I said.

"What do you mean?"

"Well, for one thing, you don't have a death certificate, and I can't apply for a certificate if you're not my customer because I don't work for free. Secondly, the company knows they have to pay out the claim because Winnie died and she had this policy for longer than two years, but they can take up to six months to send out the money if they want to. It's in the contract. So, they keep the money as long as they can because they make extra interest on it. Plus, they won't even start the paperwork until they get the death certificate, so it's up to you, Willie. You know how big business works."

"I's sure do. They always got a way to fuck the little guy," he snarled.

"Exactly!" I said, pointing at him with both hands as if he knew the hidden secret.

236

"So, we have to be smarter than them, and the way we do that is by writing you up an insurance policy and paying it for two years. Do you follow me?"

"I ain't got no money for no 'surance," he said, shaking his head.

"You don't need any. We'll assign the company authority to withdraw two years of payments from the death benefit so you don't have to pay anything. That would make me… your 'surance man, so I can apply for the death certificate. Once the company sees that you're making an investment with them, they'll write you a check in the next few weeks so they can take their cut. It's really a pretty good deal if you think about it. You get your money, and you get to make an investment at the same time."

"That sounds alright, then," he said with a nod.

"Okay, come on up to the window and sign these forms, and I'll get this thing started," I said, leading him to Mrs. Bolger's window. I helped him find the signature lines on the forms and watched as he scratched his name into the paper. I don't know why, but for some reason, I actually began to feel sorry for the guy. Though it galled me to admit it, Teddy was probably right; just looking at him, I knew that Willie was going to blow through this money as if there were no tomorrow. I wondered if there was some way I could get through to him and convince him to spend it wisely.

"Willie, it's your money, and I know you probably need to get some things for yourself and all, but it might be a good idea to put some of that money away in the bank, you know?" I said with a suggestive tone as he signed the last form. I picked up the paperwork and walked with him out to the elevator.

"Yes sir, Mr. Pickles, I'm going to be making me some smart investments. You can be sure of that," he said with a smile. "When did you say I'd be getting my money?"

"It will be sent out in a few weeks from the home office. I have to get the death certificate first, but you should have it by the end of the month. Don't forget, I'm your 'surance man now, so I'll be stopping by with your new policy."

"That's good. I'll be looking forward to seeing you then," he said.

"Okay, see you, Willie," I said, escorting him out to the elevator.

CHAPTER 16

The phone woke me up early the following Monday with an anxious call from my video football playing buddy, Craig Branson. He apologized, saying he couldn't meet me at the arcade later that day as planned. It seemed that Mr. Uhlen, the only guy in the office to ever bring me a cup of coffee, got robbed and beaten up pretty badly on Saturday night. "Damn, Craig, what was he doing out there on a Saturday night?" I cried into the phone after he relayed the story.

"I don't know, Ronnie. My manager, Mr. Singh, is losing his mind right now. He just called to ask if I could come in and help rebuild Mr. Uhlen's ledger book. You know how the Jewish guys always carry it into the houses with them."

"Yeah, Meadows told me I wasn't allowed to do that," I recalled.

"Now you know why," he added.

"Jeez, how bad is he hurt?"

"I'm not sure. I guess he got smacked around pretty good."

"Are you serious?"

"Yeah. According to Singh, the doctors told his wife he was lucky he didn't get killed."

"Holy shit! I can't believe this—first Otis, now Uhlen."

"This job sucks," Craig sighed into the phone.

"I know. I'm getting to the point where I can't stand this shit anymore," I said.

"I know what you mean. It's bullshit."

"It's just one thing after another, you know? I'm starting to wonder if those crazy fuckers like Wicks, Guru, or even Meadows might not be right about this place," I said, thinking out loud.

"What do you mean?"

"I don't know. They think the black ledger is haunted by some evil entity that's out to get you," I said with a snicker.

239

"Seriously?" Craig laughed.

"No shit. Meadows claims the ledger will only leave you alone if it's convinced you are deathly afraid to be there and never lose respect for the power it possesses."

"He actually told you this?" he asked in disbelief.

"That ain't nothing. Wicks told me the ledger was the embodiment of evil that thrived by sucking the life out of poor people who couldn't escape its grasp. ...And you've been in the office when Crazy Guru goes off during a meeting and announces his refusal to work because the ledger is angry and nobody else should work either," I said, laughing out loud.

"I fucking forgot about that!" Craig cried in hysterics. "Holy shit! Remember how pissed off Hamilton was when Guru went off?" he asked.

"It was classic," I chuckled.

"Oh man, I'm so glad I talked to you," he said with a lilt in his voice that had been missing. "You made me feel a lot better. This fucking job."

"I know. But hey, all kidding aside, I hope Mr. Uhlen is okay," I said seriously.

"Yeah, me too. It sounds like he's going to heal okay. It's just crazy on our staff right now, you know?"

"I know. Hey, if you need some help with something, give me a call, okay?"

"Okay, Ron. I better get going. Sorry to call you with this shit. Thanks for making me feel better," he said.

"No, don't worry, I appreciate the call. Just take care of your business, and I'll talk to you later," I said and hung up the phone. I sat at the kitchen table for a while, rubbing my tired eyes, feeling sick over the news about Mr. Uhlen. Until that moment, I had never taken anyone seriously or attributed the seemingly endless array of violence, destitute living conditions, or lack of self-worth to an unseen evil force, but I had to admit, the swell of sad, bizarre, or horrific events surrounding me seemed never-ending and progressively worsened as time went by. Perhaps I was magnifying things in my own mind, but the mood on the ledger seemed to darken around me after losing the opportunity to become an electrician. I felt like a man in a glass bubble dodging trouble, witnessing one incident after another. I couldn't help but wonder how long my luck would hold out.

No one talked about Mr. Uhlen before the Thursday meeting, as the usual chaos of conducting business took precedence over a casualty of war. Even Mr. Hamilton chose to avoid the gory details of Mr. Uhlen's attack, probably figuring too much information might induce a mass mutiny of the office. Instead, he mentioned the hospital where Mr. Uhlen was recuperating and said the office was taking up a collection to send him flowers, to which we all donated.

After the meeting, only Craig Branson, his manager, Mr. Singh, Mr. Meadows, and I remained in the office. We worked quietly, hammering out paperwork while sitting at our respective staff positions. As if wanting to unburden himself, Mr. Singh pushed away from his desk and sauntered over by us, pulling up a chair close to Meadows. Ray looked over at me with a slight shrug as if irritated by the intrusion. I shrugged back and raised my eyebrows, just as surprised as he was.

Mr. Singh was a dark-skinned, short, plump little guy from India with a heavy accent that could be difficult to understand at times. He was all about business and rarely conversed with anyone off the topic of insurance. His staff always led the office in sales, but as Meadows would joke, "A monkey could lead that staff with the sales from those Jewish guys." He wasn't so much a manager as he was a caretaker. His job was to unburden the likes of Mr. Uhlen and Mr. Guru from tedious paperwork so they could concentrate on sales. Craig was often the beneficiary of extra sales because he was the only guy on their staff willing to be managed by Mr. Singh.

"I don't get these guys, Ray," he said loud enough for both of us to hear. I immediately looked across the room at Craig, who jumped from his chair to come sit by us. Singh waited for Craig to sit down, then leaned back and sighed, "You don't know how competitive these Jewish fellows are. Did you know that it is a personal affront to them if someone other than a Jew is beating them in sales?" he stated as the three of us gathered close to hear what he was saying.

"You mean Otis Wahl," Meadows said, pointing to the leader board with his pipe.

"He was very upset last week. I tried to calm him down. I tried to tell him he needed to start selling more MDO like Otis, but he would not listen. All the old Jews were taught to sell the weekly insurance, and that is all they know. I tell them… you have to sell twice the amount of people that Otis does just to keep pace. Mr. Uhlen got so mad at me last week, you would not believe. He was going to prove me wrong and began canvassing at night to get extra sales," he said to the blank expressions on all three of our faces. "So, by Saturday, he had already sold more than $40 of weekly premium."

"No shit," Meadows cried out at the incredible number.

"It is true. He was even talking about going for the company record," he said with a chuckle.

"Hamilton's record?" Meadows questioned in disbelief.

"Who knows what he was thinking," Singh said.

"What is the record?" Craig inquired.

"Three hundred," Meadows replied.

"Are you fucking serious?" I asked.

"That's why he sits in the big office, Ronnie," Singh said with a chuckle.

"He wasn't even close," Craig interjected.

"I'm just saying that was his mentality. That's what was driving him. Making him nuts," Singh said.

"Greed, that's all. The motherfucker got his ass kicked because he was greedy," Ray said unsympathetically. Craig and I turned towards Meadows, bewildered at his callous response. He had already picked up his pipe and begun preparing for the never-ending cleaning ritual. "Where did he keep the collection money from the weekend?" Ray asked as an afterthought. We looked back at Singh, who dropped his eyes as if embarrassed to say.

"He had it on him," he finally admitted while shaking his head with disgust.

"How much?" I asked.

"Over two grand," Singh replied sheepishly. Simultaneously, we all dropped our mouths in amazement at the stupidity of carrying that kind of money on your person while canvassing.

"Oooooh, I bet the company ain't happy about losing that kind of cash," Craig said with a grimace.

"Crazy Jew knows better than that," Meadows sighed while digging hard into his pipe.

"That's just ridiculous," I said.

"You can bet fucking Hamilton is already planning a meeting to discuss the amount of cash someone should carry," Meadows added. "What did I teach you the first week you were hired, Ron?"

"Never carry more than $500 at one time. Put the rest in the car. If it gets stolen there it doesn't matter," I said dutifully.

"...And why do we do that?"

"Because crooks aren't stupid," I finished.

"Exactly, because crooks aren't stupid. They know what crime they're committing and how much time they'll have to do if they get caught. Uhlen ain't no goddamn rookie. He knows how this shit works," Ray said with disgust to Mr. Singh.

"I don't know what he was thinking, Ray. It was stupid," Singh confessed.

"He should be dead," Meadows deadpanned.

"Why do you say that? They got their money. What good does it do to kill the guy and risk getting fried in the chair?" Craig asked with a frown. Ray Meadows turned his attention to Craig and lectured him in a stern tone.

"Did you hear what I said? Because motherfuckers know what crime they're committing and how much time they'll have to do if they get caught. Hitting some nigga on the head and grabbing a hundred bucks might cost them a year," Ray said, glancing at me in reference to Otis. "That's if, and I mean IF, anyone bothers to report it. But aggravated grand theft on a white man by a Negro is a big-time felony. The police WILL come looking for you. Trust me. It may take time, but someone will blow on your ass when it gets hot, and you will get caught. That shit could cost you twenty years to life, and these motherfuckers know it. They're better off to kill a motherfucker so he can't testify against you. Shit, even if you get caught for the murder, you're better off copping a plea," Meadows said to a captivated audience.

"You know your shit," Craig laughed.

"Hell yeah! They don't want you to testify. A motherfucker would probably get less time for killing the guy than leaving him alive," Ray said with a satisfied flourish.

"Did he actually see who attacked him?" Craig asked in Singh's direction.

"It is still a big blur for him," Singh said. "He cannot say if he was followed or set up or anything. All he can remember is walking into the hallway of the apartment where several large men began to beat him, and... beat him they did," he emphasized before Irene interrupted, saying that Mr. Hamilton would like to see Mr. Singh in his office. Mr. Meadows, Craig, and I just sat there looking at each other in disbelief as Mr. Singh walked away. As soon as Singh left the room, Meadows stood up, peeked into the office window, and sat back down and leaned towards me and Craig. "That's a load of bullshit is what that was," he said in a hushed tone.

"What do you mean?" I questioned.

"That shit didn't go down that way," he said.

"The guy is in the hospital, Ray," Craig pointed out as if exasperated by his logic.

"I'm not saying he didn't get fucked up. I'm saying that shit you just heard don't jive."

"What doesn't jive?" I asked incredulously.

"I don't believe it. That old Jewish motherfucker has been working in the ghetto for twenty years. Why would he carry $2,000 in his pocket while canvassing?" he asked indignantly.

"It really doesn't make sense when you put it that way," I added.

"Why would Singh lie about it?" Craig asked with shrugged shoulders.

"I didn't say he was lying," Meadows said with raised eyebrows. "I'm saying I don't believe the story he's telling is accurate or that the story he was told is exactly what happened," he continued.

"I'm not following you, Ray," I said honestly.

"Me neither," said Craig.

"Look, you two are both fairly new around here and haven't seen half the shit that I have, okay? But one thing you should both know is that a lot of shit goes down in this office that we never know the truth about, and getting ripped off to the tune of two thousand bucks while claiming you were trying to break a sales record is pure bullshit."

"You think Uhlen deliberately hurt himself to steal the money?" Craig asked.

"Could be, but I doubt it. I think it's something else," Meadows replied.

"Like what?" I chirped.

"Some kind of setup is what I think," he said.

"Set up for what?" I asked.

"I don't fucking know, Ron," he shot back at my persistence. "I'm just saying you shouldn't be too quick to believe this 'holier than thou' story that ended in a tragedy. It's too contrived, and there is no way Uhlen carries that money with him on a Saturday night," he said while wrapping up his stuff and preparing to leave.

"Well, that's fucked up," I said.

"It is what it is," Ray said with a sigh while picking up his stuff and heading for the door. Craig and I watched as he left the room before we turned towards each other with bewildered looks on our faces.

"What the fuck was all that about?" Craig asked.

"Oh, that was Mr. Meadows telling us that he thinks your manager and Mr. Uhlen are full of shit," I said politely.

"Yeah, I got that part, Ron," he replied with a blank expression. "But why do you think he doesn't believe the story?"

"Honestly, Meadows is kind of weird, but he's really good at common sense and intuition. If he doesn't think something is right, it probably isn't, you know? He ain't buying this shit at all," I said, pausing for a moment and pondering the logic of Meadows' argument. "Truthfully, after listening to him, I'm not so sure I am either," I said while scooping my papers into a pile and sliding them into my briefcase.

"It's definitely fucked up," Craig said with a sigh as he pushed away from the desk and stood up. "Gotta do video football real soon," he said, walking back to his desk.

"Let's get together next week," I said as I headed for the door.

"Sounds like a plan."

CHAPTER 17

November 1980

I've never smelled the ocean, never heard the rustle of palm leaves as they gently caressed each other in a warm tropical breeze, and most certainly never rode in an airplane, much less a cruise ship. For the first time in a long time, I forgot my troubles and even shared my exuberance with Jessica, greatly anticipating the Bahamas trip coming up that second weekend in November. Unfortunately, neither one of us knew the first thing about traveling. When we were told that the company paid for everything, we figured $300 would be more than enough spending money for a weekend trip. However, less than six hours into the cruise, we stumbled into the shipboard casino and shortly thereafter we had to make do with about $20 for the rest of the weekend.

From the pool deck, we watched with envy as just about everyone else in our group disembarked the ship and took part in the offshore excursions the cruise line offered at an additional fee. Other than taking a quick walk around Nassau, we spent most of our time on the ship, sitting by the pool, trying to ignore the server's desperate attempts to sell us drinks.

Mr. Uhlen had recovered nicely from his injuries and spent most of the weekend just lounging poolside with his wife, baking in the sun. Jessica and I were grateful for their company and pulled up chairs next to them, pretending to be relaxing by choice rather than circumstance. I was dying to ask him what happened the night he was robbed, but the whole office agreed not to talk about business on vacation, so I refrained. Instead, we stretched out, took in the ambiance of the tropical paradise, and enjoyed the occasional chitchat of friends soaking up the sun.

"This is the life, Ronnie, my boy."

"It is when you blow all your money in the casino," I said somewhat sarcastically.

"If you need some money…"

"No thank you, Mr. Uhlen. We have everything we need. I was just joking," I laughed.

"You're a good boy, Ronnie. Someday, you will be a very wealthy man, and none of this will matter," he said. trying to comfort my loss.

"Well, according to my mother, Swedes are horrible drunks and bad gamblers, so if this weekend is any indication of my future earning potential, I'm in big trouble," I said to everyone's amusement.

"So, you're Swedish?" he asked.

"Partly. I think I'm pretty much a mutt, but my mom said I was Swedish on her side and Pennsylvania Dutch on my dad's side, whatever that is," I laughed.

"That is German," he said gleefully. I opened my eyes and looked over to find him smiling in my direction. I felt uncomfortable for a moment, wondering if he thought badly of me for being part German, considering his history in the concentration camps and all.

"I didn't know that," I said humbly.

"Yes, the Pennsylvania Dutch were a group of Germans that immigrated to the United States in the early 1800s and settled in Pennsylvania," he said.

"Wow, how did you know that?" I asked.

"Well, I'm Jewish by faith but German in heritage. German history was taught in grammar school, just like American History is taught here," he said with a coy smile.

"You know more about me than I do," I chuckled.

"It's our business to know people, Ronnie," he said with a smile.

"Oh God, you're not going to try and sell me insurance, are you?" I said with a feigned look of horror on my face.

"Only $5 per week, Ronnie. I'm sure you can afford it if you stay out of the casino," he said dryly. I shook my head and snorted my approval before closing my eyes and drifting into a semiconscious state without a care in the world.

The three-day vacation came and went so fast, we were home Monday afternoon, suffering jet lag, before we knew it. A bunch of tired agents lumbered into the office Tuesday morning as more of a courtesy than anything else. Otis regaled everyone about the size of a marijuana joint a Jamaican guy gave him at a reggae club, and Teddy Lobranski chimed in with a hoot, exclaiming he met the same guy. We were all bantering about the great time we had on the trip, laughing and joking, when I got up to return a wayward piece of mail to Irene.

I sauntered up to the counter, about to call out her name, when I noticed a vaguely familiar woman standing in the reception room through the other window. She was tall and pale with brown hair, nicely dressed, but not really attractive, with a grim look on her face. I stared at her for a moment, then realized she was T.J.'s wife. A somber-looking Roger Hamilton greeted her a moment later with a familiarity reserved for family members, then escorted her into his office. I called out to Irene that I was leaving the mail on the counter and returned to my desk, feeling as if something was really wrong.

My instincts proved correct when Mr. Hamilton came into the agents' room a bit later, closed the big oak doors behind him, and asked for everyone's attention as he walked up to the podium. He informed us there would be no meeting today and that poor old T.J., who was fired after the hot dog incident, was found dead over the weekend. He went on to say that Mrs. Bolger would have information on the funeral arrangements if anyone cared to attend. We all watched in stunned silence as Hamilton lowered his head and started to leave.

The news caught everyone off guard, except for Craig Branson, who seemed perturbed that Hamilton didn't give more detail. "Wait,

Roger. What happened?" he called out from his desk as Hamilton reached the doors. I think everyone in the room was grateful to Craig, glad he had the nerve to challenge Roger and demand more information. Hamilton came to a stop and turned towards us with a look of exasperation on his face, as if hoping he could escape without going into details. He looked around the room at the somber faces staring back at him and realized we needed more. He walked back to the podium to address us properly. Pausing for a moment, he looked around the room and took a deep breath before speaking.

"You know, gentlemen, in this business we deal with death all the time, and we teach ourselves to accept death as a part of life. Our business is death. We profit from selling people on the idea of dying and protecting their loved ones from the financial loss that occurs when they die," he stated, as if this were the perfect time to take a tragic occurrence and turn it into a sales lecture. Otis and I looked at each other and rolled our eyes, instantly recognizing the bullshit Hamilton was doling out. "However, I think it's pretty well known that T.J. had some problems and some difficulties dealing with those problems. We don't know any of the particulars, and it's impossible to speculate as to someone's frame of mind, but it appears T.J. committed suicide," he said to a chorus of collective gasps. "Apparently, he drove his car into Green Lake, south of the city, and was found when some debris floated to the surface. I'm sure you all can appreciate the sensitivity of this situation and will demonstrate your professionalism by respecting the privacy of the family during this time," he said with a stern expression on his face before leaving the podium and exiting the room.

The jubilation from our trip died the moment he made the announcement. A few agents murmured amongst themselves, but mostly everyone, even Otis, went quiet. A few minutes later, I found myself standing in line behind Mr. Wicks, waiting for a cup of coffee, when he turned to me with a worn look on his face.

"That's nice to come back to," he said with sadness in his tone.

"I know what you mean," I replied. "Well, if you believe things happen in threes, maybe this will be the end of it," I pondered out loud.

"What do you mean?"

"Well, first it was Otis, then Uhlen, and now T.J.," I said.

"Maybe you're right. I never thought about it before, but each one worse than the last," he added.

"It is kind of weird. It's actually scary," I said.

"Seems like the ledger will hang on and get you even after you leave this job," he said softly.

"You mean T.J.?"

"Uh huh."

"I don't know, Mr. Wick's. The guy was pretty messed up," I said.

"What made him that way?" he asked rhetorically. I looked at his tired face for a moment, contemplating a response. I didn't necessarily agree that it was an entity from the black ledger that followed him around and caused him to commit suicide, but I had to admit, it sure seemed that way.

"This may shock you, Mr. Wicks, but I'm starting to think you may not be as crazy as I once thought you were," I said with a smile as I emptied the last few drops of coffee into my cup. He just looked at me and chuckled before returning to his desk. Later that afternoon, I was alone in the office, filling out a route card for collections, when Meadows came out of a meeting from Hamilton's office and sat down at his desk. He didn't say anything, but the look on his face was positively grim.

"Is everything alright?" I asked as he began to spread out his pipe-cleaning equipment.

"I just found out about T.J.," he said.

"Oh, I thought you were here when Hamilton made the announcement," I said.

"I was, but that was all Roger wanted the office to know," he said.

"What, is there something else?"

"Oh yeah..." Meadows sang out with a nervous laugh as he began to stuff the pipe.

"Well..."

"This is between you and me. Do you understand?"

"Sure, Ray, what's up?

"T.J. became fish food," he whispered as if telling me a state secret. I stared at him with a blank expression. "You know what fish food means, don't you?" he asked at my obvious lack of excitement in his revelation.

"Ray, I hate to steal your thunder here, but I understand the reference of becoming fish food if you commit suicide by driving your car into lake. It's not a hard reach," I said sarcastically. He looked at me and snorted his disgust at my response.

"Why do you always have to be a smartass when I'm trying to tell you something?" he grumbled. "You don't know shit!"

"Okay, Ray. What does it mean to turn into fish food?" I said, surrendering with my hands in exasperation.

"It means the motherfucker has been in the bottom of the lake for six or seven weeks," he said with an animated expression.

"What? I thought this just happened over the weekend while we were gone," I asked in disbelief.

"Exactly! That mother got eaten down to the BONE!" he said with the necessary dramatic emphasis, ignoring my question.

"This don't make sense, Ray. How come we didn't hear about it before now?"

"They just found him over the weekend."

"That's what I wanted to know," I said, thinking our conversation was turning into a macabre version of Abbott and Costello's "Who's on First?" routine. "How come no one mentioned he was missing before this?" I asked.

"I guess nobody knew or cared. His wife gave up on him after she caught him cheating on her again," he said while stuffing his pipe with tobacco.

"You mean back when he threw the hot dog at me?"

"Naw, this was just a couple of months ago. Roger said he was still shacking with that woman over on 38th and Prairie."

"That slutty whore!" I cried in disgust. "Don't tell me he was still seeing her?"

"Listen up," he said, putting a match to his pipe and sucking hard to get it lit. Once the air was filled with a plume of smoke, he continued. "He got himself a job as a truck driver for some company that distributes bread. Roger said he was stopping by this broad's house during the day to get laid and drugged up before finishing his route. You know his wife has been on his ass ever since he pulled that shit working here."

"I can imagine."

"So, he stops by the girl's house a couple of months back, and guess what?"

"What?"

"His wife was waiting outside for him and goes crazy on his ass when he walks out the door."

"Holy shit, are you kidding me? I can see where this is going already," I said, shaking my head at the thought of it.

"You might think you do, but you don't," he said, pursing his lips. "You know those step vans that only have a driver's seat?"

"Sure, with the big windows in front."

"Right, well, that's the kind of truck he was driving. So, he freaks out when he sees his wife, jumps in the truck, and speeds away. His wife starts chasing him in her car, and she's got their two kids in the back seat."

"You got to be kidding me," I said in disbelief.

"I wish I was," he sighed. "Yeah, T.J. thought he'd be slick and lose her by jumping on the Dan Ryan Expressway, but he turned the truck so fast that he lost control halfway down the ramp and just barely missed slamming into the back of a broken-down car on the shoulder."

"Wow!"

"Roger said he had to be going about forty or fifty miles an hour."

"Where were the wife and kids?"

"Right behind him," he said.

"Damn!"

"Yep, she ends up slamming into the broken-down car while that motherfucker just keeps on driving," he said with contempt.

"I take it they were okay since I saw his wife in the office this morning.

"Yeah, they got banged up a little, but that was the end of that marriage," he said.

"Oh my God," I murmured under my breath, in total dismay at the story he had just relayed.

"That was the last time anyone saw him alive," he drawled.

CHAPTER 18

Later that week, I pulled up and parked in front of the liquor store on Madison Street. I had been driving around with Willie's life insurance policy in my car since before the Bahamas trip and figured this afternoon would be as good of a time as any to drop it off. I didn't feel any urgency to deliver it for several reasons, not the least of which was the fact that I really didn't like the guy. I was still feeling kind of down about T.J., and even more so when I looked up at Willie's apartment above the liquor store, realizing that a smiling Winnie wouldn't be there to greet me.

It was kind of chilly outside, so I reached into the back seat and grabbed my leather jacket, stuffed the policy inside my pocket, and got out of the car. There was the usual array of unemployed and homeless people meandering around the store. As customary, I had to ask one of the occupants spread out across Willie's door to temporarily vacate in order for me to ring the bell.

As I waited patiently for Willie to buzz me in the building, a younger looking black man dressed in typical homeless fashion approached and asked if I could spare a dollar. He seemed pleasant enough and asked with a polite manner. I usually gave somebody in front of the liquor store a couple of bucks to watch my car anyway, so I figured on giving this guy a buck and asking him to do the same.

I knew I had forty or fifty dollars in different denominations folded in my front pocket, but I sure wasn't going to pull out that wad in front of everyone at the liquor store. I always kept my singles outside of the fold, so I reached into my pocket and separated one bill from the rest with my fingertips, figuring I would produce a dollar for the guy. Pulling my hand from my pocket, I cringed when I saw the ten-dollar bill. I felt bad seeing the smile on the guy's face, but there was no way I was going spot this guy a ten to watch my car, so I just shrugged my shoulders and said, "I'm sorry, man. All I got is a ten-dollar bill."

"Not a problem," he said, reaching into the back pocket of his pants and producing a fist full of bills. Without hesitation, he snatched the ten from my fingers, then peeled back $9 in change and handed it to me like a clerk at a store. He nodded his appreciation and then walked away. I looked around quickly to see if anyone had been paying attention, relieved that no one else saw me get hustled out of a buck. The buzzer finally went off, and I pulled the door open as another guy sitting up against the building called out to me.

"Hey, y'all tell Willie to get his sorry ass down here so's we can do some drinking," he said.

"I'll be sure to pass that along," I said with a courteous tone as I entered the stairwell and walked up the stairs to what now was just Willie's apartment. I must have pounded on the door at least five times and stood there for what seemed like an eternity waiting for him to let me in. When he finally opened the door, I almost gagged with the stench that blew past me like a pent-up burst of fire looking for much-needed oxygen. It literally burned my eyes while practically suffocating me as I took in the polluted air. The stink was so heavy that it pushed me back a few steps, forcing me to turn my head and close my eyes trying to adjust to it. For the briefest of moments, I actually wondered if Winnie's decomposing body was still in the apartment, knowing Willie's adamant refusal to part with any cash to bury his dead wife. After a moment, I opened my eyes to find a smiling Willie standing in front of me, dressed to the nines in a brand-new suit with shoes to match. Even though the cloud of stink surrounding him took much of the luster from his new duds, I had to admit that he looked pretty good.

"Wow! Now that's quite an improvement from the last time I saw you," I complimented his new look while trying to breathe through my mouth.

"Yes sir, Mr. Pickles," he said with a mile-long grin.

"Willie, I have to admit, you look real sharp," I said, thinking to myself that a new suit of clothes was better than drinking the money away. "But, um, not to be rude or anything, ah, you know when sometimes you're in the house for a while, and sometimes the trash needs to go out, and you don't even realize it because you're used to it? You know what I mean?" I said, nodding my head with a smile, trying to be as polite as I could without telling him that his house smelled like a garbage dump.

"Yeah, it's probably something outside," he said, oblivious to my point. "Them ol' drunken nigga's always pissing down there stinking up the place," he continued. "Now, come on in so that smell don't bother you," he said, holding the door open as if offering me sanctuary. With all the inner strength I could muster, I stepped into his apartment, grieving more than ever for the passing of Winnie who, for in that moment, I gained unwavering admiration.

"Yes sir, you remember what I told you in your office?" he asked.

"I'm sorry, Willie. I have trouble remembering what happened yesterday," I said, delusional from the stink.

"I told you I's going to make an investment with that money," he stated firmly.

"Oh yeah, I remember."

"Yes sir, Mr. Pickles. I's told you I was going to take that money and make an investment, and that's just what I done," he said proud as punch while I almost cried when he shut the door.

"Really? Did you put some of that money away in the bank?" I asked, desperately trying to get my mind off the smell.

"No, I told you that I made an investment with that money. Wait here, I'll show you," he said, disappearing into another room. While he was gone, I walked over to the kitchen, hoping to find a bubble of oxygen that didn't reek. For the briefest of moments, I was distracted from my agony when I spotted the old insurance receipt book still tacked up on the wall where Winnie put it the last time I was there. I could almost see her running around the kitchen looking for her purse, or cleaning a jar until it sparkled, then pouring me some ice water - fond memories I wanted to keep for Winnie's sake.

Unfortunately, there was nothing fond about the kitchen table where Winnie and I would sit and chat for a while on my visits. It was loaded with discarded carryout containers and spilled food that had rotted and dried to the table. Bones from several species of animals had been chewed clean and piled on top of each other, giving the appearance of a miniature elephant graveyard. For a moment, I thought the dim light of the apartment was playing tricks on my eyes, as the bones seemed like they were moving. A little closer inspection backed me up in a hurry when I realized that a colony of cockroaches had claimed the remains for themselves.

I quickly turned and walked into the front room by Willie's famous chair and TV tray, amazed at the odd physics allowing such a feeble table to withstand the weight of the television sitting upon it. Willie's original chew jar, overflowing with tobacco spit, remained ever so vigilant on the floor next to his chair, but Winnie's positive influence was definitely missing, as it was now accompanied by several other jars in various stages of use. I wasn't about to get any closer to the jars, so I couldn't quite tell what type of flying vermin was swarming around them, but whatever they were, they seemed to be keeping the cockroaches at bay. With the jars in front of me and the roaches behind me, I found it prudent to keep myself planted in the middle of the floor as close to the door as possible.

Willie came back into the room carrying two large plastic garbage bags, surprised that I hadn't made myself comfortable by taking a seat in his chair.

"Thank you, Willie," I said, apologizing profusely. "...But, ah, I've been sitting in my car all day, and it really feels good to stand up," I said, taking an unencumbered breath, worried that I might be getting accustomed to the odor. "What's in the bags?"

"This is the investment I told you about," he said, placing the bags on the floor. He dragged one of the bags in front of me and carefully untied a knot at the top, pulling the sides apart to expose the valuable treasure inside. As if removing a treasured artifact from some undisturbed tomb, he deliberately placed both hands in the bag and carefully removed what appeared to be a handful of men's socks, still folded and held together by the plastic clips used to hang them in the store. With a knowing look on his face, he cautiously held out the socks for me to appraise. Upon examination, I nodded my head with encouragement at the different varieties and colors of thin nylon stockings he was holding.

"Those are nice socks, Willie," I said, not totally sure what he expected from me.

"This is my investment," he said proudly.

"These are socks," I said back.

"That's what I invested in," he countered.

"Socks?"

"Yes."

"Socks are your investment?"

"That's right."

"Okay, Willie, I'm a little fuzzy on the whole 'socks are an investment' thing. Can you explain that for me?" I asked, trying not to laugh.

"I invested in me, see? These socks are for me," he said seriously.

"Okay, I can see that. How much did you invest in the socks?" I asked.

"About $1,000," he said coolly.

"You bought $1,000 worth of socks?!" I called out, almost choking on the amount of putrid air I had to suck into my lungs.

"These are the best socks money can buy," he said at my reaction.

"…But $1,000! Willie! Willie… how much money do you have left?" I asked in a stunned voice, not knowing what else to say.

"The rest is gone," he said almost cheerfully.

"Gone?" I lamented. "Willie, you had $4,400 left after we bought your insurance policy. It's been like three weeks since you got the money."

"I did good, Mr. Pickles," he said, addressing the contorted look on my face. "I's had me some bills that I took care of, and you know I had to do me some drinking," he said with a smile.

"Forty-four hundred dollars on socks and booze?" I said incredulously.

"Well, since we both men's," he droned on with a bashful tone, "I don't mind telling you that I had some needs to take care of since Winnie been gone," he said with a wink and a nod.

In that moment, I despised Willie Hawkins as much as any human being I had ever met. I wondered if he was even capable of knowing how wretched of a human being he was. The way he was looking at me, I got the distinct impression he was waiting for a hearty congratulations from me for purchasing whores with his wife's death benefit. For me, it was the straw that broke the camel's back. Investing in socks was one thing, weird, but somewhat understandable considering the source. Even Winnie told me she was afraid Willie might drink away the money, so that was pretty much expected, but spending his dead wife's death benefit to buy hookers was more than I could stand. I have no idea what the expression on my face looked like, but he took two steps back when he saw it. I desperately wanted to tear into him and bit down on my lips so hard I could taste blood.

I looked at him for a moment or two longer with an anger swelling inside of me that I knew was going to get ugly if I didn't get out of there. Without saying another word, I took the newly issued policy out of my coat pocket and laid it upon the sock bag, turned away, and left the apartment. A second later, I heard him ranting and raving as he came to the top of the stairs, hurling obscenities at me as I walked down the stairwell. Not satisfied that I understood his true feelings on the matter, he ran back into the apartment and took up a position out his front window above the liquor store, screaming at the top of his lungs for all to hear. "Mr. Pickles, you can kiss my mudderfucking ass!! My mudderfucking ass! You hear me…? Kiss my MUDDERFUCKING ASS!"

CHAPTER 19

December 1980

The next few weeks went by like a blur, and, before I knew it, Thanksgiving was over, and I began to look forward to Christmas. Things seemed to be going pretty well. Nobody at the office had been beaten, robbed, or killed in a while. My friendship with Sandra continued to blossom, and things at home were relatively calm. I began to wonder if losing the opportunity to go to electrician's school might not be a blessing in disguise. I was actually doing well money-wise, as my collections and sales commissions were paying me almost $500 per week, which wasn't bad for a guy who had just turned twenty-two years old. I had full health insurance benefits, didn't have to punch a time clock, and, with the exception of Tuesdays and Thursdays, made my own hours. It seemed like any time I started feeling comfortable about the job, something bad would happen, snapping me back to reality, and this time was no exception.

I very seldom watched Monday night football, but for some reason I found myself on the couch, half asleep, listening to Howard Cosell call a meaningless game. I perked up when he stopped in the middle of his presentation as if disturbed by something. As poised and polished of an announcer as he was, even Cosell's voice cracked a bit when, in his trademarked nasally, East Coast accent, he proclaimed something to the effect that "nothing like this should ever happen!" His change in tone startled me, but his next words literally shook my very foundation: "Ex-Beatle John Lennon was shot to death this evening outside his apartment in New York City."

Though I couldn't blame the black ledger per se, the murder of John Lennon on Monday, December 8th, 1980, was like a dagger through my heart all the same. I wasn't alone, as millions of fans around the world lost a kindred spirit that day in a senseless act of brutality that no one could understand. For me, the loss was so personal, I felt like a member of my family had been taken from me. Growing up without much of a mother or father, I always counted on the music of the Beatles to get me through.

In 1964, at the tender age of five, I didn't have a clue about the Beatles or the significance of their appearance on the Ed Sullivan show, my dad's favorite program. It wasn't until five years later when I got a cheap little plastic record player for Christmas and one of Judy's friends gave me a handful of 45rpm singles to play that I discovered the Beatles.

With Mom passed out on the living room floor and Johnny Mathis records skipping in place hour after hour on our old console stereo, I was huddled in my bedroom, listening to the Beatles tell me about this great place called Strawberry Fields on my little plastic record player. Life was kind of dark for me as a kid, not knowing what to expect when Mom and Dad drank, but the Beatles convinced me there was a "Good Day Sunshine" if I could just get through another night. They became good friends who told me through their music to hang in there because everything would be okay.

By the time I got into high school, the Beatles had broken up, but each band member's solo career was flying high, and I could still remember how jealous I was of a girl who sat behind me in World History, bragging about the tickets she got to see Paul McCartney and Wings in concert. I got even with her, though, as we also shared a drama class together, and one of our assignments was to split into groups and act out a popular song in pantomime. Her group picked out an old song about going to a chapel and getting married, while my group unanimously agreed upon my selection of the Beatles' "Maxwell's Silver Hammer," which, of course, blew everyone away.

Their music had become part of me, and I would perk up whenever a song of theirs came on the radio, but, of the four, John Lennon meant the most. The poetry he put to music was honest without pardon yet inspirational without discourse. He told us when he needed "Help," asked us to "Imagine" a better world, and suggested that we all just "Give Peace a Chance." He was a kindred spirit, communicating his message through the art of music. He believed in the hope of a better day. I sat up to the wee hours of the morning watching the news coverage of his death, completely baffled at the insanity of the act that took his life.

The world was in shock at John's passing the next day, with radio and television news providing non-stop coverage or tributes. Jessica woke and said, "It's too bad about Lennon," because she liked some of his songs, even though her favorite group was Herman's Hermits. "…And by the way, can you take Rudy out for a walk before you leave?" she asked, hardly understanding the sorrow I was feeling.

The office was different. Everyone there knew I was a huge Beatles fan, and throughout the morning, into the afternoon, people came up to me and offered their condolences as if I truly did lose a family member. After a while, it dawned on me that many of them had been touched by the loss of John and just wanted to express themselves. Even Mr. Meadows chipped in by dragging out his pipe and telling me how intrigued he was about the disease song the Beatles wrote.

"I got to tell you, Ray, I thought I knew every Beatles song backward and forward, but I don't ever remember one about disease."

"Come on… They play it all the time," he insisted with a furled brow.

"I'm drawing a blank here, Ray. Do you know any of the words?"

"I know you know, the disease crawling all over him and stuff," he argued.

"Wait a minute! Does it go, 'Hold you in his armchair, you can feel his disease'?"

"That's it!" he exclaimed like he had just struck gold in the Yukon Valley.

"It's called 'Come Together,' Ray, and I don't think it's actually about disease," I said.

"That shit's messed up," he said as if pondering the lyrics, while puffing away at the pipe. "It's too bad about your guy, Ron," he finally offered before sticking his head in a ledger book to do some work. I looked at him and smiled, appreciating the expression of emotion, knowing it was as heartfelt as he could muster. The real surprise came that afternoon when Irene stuck her head in the agents' office and told me that a Sandra Wesley was on the phone for me.

"Hey, Sandra, is everything alright?" I asked, answering the phone.

"I called to ask you the same thing," she said.

"What do you mean?"

"Everybody at school was talking about the Beatle that got killed last night, and I remembered how much you liked them. So, when I got home, I asked Mrs. Brown if I could use her phone to call and see how you were doing," she said.

"Oh, that was sweet, thanks. It's sad, it's been kind of a rough day thinking about it, but I'm getting better," I said to put her at ease.

"Well, that's good. A couple of the girls in school were really upset, and the instructors actually stopped the class for a while and talked about it. This one girl knew everything there was to know about the Beatles. I swear, you'd love her."

"Is she cute with a great body and good legs?" I teased.

"No, she's fat and kind of homely, but she has a great personality. It shouldn't all be about looks, you know?" she giggled.

"Fat can be good, and I don't have any problems with homely. I just hate girls with personality," I joked.

"You're terrible, you know that?" she laughed.

"Honesty can be a terrible thing."

"Well, truth be told, my favorite thing about you, Ron, is your honesty," she said poignantly.

"Really? How do you know I'm so honest?"

"Well, when you sold me my insurance policy and told me the difference between what my mom had and what you wanted to give me, I knew you were an honest guy," she said in a way that embarrassed me a little.

"It was a weak moment, it was hot outside, I was suffering from heat exhaustion, I had a stubbed toe, I…"

"Oh, stop it!" she cried into the phone. "Hey, I got a question for you."

"Question me!" I said like an all-knowing soothsayer.

"Did you know the Beatles wrote a song about black girls?" she asked.

"Black girls? No, but it's been a weird day. I'm starting to learn they wrote songs about all kinds of things I never knew," I said glancing over to Meadows.

"It's called 'Blackbird,'" she said.

"Oh, I know that one. It's a great song. Who told you it was about black girls?"

"The girl in class with the personality, silly."

"Really? Now you got me curious. I'll have to listen to it again."

"I want to hear it too," she said.

"I'm pretty sure it's on the White Album," I said, trying to remember.

"The song about black girls is on the White Album?" she asked with a healthy amount of skepticism in her voice.

"Ironic, huh? It's hard to explain. It's not actually titled the White Album. It's actually just called *The Beatles*, but the album cover is all white, so it's easier to call it the White Album."

"Oh, you'd love this girl in my class. I can't understand a word she says either," she said with a laugh.

"You're right, Beatles fans have their own language," I agreed. "Do you have a tape player?"

"No, but I have a record player," she replied.

"Well, let me see if I can find the album somewhere. I think you'd like the song," I said.

"It won't turn me into a Beatles freak like you guys, will it?" she joked somewhat hesitantly.

"You never can tell. Six months from now, you might be sitting at home, spinning records backwards, and trying to find the meaning of life in a Beatles album."

"How come it doesn't sound like you're joking?" she asked seriously. I started laughing and couldn't speak when she yelled into the phone, "Oh my God, it's some kind of cult or something!"

"Okay, okay, already. Enough about the Beatles," I said in surrender.

"Hey, since I got you on the phone, I wanted to tell you not to stop by the house for the next couple of weeks," she said seriously.

"Come on, Sandra. It's not really a cult."

"No, I mean it. I decided to take the kids and go down South with my parents to visit my grandma for the holidays," she said.

"Oh, where are you going?" I asked, startled by the news.

"She lives in Mississippi. I haven't seen my grandma in such a long time, and I can't wait to go," she said with excitement.

"Absolutely, I think that's great. When are you leaving?"

"Thursday after school."

"Wow, are you guys going for a long time?"

"We come back after New Year's. Mom and Dad drive down every year," she said.

"You're almost finished with school, aren't you?" I asked.

"Yep, Thursday is my last day. That's something else I wanted to tell you. I have some news," she said.

"What news?"

"I got a job!" she yelled into the phone.

"Are you kidding? That's great. Tell me about it."

"Well, one of the instructors at school said she thought I was a good student and recommended me to the owner of a beauty salon she knows. I had an interview with him yesterday, and he hired me on the spot. I start when I get back from my trip. I'm so excited!" she said with exuberance in her voice that was positively infectious.

"Sandra, that's fantastic! See, it's everything we've been talking about for the last six months; if you work hard, good things happen."

"You are so right. It's like I'm actually getting my life together, and I'm so happy, but I'm sooo sorry…" she said, quickly changing her tone.

"What are you sorry about?" I asked, confused.

"I hate to tell you how happy I am when I know you're feeling sad," she said thoughtfully.

"My darling Sandra, you have no idea how much you cheered me up today. I feel a thousand times better than I did before you called. I mean it."

"I hope so," she sympathized.

"I do. Thanks for calling. And I hope all you guys have a wonderful trip and a great holiday, okay?"

"Same to you and your family, Ron. I'll see you when I get back," she said.

"Okay, bye, bye." I hung up the phone and looked around the office, realizing that everyone, including Meadows, was gone. I sat back in my chair, took a deep breath, and thought about the way I felt every time I talked to Sandra. I didn't know if it was the sound of her voice, the thoughtfulness of the phone call, or her eagerness to comfort me about something she knew was important, but Sandra's call lifted the burden of sadness off my heart that day like nothing else could.

CHAPTER 20

January 1981

It was the 10th of January, and, regardless of the weather conditions, I had to be at Linda, Pauline, and Theresa Goodall's house by 10:00 a.m. to collect their premiums or risk losing them as clients. I stood at the bottom of the porch that gloomy Saturday morning, looking up at the three floors of ice-encrusted, snow-packed, wooden stairs I needed to climb to make this collection. Determined not to fall, I grabbed the handrail and carefully placed one foot securely after the other, like a skilled climber ascending a mountain. I tried to mimic the footprints of the brave souls that climbed these stairs before me, looking for any sort of notch or cut in the ice that would improve my footing and keep me from a nasty fall. Cold and exhausted from my treacherous climb, I finally made it to the third floor, hating Chicago's weather and life in general.

The 10th of the month was significant because it was "package day" for a good many welfare recipients and almost all of my clients. Though most of my customers had the self-discipline to put the insurance money on the side for a day or two without spending it on something else, the Goodall's could only maintain self-control for about two hours. Far from being annoyed at such lack of discipline, I was actually impressed that they had the wherewithal and good sense to purchase insurance in the first place.

Linda and Pauline were twenty-year-old fraternal twins. I never knew how the science worked, but each was predisposed to have twins of their own, and they did. Linda had a pair of three-year-old boys, and Pauline had a pair of two-year-old girls. Neither was married, nor had they seen the fathers of their children since they were born. Along with their forty-year-old mother, Theresa, the seven of them shared a three-bedroom apartment just north of Madison Street on St. Louis Avenue. The two girls ran the

269

household, paid the bills, and took care of their kids. They even took turns establishing a social life, knowing their chances of finding a husband under their circumstances were somewhere between slim and none. I thought they did a remarkable job of keeping up with the four toddlers as well as watching out for their mother, who was definitely a little off.

The first time I met Theresa, I thought she was just shy, but after a few minutes, I realized there was something wrong. She wouldn't look directly at you and never made eye contact. If by chance you did accidentally make eye contact, she would turn her head and look in a different direction, as if distracted by something else. She never initiated conversation and only responded with one- or two-word answers when she did say something. Linda and Pauline would always speak for her if I asked a question they thought she couldn't answer.

I had to admit, it was always kind of fun collecting from Linda and Pauline because their house was literally charged with the energy of a school playground during recess. It was like a circus with the two sets of twins running back and forth through the apartment, getting into all kinds of trouble while Linda and Pauline (who were barely adults themselves) kept pace stride for stride, cleaning up their mess. Both of the girls were thin and pretty in their own way, hardly inhibited by my presence. Their morning attire throughout the year consisted of an oversized T-shirt, worn like a nighty, with panties and slippers. The only difference between their summer and winter wardrobes was the addition of knee-high socks when it was cold outside.

Linda was the most outgoing and generally handled the insurance business while Pauline handled more of the domestic chores. While the girls were running around the house like maniacs trying to keep up with the chores and the kids, Theresa would be seated somewhere out of the way, taking in her surroundings as if waiting for an appointment in a doctor's office. She had a bigger build than her daughters and appeared a little older than her forty years but was an attractive woman all the same. Unlike the girls, she was always dressed in slacks and a sweater or a nice top, and if you didn't know better you would think she was just visiting instead of living there.

I tugged at the screen door, kicking at the accumulated snow that was blocking it from opening all the way. Eventually, I managed to open it far enough to wedge my head and shoulders between the screen and back door. I stuck my face up to the door's window and knocked hard while peeking inside. Steam from my breath fogged up the glass, but I could see Linda coming into the kitchen through a crack in the partially closed curtains. She was dressed in her winter attire, complete with the knee-high socks. "Come in out that cold, Mr. Pickles," she said, pulling the door open and quickly shutting it once I stepped inside. The kitchen was small, with a refrigerator and stove to the left when you entered and a small countertop, sink, and cabinets to the right. A blast of hot air bowled me over when I walked in, and it felt like I had just walked into a sauna compared with the freezing temperatures outside.

"Man, it's hot in here," I said, stepping out of her way and stomping the snow off my shoes.

"I got the oven and burners going," she said, pointing to the stove that was literally ablaze in fire.

"Is that safe?" I said with a grimace.

"Oh yeah, we do it all the time. It's 'cause that mean, old landlord is so stingy with the heat," she said.

"I see. Hey, do you have something I could dry these shoes with? I don't want to track water all over the place."

"Here, just use this," she said, passing in front of me and pulling a dish towel off the sink.

"I can take them off if you prefer?" I asked while balancing precariously on one foot, trying to dry one foot and then the other.

"No, they look fine. Boy oh boy, I bet it feels good to be out of that cold," she said with a smile.

271

"Well, yeah, it sure does," I said hesitantly, not entirely sure that an open blast furnace was a better alternative.

"I know you are," she giggled while taking the towel from my hand and draping it back over the sink.

"So, how have you guys been doing since the last time I saw you?" I asked while unbuttoning my leather coat and following her through the oversized door into the dining room.

"You know how it is, same ol' same ol', Mr. Pickles. Seems like the only thing that ever changes around here is the weather," she said with a laugh.

"I heard that," I agreed.

Their apartment was old-school Chicago style, where the kitchen, dining room, and front room all joined together into one long, narrow living space. I couldn't see into the front room because Pauline was folding laundry and stacking piles sky high on the dining room table.

"I'll be right back. Get yourself a seat," Linda directed. "I gotta get them books out of the bedroom," she said before scampering off into another room.

"Now that's a load of laundry," I said, walking up to Pauline, who was walled in by a mountain of folded clothes on each side of her.

"These kids sure can go through it, Mr. Pickles," she said, stopping for a second to catch a breath before continuing.

"Speaking of which, it seems awfully quiet in here. Where is everyone?" I asked.

"Momma's sitting in the front room, but you know you won't see them kids until the Saturday morning cartoons are over," she laughed.

"How could I forget?" I chuckled.

"Get yourself a seat," she said, mimicking her sister and pointing to a chair on the other side of the table.

"In a second. Let me say hi to your mom first. I'm afraid I might get buried by laundry over here," I joked.

"Suit yourself," she giggled before bending down to retrieve some more laundry and plopping it on the table. Out of courtesy, I always made it a point to greet their mom, even though I wasn't entirely sure she welcomed it. I carefully navigated around the laundry baskets and piles of clothes, snaking my way towards the front room where Theresa was sitting on the couch with her feet up on the coffee table. The dim lighting made it hard to see, but I felt like something was uncharacteristically wrong as I approached her.

"Hi, Theresa!" I called out with a cheery voice ahead of my arrival. I thought she heard me come in and didn't realize that she was asleep on the couch. I felt bad that I woke her and even worse at the feeble attempt she made to cover herself with a blanket. Slowly, I walked closer to the woman, thinking the poor lighting in the house was really distorting my vision. The smile I reserved to greet her slid off my face when I stopped dead in my tracks and realized that lighting had nothing to do with what I was witnessing. "My God! Theresa! You poor lady, were you in a car accident?" I cried out in horror at the damage to her face and body. She didn't move a muscle at my reaction and just stared aimlessly into space, as if her mind were a million miles away. I took a deep breath and studied her from head to toe, in shock at what I saw.

Her eyes were practically swollen shut, and her face had looked as if it had been used as a punching bag. She was wearing a blue nightgown that had been pulled up to the waist, exposing her bruised and battered legs; they were covered with damp washcloths, stained with blood, and placed over her knees, thighs, shins, and feet. Some of the rags had fallen to the floor or bunched up between her legs, exposing giant welts and cuts as if she had been beaten with a belt. A plastic wash bucket sat on the floor next to her with several washrags draped over the side. I took another step closer and watched as she dropped her eyes and turned away, as if embarrassed by my presence. Then, she did something she hadn't done in all the time I knew her: Theresa turned back towards me and woefully brought her eyes to mine, as if pleading for help. In that moment, Linda appeared and quickly came to Theresa's side, kneeling on the couch and stroking back her hair to comfort her. "Linda, what happened to your mom?" I asked, literally drained at the sight.

"Oh, Momma's going to be all right, aren't you, Momma?" She took a washcloth off Theresa's leg and used it to gently pat her face.

"Linda, what happened?!" I asked more forcefully.

"Oh, it ain't anything for you to worry about, Mr. Pickles. Them boys got Momma, that's all," she said as if annoyed at the question.

"Oh, I see," I said, taking a step backwards without comprehending her meaning. A moment later, my mouth dropped open as her words finally registered with me. "Wait a second, Linda. What are you trying to tell me here?" I asked again, wanting to make sure I understood her correctly.

"Momma knows. Don't you, Momma?" she asked sympathetically while attending to her mother's needs. I watched in dismay as Linda carefully removed each washcloth from her mom's legs, then dipped it in the bucket, wrung out the water, and gently put it back. I couldn't believe the severity of the wounds to Theresa's knees. "There now, Momma. Everything is going to be all right. You just sit here and relax and let me and Pauline take care of everything," she said as if talking to one of her babies. "Momma knows she can't be outside past nine o' clock on a Friday night. Don't you, Momma?" she asked, as if scolding a child. Theresa nodded her head in agreement while watching Linda tend to her injuries. "Momma knows them boys will get her if she doesn't follow the rules. Ain't that right, Momma?" Linda continued.

"My God, Jesus," I whispered under my breath while feeling weak in the knees. I dragged my hand through my hair several times and swallowed hard, feeling as if blood were leaving my face. "Doesn't this shit ever end?" I mumbled to myself while looking on, sick to my stomach. "Linda, can I please have a word with you for a moment in the kitchen or someplace?" I asked, not wanting to talk in front of Theresa.

"Sure. I'm going to go talk with Mr. Pickles for a minute, so you call for Pauline if you need anything, okay, Momma?" she said, stroking her mother's head a few times before following me into the kitchen. Linda knew by the look on my face that I was more than just a little upset when she met me in the kitchen.

"Don't you worry, Mr. Pickles. Momma's going to be just fine. We're taking good care of her," she said as if that should be the end of the conversation.

"Linda, let me get this straight," I said, trying to control my panic. "I don't want there to be any possibility that I'm misunderstanding something. Are you telling me that your mother was beaten and raped?" I asked point-blank, praying I was wrong. Linda's eyes told the story as they flinched to the side before she spoke.

"Yeah, those boys downstairs messed with her last night," she said with a sigh. I stood there for a moment, speechless, before realizing that Theresa must be okay, or they would have never released her from the hospital.

"Okay, I understand what happened, and I'm so sorry. This is just unbelievable. But, ah, what did the police say? Do they have some idea who did this? Did the doctors say that your mom was going to be alright?" I asked nervously. She gave me a strange look while shaking her head.

"We didn't call no police," she said as if I were insane for even suggesting such a thing.

"No police! What... did this just happen? I thought you said it happened last night?" I asked quickly.

"It did happen last night, but we ain't calling no police," she said.

"What about a doctor?"

"Momma don't need no doctor. We're taking care of her just fine," she said.

"Linda, your mom needs a doctor," I said forcefully. "She could be hurt inside. This is a serious crime. You can't let these guys get away with something like this. They'll just do it again," I said angrily.

"I know what you're saying, Mr. Pickles, and I appreciate it, but you got to understand something. The police ain't going to do anything around here. They got way more important things to worry about than some ol' nigga gal came home too late and got herself messed with by some boys."

"But Linda…"

"No sir! What do you think them boys will do to us if we call the police on them?" she asked incredulously. I looked into her eyes with a blank expression on my face, trying to understand her logic, completely disillusioned that she couldn't understand mine.

"I don't know," I said, fumbling for something to say.

"No sir, Mr. Pickles. All calling the police will do is make those boys mad, and then they'll be looking to take it out on the rest us," she said seriously. I felt paralyzed. I was trying to make some sense out of what she was saying, but I couldn't. It was almost like we lived under different rules. If something like this had happened to my mother, I would be beside myself with rage. I'd be demanding the police use every resource at their disposal to hunt down the animals that committed such a heinous crime. These girls had absolutely no faith in the police or in the rule of law, choosing instead to blame themselves because their mother was in the wrong place at the wrong time.

"Okay, listen to me. I understand you don't want to call the police or anything, but don't you think we should take your mom to a doctor, or to the hospital, or something?" I asked, trying to appeal to her sensibilities. "We could take my car; I'd be happy to drive," I said, hoping she'd compromise at least that far.

"If Momma goes to the doctor, they'll know she got raped, and we'll have to report it to the police," Linda said as if schooled in criminal law.

"But what if she's seriously hurt?"

"Momma will be all right," she said, dismissing my concern. "We know how to take care of Momma, so don't you worry yourself," she said with a smile as she walked back in by her mother. I followed as far as the dining room table and stopped where she had left their receipt book on top of a pile of folded laundry. "You hear that, Momma? We gots the best 'surance man in the whole world. He's real concerned about you and even said he'd take you to the hospital if you needed." Theresa looked over at me with fear in her eyes, shaking her head to let me know that she didn't want to see a doctor.

"It's okay, Theresa. Don't get upset. I just want you to know that I'm here if you need me, that's all," I said with frustration. I was furious with the situation yet realized that I couldn't do anything about it, especially if they refused my help. I was deflated, with a feeling of helplessness, resigned to the idea that any unwanted interference from me might cause more harm than good.

I pulled a chair out from under the table and sat down. I took the receipt book off the top of the folded laundry and pushed the unfolded laundry forward to clear a spot on the table. "Linda, I'm going to write my home phone number on the back of my card and leave it here in your receipt book," I said, quickly crediting their premium book with the money Linda left inside. "Look, if you guys change your mind about any of this and need a ride to the doctor or something, I want you to call me, okay?"

"Thank you, Mr. Pickles, and I know Momma thanks you too," she said without looking at her mother for a reaction. I took a deep breath and pushed myself away from the table, pausing a moment to collect my thoughts. I stood up and slowly walked over by Theresa with a feeling of total despair. I looked at the poor lady, feeling helpless in every way imaginable.

Rape was something I heard about on the news. I never paid attention. I didn't even know what victims meant when they said they had been violated or felt dirty. Until today, I could never imagine what it would be like to be a victim of rape, and now I couldn't image how someone could live with such a thing. The empathy I felt for Theresa almost brought me to tears as I looked upon the battered soul that sat before me. I was actually surprised when she looked up to make eye contact with me again. This time it was different. Instead of tears and sadness, there was a look of gratitude. Without saying a word, she conveyed an appreciation that only the two of us understood. I drove away from the girls' house that morning with my head spinning in a million directions. Before I knew it, I was sitting on Sandra's couch, explaining to her how upset I was that the daughters wouldn't let me take Theresa to the hospital, call the police, or do anything to report the crime.

"I know it's hard for you to understand, Ron. I know you won't like this, but it's because you're not black," she said, looking into my eyes. "You see, Ron, for black people, it's really hard to look at things the same way white people do," she said. My jaw dropped open, and I stared at her in disbelief.

"This ain't about racism, Sandra!" I shouted in frustration. "Didn't you hear me? This is about a woman who was brutally raped by a bunch of guys," I said with exasperation.

"…And you're not hearing me, Ron!" she shot back, determined to make her point. "It's different for black folks, okay! Like you said earlier, if that had been your mother that was raped, the police would have been working overtime to find out who did it. She'd be taken to the hospital and given counseling and treated like a queen. Do you know what would happen to this lady if she reported the rape to the police?"

"I don't know. I imagine they'd take her to some hospital," I said, caught off guard by her question.

"The police would get a report. Then, they'd take her to Cook County Hospital, where she would sit in the emergency room for hours because she ain't bleeding bad enough to be moved to the front of the line."

"But she's been raped!"

"It don't matter when you're on welfare, Ron. It's like what they say on television, 'If it bleeds, it leads,' and this woman would be waiting her turn just like everyone else. Then, after they finished treating her, they'd put her on a bus and send her home, where the guys that raped her would be waiting to kill her," she said with a seriousness I'd never seen before.

"So, you're saying the police wouldn't do anything?" I asked sarcastically.

"Ronnie, it's like a war zone around here! People get shot and killed here every day. Nobody cares. You don't see a news flash every time something happens. The police might go through the motions to cover themselves and make sure they don't end up on the television, but, to most of them, a dead black man is just another 'nigga' off welfare," she said.

"That's not fair to say," I said, shaking my head.

"...But it's true," she pleaded. "Honestly, nobody cares if a black woman gets raped in the ghetto," she said, placing her hand on mine and positioning herself a little closer. "I think it's hard for you to understand because you are a good person and it broke your heart to see this happen. But you got to understand that there's a difference between being born white and being born black," she said.

"...But how can you say that if you're not white?" I asked, challenging her.

"People don't look at you differently because you're white, silly," she said as if amused at my ignorance. "It's like Dr. King said, 'Judge me for my character, not my color,' you know? People don't treat you differently because you're white. But they do if you're black," she said with conviction.

"It shouldn't be like that," I said with a sigh, sadly knowing that she was right.

"I like to think that someday it won't," she said with an upbeat tone.

"So, now you're the eternal optimist?"

"Well, as bad as it may be for black people today, it's a damn sight better than it was a hundred years ago," she chuckled.

CHAPTER 21

May 1981

By the time May rolled around, I was almost at my wit's end. I didn't know if it was Mr. Wick's "evil entity" or just the fact that every other week something crazy seemed to happen. If it wasn't death defying, it was comical, but it never stopped. To complicate matters, I contracted a terrible case of "call reluctance," which is a condition that kills anyone who makes sales for a living. Something inside kept me from knocking on doors or looking for new business. Whether consciously or subconsciously, I didn't want to get in the middle of anyone else's pain and suffering. Since my sales had gone down, the paycheck justifying the job had been cut by a third. Lapses were killing me, but I knew better than to hold someone's insurance, so I continued to lapse everyone who didn't pay, which wiped out the occasional sales commission I did make. Every day I thought about quitting, and every day I asked myself what I would do for money if I did. I still had my baby to think about, and, whether I liked it or not, I had to support Jessica as well.

The time I spent working the black ledger had matured me and opened my eyes to a world of possibilities I never knew existed. It also opened my eyes to the importance of making good decisions, thinking about the future, and taking responsibility for myself. I began to realize that a life partner, chosen by a seventeen-year-old mind based on a physical attraction, was a mistake. I wasn't in love with Jessica, but it wasn't just about Jessica and me; it was about the precious little girl we brought into the world that weighed heavily on my mind. My little girl, Jeannie, meant the world to me, and I didn't want her to grow up without a father like I did. "Be more of a father to her than your father was to you, and she'll be happy the rest of her life," my Uncle Bud once told me. Those words were cemented in the back of my brain as I struggled with the emotional dilemma I was having over Sandra.

Sandra had become my support system, my confidant, and my best friend. My ability to open up and express myself to her was something I couldn't do with Jessica. Ironically, it actually helped my relationship at home improve. I got what I needed emotionally and intellectually from Sandra and what I needed physically from my wife, but I wasn't happy. I knew that any attempt to get out of my marriage and begin a serious relationship with Sandra would send my little girl's life into a state of chaos, which I wasn't prepared to do. With the patience of a saint, Sandra would listen as I danced around the subject, trying to imply what I wanted, but couldn't for my daughter's sake. Seemingly, she understood and told me not to worry; she assured me that I'd find my own way and do the right thing if I just "gave it time."

Sandra's new job was both a blessing and a curse. She really loved it and was doing well, but the schedule had her working six days a week, which made it difficult for me to see her on a regular basis. Having just picked up a desperately needed collection, I found myself driving right past her house that first Monday morning in May and decided to stop and see if I could catch her at home. I pulled up and got out of the car just as she was running out of her apartment in a mad rush.

"I'm sorry, Ron. I feel terrible, but I don't have time to talk right now. I got to go! If I miss this bus, the next one doesn't come for an hour, and I can't be late for work," she cried out.

"Hold on! Relax. I don't have anything to do for a couple of hours. Let me give you a ride to work," I said, trying to calm her down.

"Are you sure? It's way up north, Ron. I don't want to mess you up," she replied.

"You'll mess me up more if you don't let me give you a ride. I haven't seen you in ages, for crying out loud. Come on," I ushered her to my car and held the door while she got inside.

"Thanks, I really appreciate it. You have no idea what I have to do to get out of the house in the morning," she said, taking a deep breath.

"I can only imagine," I chuckled.

"Seriously, those children of mine do not like to cooperate, and everyone is on a different schedule," she was talking a mile a minute.

"What do you mean?"

"Well, first I have to get them all up, which is a chore in itself. Lucy has to get dressed, eat breakfast, and be ready to leave the house at 8:30 sharp, or she misses her chance to walk with the neighbor lady and her kids to school. I don't want that child walking to or from school by herself, you know?" she asked rhetorically.

"Oh, I totally agree," I said quickly, trying to keep up with her pace.

"Then, I have to have Lee and Liz fed, dressed, and over at another neighbor's house by 10:00 a.m., which gives me exactly one-half hour to get back home, ready for work, and out the door by 10:30 to make my first bus and then transfer to the second," she took a deep breath in exasperation.

"So, what's the problem?" I asked with a frown, while playfully smacking her on the shoulder. She just looked over at me with a smile and shook her head. "I'm not complaining," she laughed. "I'm just telling you what it is."

"I hate to harp on this, but if you had a phone, I could call you when I'm out here and give you a ride more often," I said with a soft, suggestive tone.

"I know, I'm just not ready yet," she sighed. I knew she didn't like to talk about her finances, so I dropped the subject. Otherwise, we laughed and joked all the way up to the North Side of the city, though traffic was miserable, and I got her to the salon just in the nick of time.

"Lordy be! I wouldn't have even made it to the second bus yet," she said as I pulled the car up and parked in front of the beauty salon.

"My God, is traffic always that bad?"

"No, I never seen it like this before. Thank God you were able to take me."

"Jeez, I didn't realize you had to leave so early to get up here," I said.

"Yeah, getting here is a pain, but at least I get to hitch a ride back home with one of the girls that works here."

"Does she live by you?"

"Close to my mom and dad," she said, dropping her eyes and smiling. "Ahh, speaking of which, I've been meaning to ask you something," she said with a slight hesitation in her voice.

"Sure, go ahead," I assumed from the way she segued into the question that it had something to do with her mom and dad's insurance.

"I have an offer for you," she said.

"An offer?"

"Yes, an offer from my mother to come over and have dinner with us," she sounded almost giddy.

"Dinner at your mom's house! With your dad?" I questioned with a hefty amount of reservation.

"What do you say?" she asked, ignoring the contorted expression on my face.

"I don't know, Sandra. I'd feel too weird," I whined.

"Come on, it'll be fun. Besides, I already told my mom that you'd come, so you have to now," she pleaded.

"How could you have told her I was coming to dinner when I haven't talked to you in two weeks?" I asked with a degree of suspicion.

"Well, I knew you would once I asked you," she said, making no sense whatsoever.

"So, you already told her I was coming to dinner though you didn't ask me until now?"

"She's thrilled!"

"I can imagine."

"Oh, come on, please," she begged.

"But it's your dad. He doesn't like me, and he hates when I come by to collect the insurance money. Sandra, I don't think he's teasing when he says I'm robbing him," I said seriously.

"You'll be fine… just don't ask him for money," she quipped.

"That's cute," I frowned. I realized immediately from the sparkle in her eyes and illuminating joy on her face that I'd be going to her parents' house for dinner, whether I liked it or not. "Alright, I'll go, but this game is under protest," I said, knowing she'd understand the baseball term.

"Great! You made me so happy. Don't worry, Ron, it will be fine, you'll see," she said, beaming as she bolted from the car and ran toward the salon.

"Hey, wait a minute!" I shouted while frantically rolling down my window and sticking my head out. "When is all this going to happen?"

"Don't worry, I'll call the office and leave you a message," she said before vanishing into the building.

Later that week, Sandra phoned me at the office and asked if the following Wednesday would work for me. Not wanting to disappoint her, I agreed with about as much enthusiasm as removing an embedded sliver.

"So, who all is going to be there?" I asked.

"Just the four of us. My sister is going to watch the kids," she said.

"And your dad is okay with this?" I asked to reaffirm one more time.

"He's fine, silly. He's looking forward to it," she insisted. "I'll see you next Wednesday."

"Okay, bye," I hung up the phone and pondered the impending doom of having dinner at her parents' house. Though neither of us brought it up in conversation, the significance of dinner with her parents, innocent as it may be, was tantamount to our first date. Everything about it felt strange. Considering I was married and had a kid, that she was divorced and had three kids, that they were all my clients, not to mention the fact that we were falling in love with each other, and the whole black and white thing… It was all very weird.

I told Jessica I was having dinner at a client's house that Wednesday evening. She feigned some concern about me going to the ledger at night, and I acknowledged that it was always dangerous but assured her that this was completely different. About the only real conversation we had on the subject was when I sat at the kitchen table and gift wrapped the presents I was bringing to them.

"Aren't you going a little bit overboard for these people?" she said with a smirk while looking at the stuff on the table.

"Nah, these guys have been pretty good to me about referring clients, and as bad as my sales have been, I need all the help I can get," I said convincingly.

"Who's the album for?" Jessica asked.

"My client's daughter."

"Really? I didn't know black people liked the Beatles," she remarked sarcastically before plopping herself down in the living room and watching television. I wanted to pick up the challenge and lay into her but thought better of it. The last thing I wanted to do was ruin my mood by getting into a battle with Jessica before going to see Sandra.

I had to admit, it felt very awkward coming out of our bedroom and walking past Jessica dressed in the blue suit and tie I wore exclusively to the office on Thursdays.

I began to feel guilty and wondered if she was going to say anything about the cologne I splashed on, my hair being combed perfectly, or that I had shaved for the second time that day. My fears were laid to rest fairly quickly as either Jessica didn't care or was too preoccupied with herself to realize she could be losing her husband.

Jessica broke her concentration from the television just long enough to wish me luck as I was preparing to leave. I leaned down and gave her the required kiss on the cheek before gathering the gifts and heading out the door. I couldn't help but think Craig Branson was right; you could do practically anything you wanted on the ledger because no one figured you would.

Clarence and Othra Buckley lived on the first floor of an old brick three-flat, right smack in the heart of my ledger territory. It wasn't spectacular in design or different from any other three-flat in the area, with the exception that it was meticulously maintained. The doors didn't have any broken glass, all the little square tiles were set in the floor, and all the lights in the halls had lampshades and worked perfectly. The floor was spotless, and instead of being welcomed by the almost obligatory stench of urine present in most of the buildings, you were met with a somewhat musky, but pleasant, scent of wood cleaned with oil soap. Carefully, I scanned the column of buttons next to the mailboxes making sure to press "the Buckley's" good and hard to make it ring inside their apartment.

As I stood in the hallway with an armful of gifts, waiting for someone to either buzz me in or come down and open the door, I couldn't help but think about Sandra's parents. Months before I met Sandra, I was sitting at her parents' dining room table, listening to Othra regale me with the tales of her flirtatious love affair with her husband Clarence thirty years ago. They met while working in the same office building in Chicago's downtown financial district. Clarence was the building's janitor, and Othra cleaned offices, the same jobs they had today. Othra insisted that God brought them together, going on and on about how she had to "chase that stubborn old man" of hers before he came around to asking her out.

Othra was a gem, and I knew that Sandra took after her most. Clarence, on the other hand, was a bit stuffy and didn't seem to like too much of anything, but all in all, they were good people with strong values. They seemed so out of place living in such a run-down area yet happy with what they had. Sandra told me her parents had some money saved up but not enough to buy their own home and seemed content to live in the same apartment for as long as she could remember.

I didn't know what to expect and was more than a little nervous while standing there waiting for someone to let me in. My anxiety was soon replaced with anticipation when the buzzer sounded and I opened up the door to see Sandra standing at the top of the stairs, outside of her parents' doorway, smiling.

The light from inside the apartment engulfed her frame and created a soft aura around her, electrifying her presence. Only the absence of gossamer wings betrayed what otherwise appeared to be an angel from heaven. For a moment, she stood motionless, as if allowing me to take in all she had to offer, and I wasn't disappointed. She looked wonderful. Her jet-black hair bounced atop her shoulders, soft and shiny, parted in the middle, and turned away from her face. A touch of blush, softly powdered over her cheeks against the backdrop of a coffee cream foundation, brought to a pinnacle the most beautiful of all her features, those magnificent eyes. She wore a bright red sweater, fit snuggly against her hourglass waist, that cupped her breasts in a way that was both conservative yet sensual. The black dress slacks she was wearing looked as if they had been cleaned and pressed moments before I arrived. They hung perfectly and were cut to include the height of her black pumps, showing just the tips of the shoes.

If Sandra had a hidden talent, it was her ability to accessorize every outfit she wore, and tonight she went the distance. A small white flower, just above her ear, gave her appearance a playful dimension that otherwise may have been missed. Silver earrings peeked out from behind her hair and sparkled from time to time, like beacons directing your attention to her face. She had a playful side to her, but a simple silver cross and chain displayed just above the rounded collar of her sweater let you know that she was a good girl all the same. Her hands were meticulous, and as one might expect from a recent graduate of beautician's school, her fingernails were perfectly manicured and glossed to highlight their natural beauty. I was amazed at how beautiful she appeared and didn't hesitate to tell her so. "Wow! Now that's an outfit," I said, grinning from ear to ear.

"Well, thank you, Mr. Pickles. I'm sure you're as gracious to all your clients," she said like a Southern belle.

"I'm not kidding… you really look beautiful," I said sincerely. She smiled slightly, looking away for a moment as if embarrassed by my compliment.

"My goodness, what is all this stuff?" she asked with a perky tone as she looked at the armful of gifts I brought, conveniently changing the subject.

"Well, the plant is for your mom, the wine is for your dad, and this present is for you," I said, shifting the presents around in order to hand her the gift. With a big smile on her face, she guessed instantly that the flat, gift-wrapped package was the Beatles album we had talked about months before.

"I wanted you to have it for Christmas, but when you guys went out of town it kind of slipped my mind," I said with a shrug.

"Oh hey, don't worry about it. You got it for me now," she said. "Come on in. Momma's almost got dinner ready," she said, stepping to the side and allowing me just enough room to squeeze past while brushing lightly against her. I couldn't believe how uncomfortable I was stepping inside as an invited guest instead of their insurance man. I felt like a total stranger. Everything seemed different. I was surprised at how elegant the table looked with Othra's fine china adorning the top instead of in its usual place: in the china cabinet. The place was immaculate, and the hardwood floors under my feet were waxed so clean that they actually felt slippery. Sandra entered behind me and closed the door, making sure to slide the safety chain into position before skipping past me and placing the record on the buffet against the wall. Then, she came back and took the gift-wrapped plant out of my hands. "Mom, Mr. Pickles is here, and he brought something for you," she called out into the kitchen.

"Lordy! Lordy! Lordy!" Othra exclaimed with a big grin as she hurried out of the kitchen to greet me. Sandra's cherub-faced mother stopped for a moment to remove the apron from around her plump waist and laid it upon the buffet, partially covering the gift-wrapped record Sandra had just put there. She bounced over to greet me while smoothing out her quaint black dress where the apron had bunched up some of the material. She was wide-eyed and overjoyed with the plant I gave her and beamed with delight as she took it and headed for the dining table. Though she had slowed slightly by age, I got a kick out of her bubbly personality that reminded me so much of Sandra's. "Mr. Pickles, this is beautiful," she said, replacing the centerpiece already on the table with my plant. "Sandra, go put this away," she said, pushing the old one to the side.

"Boy, something smells good," I said at the delightful smell coming from the kitchen.

"I hopes you like smoked butt and greens," she said, stepping back from the table and admiring the plant with a smile. "Don't worry, Ron," Sandra remarked at the twisted grin on my face. "You'll like it, and..." she leaned into me and whispered in my ear, "you'll thank me for talking Mom out of chitterlings."

"Right," I whispered out the side of my mouth before telling Othra I was sure anything she cooked would be just fine.

"Sandra, you take Ron in by your father and come help me get supper ready," Othra said, grabbing her apron and heading off into the kitchen.

"Okay, Momma," Sandra replied.

"Daddy, Ron is here," Sandra called out as I followed her into the front room where her dad was lounging back with his feet up, watching television.

"Look, Daddy, Ron brought you over some wine," she said, taking the bottle from me and holding it up in front of her dad.

"That's nice," he said with little enthusiasm. Looking at the perturbed expression on his daughter's face, he knew a simple hello would not suffice. Dressed in a green flannel shirt, blue work pants, and brown slippers, he slowly leaned forward, collapsing the reclining footrest and grunting with discomfort as he pulled up his aged, lanky frame to shake my hand. From the expression on his face, I could tell that he was somewhat annoyed at the formality of the whole thing.

"Thanks for inviting me, Mr. Buckley."

"Nice to see you, Ron. Why don't you grab yourself a seat and watch some television with me while the women folk get supper on the table," he said, raising a partially graying eyebrow to Sandra, hoping his attempt at civility would satisfy her. She smiled her approval and guided me to the couch before heading off to help her mom in the kitchen. I looked at her lean-faced dad and smiled, knowing he hated this as much as I did.

"It was really nice of you and Othra to invite me over tonight. I'd like to thank you again," I said to break an uncomfortable silence.

"That was Sandra and her mother who did that," he said in a deep monotone voice, letting me know his feelings on the matter.

"Well, thanks anyway," I said, trying to be gracious. Realizing that talking wasn't his strong suit, I leaned back on the couch, crossed my legs, and turned my attention to the television, praying that Sandra would rescue me. Unfortunately, the good Lord and Sandra both had more pressing matters and ignored my request. After a few minutes, the program we were watching ended, and I could feel the tension in the room encroaching upon me like it was high tide.

"What do you want with my daughter?" her father suddenly asked out of the blue while casting daggers with his eyes. The unexpected question caught me off guard, and I decided to feign ignorance instead of stuttering and stammering for an answer.

"I'm not sure I understand what you mean," I said, trying to buy some time.

"What are you doing with my daughter?" he asked like I was an idiot.

"Well, ah, nothing really," I said innocently. "I think your daughter is a wonderful girl, and she's become a really good friend," I said.

"Good friend! You're the first GOOD FRIEND she ever invited to dinner," he snorted as if insulted that I couldn't come up with something better. I gathered from his tone that Sandra had obviously been talking about me to her parents, and I wondered what she told them. Just then, Sandra came sauntering into the room, and I was grateful that my prayer was finally answered.

"Dinner is ready, gentlemen," she said with a glow.

"Thank God," I muttered under my breath.

"What was that?" her father demanded.

"Thank God the food is ready; I'm starving," I said, amazed at the acuteness of his hearing.

Her parents sat at each end of the table while Sandra sat across from me in the middle. The plant I brought over was moved to the buffet to make room for three huge platters of food and a basket of freshly made biscuits. There was a platter of potatoes, a platter of meat, and a pile of green stuff, which I presumed were the greens Othra mentioned. We passed the platters around the table, and once our plates were filled, Othra informed us that she would be saying grace before we started to eat. I thought the three minutes of prayer was nice, though the theme of alcohol abuse and sobriety didn't quite fit the occasion. I actually felt like I needed a drink by the time she finally concluded and we began to eat. "Did you guys ever see that movie with Sidney Poitier?" I asked, figuring I'd get the conversation started after the temperance lecture.

"You mean, 'Look Who's Sitting in My House at Dinner Time'?" Clarence drawled with a dry wit I didn't know he had.

Sandra began laughing so hard she almost choked on her food, and even Othra couldn't help but be amused by the comment.

"One of your favorites, I'll bet," I added to the delight of her father.

"Son, let me ask you something. Do you know what soul food is?" Clarence asked with a serious look on his face. This I was prepared for, and I couldn't wait to shock him with the answer drilled into me over and over by Meadows, Otis, and every other black guy I met since working on the black ledger.

"Yes, sir," I said proudly. "Soul food is whatever the hell a black man says it is," I said with authority to three stunned faces.

"Who the hell told you that?" he wanted to know.

"I won't have no more cussing at the Lord's dinner table," Othra injected.

"The boy started it, Momma," Clarence complained.

"I'm sorry, Othra. I thought it was the answer he was looking for, like a saying or something," I said with an apologetic tone, kicking myself for repeating anything Otis or Meadows told me.

"I asked you if you knew what soul food was, not what you heard some ol' nigga on the street said," Clarence chided me while shoving a fork full of the green stuff in his mouth.

"Daddy, I think you made your point!" Sandra spoke up.

"You're right, Clarence. I was just repeating what I heard. I really don't know what soul food is exactly," I said, glancing over at Sandra in time to see her shaking her head as if amused.

"What are you smiling at?" I asked her.

"You stole Daddy's thunder," she chuckled.

"Nobody stole nobody's anything," Clarence insisted.

"We all know it's your saying, Daddy," Sandra said.

"It just don't sound right coming from a white boy, that's all," Clarence said with a tone that made us all laugh at his conclusion.

"What are you guys talking about?" I snorted.

"Only black men should say, 'Soul food is whatever in hell a black man says it should be,' not white men. White men don't know what soul food is and shouldn't ever repeat a black man's sayings if he don't know what in the hell he's talking about," Clarence said, continuing a rant that we all enjoyed.

From that point forward, I realized that Clarence was actually a pretty nice guy who just wanted to appear tough. His humor was a welcomed relief as it broke the ice and gave us a chance to settle in and enjoy the rest of our dinner over good conversation.

When we finished, Clarence announced that he was tired and hoped we wouldn't mind, but he had to get up early in the morning for work and excused himself. I helped Sandra and Othra clear the dishes before Othra told Sandra to go visit with me in the living room.

"Are you sure, Momma?" I heard Sandra say as Othra pushed her out of the kitchen.

"You didn't bring him all the way down here to make him sit in the other room by himself, did you?" Othra said.

"Thank you, Momma. You leave them pots for me, you hear?" Sandra said, walking in to see me.

"Hey, we used to have a stereo just like that. Does it still play records?" I asked Sandra, pointing to the council cabinet up against the wall.

"I'm sure it does. Let me get my present," she said, catching my drift immediately. She went into the dining room, took the record off the buffet, came back, and sat down beside me on the couch. I watched as she carefully peeled off the tape holding the folded edges of the brightly colored wrapping paper, proclaiming it was too beautiful to ruin and that she wanted to save it. A look of astonishment came over her face when she finally removed the album and examined it.

"You weren't joking—it is a White Album," she said as we both started laughing. "...And it's a two-album set," she said, removing the protective plastic and opening up the jacket. She opened up the cover and held it on her lap so we could both look at it.

"Which one died?" she asked, looking at the pictures inside the cover.

"That's John, right there," I pointed out.

"He was a nice-looking guy."

"He was an amazing talent. I don't think the world will ever see the likes of someone like him again," I added soulfully.

"Oh, here is that song," she said, pointing to Blackbird on the song list. Carefully, she slid the right record out of its sleeve, got up, and walked over to the stereo cabinet to play it. "Oh shoot," she said.

"What's wrong?"

"It's the third song down, and I don't want to scratch it. Do you mind if we play through the other songs?" she asked, looking back at me.

"Are you kidding? This is how we get you started in the cult."

"I figured as much," she said with a smile, turning her attention to the stereo. I watched as she opened the top of the cabinet and carefully slid the record over the center post, then moved the stabilizing arm in place over it. The amplifier came to life with a "thud" when she turned on the power knob. She hovered over the console, waiting for the old turntable mechanism to activate and drop the record into place. Satisfied that everything was working properly, she came back and sat down beside me while the stylus automatically moved over the record, and it began to play.

"This music won't bother your father, will it?"

"No, it's turned low, and once his head hits the pillow, it would take an earthquake to wake him," she said as we both leaned back on the couch, shoulder to shoulder, listening to the music.

"I've heard this song before," she said.

"You've probably heard them all before but just didn't know they were Beatles tunes," I said as we heard a clang come from the kitchen.

"Momma, I told you to leave those pots and pans for me," Sandra sat up and called out before leaning back again.

"You just mind yourself, child," Othra shouted back as we looked at each other and laughed.

"I guess dinner wasn't such a bad idea after all," I said sheepishly.

"It was nice. I'm glad you came over," she said.

"Me too."

"I suppose I shouldn't ask this, but what did you tell your wife you were doing tonight?"

"Actually, I told her the truth."

"Really?"

"Yeah, I told her that I was having an affair with this hot black chick and that I'd be home later," I said, trying to keep a straight face.

"You did not!" she elbowed me in the side.

"Okay, I didn't say you were hot, because I didn't want her to feel bad, so I told her you were a little frumpy."

"Oh! I don't believe you said that," she said, grabbing a pillow from the corner of the couch and smacking me with it.

"Okay, okay, stop! I'm just messing with you," I said.

"So, what did you tell her?" she demanded.

"I really did tell her the truth. I told her I was coming over to your parents' house for dinner."

"She was cool with that?"

"Well, I didn't go into detail; I just told her that your mom and dad invited me and that I didn't want to be rude, so I had to go."

"May I ask you a question?" she asked with a hint of melancholy in her voice.

"Anything," I replied.

"Do you feel okay about being here?" she asked, softly arching her head to look at me. I turned to look at her and then turned back, pondering my answer.

"Honestly, it felt a little weird. I wasn't sure what to expect from your dad, but, after a while, everything was okay," I said, still looking straight ahead, thinking that I answered her question.

"Well, that's not really what I meant," she sat up and faced me, half smiling. "I meant… do you feel okay about being here with me?" she asked with a shy smile.

"Trust me, I wouldn't be here if it wasn't for you," I said with a chuckle. Looking up, I noticed that her expression changed, as if she were saddened by my response.

"Is there something wrong?" I asked.

"No, I just think that you're missing my point," she said. I looked at her thoughtfully, about to speak when her mom came into the room and told us she was finished in the kitchen and getting ready for bed.

"Momma, do you mind if we wait for this one song to come on before Ron leaves?" Sandra asked.

"That's fine. If tomorrow wasn't a workday, we'd be staying up with you, but you know us old folks got to get our sleep," Othra replied.

"Thank you so much for having me over. I can honestly say that was the best smoked butt I ever ate," I said, standing up and putting my arms around her for a hug.

"Just don't tell anyone that you're eating butt at my house," she said with a wink, catching Sandra and me by surprise. "Good night, all," she said, disappearing around the corner.

"Oh my God, that was hilarious," I said to Sandra after her mom left.

"Momma doesn't do it often, but every now and then she'll come up with a good one," Sandra giggled. Just then, the first strains from "Blackbird" played on the stereo.

"Oh, sit back. I want you to hear this," I said, excited for the song. When it finished, Sandra got off the couch and removed the record from the stereo, came back, and stood over me while she put it back in its sleeve.

"Wow, I think I may have a new favorite song," she said.

"Pretty cool, huh?"

"I liked it a lot… and you never knew it was about a black girl until I told you?" she asked.

"Nope, never had a clue," I said, getting up off the couch. "It's getting late. I should probably get going. I don't want to wear out my welcome with your mom and dad."

"I'll walk you out to the hall," Sandra offered as I followed her to the door.

"Do you need a ride home or to pick up the kids or anything?" I asked as she slid the chain off the door and opened it up.

"No thanks, I'm going to spend the night here, and my sister is going to pick me up in the morning," she said, following me into the hall.

"Can I ask you something?" I said, turning to face her as she kept her hand on the door to prevent it from closing.

"Sure."

"You were about to say something about me 'missing the point' when your mom interrupted you," I said, hoping to jog her memory. She looked at me for a moment, as if deciding what to say. After a couple of deep breaths, she finally spoke up.

"Well, I was trying to ask you something, and I wasn't sure you understood what it was I was trying to ask."

"Sandra, I've never felt more comfortable talking to anyone in my life. Ask me whatever you like," I said with anticipation of her question.

"That doesn't exactly make it easier," she joked.

"I remember you asked something about whether or not I was glad to be here with you, and maybe you misunderstood me, but the answer is most definitely yes," I said, trying to help her along.

"Then you agree that we get along pretty well and seem to like each other a lot," she said nervously.

"I think that would be safe to say," I said with a smile, nodding my head in agreement.

"So, you agree?" she asked again.

"Yes, I do," I stated with resolve.

"So..."

"So, what...?" I asked playing along.

"So, what happens next?" she asked, shrugging her shoulders and grimacing, as if she had said something she shouldn't have. I could tell by the anxiety written across her face that she was afraid of what I might say. She arched her back against the doorframe like a shy little girl, patiently waiting for my response, but her eyes, ever expressive, continued to speak volumes, imploring me to answer her. I knew what she wanted to hear, and it took every ounce of willpower I could muster to keep from making a commitment to her. I was afraid to let go and trust my instincts. I almost felt like something was deliberately keeping me from expressing my love and desire for her by hammering my brain with what an enormous mistake it would be to make that choice.

"I wish I knew," I said, dropping my eyes to the floor. "I'd be lying if I told you I don't think about it every day," I finally said with a deep breath. "I don't know, Sandra. There is so much involved here that I don't even know where to begin. Maybe the best thing to do is just wait and see what happens," I said with a sigh.

"How long do I have to wait?" she asked before looking away and flicking at her eye with her free hand as if she had something in it.

"Honestly, I don't know," I said, hating what was coming out of my mouth. "I don't know what I'm going to do for a job, and I don't know what I'm going to do about Jessica. Don't forget I have a child at home too. I'm scared of making the wrong decision again..."

"I know that, silly. That's why I think it's good to talk about it. I think it's time we figure out where this is going," she said, noticing my discomfort and trying to put me at ease.

"Why does this shit always have to be so complicated?" I said, raising my hands with frustration. "So many mountains to climb. Money, always money, the children, my job, and don't kid yourself into thinking this is going to be some kind of a picnic either," I said, pinching the lily-white skin on my arms while looking into her eyes for an answer.

"You can make it as complicated as you want, or you can accept the fact that we're going face some difficulties and deal with them the best we can," she said, staring at me with penetrating eyes. "Sometimes, you just have to follow your heart."

"What are you supposed to do if your heart says 'yes' and your brain says 'no'?" I said, feeling my eyes begin to well with emotion.

"We all make mistakes. Not just you!" she cried out with more than a hint of regret in her voice. "It's true you need to learn so you don't make them again, but you don't stop taking chances because you're afraid. How would you grow as a person if you didn't follow your heart or your dreams once in a while? Life is a risky business; bad stuff happens all the time. You just can't stop living for fear you might screw up. You know that," she said with a smile.

"Sandra, it's not that simple. I want to follow my heart. I really do, but I have too much respect for you to start something I can't finish. I can't hurt you that way," I said, feeling the muscles in my face getting tight with emotion.

"That's just an excuse," she said, choking back her emotion. The sadness creeping across her face tore me apart inside, and it was hard to look at her. I could see a teardrop start to form at the corner of her eye, and I thought desperately hard for something I could say that would give her hope but make her understand that I couldn't commit to her right now.

"Would it help if I told you how much I cared for you?" I asked with a humbled expression.

"It won't if you can't do anything about it," she said with a cracking voice. Our eyes locked as we searched for ways to convey thoughts that words simply wouldn't do justice. I moved toward her and held out my arms, hoping to comfort and let her know that I wasn't going anywhere. My expression was pained at the tears beginning to run down her face. I laid my hands on her cheeks and gently brushed them away with my thumbs, never losing sight of her eyes. "You have no idea how much I care for you, but..." Before I could say another word, she let go of the door and threw her arms around me, burying her head into my chest. Instinctively, I cradled her in my arms and pulled her tight.

After a moment, she loosened her grip and brought a hand to my face, gently caressing the side of my cheek with her fingertips, all the while snuggling close to my heart. Slowly, she tilted her head upwards while moving her hand to the back of my head and gently pulling my face toward hers. She began kissing my neck with soft, subtle pecks that grew into gentle bites as her mouth set sail on a deliberate course, anxious to reach its destination. Our lips met, and her mouth embraced me with the most passionate kiss I had ever experienced. She took the lead and waltzed my tongue back and forth between our lips with a swirling motion that took my breath away. After a few moments, we allowed our lips to part, and fell into a long, silent embrace. I closed my eyes and pulled her even closer, gently massaging her back as I lost myself in the serenity of her arms.

In those precious moments, my desire for Sandra was stronger than anything I had ever felt in my whole life. I was in a trance, and it was all consuming yet incredibly fulfilling. It was like taking that first breath of life after you're born, except better, because now you can actually envision the wonders of life to come with this beautiful woman by your side. I was in love, and I knew she loved me back. I began to tremble with the thoughts and expectations this amazing relationship could mean for our futures, when suddenly, a cold chill ran down my spine, as if waking me from a heavenly dream. I could feel my body stiffen and separate ever so slightly from Sandra's embrace. It was like some invisible force grabbed me by the collar and tugged me back to reality.

Sandra reached up to kiss me, as if sensing I was drifting away. With every breath, I swear, I wanted to kiss her more than anything in the world, but somewhere in the back of my mind it felt wrong. "Sandra, please. Sandra," I whispered softly as I struggled against her embrace, pushing her back just enough to gaze into the majesty of her eyes. They were pleading with me to kiss her with twice the passion we had just experienced. She would never know how badly I wanted to cross that line and unleash the feelings locked in my heart, but at that moment, knowing I had a wife and child at home, I couldn't.

Slowly, I released my hold and gently, but firmly, pushed her away, watching as her expression changed like a fast-moving storm, from wanton desire, to confusion, then sorrow. She allowed herself the vulnerability of a woman faithfully surrendering her heart to a man she wanted to love, and I turned her away. The rejection was more than she could take. There was so much I wanted to say, but I couldn't speak, and every moment that passed put miles of uncharted territory between us. Her eyes that just moments before had showered me in a bath of loving affection now turned cold, as witness to a betrayal she didn't understand. My hands fell off her shoulders and dropped to my sides, limp with frustration. She turned away for a moment, then shook her head in disbelief, trying to understand what had just happened. I watched as she slowly backed into the apartment, her head tilted slightly, staring away from me with a contemplative, almost somber look upon her face.

"Sandra, wait!" I begged as the door began to close. I was ashamed of my behavior, already regretting the moment, but it was too late. She disappeared behind the door without so much as glancing in my direction.

CHAPTER 22

Wednesday, July 1st, 1981

It was an incredibly bright and beautiful Wednesday afternoon, with a warm, comfortable breeze and the smell of summer you'd expect on the first day of July. The distant wail of a police car siren, an occasional barking dog, and the playful shrills of children's voices joined together and blended into a harmonious melody that defined the essence of a Chicago neighborhood. I had been roaming around my ledger that afternoon, making a last-ditch effort to collect from anyone who wasn't paid for June. Tomorrow was July 2nd, the official lapse day when I actually had to report who hadn't paid. Sandra was on my list, and I was sick to my stomach trying to figure out what to do.

It had been seven weeks since we had dinner, and she still refused to see me. She wouldn't open the door when I knocked. She wouldn't return the messages I left with Mrs. Brown, and she refused the flowers I sent her. The one time I called her at the beauty salon, the owner said he didn't allow personal phone calls and not to call anymore. Now, I was forced to confront her in some way about this fucking insurance policy that she probably didn't want any more because of me.

I knew she was hurt, but I didn't know how much until I heard it from her mom. "You need to give her a little time. Let her settle down, think about things. People don't see it too often, but I know; Sandra was born with that same stubborn streak of her father," Othra said when I stopped by to collect her insurance money a few weeks earlier. "...But," she added, "you did hurt her feelings pretty bad."

Until that moment, I only thought about what Sandra meant to me but never considered what I meant to her. It began to dawn on me that I had been the foundation for a new beginning in her life, a chance to start fresh and forget about past mistakes. I was the first person to value her opinion and look upon her as an uncut jewel with incalculable worth. I encouraged her to go to school and follow her dreams when others told her to be content on welfare. I put her on a pedestal and made her believe that she could reach for the stars because I'd be there in case she stumbled. Not only did I break her heart, but I also crushed her spirit. I cringed every time I thought about the way I pushed her away that night. She had a right to expect better from me; instead, she got the immature ranting of an idiot spouting self-righteous nonsense. I acted so childishly. It was no wonder she refused to speak to me.

I pulled up and parked on the opposite side of the street from Sandra's house, feeling like a complete jerk. I turned off the engine and leaned across the front seat to get a better look at her house while trying to figure out what to do. I was sure she was at work and thought about sticking some kind of note on her door. Her due date was the 2nd of the month, and she hadn't paid her premium since April, so technically her insurance had already lapsed, and her thirty-day grace period had expired. I had to find out if she wanted to keep the policy because lapsing it was going to cost me over $200 in commissions. On the other hand, I would have gladly paid the thirty-five bucks out of my pocket if I knew she wanted to keep it. I just didn't want to get stuck for the premium if she didn't want it. After all, she could buy the insurance anywhere.

I pulled my briefcase off the passenger-side floor and propped it open on the seat next to me. The inside was a rat's nest of old route cards, "while you were out" notes, undelivered insurance policies, and an assorted collection of junk and garbage that I should have thrown out long ago. I was looking for a small note binder I had used to keep track of new prospects and frequently needed phone numbers. I knew it was floating around inside the case somewhere. Finally, I found it sandwiched between some policies and bubble gum. I yanked it out before closing the briefcase and started looking for an unscathed piece of paper. I started flipping through the little notepad in a panic, realizing that I managed to fuck up every piece of paper in the book. I shuffled through, just about to the end, when at last I found a piece of paper in pristine condition. I carefully tore the paper off the little ring binder and laid it on the briefcase. I took a pen from my pocket and pulled the briefcase towards me, thinking carefully about what I wanted to say before writing:

***

Dear Sandra,

I've stopped by several times to collect your insurance premium but seem to miss you each time. The 30-day grace period has expired, and the policy has already lapsed. But tomorrow is the official lapse day. I have to turn in the lapse card or pay your premium out of my pocket. I will gladly pay your premium if you call the office either today or tomorrow and make an appointment for me to pick up the money. However, if I don't hear from you by 10:00 a.m. tomorrow morning, I'll have to assume you no longer want the insurance or for me to be your insurance agent.

Love, Ron

P.S. - I think everyone deserves a second chance. I hope you give me one.

I read the note once more, then carefully folded it in two before tugging at the door handle and throwing my shoulder against it to get out. It didn't even occur to me that I parked on the wrong side of the street until the car door swung open and took out a sizable chunk of concrete when it smashed on top of the curb. In addition, the horrible scraping noise seemed to echo through the quiet neighborhood like a shovel being dragged over an ice-covered sidewalk in the wintertime.

Undeterred, I crawled out of the car and lifted up on the door and heaved it shut with a mighty tug and ear-piercing scrap that could have woken the dead. I didn't care. I just wanted to get this note on her door and hurried across the street with my head down as if I were on a mission. I jumped up on the curb and just about made it to the sidewalk when the door to her building swung open and Sandra emerged in the doorway. I was shocked and came to an abrupt stop, frozen in place, completely taken aback by her presence. Her face filled with emotion the moment she spotted me, and, for a moment, I thought she was going to turn around and go back inside. Instead, she turned and held the door for two men who followed her outside.

One of the guys was tall, the other short, neither of which I recognized. The sight took my breath away, and I felt as if my knees were going to buckle at any moment. I was dumbfounded; I never even imagined the possibility of her being with someone else. I tried to make eye contact with her, but she looked away, seeming to ignore me. She was dressed nicely in blue jeans and a white blouse, but her hair was pulled tight against her head and tied off in the back like she didn't want to bother with it. She looked tired, and her expression seemed cold and indifferent. She headed down the stairs towards me, walking side by side with the tall guy while the shorter one trailed behind. Without blinking, she sped up and walked right past me, as if I didn't exist, while the other two followed. For the life of me, I couldn't understand what she thought I'd do, but I sure wasn't going to stand there like an idiot and say nothing.

"Sandra! I need to talk with you," I called out, startling the two guys more than her. I raced in front of them and cut them off, forcing all three to come to a stop. The tall guy looked down and frowned at Sandra, waiting for an explanation. He was older, with dark black skin and a hard look to his face. The small guy was younger and appeared to be tagging along for the ride.

"This is my 'surance man, Gregg. I'm late with my bill. Y'all go wait in the car. I'll be there in a second," she said with a slang that was so out of character. From the look on his face, the tall guy wasn't happy, but he didn't say a word and continued to the car, just nodding for the other guy to follow.

"I don't have time for you, Ron," she said with indignation and a distressed look on her face.

"Sandra, please, I have to talk with you for just a minute," I pleaded.

"There's nothing to talk about," she said coolly while avoiding eye contact.

"There is!"

"There isn't! You don't have to worry about soiling yourself with this little ol' nigga gal," she lamented in a hushed, angry tone.

"I was wrong. I'm sorry..."

"Come on, woman, we going to be late!" the tall guy hollered from inside the car.

"Just wait a minute, baby. I'll take care of this," she called back. "I have to go," she directed at me.

"You're not being fair," I pleaded while trying to keep up with her as she hurried around me to the car. I followed behind desperately; trying to think of something she would respond to. "Sandra, forget about me for a second. Think about your kids. Your insurance is going to officially lapse tomorrow. Don't you want to keep it for their sake?" I asked, hoping to appeal to her common sense and get something positive from her. She opened the car door and slid inside before slamming it shut behind her. The window was rolled down, and I stopped a few feet away with a somber look on my face as she stared straight ahead. The car inched forward as the driver turned the wheel, about to pull away, when she reached over and touched his arm, asking him to stop a moment. She turned toward me with a sullen expression on her face.

"When do you need to know about the insurance?" she asked with a sigh.

"Everything you need to know is right here," I said, handing her the note. She glanced up and looked into my eyes without emotion before turning away and patting the driver's arm to let him know it was okay to go. I stood there watching as their car drove down the block and disappeared from view.

The next morning, I was sitting at my desk, slumped back in my chair, stoking a slow burn about Sandra while twiddling her lapse card between my fingers, as if contemplating my discard in a game of poker. I didn't have a right to be jealous, but I was all the same. It must have hurt her to no end that I went home and slept with my wife every night, but she knew I was married, and neither of us figured on falling in love. Seeing her with this guy was different. Though our total encounter lasted less than five minutes, I took an instant disliking to the man, wondering why she would lower herself and date such a guy. It was like she was afraid to upset him, even changing her speech pattern when she spoke as if to impress him with her ignorance. She never called me the "'surance man" or twanged her words like she had a fifth-grade education. The thought of it made me mad, and I seriously began to wonder what she was thinking. I knew she was hurt, I understood that part, but she never even gave me a chance. I couldn't understand why she would just give up without at least hearing me out. It was no wonder she wouldn't speak to me if this was what she wanted in a man.

I glanced over at the clock above the door one more time to see it was a quarter past ten, and she still hadn't called. Just then, Hamilton walked in to announce the meeting would begin in fifteen minutes, insisting that everyone get their lapses to the managers and their settlements in Mrs. Bolger's window before it started. Chaos erupted around me as everyone scrambled to get their accounts up to the window.

"Ron, you going to play with that lapse card all day or give it to me?" Meadows called out with annoyance.

"What?"

"Shit, Pickles, what the fuck's the matter with you? Give the man the fucking card so we can get the meeting started," Otis chided when I didn't respond to Meadows quickly enough for his liking.

"Fuck off," I told Otis with disgust. Mr. Uhlen was standing at the window and took a giant step towards me, then bowed his head and reached out, gently taking the lapse card from my fingers and passing it to Meadows, like he was doing me a favor.

"That's a good boy," Uhlen said with a smile before returning to his position at the window.

"What's your problem, goddamn it?" Otis growled at me in a low voice.

"My problem is that this fucking broad was supposed to call me this morning and tell me she was going to pay for her insurance," I said, pointing at the card in Meadows' hand.

"Fuck it, lapse that shit," he said. Without missing a beat, Mr. Guru jumped to his feet and blurted out his famous saying: "IN ORDER TO LIVE, YOU HAVE TO EAT. IN ORDER TO EAT, YOU HAVE TO SHIT. IF YOU DO NOT SHIT, YOU DIE. THAT IS ALL!"

On cue, Otis turned toward him and said, "Shut the fuck up, you crazy motherfucker. Nobody asked you shit!"

"You listen to me and be quiet!" Guru shouted back.

"How the fuck did Hitler miss your ass!" Otis turned back with disgust.

"You shut your black ass up," Guru replied before sitting back at his desk and burying his head in his ledger book. I stood there listening to the exchange for what must have been the umpteenth time in the last year and a half before glancing over at the coffee pot. "Holy shit! Will you look at that," I said, quickly running over to a freshly brewed pot of coffee that no one had touched yet.

"Get me a cup, Ron!" Meadows yelled out when I took off. The thought of having a hot cup of coffee to sip during the meeting was a rare thing indeed, but tapping the first cup from a new brew bordered on biblical. The excitement was too much, and I couldn't control the adrenaline rush to my extremities with any amount of accuracy, so in addition to filling both cups, I poured an extra one all over the counter to the chagrin of those who rushed in behind me.

"Jesus Christ! Pickles just poured half the fucking pot on the floor," Vinnie from the stoner staff announced to a stunned office.

"It's two drops!" I called out to the angry mob glaring at me as if ready to impose vigilante justice. Content with my victory, I proudly walked my two steaming cups back to our staff like a conquering hero, ignoring the snarling faces of those standing in line with little hope of achieving such glory. Unfortunately, Mr. Meadows seemed to suffer from the same anxiety of anticipation over the coffee as I did and surprised me by reaching out with both hands for the cup, which caused a fumbled exchange, and spilled most of the hot liquid over his deformed hands.

"Damn, Ron, that's hot!" he cried out.

"Stop being such a baby," I said, watching as he wrung the spilled coffee from his fingers.

"Be an improvement to burn those motherfuckers off and start new," Otis called out unsympathetically.

"Fuck you, Wahl," Meadows shot back. ...And so began the verbal jousting we had come to expect on a weekly basis from Otis Wahl and Ray Meadows, two gentlemen who perfected the art of destroying each other's characters by using colorful metaphors to describe each other's plentiful shortcomings.

After sitting through an uneventful meeting, I gathered my things and headed out the door, stopping one more time at the window to ask Mrs. Bolger if she was sure no one left me a message. "I don't think so, but let me check your box again," she said. I watched as she slowly backed away from the desk and swirled the old secretary's chair in the direction she wanted to go. With a grunt that emanated from somewhere in her body, she heaved herself out of the chair and headed for the folders where the agents' messages were kept, with a pace too slow for snails. She obviously didn't see the urgency on my face, and, instead of just calling out from the other side of the room, I had to wait patiently as she strolled back and repositioned herself in the chair before she'd speak. "Nope, nothing," she finally said.

"Thank you so much, Mrs. Bolger."

"Anytime," she growled as I turned and left the office. I was tempted to drive out to Sandra's house that afternoon but thought better of it, figuring that she was probably at work, and I would just be wasting my time. I was depressed and really starting to think things might be over between us before anything actually began. It really didn't make any sense, and I decided that whether she liked it or not, we were going to sit down and talk this thing out. If she really didn't want to be with me, that was fine, but at least I wanted to hear it directly from her.

CHAPTER 23

Friday, July 3rd, 1981

Earlier Today

I pulled up in front of Sandra's house at 8:30 sharp the next morning with a strange feeling. I didn't know if it was nerves or the fast food I ate for breakfast, but something about being there felt wrong. I began to wonder if, perhaps, I wasn't pushing this thing a little too far, wondering if I should just back off and let things go. There was no excuse for her not to call me yesterday, even if it was just to say she didn't want the insurance anymore. Her coldness bothered me, and I was just about to drive off when something inside told me to give it one last try.

I leaned over and rolled up the passenger-side window, then did the same with the driver's side before looking in the rearview mirror to check out my appearance. I always thought I looked good in my short-sleeved white shirt and black slacks, but my hair was a rat's nest from having the windows open and needed to be fixed. Removing a comb from behind the sun visor, I raked it through my hair a few times until satisfied that I looked presentable, then exited the vehicle, making sure to lock it as always. I took a moment to stretch my arms and take in a couple of long, deep breaths before heading up to her building. I could see her window shade was pulled down, so I wasn't worried about getting caught in another moment of indecision like the first time I was there, but I really started to have second thoughts about going any further. I backed up a couple of steps and looked around the neighborhood, trying to get my nerve, thinking that it seemed eerily quiet for the start of what was going to be another beautiful day. After a moment, I regrouped and walked up the stairs, figuring, at worst, she would call me a jerk and tell me to leave her alone. As painful as that might be, at least I'd know for sure it was over, and I could move on.

I climbed the stairs and walked over to the window where the shade was drawn, trying to peek inside to see if anybody was around. It all looked pretty dark, and I wondered for a moment if everyone was still asleep, quickly dismissing that possibility with three kids running around the house. I pulled the door to the hallway open and walked inside the building, just as I had just about every week for the past year. Stepping up to her door, I knocked with more than a little apprehension at what she might say when she saw me.

I stood motionless outside her door, waiting for a response, somewhat disturbed when there wasn't any. I knocked at least a half dozen more times before putting my ear to the door to see if I could hear anything on the inside. There wasn't so much as a peep, so I went back outside and banged on the window, calling out her name to let her know I was serious about seeing her. I went back inside and pounded on the door, pissed that I got all worked up just to discover she wasn't even home.

I walked out of the building and down the steps, heading for my car, when I suddenly stopped, changed direction, and made a beeline for Mrs. Brown's house next door. "One way or another, you're going to know I was here," I said to myself, walking up the stairs of Mrs. Brown's porch and knocking on her front door. Within seconds, the door opened, but instead of Mrs. Brown, a tall, light-skinned, lovely young lady in a black business suit appeared.

"Can I help you with something?" she asked with a somber tone. Startled by the lady I had never seen before, I quickly looked around to get my bearings, making sure I walked up to the right house.

"I'm sorry to bother you. I was looking for Mrs. Brown?" I asked apprehensively.

"She's not here right now. May I tell her who called?" I was taken aback by her formality and even more so by her demeanor, which seemed positively glum for 8:30 in the morning.

"My name is Ron Pickles. I'm Mrs. Brown's insurance man. I'd appreciate it if you'd tell her I stopped by."

"Okay, I'll tell her," she said teary eyed, about to close the door.

"Wait just a second, miss," I called out.

"Yes," she said through a crack in the door.

"Is everything okay with Mrs. Brown?" She could tell from the look on my face that I was concerned and nodded her head, slightly re-opening the door to explain.

"I apologize. I didn't mean to imply anything. It's been a difficult morning. Yes, my mother is fine, but we did lose a close friend of the family yesterday," she said, pursing her lips.

"Oh... I'm so sorry to bother you," I said.

"Thank you."

"Just out of curiosity, your name wouldn't be Cynthia, would it?"

"Yes, it is, but how did you know?"

"Your mom talks about you all the time."

"That's my mother," she said, forcing a smile over her sullen face.

"You know she adores you, and so does a mutual friend of ours," I said.

"Who would that be?" she asked.

"Well, actually, that was the reason I stopped by. I was hoping to leave a message for the girl next door, Sandra..." Without warning, a gasp of air burst from her lungs, cutting me off in mid-sentence. Her face began to quiver with emotion, her eyes welling up before bursting with tears.

"Are you okay?" I asked with a feeling of dread coming over me. Covering her mouth, unable to speak, she motioned for me to come into the house. Cautiously, I followed her inside without closing the door. I watched as she took long, quick strides into the dining room, grabbing at a box of tissues for her nose and wiping her tears. I turned back and closed the door, returning to the living room with a sick feeling in my stomach. I couldn't believe what was going

315

through my mind and tried hard to suppress the thought, hoping that her reaction was just a coincidence and had nothing to do with Sandra. After a moment, she turned and slowly walked back into the living room, placing the box of tissues on the couch.

"Please, Cynthia, tell me what's wrong?" I asked, bracing myself for the answer. She stared at me for a long moment, as if struggling to gather the strength she needed to speak. From the look in her eyes, I knew something terrible had happened.

"Sandra passed away Wednesday," Cynthia said with a cracking voice. I studied her face, confused by what she said.

"That can't be," I said, a momentary wave of relief washing over my body. "You must be mistaken. I saw Sandra Wednesday. She was fine. You must be thinking of someone else," I said, demanding that she correct her statement.

"We lost Lucy too!" she cried out.

"Lucy! What do you mean Lucy? Her little girl?"

"Yes, she's gone too," she said, wiping more tears and gulping large amounts of air. I dropped my eyes to the floor, completely flustered at what she was trying to tell me. I heard her words, but they didn't register.

"This can't be... I saw Sandra on Wednesday," I muttered. "No, there has to be something wrong here," I said slowly and deliberately, struggling to breathe. "I saw Sandra on Wednesday," I said with an angry tone.

"Listen to me! You're not listening to what I'm saying," she said sternly with deep, soulful eyes that penetrated deep into my body, cutting the legs from out beneath me. "It happened sometime Wednesday evening," she said.

"Wednesday evening? But I told her to call me yesterday. I mean she was supposed to call me... oh my God!" I cried in a pitch so high I didn't recognize it as my own. I began to feel lightheaded and dizzy. Cynthia grabbed my arm and guided me to the couch before I lost my balance. I couldn't catch my breath as my chest went into a spasm, my face contracted, and I cried out without any audible sound. Cynthia put her hand behind my neck and pulled my head against her chest, holding me there until I could breathe again. After a minute or two, I stopped hyperventilating, and she helped me up with a look of recognition on her face.

"I know who you are now," she said. "Sandra talked about you all the time. You're her blue-eyed, blonde-haired insurance man," she said with an understanding that made me feel as if I had known her forever. "Sandra told me how close you were. I'm so sorry," she cried, holding out her arms.

I was beyond stunned, beyond shocked, and even beyond tears. I looked into Cynthia's swollen eyes and forced myself to nod, unable to speak. My arms were so heavy, they felt like anchors embedded deep beneath the ocean's surface. It took all the strength I could muster to reach out and accept her embrace, but when I did, I held her tighter than anyone I had ever held before. Comforting me with sympathetic strokes to my back, she allowed me to hold her as long as I desired. Two strangers brought together in a moment of loss so powerful that we gratefully took comfort in each other's embrace.

When I finally released her, the tears were flowing from my eyes uncontrollably, and she was quick to dab them with a tissue before handing me the box. I sat upright as best I could and took several deep breaths, trying to compose myself before attempting to speak. I couldn't believe I was sitting face-to-face with someone who knew of my relationship with Sandra and knew why I was feeling the incredible sense of loss in that moment.

"Were they in a car accident or something?" I asked, forcing the words from deep in my throat while peeling away a handful of tissues and wiping my nose.

"It's so terrible, I don't even want to say," she said, not wanting to be the bearer of any more bad news.

"Please tell me," I begged of her. She shook her head, then looked out across the living room. She paused, grabbing more tissues from the box and wiping her eyes one more time before turning towards me and swallowing hard before she spoke.

"They were strangled to death sometime Wednesday night," she said, barely able to form the words with her lips. I looked at her with a solemn expression and nodded my head in understanding, though my thoughts seemed miles away. The thought of them being murdered was so incomprehensible that it took several moments for it to sink into my system.

"Where did it happen?" I asked, still not equating their deaths with murder.

"In their house," she choked out. Suddenly and without reason, the full impact of Cynthia's words struck me like a sucker punch to the stomach.

"Oh my God, Jesus, NO!" I howled out, covering my mouth with my hand. We looked at each other in disbelief. A cold chill ran up my spine as the horror of their last moments came over me in vivid detail, stunning my senses with the notion that someone had strangled the life out of those two precious girls.

"I can't believe this. Someone killed them?" I asked with a tone of disgust at the thought more than looking for an answer. Cynthia knew what I meant and just nodded her affirmation as I looked on in a state of shock.

"What about the two little ones, Liz and Lee?

"They spent the night at her sister's house. They're fine," she said. My mind was spinning out of control, so thick with concentration that retrieving a thought was like wading through a slew of mud, every step more difficult than the last. The nervous anxiety pummeling my senses at the news of their death quickly escalated to gripping fear with the realization of their murder. It felt like the room was closing in around me - I needed to escape. I didn't know what else to say to Cynthia, but I was going to jump out of my skin if I stayed there one minute longer. I reached over and took her hand off her lap, cupping it between mine.

"Cynthia, please don't be angry, but I have to go. I have to get out of here right now," I said, tenderly squeezing her hand. Her expression turned sad, and I knew she didn't want to be left alone, but I couldn't stay.

"I understand, Ron, but I want you to know something."

"Sure, what?" I said, releasing her hand and standing up.

"Sandra knew how much you cared for her," she said, looking up at me with a knowing smile. I returned the smile and nodded my appreciation, wishing I had the strength to tell her how grateful I was for her kindness, but I had to go.

Darting out the door, I glanced over at Sandra's building, only once horrified at the thought of my own actions that morning, banging on her door and demanding that she let me in to talk to her. A strange feeling came over me as I crossed the same patch of grass next to the sidewalk that Sandra and I occupied together only forty-eight hours earlier. For me, it was like passing over hallowed ground, still fresh with the spirit of her soul lingering in the air. I picked up my pace, running to my car while fumbling for the keys in my pocket. I dropped them on the ground twice before unlocking the car door and getting inside. I started the car and began to drive. I had to get away, and I had to get off the ledger. I didn't know where to go; I just knew I had to keep going somewhere - anywhere but there. It felt like I was driving in a fog. I drove the wrong way down one-way streets, blew through stop signs, and came within inches of hitting a pedestrian in a crosswalk. I turned south on Western Avenue and weaved through traffic until I came upon a McDonald's where I pulled into the parking lot, turned off the car, and slammed my head against the steering wheel, crying until I couldn't cry any more.

It was about 11:00 when I walked into the restaurant, headed for the bathroom, and drowned my face in the sink. I turned off the water and looked around, realizing that the bathroom didn't have any paper towels to dry my face. Dripping wet, I went to the toilet stall and unrolled as much toilet paper as I could, taking it back to the sink and looking in the mirror while pat drying the raw skin on my face. It was red and swollen, my eyes were bloodshot, and my hair was matted back with what I hated to admit was probably a combination of tears and snot that I had continuously wiped from my face for the last hour. I stood there for a few minutes, picking tiny shards of toilet paper off my face, feeling as if I was finally beginning to get a hold of myself when another horrific revelation washed over me, sending my back hard against the bathroom wall. "GOD! I lapsed her fucking policy yesterday!" I screamed at the ceiling. Running out of the restaurant, I jumped in my car, started it up, and threw it in reverse. I was about to tear out of the parking lot when I spotted a public phone standing alone at the end of the driveway. Quickly, I pulled back into the spot, yanked open my ashtray, and dumped all the loose change into my palm, scattering much of it across the front seat of the car. I jumped out of the car and ran over to the phone, frantically putting coins in the slot before dialing the office.

"Unified Insurance Company, may I help you?"

"Irene, this is Ron Pickles."

"Oh, Ron, I'm glad you called. You have a ton of messages this morning," she said.

"Okay, I'll get those in a minute, but right now I have to talk to Hamilton. It's an emergency."

"Okay, hold on. Let me transfer you," she said, putting me on hold. I looked around while waiting for Hamilton to answer, realizing that I had driven all the way back to the South Side of the city. I was actually closer to home than I was to the ledger.

"Ron, what's going on?" Hamilton's voice finally came through from the other end.

"Roger, things are so fucked up, I don't even know where to begin, but I need your help!"

"Okay, well, slow down and tell me what the problem is, and we'll see what we can do," he said in a calm, soothing voice.

"I just found out that a client of mine and her child were murdered."

"That explains all the phone calls for you today," he said.

"Yeah, well, the problem is that I lapsed her policy yesterday," I said. There was a long pause before he responded.

"How long did they have the contract?" he asked.

"Less than a year," I replied.

"How much coverage did they have?"

"I wrote them MDO. The mom had $15,000, and the child had a $5,000 term rider," I said.

"Wow, that's too bad," he said as if dismissing any more conversation about it.

"What do you mean it's 'too bad'?"

"Well, the policy is too new to have any extended term benefits or cash value to keep it going, so we won't be able to pay a claim," he said.

"But Roger…"

"I can imagine how upsetting this day has been for you," he said, cutting me off.

"I really don't think you can, Roger," I said with a tense voice. I knew I was walking a fine line with Hamilton. I had to maintain some kind of self-control, or I had no chance of making him understand my predicament. He had no idea about my relationship with Sandra, which meant I was going to have to talk about her in third person terms relating to insurance as opposed to a personal loss. "This is really important to me, Roger. I have this woman's entire family insured with me," I said, trying to justify my case.

"I understand the situation, Ron, but if the woman didn't pay her premium, her insurance isn't in force, and we can't pay the claim. You have to accept the facts," he said, pissing me off to no end with his condescending tone.

"Okay, Roger, here are the facts: I saw this woman on Wednesday afternoon, and she promised to pay me on Thursday. She always kept her word, but she was murdered sometime Wednesday night. She and her daughter were strangled to death, so she couldn't exactly keep that promise, do you understand that?!" I yelled into the phone.

"Okay, you have to calm down, Ron."

"I'm not going to calm down. This is bullshit," I fired back.

"What do you want me to do, Ron... pay the claim?" he said with an incredulous tone that immediately put me on the defensive.

"Yes, and you know why? Because if we don't, everybody on my ledger is going to think that Unified Insurance Company is a shit company that doesn't pay when you die," I said, hoping to strike a chord that might make him reconsider.

"I don't see it that way. As a matter of fact, I see a tremendous opportunity for you right now," he said.

"Oh really?"

"Absolutely. If I were in your position, I'd make a point of telling everyone how important it is to keep your insurance paid up to date. You can explain to people that you had a tragic circumstance where a lady was murdered and her family got nothing because she didn't pay her bill," he said. I bit my lip when I heard him, not believing what a cold-hearted bastard he was.

"You know something, Roger? That might sound real good at the meeting Tuesday or Thursday, but it's going to sound like bullshit to the people on the black ledger!"

"You're right, Ron; this IS what we talk about at the meetings because it's important to keep people paid. When did you say you saw these people last?" he asked. I took the receiver away from my ear for a moment in frustration, realizing that he wasn't paying attention to a thing I said.

"That's just what I've been trying to tell you. I saw her on Wednesday, and she told me she would call me to pay yesterday, but she couldn't... because she was killed sometime Wednesday night," I said, sucking up air to control myself from breaking down again.

"Well, then, she could have paid you on Wednesday, Ron," he said without emotion.

"Jesus Christ, Roger, I know that, but this is the black fucking ledger. You know how it works out here. Roger, she was two days late, for Christ's sake. Look, I'll take whatever punishment the company wants to dole out, but let me re-do a deposit slip so this family can get paid."

"I've heard enough, Ron," he said with an angry tone. "I feel bad for your client's family, but the fact of the matter is that this lady had all of May and all of June to pay her insurance and chose not to. You did everything you were supposed to, and she still didn't pay. It's a tough situation, but there isn't anything I can do about it," he said. I stood there with the phone plastered to my ear, not able to think of a response. "Hey, Ron, you there?" he said after a moment.

"Yeah, Roger, I'm here."

"Okay, hold on a second. Irene wants to give you some messages," he said, putting me on hold.

"Ron, it's Irene again. Okay, you ready?"

"Go ahead."

"The Buckley's have called several times, as well as a Mrs. Brown, and Mr. Meadows wants you to call him at home as soon as you can," she said. "Do you need the numbers?"

"No, I got everything, thanks," I replied, dropping the phone to my side momentarily while clicking the hook a half dozen times with the other hand in order to get a dial tone so I could call Mr. Meadows.

"Ray, it's Ron," I said upon hearing him answer the phone.

"You hear what happened?" he asked.

"Yeah, how did you find out?" I asked.

"What do you think...? I was the Buckley's insurance man for ten years. They called me at home, wanting to know about Sandra's insurance," he said.

"They left messages for me at the office," I said nervously. "They want me to call them back, and I don't know what to tell them. Did you tell them that I lapsed her insurance yesterday?"

"No, I didn't tell them anything yet. I'm trying to think of some way we can get that lapse card back."

"I fucked up so bad," I cried into the phone. "It won't work. I just got off the phone with Hamilton and told him that I saw her Wednesday afternoon and she promised to call me yesterday morning but... well, you know," I said.

"Damn, Ron! Why didn't you talk to me first?" he yelled into the phone. "I left fifteen fucking messages at the office and at your house this morning."

"I'm sorry, Ray. I didn't know. I came out here first thing this morning to see her."

"Shit, where are you now?"

"67th and Western."

"We got to talk. Meet me over at the Lake Street Diner in a half hour," he said, hanging up the phone.

"Shit! Shit! Shit!" I screamed at the top of my lungs, slamming the phone down on the hook. I got in my car and headed back for the ledger, feeling like a condemned man riding to his execution. I was dying on so many levels that I felt like my body was merely going through the motions of life. I could not believe this day was happening.

Lunch hour was winding down, but the diner was still crowded, and it felt refreshing to be around people after spending most of the morning grieving by myself inside the car. I spotted Meadows sitting in a booth at the back of the restaurant and rushed to greet him, relieved to be with someone I could talk to. I slowed my pace slightly when I saw the grim look on his face accompanied by the black suit he was wearing. It reminded me all too well of why I was there. A waitress met me at the table and waited impatiently as I slid into the seat opposite of him and got myself situated.

"Coffee?" the waitress asked.

"Please," I said, flipping over the mug in front of me.

"Menu?"

"Not right now, thanks," I said. Ray and I watched as she poured the hot coffee. Once she left the table, he shook his head in disgust.

"Why didn't you call me first? I'm your supervisor, damn it! You should have called me."

"...And what could you have done? I handed you the lapse card yesterday, don't you remember?"

"I might have been able to think of something," he said.

"Let me tell you something, Ray; you have no idea what I've been through today," I said, pointing my finger at him. "I don't even know what I'm doing. I'm losing my fucking mind. This thing is tearing me up inside, so there ain't nothing you can say that can make me feel any worse than I already do," I said, feeling my eyes beginning to well up again.

He looked away when he saw me struggling, as if embarrassed at my reaction. I lifted the coffee cup slightly off the table and put my head down to meet it, taking sips of hot coffee, trying to stem the tide of emotion before it came flowing out again. I put the coffee down, pulled the napkin out from under the silverware, leaned back in the booth, and blew my nose. He removed his pipe and cleaning equipment from his jacket pocket and placed it on the table, as if pretending not to notice my struggle, but I could tell by the look on his face that he knew something was wrong. He had an acute intuitive side to him, almost like a sixth sense, and could spot bullshit or trouble a mile away. I watched as he turned the pipe upside down and tapped it against the table a few times before using his cleaning tool to scrape the inside.

"Ron, do you want to tell me what was going on between you and this girl?" he asked as if it were an afterthought, slowly raising his eyes to meet mine. For a moment, I thought about lying to him, but I just didn't have the strength. Besides, I really needed to talk to somebody. I think he was taken aback by the sadness in my eyes because he stopped tinkering with his pipe, folded his hands on the table, and gave me his complete attention.

"It wasn't sexual, if that's what you're thinking," I said with a deep sigh. I closed my tired eyelids for a moment before taking several deep breaths and continuing. "...But up until these last few weeks, we were becoming close," I said. He had a confused look on his face, and I could see that something wasn't making sense to him.

"Then why didn't she pay the insurance?" he asked somewhat incredulously.

"I don't know, Ray, and I don't know if I'll ever know. About six weeks ago, she invited me over to her parents' house for dinner, and something happened at the end of the night that made her angry with me, and she hasn't wanted to talk to me since."

"What made her angry?"

"It was my fault. I, ah..."

"Take it easy, Ron. You don't have to tell me if it's too hard," he said as I fought back the tears.

"No, I want to tell you. It's important to me. Trust me, I need to talk to somebody about this, or I'm going to explode," I said, gesturing with my hand for him to hold on a moment and let me regroup. "Ray, she was unbelievable. I never met a girl like her before, and over the past year we just became great friends. We shared some things I couldn't even talk to my wife about and just became really close, you know?"

"So, what happened after the dinner?"

"I don't know, Ray; it's going to be one of those things that stay with me for the rest of my life," I said, looking down at my coffee and fiddling with the cup. "We had a great evening, and when it was time to go, she walked me out of the apartment into the hallway. You've been to her parents' house a million times - you know what I mean?" He nodded in agreement. "So, we're in the hallway, and she wants to know if, um, we had a future or something. Jesus, Ray, I don't even know how to say it. The bottom line is that I pushed her away, and she didn't want to have anything to do with me after that," I said.

"You haven't seen her since?"

"I've tried. I called her at work. I left messages with her neighbor. I talked with her mother. I did everything I could, but she didn't want to see me. It was a fluke that I saw her on Wednesday."

"Why is that?"

"I figured she was at work and…"

"She quit her job," he said, cutting me off.

"How do you know…?"

"Her father told me when we spoke this morning."

"Okay, at least that makes sense," I said with a sigh. "I stopped by Wednesday afternoon to leave a note on her door when she came walking out of her house with these two guys."

"Did you talk to her?"

"I tried, but she didn't want to talk. I doubt she said ten words to me, but I did hand her a note that told her to call me by yesterday morning or her insurance was going to lapse. …And she couldn't… because she was dead," I said, barely able to speak before hunching over my coffee in a crying jag I couldn't control.

"It's all right, man. It's all right. Just let it go," Ray kept saying as he leaned across the table and grabbed my elbow for support. After a few moments, I got control and pawed the table for anything I could use to wipe my face. Meadows jumped up and ran over to some empty tables, grabbing handfuls of silverware wrapped in napkins, then quickly returning and dumping them in front of me for my use.

"Thanks, man. I appreciate that," I said, fumbling to unwrap the napkins from the spoons, forks, and knives to blow my nose.

"Take your time, Ron."

"I'm sorry, I just never had to deal with something like this," I said, feeling as if my head were going to explode from the congestion. The waitress came by and stood over me with a suspicious look on her face and dropped off a huge stack of napkins in front of me.

"You okay, sweetheart?" she drawled.

"Oh yeah, thanks. I get allergies, and when they flare up, it's like a waterfall," I said, trying to force a smile at her concern.

"Hmm, looks like you got them pretty bad," she said, knowing I was lying. "You gentlemen ready to order some food?"

"I just want coffee," I said, wanting her to leave.

"Yeah, just coffee," Meadows concurred. I waited for her to fill our cups and leave the table before raising my head and looking at Ray straight in the eyes.

"Jesus Christ, Ray. I was so fucking pissed off at seeing her with those other guys. I thought she was being such a bitch and really unfair by not giving me another chance," I said with my voice cracking. "But I swear to you with all my heart, I never would have lapsed her insurance if I thought something like this was possible in any way, shape, or form," I said, beginning to get my control back.

"Ron, you did everything you could," he said, dropping his eyes and nodding his head. "She didn't give you much of a choice, did she?"

"Ray, I'm so fucking sick to my stomach, I can't even explain. Not just the insurance, Ray... I loved this girl, and I can't even..."

"Take it easy, Ron. I understand, but it's not me you have to convince," he said with a forced smile. We stared at each other for a moment, knowing exactly what he meant.

"Her mother and father? I don't know how to face them, Ray," I said like a zombie.

"I'll go with you. All we can do is tell them the truth," he said. I looked at him with grateful eyes and nodded my head.

"I'm sorry I didn't get in touch with you before talking to Hamilton, but I thought he might understand and try to help," I said, trying my best to apologize for the slight. "This is just unbelievable,"

I leaned back in the seat and took in deep breaths of air. "Did you say you talked to her father today?" I asked, wondering if he knew more about what happened.

"Yeah, remember, I've known these people for a long time."

"I know."

"He called early and told me what happened," he said.

"Did he go into any detail? Do they know who did this or anything? Could those guys I saw her with have anything to do with this? I mean, this is a fucking nightmare."

"He didn't say anything about that," Ray said with a deep sigh, as if hesitating to say anything that could start me off again.

"I'm okay, Ray," I said at his reluctance. He chewed on his lower lip and looked around the restaurant, clearly deciding whether or not he should tell me more.

"This shit is fucked up, Ron."

"I know, I can't imagine what these poor people are going through," I said. "What did Clarence tell you, Ray?" I asked again. He looked at me and took a deep breath before speaking.

"He said it happened late Wednesday evening, but nobody found out until sometime yesterday morning, and even then, I guess everything was fucked up," he said.

"What do you mean?"

"You know Mrs. Brown next door?"

"Yeah, her daughter is the one who told me what happened when I went by Sandra's house this morning."

"Well, she got concerned when Sandra didn't answer the door yesterday morning. They had some plans or something. So, she called the landlord, who came over with a spare key and let her in to see if anything was wrong. They found the little girl unconscious in the bedroom and called the police. They rushed her to the hospital, but she was already gone."

"What about Sandra?"

"That's the fucked-up part. I swear, the fucking cops out here just don't give a shit," he lamented.

"So I've been told," I replied.

"These fucking guys didn't even bother to search the apartment when they found the little girl."

"Whoa, back up a minute… What are you saying?"

"Ain't that something? They find a dead kid in the house, wrap her up in a blanket, and call it a day," he said.

"…And Sandra's body was in the house the entire time?" I asked in disbelief.

"Can you believe that?" he said, shaking his head.

"When did they find Sandra?"

"A few hours later," he said.

"You got to be shitting me!"

"Nobody knew where she was, so her mom called the police again. This time they went back and searched the house. They found her body tied to a chair in one of the closets," he said.

"Jesus Christ!"

"The old man said it was pretty bad. You sure you want to know?" he asked, looking at me with sympathetic eyes, as if wondering whether or not he should say more.

"I want to know."

"Well," he said with a long sigh. "I guess these assholes tied her up to a chair in the kitchen then shoved a rag in her mouth. They pulled an extension cord out of the wall and strangled her, then dragged her body into the closet still tied to the chair."

"My God, do they know where Lucy was during this?"

"The cops think she probably woke up and saw what was happening, so they killed her too," he said with disgust.

"So, Lucy was killed after seeing her mother die," I said with a stunned expression, imagining the terror the poor little girl experienced in her final moments. "The other kids weren't home?"

"No, they were with her sister. Thank God, but…"

"But what?"

"I, uh, I don't know," he began to stutter.

"Ray, what the fuck?" I demanded.

"Her father told me something else that's been creeping me out," he said, squirming in his chair.

"Please, I don't want to know if they were..."

"No, nothing like that, but whoever did this smeared some kind of cold cream all over Sandra's face and hands after she was dead," he said as I listened in shock.

"Cold cream?" I asked as my mind flashed back to the time Sandra had plucked my eyebrows and dabbed her finger into the big jar of cream, gently applying it above my eyes while little Lucy looked on.

"Yeah, she was painted white with that shit when they found her," he said.

"Are you shitting me?"

"I know, shit's fucked up, but that's what her father said."

"My God, Ray, this is un-fucking-believable. I seriously can't believe it. I was in that apartment so many times. What kind of sick motherfucker does something like this?" I cried.

"It don't make sense, Ron. It's just the way things are on the ledger. Come on, let's go." We took Meadows' old Pontiac Catalina over to the Buckley's apartment. It was a short trip over to my ledger, and we both remained quiet, contemplating the task ahead of us. The last thing either of us wanted, especially me, was to face Othra and Clarence. The street outside their place was packed with cars, so we ended up parking halfway down the block. "You going to be okay?" Meadows asked before I stepped out of the vehicle.

"Ray, I'm so numb right now, I can't feel anything," I said. It was true. I had expended so much emotional energy that I was drained to the point of exhaustion and felt like I was walking around in a state of limbo. The inner door of the apartment vestibule was propped open, and the murmur of people's voices met us at the doorway. The sounds grew louder as we climbed the flight of stairs to the Buckley's apartment. Meadows waited for me to climb up the stairs and stand next to him before knocking on the door. A young man opened the door and greeted us with a sullen smile while motioning for us to come in. As one might expect, the place was packed with relatives and friends contemplating the tragic events and lending support to the grieving family. Every possible spot at the dining room table was taken as people were milling back and forth between the three connecting rooms, consoling each other and murmuring in low voices about the incident.

No one seemed to notice as Meadows entered the apartment, but when I stepped in behind him, it was like someone flipped a switch. The room went dead silent when I shut the door. You could hear a pin drop as every black face in the room turned its attention to me. I was horrified, not afraid of bodily harm, just at the realization that every person there was aware of the significance my role played in Sandra's life. Even though we talked about it at the restaurant, I don't think Meadows realized the extent of my relationship with Sandra until that moment. I could never imagine a more God-awful, uncomfortable experience in my life, but I was truly not prepared for what happened next. As if it had been staged, the sea of glaring faces surrounding us parted as people stepped away to make a path for Sandra's father. Clarence—the stoic man with the dry wit, whom I had dined with weeks before—came running at me in hysterics.

"Mr. Pickles! Mr. Pickles! It was here all along! She left it here for you! It's here, see, see," he said, holding up a personal check from Sandra made out to the insurance company. "Here, you take this and make it right," he said, grabbing my hand and stuffing the check in my palm. He stood there, forcing a grin while nodding his head and pointing at the check he gave me. "Look, look, it's been here waiting for you," he said, shaking.

"I don't understand, what is this?" I asked. Ray and I looked at each other with puzzled expressions. We were coming here to tell him that she didn't pay her insurance and that it had lapsed. How did he know already?

"See, Mr. Pickles, she came over here and dropped off the check at our house after you left her the note. You was suppose to pick it up, so see, it's your fault 'cause you didn't pick up the check, but it's been here all along," he said, trying to catch his breath as he spoke.

"Clarence, it's too late," I said bewildered at his actions.

"No, you don't understand. See, after you left her the note…"

"Note! How do you know about the note?" I demanded.

"That's what I'm trying to tell you. See, she got your note thinking you were going to stop by here and pick up the 'surance money, you see?"

"I didn't leave her the note, Clarence. I saw her Wednesday afternoon and handed her the note, telling her to follow the instructions if she wanted to keep the insurance. She wouldn't even talk to me," I said.

"But she left the check at our house, you see," he begged.

"She was supposed to call me yesterday morning," I lamented.

"She was dead yesterday morning!" he said harshly with tears rolling down his cheeks.

"Don't you think I know that?" I hollered back at him.

"Wait, Ron!" Meadows called out while stepping between us, so as not to let the situation escalate. "Clarence, Ron talked to Sandra on Wednesday," Ray said, trying to help him understand.

"No, she left this money for you, and you didn't come and get it. See, it's your fault, so you got to do what's right," Clarence demanded.

"Clarence, Clarence, you know me," Meadows said forcefully. "Now, listen to what I'm saying. I know what this means to you, but Ron did everything he could. It's nobody's fault, you hear?"

"No, see, this is the check you wanted," Clarence directed at me with an angry tone, ignoring Meadows completely. "Mr. Pickles, you told me that you wanted to be the best 'surance man she ever had, and now you got to do what's right by her. You see that, don't you?" he pleaded. "I got to bury my babies the right way. You see that, don't you? You see that... Momma and me got to take care of the little ones. Mr. Pickles, you see it, don't you?" he begged while dropping to his knees with his face shaking and tears rolling down his cheeks. Everyone in the room watched in agony as Sandra's father broke down before our eyes. I stood there, frozen, drowning in his pain, while daggers were plunging into my body from the angry eyes of every person in the room.

From somewhere out of the crowd, the family minister excused his way to Clarence's side and helped him to his feet. He put his arm around him, then asked a woman seated at the dining room table if she wouldn't mind moving for a moment so Clarence could sit down. The minister pulled the chair over by Clarence, who fell into it, leaning forward, placing his elbows on his knees, and burying his face into his hands. The minister looked at me and recognized the anguish written across my face, offering a nod of understanding, which I took in like a breath of fresh air. After a few moments, Clarence lifted his head and brought his tired eyes in contact with mine, as if ashamed by his behavior. "I don't know what we're going to do. I just don't know," he said in a voice that was barely audible.

"Clarence, how did you know about the note?" I asked in a hushed tone while squatting down to his level. His face was defeated and his spirit so crushed that it hurt just to look at him.

"The funeral home found it in the pants she was wearing and gave it back to us this morning," he finally admitted. The muscles in my face tightened. I closed my eyes and pictured Sandra's final moments. The last words she would ever see from me warned of the consequences to her children without the insurance while she was being strangled to death. Meadows tapped me on the shoulder and gestured slightly with his hand that it was time to leave. He reached down and grabbed me under the arm to help me up before opening the door and saying goodbye. I followed him halfway out the door, standing inches away from the spot I left Sandra weeks before when I turned around and looked at Clarence, who was staring into space with a glazed expression on his face.

"Clarence, just one more thing. Did you read the end of the note?" I asked. Slowly, he turned towards me with an expression that seemed puzzled.

"That's what I don't understand, Mr. Pickles. Why you taking this money away from us if you cared about her so much?" he asked. I looked away and closed my eyes as a lone tear bubbled out and rolled down my cheek. I took a deep breath and turned back, taking in the man's face, knowing it was for the last time.

"You can think whatever you want, Clarence, but there ain't anyone here who wishes I could change this more than me. I'm sorry. I'm so sorry."

CHAPTER 24

The Next Day – Saturday, July 4th, 1981

It didn't even occur to me that it was July 4th when I rolled out of the recliner the next morning. I was on autopilot and found myself parked outside Lanni Tisdale's apartment, ready to make my first collection of the day, as I had done every Saturday morning for the past two years. Only a day after experiencing the most horrific event of my life, I was attempting to function as if nothing had happened. My physical presence was there, but my mind was a million miles away. I was in a zombie-like state, mimicking past behavior and actions without thought or reason.

Without hesitation, I opened the car door and exited without scanning the area for signs of danger, oblivious to my surroundings. It was still early, and the July sun hadn't quite burned off the lingering odor of humanity indulging themselves on a Friday night. Instead of being repulsed by the faint whiff of stale beer, melted rubber, and urine, I perked up and took a deep breath, as it seemed to fuel the lifelessness in me.

I climbed the back stairs and knocked on Lanni's apartment, waiting patiently as her little boy Max struggled with the locks and chains securing the door. Once he got it unlocked, the warped door stuck as he pulled on it, and I tried to help him by shoving it from my side, which worked a little too well and pushed Max to the floor with a giggle.

"Sorry, Max," I said, reaching out to help him up.

"That was fun," he said, jumping to his feet.

"Mom in the bedroom?" I asked.

"Yep, you want me to go get her?"

"Don't worry, Max. You watch your cartoons. I'll take care of it," I said.

"Okay," he said without a care in the world as he bounced back into the living room and flung himself to the floor in front of the television next to Takesha, who was too engrossed in her program to acknowledge me. I walked past them and opened the bedroom door to find Lanni face down, spread out naked across her bed with a sheet pulled partially across her back.

For almost two years now, I had been coming up to Lanni's apartment every Saturday morning to collect her weekly premium. In all that time, I completely distanced myself from the fact that she was an incredibly sexy woman who almost seemed as if she were testing my restraint. The ritual had become so commonplace, I didn't even think about the implications of intruding into the woman's bedroom anymore. This was just the way we conducted business. But today was different. I was different. "It's just me, Lanni," I said, announcing myself before grabbing her purse from the dresser and walking over to the side of her bed. She acknowledged my presence with a feeble attempt at pulling more of the sheet over her back. Her lame effort inadvertently uncovered her long, curvy legs and half her ass while she squirmed for a more comfortable position. I stood by the side of her bed and swallowed hard, taking in every inch of her jet-black, silky skin. I was dizzy with desire, barely able to restrain myself at the pure savage lust that overtook my senses and delivered the first pleasurable feeling I had experienced in two days.

Momentarily, the crushing pain of sorrow was lifted from my soul and replaced with a primordial urge to fuck this woman with all the anger in my heart. I stepped closer and ignored the usual routine, which was to drop her purse on the bed and wait while she rifled through its contents in search of money and her receipt book. Today, I acted on impulse, without regard to consequence. I sat on the bed and gently touched her shoulder to get her attention. "I have your purse, Lanni," I said, watching with delight as she tussled around in the sheets for a moment before lifting her head off the pillow and looking at me with a smile. She studied my expression for a long time, as if sensing the desire in my face. Slowly, she turned her body towards me, while twisting and tugging out of the sheets, like a butterfly emerging from a cocoon.

"Mr. Pickles, do you want anything to do with me?" she asked seductively. Without waiting for an answer, she placed her hand between my legs, cupping and squeezing my crouch. She slid closer and began rubbing and twisting me into a frenzy. I put her purse on the floor and pulled the sheet back, exposing her delightfully large breasts. Her nipples were black and hard, rising high above her glands like small handles on a bell. I pinched one between my thumb and forefinger, pulling it hard and letting it snap back like a rubber band. She moaned in delight and rubbed me harder, as if I needed any encouragement to do it again. I bent over and took the nipple in my mouth while running my hand under the sheet in search of her pussy, when, suddenly, the door to her bedroom burst open. Instantly, I pulled away from Lanni's tit and turned with a gasp at the face of her astonished little boy, Max, as he stood dumbfounded in the doorway.

"Boy! Shut that goddamn door and get out of here!" Lanni screamed at the top of her lungs as she jumped to her feet while wrapping the sheet perfectly around her body. Max didn't wait to be told again, slamming the door shut and running away before Lanni could get there. She twisted the lock on the door, then turned toward me, smiled, and let the sheet drop to the floor as if nothing had happened. Lanni took a step towards me but backed up when she saw the expression of disgust written across my face. Embarrassed, she bent down and picked up the sheet to cover herself once again. I stood up and walked past her with my head hung in shame as I reached for the door.

"I'm sorry, Mr. Pickles. That boy just don't know his manners," she said.

"No, it's me that's sorry, Lanni. I don't know what came over me. I got to go," I said humbly.

"Well, wait just a second," she said, hurrying over to the side of her bed and retrieving her purse.

"I got to get you that 'surance money," she said, digging through her purse. I stood there waiting for what seemed like an eternity, unable to fathom my own actions. I collected her money, marked her receipt book, apologized again before hanging my head in shame and walking out past the kids to the back door. As I was stepping outside, Max appeared in the kitchen standing tall, hands by his side, not saying a word. I forced a wink and a smile in his direction, but the look of betrayal on the little boy's face served as a mirror into my soul, reminding me of those famous words: "To thine own self be true." I felt dirty. I dropped my eyes and pulled the door shut in disbelief at my own insanity.

My frame of mind sunk to a new low as I drove around the black ledger in a literal vacuum of consciousness. I was disgusted by my actions at Lanni's house, consumed by the loss of Sandra, and plagued with the responsibility of the job that had now become tortuous. At every collection, it felt as if people were staring at me like a criminal, guilty of the most heinous of crimes. No one mentioned the murders, but they knew. They knew who was killed, how they were killed, and more than likely who was responsible. They also knew that I was the "'surance man" whose company wouldn't pay. Killings happened so frequently it became a way of life, but getting cheated by the white-owned insurance company was viewed as a racial indignity suffered by all.

I managed to collect most of my route card before feeling like I was going to literally collapse if I didn't get off the ledger and rest for a while. I pulled off in the direction of the Lake Street Diner, hoping that some lunch might help bring me back to life. I drove as far as Central Park Avenue, about to turn right, when a Chicago Police car passed in front of me, heading in the opposite direction. The squad car was gone in a moment, but it left a faint beacon of light that flickered in my mind as if guiding me back to reality. All the while I'd been wallowing in a puddle of emotions, I completely lost sight of the fact that somewhere out here was a killer who murdered two innocent people. I realized that I was becoming my own worst enemy when it dawned on me, *I wasn't the bad guy in all of this.* I didn't have a ton of information, but I did see her with those two guys the day she was killed, and that might be something. Without hesitation, I flipped the directional lever down for a left-hand turn and headed for the eleventh district police station down the block. I truly did love Sandra, and I needed to do something, anything, to ease my conscience. The guilt was unbearable, made worse because I felt completely helpless in a situation that was totally out of my control. I immediately felt better about myself just thinking that I made some effort to help.

It was weird, almost eerie, pulling into the parking lot of the police station. Even though the lot was jammed with cars and police officers were everywhere, the place had a foreboding sense about it. Just knowing the building contained every morbid detail of Sandra and Lucy's deaths, chronicled and stored with absolute indifference, gave me pause as I parked the car.

I walked inside the building wondering how exactly someone was supposed to go about reporting information to the police. There was a long, glass-enclosed counter with several officers mulling around inside and one sitting at a window assisting a line of people, which is where I figured I'd start the process. The lobby was packed with people, mostly degenerates and hookers, who were crowded together on wooden pew-like benches aligning the walls of the station. It was loud and unruly, with cackles of laughter erupting from time to time and people jabbering away like a Sunday meeting place.

I stood in line for fifteen or twenty minutes before stepping up to the window and waiting patiently while the desk sergeant filled out forms, a positively grim expression on his face. He was an older white guy with thick, black reading glasses, a buzz cut, and rough looking face, and I immediately realized that customer relations were not his top priority. After a few more moments, I cleared my throat in hopes of getting his attention. He barely acknowledged my presence by lifting his eyes over his glasses with an expression that seemed pained by the effort.

"Can I help you?" he finally grumbled.

"Yes, sir. I'm not sure exactly how to do this, but I may have some information about a murder I witnessed two days ago."

"You witnessed a murder?" he asked with alarm.

"No, no, not exactly, that's not what I meant…"

"Well, what then?"

"I'm sorry, officer. I meant to say that I had some information that may be helpful in a murder investigation," I said, realizing my mistake. He stared at me for a long moment, then finally stood up, dropped his glasses on the desk, and walked back to a doorway labeled "DETECTIVES" and disappeared. A moment later, he returned and pointed to a plainclothes officer who followed behind. The sergeant then motioned for me to move towards a glass door that led into their enclosure where the plainclothes officer was waiting.

"I'm Detective Randall. The sergeant said you wanted to report something," he said, opening the door and holding it as I walked through.

"Yes, sir. It's been sort of bothering me, and I just wanted to tell somebody in case it helps," I stammered for words.

"…And your name, sir?" Detective Randall asked.

"Um, Ron. Ron Pickles."

"We can talk in the office," the detective said, abruptly marching me back to the detective's room. The office was narrow with several desks on each side of the wall and a walkway down the middle. A few detectives were standing around a coffee machine at one end of the room, while several others were doing paperwork at their desks or talking on the phone. No one even glanced in my direction as the officer led me to his desk and asked me to have a seat before positioning himself behind the desk. He took a yellow legal pad out his drawer, flipped over several pages with writing on them, then searched the middle drawer for a pencil.

"First name is Ron. How do you spell that last name?" he asked.

"It's just like pickles: P-I-C-K-L-E-S," I replied.

"You catch some shit about that, huh?" he asked with a smile.

"It's unique," I replied.

"Okay, Mr. Pickles. Why are you here?"

"Well, this is in regards to the murders of Sandra and Lucy Wesley."

"Oh, let me stop you right there!" he said, jumping to his feet and turning around. "Hey, Hodges, you want to take this? It's about the Wesley case," he yelled toward another detective a few desks down. "Come on, Mr. Pickles, follow me, this is Detective Hodges' case. It's probably better if you talk to him. I'm going to take you to his desk," he said, motioning for me to follow.

"Hodges, this is Mr. Pickles. Detective Hodges will take your information," Randall said before walking back to his desk. My eyes practically rolled up into my head as the detective stood up and towered over me. He puffed out his chest as if daring me to wilt from his intimidating presence, which I considered in earnest. While Detective Randall was dressed comfortably in jeans, gym shoes, and a white T-shirt, Hodges' huge frame was uncomfortably stuffed into a shabby gray business suit that hadn't seen the dry cleaners in a long time. An expressionless handshake and a motion to sit was all the courtesy I was to be afforded by the aged veteran, who had already dismissed me as an incredible waste of his time.

"My name is Hodges," he deadpanned. "I'm the detective in charge of the Wesley case. Detective Randall says you have some information?"

"Yes, sir. I don't know how helpful it will be, but…"

"So, how did you know Ms. Wesley?" he asked, cutting me off.

"I was her insurance agent," I said.

"Okay, I got to get some information, so I know who I'm dealing with."

"Yes, sir, I understand."

"Here, write your name, address, and phone number on this," he said, tossing a legal pad and pencil in my direction. I quickly wrote down my information and pushed the pad and pencil back to his side of the table. He studied the paper for a moment then looked up at me with a raised eyebrow.

"You're from the South Side?" he asked.

"Yes, sir."

"So, how do you know Ms. Wesley?"

"I was her insurance agent," I said, stinging with the realization that I was talking about her in the past tense.

"You one of those ledger agents?" he asked.

"Yes, that's right. You know about the ledger?" I asked, surprised that he knew the term.

"Yeah, those assholes are always getting beat up and robbed out here," he said with a sly grin, as if amused by the story.

"Sad, but true," I said.

"It's not sad, it's stupid," he said. "It's like I told the last guy. You don't want to get beat up, stay the hell out of the ghetto, you stupid son of a bitch," he blurted out with a bellow of laughter as if very satisfied with himself.

"It's my job," I said somberly, dropping my eyes at the realization that I was dealing with a stone-aged relic of the police department.

"Yeah, that's too bad," he said unapologetically. "Alright, hold on a second, I need a witness report," he said, pushing himself away from his desk and fumbling for some paper in a bottom drawer. "Randall, you got a witness report?" he shouted across the room.

"Yeah, right here," the other detective said, waving some papers over his head. Hodges pushed himself away from his desk with a groan and walked over to Randall, grabbing the report from

Randall's hand and returning to his seat with another moan as his massive frame plopped behind the desk. I watched as he scribbled his name at the top of the report, then quickly transferred my information from the legal pad to the official report.

"That looks about right," he said, glancing over the form before looking up at me. "So, what did you see, Mr. Pickles?" he asked bluntly.

"Well, um, like I said, I don't know how helpful it will be, but I saw Sandra with a couple of guys the day she was killed, and I thought I should tell someone."

"Two guys?"

"Right."

"Two black guys?"

"Yes."

"So, you saw a couple of black guys with Ms. Wesley?" he asked as if correcting me.

"Right, black guys."

"When?"

"It was Wednesday afternoon," I said.

"At her house?"

"Correct."

"Why were you at her house?"

"I was there to collect her insurance money. Like I said, I was her agent."

"Alright, so, you saw a couple of black guys at her house, so what?" he asked impatiently.

"Well, actually, the reason I thought it was weird was because I had never seen these guys around her before and…"

"How often you see her?" he asked, cutting me off again.

"Usually once a month, but sometimes more, you know, if she's at her folk's or a neighbor's house when I'm collecting," I said, feeling a bit uncomfortable that he wouldn't let me explain myself.

"How long have you been collecting from her?" he asked.

"Little over a year."

"Okay, so let me get this straight. You're her insurance agent, and you see her on average once a month for a year, correct?"

"Yes, sir."

"Right. Now, I hope you don't mind me pointing this out again, but you are Caucasian, and she was a Negro, correct?"

"Well, yes, but what does that have to do with anything?" I begged the question.

"Well, Mr. Pickles, you're a white man, a white man that sells insurance to black people in a black ghetto, correct?"

"Yes."

"So, the day she is murdered, you see this black woman with two black guys in the ghetto where these people live and assume the two black guys killed her. Is that correct?"

"Well, no, I don't know. She seemed nervous, and I thought..."

"Is that correct?" he demanded.

"I don't know! I just thought it was something the police should know," I said defensively. He leaned back in his chair and looked at me as if I were a complete moron.

"Yeah, let me ask you something. You're probably a good guy trying to help out, right?" I nodded my head, then looked away and sighed, not wanting him to see the pain I was feeling.

"That's exactly what I mean," he said, going into a stretch as if bored with the conversation. "Here you are, a white guy who sees this broad once a month. She gets killed, and you show up here with some information you think may be important to the case. Do you see a line of 'Willies' from 'the hood' out there wanting to tell us what they saw?" He pointed to the lobby. "Nobody gives a shit!" he said, emphasizing his point. I shook my head as if agreeing with him, all the while remembering that Sandra said the same thing about the police.

"Listen to me. I deal with these people every fucking day, and you want to know something? Every single one of these sons of bitches knows what's going on out there, yet not one person comes in here," he said, leaning forward and tapping his desk hard, as if driving home his point. "These people treat cops like we're the fucking enemy while they blow each other's brains out. I don't mind telling you that the sadistic bastards fucked up this woman and her kid pretty bad, but nobody in that neighborhood says shit. These fucking people... Come on, you know somebody knows something," he said with disgust. His callousness sawed at my raw nerves but also woke me up to something I hadn't realized.

"So, wait a minute. You know about the guys I saw her with, don't you?"

"We do."

"They didn't have anything to do with this?" I asked.

"Nope. Nothing. Look, Mr. Pickles, I'm not supposed to share information about the investigation, but they didn't kill this woman or her kid."

"How can you be so sure?" I asked incredulously.

"We interviewed both of them. One of the guys you saw her with was a cousin, and the other was his friend. They didn't have anything to do with killing them," he said dismissively. Just as abruptly, he pushed himself away from his desk and stood up. "We appreciate you coming in. Now, if you'll excuse me, I got work to do," he said with a strained look on his face while pointing me in the direction of the door. I took a deep breath, stood up, turned, and left, feeling very unsatisfied with the Chicago Police Department.

CHAPTER 25

Sunday, July 5th, 1981

For the first time in a long time, Jessica and I actually had a civil conversation over supper Sunday night. We talked about the baby, our parents, and some silly family gossip she learned from her sister the night before. Once or twice, work crept into the conversation, and, just as quickly, I would change the subject onto something else. The conversation was pleasant because we spoke to each other more as acquaintances than as husband and wife. It was as if civility had emerged from the ashes of a burned-out relationship, and it was quite refreshing.

After dinner, Jessica put Jeannie in the crib and headed into the bedroom to lie down. I sat down on the recliner, mindlessly flipping channels on the television, not the least bit interested in watching anything. Just as I had begun to nod off, the phone rang, startling me and waking the baby. I hurried into Jeannie's room and picked her up before running back into the kitchen to answer the phone.

"Hello?"

"Hey, Pickles, that you? It's Teddy."

"Lobranski, what do you want?" I asked with annoyance.

"I got something I need to talk to you about, and I was wondering if we could get together tonight and get a beer?"

"Are you out of your fucking mind?" I shouted into the phone. The harshness of my voice upset Jeannie, so I put the phone on my shoulder and reassured the baby that everything was all right before continuing to talk in a subdued tone. "Teddy, if this is about the death claim we talked about Friday, I've already told you that the policy was lapsed, and that's it."

"Wait a minute, Pickles. Listen to me for a second, will you?"

"Teddy, I got the baby here, make it quick," I said.

"There's a way out of this if you're willing to listen," he said.

347

"Teddy, you're the one not listening to me. I've already talked about this with both Hamilton and Meadows. The policy is lapsed," I said forcefully.

"Fuck Meadows. He don't give a shit about you," he shot back.

"You're missing the point, Hamilton…"

"Ron, the big guy's on your side," he said, cutting me off. I stood dumbfounded for a moment, not knowing how to respond.

"I don't understand. What do you mean he's on my side?"

"You heard me. The big guy knows what you're going through and wants to help you out," he said with a sympathetic voice.

"Hamilton? Bullshit, Teddy, I talked with him yesterday, and he…"

"What's he supposed to say at the office, Ron? Now look, I don't want to talk about this over the phone. Do you want to get a beer and discuss this or not?"

"I dunno," I half muttered into the phone. I didn't know what to say. I was in a bad way, vulnerable to a fault with my back up against the wall, and he knew it. I did tell Hamilton how much this meant to me; I wondered if maybe Roger did understand the situation better than I gave him credit for and wanted to help. I had to listen to him. I had to know if there was some way, any way, to get Clarence the money he would need for his family.

"Where do you want to meet?" I finally asked.

"Meet me at King Arthur's by the office in an hour. Fuck that liver and onion shit. I'll buy you a double cheeseburger on French bread and a beer," he said with a chuckle. I hung up the phone and took Jeannie back into her room. I laid her down on the bed where she seemed eager to roll over and go to sleep. Jessica was fast asleep, so I wrote her a quick note, tacked it up on the fridge, and headed off to King Arthur's Bar and Grill.

The night air was refreshing, and the long drive gave me an opportunity to think about what Lobranski had to offer. I would have hung up on him had he not referred to Hamilton. I couldn't help but wonder if Roger really did understand how upset I was yesterday and if he thought enough of me to enlist Teddy's aid in getting Sandra's claim paid. Then I remembered how many times Meadows had told me to stay away from Teddy and the stoner staff because they were up to no good. On the other hand, he also told me that Hamilton knew of their dealings and ignored them as long as they produced sales. If that were the case, maybe Hamilton figured Teddy owed him a favor and decided to call it in for me. By the time I reached the bar, my mind was spinning in every direction, trying to figure out both Hamilton and Teddy's motivation.

King Arthur's Bar and Grill was housed in a dingy little brick building on Cermak Road, a few blocks away from the office in the town of Berwyn. Chances of getting one of the three parking spots behind the tavern were slim to none, so I just parked along one of the side streets and walked a block to the restaurant. The restaurant owners spared every expense when it came to decorating the exterior of the building in the style of a medieval castle befitting that of King Arthur. They figured that an arched wood plank door with a cheesy looking shield and sword nailed to it was all the customers needed to feel the ambience of the mythical ruler's home.

The inside felt a little more medieval with a dungeon-like atmosphere, dark and smoky with a long, crowded bar full of men downing schooners of their favorite ale. Wooden picnic tables adorned the floor area where two to eight people could sit across from each other and sample the limited menu choices of the establishment. There were two bartenders but no waiters or waitresses. If you wanted something, you had to go up to the bar or call out for the bartender to come to the table. I walked inside and spotted Teddy hoarding a large table, puffing furiously on a cigarette with one hand while clutching a mug of beer in the other. He was still dressed in his business suit and looked as if he had just walked off the ledger.

"Jesus Christ, Pickles. I was starting to think you weren't going to show," he said, reaching out to grab my hand as I sat down on the other side of the table.

"I told you an hour."

"Yeah, that's right. I forgot," he said with a shrug. What are you drinking?"

"I don't care. Beer is fine," I said, watching as his eyes danced around the room.

"Stosh! Can we get another beer over here?" he shouted in the direction of the busy bartender.

"Same thing?" the bartender called back.

"Same thing," Teddy replied before extinguishing one cigarette then lighting another. He seemed nervous and fidgety, but I couldn't tell if it was because of our meeting or just a byproduct of his well-known cocaine usage. The bartender dropped off the beer and asked if we wanted anything from the grill before they shut it down for the night.

"Hey, ya hungry? Let's order some cheeseburgers."

"No, Teddy, I just had dinner a couple of hours ago. I'm not really hungry."

"Come on, Ron! Jesus Christ! You can't come to the King's and not get a double on French," he said as if I were committing some sort of sacrilege. "Where else are you going to get a double burger cooked to perfection and split into the pocket of a delicious hunk of French bread, smothered in cheese?" he said, demonstrating with his hands as he spoke. "How 'bout it, Stosh?"

"Best burger on the South Side," Stosh agreed.

"You're killing me, Teddy, you know that?" I said, shaking my head.

"Alright, you're the man, Pickles. Hey, Stosh, how about two doubles on French bread, American cheese and all the fixings," he told the bartender before I protested further. Once Stosh walked away, I watched with interest as the expression on Teddy's face changed from a wild-eyed carnival barker into a sympathetic friend. I wasn't impressed.

"I bet it's been a tough couple of days for you, huh?"

"I've seen better," I said, taking a big swig of beer. "You working a Sunday?"

"Yeah, I was out all day. You know how it is, first of the month and all. Gotta catch these niggers before the check is gone," he said with exasperation. I just looked down at the table, shook my head without acknowledging him and took another sip of beer. He cleared his throat and pinched his nose between his thumb and forefinger, as if trying to wring it out while sniffing furiously to stop it from dripping. "Must be catching something," he muttered while reaching to the center of the table and grabbing some paper napkins out of the condiment basket. He wiped his nose with the napkins, then stuffed the napkins into his pants pocket before taking another gulp of beer. I couldn't help but find the amount of nasal work needed to sustain a good cocaine habit amusing. "Damn, Ron, I know you think I'm full of shit sometimes, but seriously, I wouldn't wish what happened on your ledger to anyone," he finally forced out in a phlegm-covered voice.

"I never saw it coming, that's for sure," I said with a sigh.

"Fuck no! Something like this blindsides you out of the fucking blue, and who's there for you?" he shot back.

"Well, I appreciate it, Teddy. It's been real hard. That's the thing, you know. I can't talk to anyone at home about it, so it just sort of sits inside your gut and eats you up," I said before taking another long swig of my beer.

"Who can you tell?" he asked rhetorically.

"Nobody," I concurred.

"No fucking way! The black ledger doesn't even exist to your friends and relatives. They don't have a clue what it's like to deal with these fuckers in the ghetto," he lamented. I knew he was trying desperately hard to suck up and cajole me into despising everything about the ledger. It was an old sales trick, sort of a "misery loves company" approach to buddy up and frame our conversation like it was me and him against the world. It was tempting too. It would have been so easy to let my hatred of everything that happened over the past few days boil into a racist rant or condemn everyone who lived there as worthless pieces of shit. But I knew the truth, and I knew that's what Teddy wanted from me, so I just dropped my eyes and shook my head as if contemplating his words of wisdom. I wanted him to think he was swaying me to his way of thinking. After a long moment, I lifted my head and looked into his eyes as if we were the best friends on the face of the planet. He bought it hook, line, and sinker and pursed his lips in anger, as if outraged by my predicament.

"See, that's what pisses me off about fucking Meadows," he grumbled while pounding his fist on the table in a mock show of indignant rage.

"Come on, Teddy, I know you have problems with Meadows, but I don't..."

"...Wait a minute, Pickles. Hear me out, okay?" he said, pleading as much with his eyes as with his words. I glanced away for a moment, then looked back and nodded my head.

"I'm listening," I said.

"This is exactly what I'm talking about when I tell you that, in this job, we need to stick together to survive. Why do you think I'm always bugging you to transfer over to our staff?"

"You mean us white guys," I said sarcastically.

"Who's talking to you right now?" he shot back.

"You are."

"Exactly, think about it. Where's Meadows? Where's Wahl, or any of the other shines on your staff?"

"Come on, Teddy, what's your point?"

"My point is that nobody, including the black guys on your staff, has a clue how hard this fucking job can be if you're white!" he said with added emphasis on each word, believing that he could strike a chord with me.

"Okay, Teddy, let's get this thing started right. The first thing you need to do is cut the bullshit," I said.

"What bullshit, Ron? I swear to God," he said, putting his hand on his heart. "Do you think you're the first one to ever have something like this happen to him?" he asked, catching me off guard.

"What do you mean?"

"Ron, every agent in the company has lapsed a policy and not been able to pay off on a death claim. You're not the first. It's a bitch because you're 'the 'surance man,' and they blame you, even though it's their own fucking fault that they didn't pay the goddamn premium." I nodded slightly, then took a few sips of my beer. I understood what he was saying but knew my situation was way different. "Add the fact that you're white, and now you've just become another honky motherfucker that stuck it to the black man," he said.

"Look, Teddy, I understand what you're saying, and you're probably right. I'm sure that's the way a lot of people look at me right now, but truthfully, the only reason I came down here was because you said Hamilton may have a way to help, which I assume means that he'll consider paying the claim?"

"Whoa, Pickles, back up a second!" he said, pushing himself away from the table and gesturing with his hands as if to slow down.

"What, is something wrong?" I asked. He didn't answer immediately, choosing instead to remove a new pack of cigarettes from inside his jacket pocket and scratch off the cellophane wrapper. He cleared his throat while tearing off the corner foil of the package and tapping the pack on the table. With eyes darting around the room, he leaned forward and motioned for me to lean in as well.

"The first thing we got to do is come to an understanding," he said in a hushed tone.

"…And that would be?" I asked, imitating his dramatics. He straightened up, seemingly annoyed that I wasn't taking his gesture of secrecy as seriously as he would have liked.

"You have to understand that the big guy is really going out on a limb for you. So, from the get-go, we never mention his name. Do you understand?" he asked while removing a fresh cigarette from the pack before returning it to his jacket pocket.

"Understand what? You know something, Teddy, this is starting to sound like bullshit, and the main reason I didn't even want to come here tonight."

"Pickles…!"

"No, fuck you. This is serious shit, Teddy. You never give anybody a straight answer about anything. You drag me down here by telling me that Hamilton wants to help, then come off with this secret bullshit like it's a cover-up or something. I'm not playing these fucking games with you!" I shouted out with exasperation.

"Pickles, Pickles, Pickles, be cool, man, okay? Get a fucking grip," he begged.

"Fuck that, Teddy. Either you're here to help me or not. Did Hamilton send you or not?"

"Come on. Pickles. Don't act like a jagoff," he said with a furrowed brow and puckered lip. "We're all putting our asses on the line trying to help you out, but that means we have to bend the rules, and you've been in the office long enough to know that MR. HAMILTON doesn't bend the fucking rules!"

"Teddy, I want a straight answer: is Hamilton going to help or not?" I asked, fully prepared to get up and walk out at the first hint of deception. He looked at me for a long moment, as if deciding what to say. He was troubled, and, for the first time, I got the feeling he wasn't sure he could trust me. I found it somewhat reassuring that we both had the same misgivings about each other.

"Yes, Hamilton will help, but indirectly," he said reluctantly. "You have to know that this shit could land us all in jail."

"Wait a minute, Teddy. I'm not asking anyone to do anything that's illegal," I said firmly.

"What are you, fucking stupid, Pickles? You lapsed the fucking policy."

"I put the card in the lapse pile, but we both know there's nothing illegal about claiming it was a mistake and that the premium had been paid," I said.

"Yeah, maybe with a $500 claim, but not a $20,000 payout. The home office would go apeshit over any discrepancy on a claim that big."

"How would they even know?" I asked in confusion. I hadn't thought about the ramifications of paying the claim, since it always seemed pretty cut and dry whenever I got one.

"Pickles, what's the biggest claim you ever turned in?"

"I don't know. Total? I think I had one for $7,500 once, but it was a combination of five or six policies on one person."

"Right, well get this straight. On any claim over ten thousand, the company does a field audit before the claim is approved. You ever hear of that?"

"No, what's that?" Teddy shifted his eyes around the room then held up his index finger and started counting off the purpose of the field audit.

"First, it's to establish definitive proof and identification of the deceased. Second, it's to verify and confirm that every payment was received and recorded properly. ...And third, it's to perform an inner-office audit and make sure the payment was recorded on your weekly account," he said with authority.

I withered back and almost slid off the picnic bench with my body aching as my brain tried to absorb the futility of this conversation. Just then, the bartender edged up to the side of the table and slammed two huge baskets of food in front of us. The greasy cheeseburgers tucked nicely into the folds of the lightly toasted French bread were still sizzling and gave off the most enticing aroma you could imagine. The food seemed to perk us both up as we immediately took to preparing the burgers to our liking.

"See, aren't you glad I talked you into the burger?" Teddy asked as I ripped off the first bite.

"It's a great sandwich," I mumbled with a mouthful of food as my thoughts turned back to our discussion. "So, tell me more about this field audit?"

"Not much more than what I already told you, except that the home office gets involved," he said.

"So, it's out of Hamilton's control?"

"The actual field audit? Yeah," he said casually while downing another bite. For the next few minutes, we both concentrated our full attention on devouring the basket of food without speaking. I finished the sandwich, then pushed the basket to the side before gulping down the rest of my beer to wash down the food.

"You want another? Teddy asked.

"No, I'm good," I replied as Teddy pushed his basket to the side, took a sip of beer, lit his cigarette, and stretched his chin towards the ceiling to exhale the smoke.

"So, what's the fucking point?" I finally muttered with exasperation.

"The point?"

"Yeah, the point. If it's out of Hamilton's control?" I asked.

"Well, the point is that we can make this thing right if you're willing to do what you're told, keep your fucking mouth shut, and be somebody we can trust," he said with an arrogance of authority. Right then, I knew it was a scam. A sinking feeling began to come over me as I realized that not only was I being played but that nobody gave a shit about me or what happened to Sandra and Lucy. I felt like a fish on the end of a line, fighting for my life, knowing that I was caught and being reeled ever so slowly into a boat where I was going to be filleted. I had two choices: I could stand up and walk out of the restaurant, or I could allow myself to be caught.

"So, it's not a done deal?" I asked almost sarcastically, knowing that it was still very much in play.

"Not yet, but time is running out," he said. I couldn't help but crack a smile.

"How much?" I asked.

"Join our staff. Learn how we do things. Learn how we protect each other and make some serious money," he said, ignoring my question.

"Teddy…"

"No, wait a minute! You need to hear me out first. Don't be an idiot. The niggers take care of themselves, and we watch out for each other. Don't you realize that you're the odd fucking guy out? Don't you know that, if you were black, there is no way Meadows would have let you take the fall in this situation?" he insisted.

"Jesus Christ, Teddy. It's not like that, and you know it," I countered.

"Oh really, Pickles?" His confidence rattled me a bit, though I knew in my heart that Meadows would have done anything he could have to help out yesterday. "Look, all I can tell you is that right now you're fucked, and so are your people. Join us, and we get these people the money they deserve and make you look like a hero. It's up to you, Ron, but this will be your only chance. If you say no, you're on your own, and there's nothing more we can do."

"Like I asked you originally, Teddy, how much?"

"Your cut?" Teddy almost asked gleefully.

"No, the family," I said sternly.

"Burial, plus twenty-five hundred," he said.

"Out of twenty thousand fucking dollars?!"

"No, Pickles! Out of the FUCKING NOTHING they have right now!" he yelled back. We both paused and looked around the room to see if our outburst had garnered any unwanted attention, which it hadn't.

"Jesus Christ, Teddy. Is this a joke?" I asked with disgust while lowering my voice.

"No, it's a business deal, and it's a damn good business deal," he countered.

"Yeah, for who?"

"For everyone. Think about it for a second. These people are looking forward to getting nothing. They just had their family members brutally murdered, and they can't even come up with the money to bury them. It isn't our fault they didn't pay the premium. You did everything you were supposed to do. You sold the woman some of the best insurance we can offer and covered her kids as well. For whatever reason, she didn't pay the contract, and you did the right thing and lapsed it, right?"

"Yeah," I said softly.

"What we're going to do now is literally give them something nobody else in this world can give them, a chance to hold their heads up with dignity and bury their people without passing a hat. Do you realize how important that is in the black community?"

"Yeah, I do," I said, knowing he was right and still hating the fact that his way was the only answer. How could I refuse? How could I turn away the only chance Sandra's family had to recover at least something? The smugness on Teddy's face was revolting and reminded me that I was about to do something that went against all my principles.

"Fuck it," I finally said. "I guess I'm part of your staff," I said while sheepishly extending my hand.

"It's a good decision, Pickles," he said, grabbing my hand with the handshake of a salesman.

"Okay, but I just can't, um…"

"What?"

"Well, I need to know how this thing is going to work. I just can't do it blindly," I said.

"Hey, no secrets between us now. You're part of the team, kid. What do you want to know?"

"Well, you said Hamilton wasn't in control…"

"…Of the field audit," he interjected.

"But all the information is already written down in our office," I said.

"Right, but the people in the office are under Hamilton's control," he said.

"So, the lapse card will be pulled?"

"Already done."

"Really?"

"He wants you on the team," he said pointedly.

"Sounds like you guys had this planned all along," I quipped.

"Like I said, Ron, this business is fucked up. We're not stupid. He knew the minute you called how bad you were hurting, and he wanted to help," he said sympathetically.

"Then what about the money? Who gets what? Because I don't mind going with the program, but I do want the family to get all they can. That's my request. That's something you can do for me?"

"Pickles, I understand, and believe it or not, so does Hamilton. He knows how much you care about your people, and that's why he wants you on the team, and..."

"The money, Teddy?" I demanded in a strong tone.

"The office gets $15,000, the funeral home gets $2,500, and the clients get $2,500 cash, plus the burial," he said methodically, as if he had known the numbers for some time.

"Fifteen thousand dollars to the office!" I blurted out in disgust.

"You think the office girls are going to lift that lapse card and make sure the payments have been recorded for nothing?"

"Jesus, everyone's involved," I said, rubbing my eyes at the scope of this deception.

"Like I said, Pickles, we have to take care of each other," he said in a reassuring tone.

"Not me. Anything you had planned to give to me goes to the family," I shot back.

"Nope, it don't work that way. You have to accept a cut, or all deals are off," he said calmly.

D.G. ALLEN

"Why?"

"You know why, Pickles. You're not stupid," he said with a sideways look that cut me to the core. I closed my eyes momentarily, sick to my stomach that I was actually doing this.

"What if I just give it to the family?"

"Can't do that. The family is going to sign an agreement with the funeral home. They will be told that we contract a lot of business with this particular black-owned funeral home that looks out for the brothers. You know what I mean? We will explain to them that, without this funeral home, we couldn't help them out, and they'd get nothing. So, if you walk into that family's house with a handful of dollars trying to soothe your conscience, they're going to know it's a scam and blow on all of us. But if they accept the funeral home money, they're part of the scam and have to eat the shit we give them."

"Eat the shit we give them!" I screamed at him.

"I'm sorry, Ron. I didn't mean it the way it sounded," he apologized. I stared a hole through him, hating this whole fucking thing, but I bit my lip, knowing that, at least for now, I could get Sandra and Lucy a decent burial. But something about this wasn't sitting well with me, and it wasn't just the scam. I couldn't put my finger on it, but it stunk. "You okay?" he asked at the look on my face.

"I don't know," I sighed.

"Look, Hamilton has been sick to his stomach after that phone call you made to him. He doesn't want to lose you. You're one of the best agents in the office. It's practically fucking impossible to get someone decent to do this job, and he doesn't make any money if he's constantly hiring new agents. He thinks the world of you, guy!" he exclaimed.

"He thinks the world of himself!" I shot back sarcastically.

"Pickles, come on, man!" he shouted. "What the fuck do you want from me?"

"The truth! That's all, Teddy," I said with exasperation, trying to absorb everything he was saying. "I need to understand the mechanics. I want to know every detail so this shit doesn't come to bite me," I said, pointing at him with determination.

"Pickles, what do you think I'm trying to do? I'm trying to tell you how this thing has to go down in order to make it right, don't you get that?" he demanded.

"I don't know. You're saying all the family has to do is sign an assignment form?" I asked quickly.

"That's all they have to do. As far as they know, it's a deal with the funeral home and has nothing to do with the insurance company. That's why you can't go in there handing them money. They might just get a little suspicious and want to know why you're handing them a shitload of cash, and that would be bad for all of us. So, now do you understand?" he asked, prodding me to answer.

"Yeah, I get it, Teddy. So, what's next?"

"Well, for one thing, you're done with these people."

"What do you mean, 'done'?"

"You're too close to the situation. You'll fuck up everything and blow the whole fucking deal. From now on, I'll deal directly with them and get them on board with the program."

"You?"

"Who do you think? It certainly ain't going to be Meadows."

"…And what about Meadows? How are you going to stop him from finding out or questioning all this? He's going to know what's happening. He used to be their insurance agent," I said.

"Fuck Meadows. For one thing, we're going to transfer that particular case to my book, which means he's got nothing to say about it. Secondly, you're transferring to our staff, so Meadows won't have an excuse to get involved with anything you do. …And lastly, don't think for one second that Hamilton doesn't own Meadows' ass. He'll do exactly what Hamilton wants him to do."

"Really?"

"Fuck yeah. Hamilton saved his ass a couple of years before you got here. The fucking nigger got shit faced at a bowling alley and started beating on people. Hamilton bailed him out, got him straight, and paid off the damages."

"No shit," I replied, figuring that Meadows' tormented youth must have bubbled over.

"Yeah, so he won't give us any problems."

"He'll feel betrayed," I said.

"Fuck him, Ron. What else do you want me to say?" After that, I left the subject alone, figuring that it didn't matter to Teddy and might serve to agitate him into forgoing any more information.

"Yeah, fuck him. Like you said, he wasn't going to help me anyway," I said with more than a dose of guilt. "So, what's the plan?" I asked. Teddy gulped down some more beer and seemed pleased that I dismissed Meadows so easily and got back on subject.

"Well, first thing is…"

"Wait a fucking minute," I stopped him cold.

"What?"

"What about your manager? Tom Minka. I completely forgot about him."

"Minka does what he's told. No problems there," Teddy dismissed, as if amused by the urgency of the question.

"So, he's in on this too?"

"I take care of Minks out of my cut."

"You got this shit down, don't you?"

"Pickles, we've been doing this for a long time."

"So, you were about to tell me what I needed to do," I said.

"Right. Well, the first thing is to get to the office really early tomorrow morning."

"Alright."

"See Roger first thing and formally ask him for a transfer to our staff. He'll be expecting you and understand that you're upset over the situation and wanting to move," he said with a smirk. "Then,

362

he'll discuss the move with you and probably have Minka welcome you to the staff or some bullshit like that," he said dismissively before taking a quick swig of beer.

"Okay, then what?" I asked impatiently, waiting for him to swallow the beer.

"Well, then Roger is going to have you transfer the case to me. He's going to want you to transfer anyone else in the girl's family you may have insured as well," he said as an afterthought.

"You know I have her mom and dad," I interjected.

"Yeah, sure, I'm just saying we don't want you in that house anymore. Give that transfer directly to Hamilton. Don't give it to the girls, or it could sit in their bins all fucking week. He'll know what to do with it and expedite it to my book. Then, we can start the process and get this mess cleaned up," he said as if it were just a minor annoyance. Suddenly, without warning, his demeanor changed, and his face contorted as if enraged by a thought that erupted from his brain.

"But! And this is very important!" he said, leaning in close with a finger pointed at me with a seriousness I didn't like. "You never fucking mention our meeting, and you don't say a word about lapses, payoffs, or anything remotely connected to what we talked about tonight, or he'll blow his fucking stack. Do you understand?" he asked while pushing his index finger into the table. I couldn't help but chuckle and shake my head at his forced antics, which threw him into a rage.

"I get it, Teddy," I said. "But if something goes wrong or I have a question about something, who can I talk to? And when do I get a chance to talk to Roger about any of this?" I asked innocently.

"You don't fucking get it!" he shouted back at me. "Nothing ever goes wrong, and you never ever talk about this shit! That's why it works. If a play comes up, then you'll be asked if you want it settled. That's it! This is the only time anyone will ever go into any detail with you about anything. Roger knows what he's doing, and we all make a shitload of money because of it. He's got this shit figured out like a science and knows how to work it. That's why nothing ever gets said in the office. Do you understand? Now do you fucking understand?" he scolded, almost in a panic.

"Yeah, I get it, for Christ's sake. Just calm down," I said, motioning with outstretched fingers to relax. "This is all new to me, goddamn it! You knew goddamn well I wasn't going to just do this without asking a shitload of questions," I said, trying to put him at ease. I studied his expression and realized in that moment that he was petrified of Hamilton and seemed as if he were under some hypnotic spell to do his bidding.

"I'm sorry, Ronnie. I get a little uptight sometimes, but as long as you know the rules and do what you're asked to do, everything will be fine, you know?"

"It's cool, Teddy, and I really do appreciate you guys helping me out with this," I said, practically gagging on the words as they left my mouth.

"So, you know what to do Monday?" he asked with a calmer tone.

"Yeah, I'm good, and I know not to bring up any of this," I replied.

"Good," he said, leaping to his feet and throwing forty bucks on the table. "I got to run, Pickles. Do me a favor and pay this, will you? You have any questions, don't hesitate to give me a call. Remember, this stays between you and I, okay, kid? See you at the office," he said, bolting out of the restaurant like the place was about to blow up.

I sat there for a few minutes and gathered my thoughts, oblivious to the raucous atmosphere of the bar. I couldn't figure it out, but something began to gnaw at me as I replayed this conversation with Teddy over and over in my head. Then it dawned on me. It was his comfort level and knowledge of the events, as well as his patented formula for profiting from the case. "How many times have they pulled these scams?" I wondered to myself as the realization and magnitude of this began to creep into my bones. This was bad. Not just the idea of pulling off what amounted to an unbelievable case of fraud in an attempt to help Sandra's family, but the realization that this entire business was complete bullshit. Everyone was corrupt. Hell, I was corrupt when I agreed to write key man insurance on Ruppert and the gang, or like what I did to old Willie, forcing him to buy insurance out of Winnie's death benefit. Self-righteous as it seemed at the time, especially when he invested the rest of the money in socks, booze, and whores, it wasn't my place to steal his money out of the guise of doing him a service. "Jesus Christ, how they brainwashed you," I muttered to myself. Suddenly, things were beginning to make a little more sense. Roger Hamilton was behind everything that went down in that office.

Our district wasn't number one in sales because we had the best talent in the industry. We were number one because Hamilton was a master thief who figured out how to play the system and steal from both the company and the policyholders. I had heard grumblings around the office that Hamilton knew what everyone was doing but figured he stayed clear as long as no one got into trouble like T.J. What I didn't realize was that Hamilton actually sanctioned and even promoted these scams to enrich himself. I kept wondering what kind of power he must have had in order to operate without fear that someday his empire would come crashing down. It just seemed unfathomable to me that this had gone on for as long as it did, and no one stopped it, or even tried. As much respect as I had for Meadows or Otis, even they knew what was going on, and they just played along like everyone else. Now, he had me by the proverbial balls.

I stood up, grabbed the money off the table, paid the bill, and strolled to my car as a different man began to emerge from within. I wasn't going to stand by and let this crooked insurance agency continue to steal from folks who could least afford to be preyed upon. People were dying and getting ripped off by the insurance agents they trusted. Poor people who invested the little money they had in hopes of maintaining their family's dignity, only to be scammed at their most vulnerable time. I decided right then and there to accept the deal, play their game, but on my terms, not theirs.

The cocoon of innocence was gone, the metamorphosis complete. I had become a man with a purpose. I was angry for sure, but never in my life was I more determined. I wasn't scared. I was emboldened. I wasn't a thief, but I knew after meeting Teddy, it would take a thief and a con artist to beat these guys at their own game. This shit had to stop, and I was going to do everything I could to end the madness.

Oh, I would do exactly as Teddy suggested and get whatever money I could for Sandra's family. I would put on the best act I could and become one of them. I wanted them to think they owned me lock, stock, and barrel. I would be the perfect soldier and someone they could trust. What they wouldn't know is, at the same time, I would document every conversation, copy every note, and get supporting evidence wherever and whenever I could to bring them down. I figured that by playing along, I would probably get in as much trouble and be accountable to some extent, but I didn't care. If I had to go to jail in the process, then that's what I had to do.

My mind was working in a thousand different directions as I headed home that night, and my driving was on automatic. I had totally missed the exit for the Stevenson Expressway while driving southbound on Harlem Avenue, which would have been the quickest way home. Before long, I was passing through the little town of Bridgeview and stuck behind a postal truck waiting to turn left into the massive postal operation located in that town. The truck finally turned, and I headed down the street when an idea hit me like a thunderbolt out of the blue. Without hesitation, I pulled a U-turn in the middle of Harlem Avenue and headed back towards the post office. It was the only post office on the South Side that stayed open till 10:00 p.m. every night of the week. I remembered this because I was just there a few months back, trying to get my taxes filed and postdated before the deadline.

I pulled into the giant facility and pulled into the first parking spot I could find. I had thirty minutes before they closed. I reached into the back seat and grabbed my briefcase, heaving it over the front seat and plopping it down next to me. Sadly, I remembered that I didn't have any paper to write on, and, for a moment, my thoughts turned to Sandra and the note I wrote her. I shook the memory from my mind, trying to focus on something my mother had told me about years before.

For all her faults, my mom was a voracious reader and once told me about a story she read about a good guy who was being blackmailed by the CEO of a company where he worked. I couldn't remember the whole story, but the good guy was in a terrible predicament. The CEO was stealing money and planted some documents that implicated him. The good guy couldn't go to the police because he didn't have proof, and he was afraid the CEO might have him killed if he didn't go along with the scam. This guy also knew that he would be guilty of theft if caught and in a situation where he would have to prove he was being blackmailed. So, he began writing letters and mailing them to himself, chronicling the details, dates, and demands of the blackmailers. When the CEO finally got caught and tried to pin the thefts on the good guy, he was able to produce these wonderfully sealed and postmarked letters proving that he, in fact, was an innocent victim being blackmailed into committing crimes. I wasn't being blackmailed in the sense that anyone had threatened me, but I was most certainly being asked to commit fraud and take money as a way of benefiting from the scam. They were using my guilt as a means to profit and making damn sure I willingly signed off on the deal. I didn't have any paper, but I had tons of blank route cards and lots of return envelopes from Unified Insurance Company. Quickly but methodically, I wrote a synopsis of the meeting Teddy and I had just conducted on the backs of a couple of route cards, focusing on the things he said "the big guy" would do for me if I pledged to work with them. Most importantly, I detailed the breakdown of the numbers Teddy reeled off to me: $15,000 to the office, $2,500 to the funeral home, and $2,500 to my clients. I sat there for a moment, mesmerized by those numbers, remembering how Sandra said she trusted me. "Jesus Christ, this is fucked up!" I cried out before jumping out of the car and running into the post office.

I stepped up to the window with the route cards in one hand and the pen and envelope in the other, just minutes before they were going to close. "You just made it," the lady clerk said with a smile.

"I know, a last-minute thing," I said, trying to catch my breath while laying out the paperwork on the counter. "Hey, would it be okay to get a postmark on the contents of the letter as well?" I asked as an afterthought.

"I don't see why not. What do you want me to stamp?" she asked.

"Umm, well, if you could stamp these two cards, it would be great," I said, pushing the hastily written cards in front of her. She pounded the stamp down on each route card, then put a postage stamp on the envelope and stamped that before ringing up my bill. I hurriedly folded the route cards and stuffed them in the envelopes, quite proud of my ingenuity before turning the envelope over to write my address and bursting into a total panic. I forgot the return address on the envelope was emblazoned with the return address of Unified Insurance Company. It would not be good if something happened to this envelope and it found its way back to Roger Hamilton. Quickly, I scratched out the insurance company's address and wrote mine underneath and again in the center of the envelope. I paid the bill, handed her the envelope, and headed back to my car. I could feel a tingling of pride seeping under my skin as my desire to make things right took root in my soul and fired my eagerness to get things moving.

THE BLACK LEDGER

CHAPTER 26

Monday Morning

When I opened the door to the agents' room that Monday morning, the lingering stench of twenty-plus men, cured in smoke, basted with dime store cologne, and slow cooked to perfection, pushed me back a step or two. With determination, I stepped forward into the dimly lit room and ran my hand up and down the wall, searching for the row of light switches. A moment later, I swiped on the switches and waited while the fluorescent lights in the office hummed to life. I walked over to my desk, drowning in the stale air that engulfed the room. I dropped my briefcase and ledger book on my desk before looking for the wall thermostat and turning on the air conditioning. Another one of Hamilton's cost-cutting measures was to turn off the air on the weekend, which made for an incredibly stuffy Monday morning in the office.

Next, I grabbed the coffee pot and headed back out to the hallway to fill it up with water. Robotically, I marched back to the coffee station, retrieved a coffee packet and filter from the cabinet, flipped on the burner switch, ripped the premeasured packet of coffee open, and poured the coffee into the filter. Without spilling a drop, I emptied the water into the machine's holding tank and quickly placed the glass pot under the spout before one drop of hot coffee escaped onto the burner. My proficiency at coffee making was only exceeded by my desire to drink the stuff, which had developed into a nasty addiction.

I stepped back, folded my arms, and watched, somewhat mesmerized by the slow drip of the coffee as it filtered down into the glass pot. Between the coffee and air conditioning, the stink in the office began to dissipate, and breathable air filled the room, helping me to relax. While standing there, I realized that the endless fog that seemed to infiltrate every corner of my being had been lifted, and a confident clarity had taken root in my mind. Somehow, I had managed to compartmentalize my grief and sorrow over the deaths of Sandra and Lucy. It wasn't that I buried my emotions or didn't care, just the opposite. I was sick to death over their loss and determined to use the intense anger boiling through my veins to fight back. I needed that anger to quell the feelings of distraught and sorrow that would come gushing over me from time to time, and I would use that anger to make things right.

I had become a man with a purpose. I wasn't going to stand by and let this crooked insurance agency continue to steal from folks. I wasn't going to avenge Sandra's death, but I was going to do everything I could to bring meaning to her life. In a strange way, I almost felt as if Sandra had prepared me for this journey and that her death was somewhat preordained and the catalyst needed to put a stop to this insanity. I couldn't bring Sandra back, but I could lead a fight to expose the fraud and deception perpetrated on people like her and countless others whose deaths were used to make others rich.

I made my coffee and settled in behind my desk before opening my briefcase and pulling out my route card from the weekend. I was actually surprised at the amount of money I was able to collect, considering my state of mind, as well as spending half the day at the police station. I had just about completed the paperwork for my deposit when the agents' door swung open, and Mr. Guru and Mr. Uhlen strolled in and headed for their desks. As usual, Guru didn't say a word as he passed my desk and went directly to his seat, but Mr. Uhlen lit up when he saw me and then glanced over at the three-quarter-filled coffee pot.

"Ronnie, my boy, you thought enough of me to come in and start a fresh pot of coffee," he said with a smile as he immediately altered his course for the coffee pot.

"I take care of my friends," I shot back with a smile.

"Good to see you here early on a Monday morning. That's how you make money—don't forget that," he said with a lilting voice like a worldly sage. Of course, Mr. Guru wasn't going to let Uhlen have the last word in anything sounding the least bit worldly and marched toward me as if daring me to defy him. With a snarled expression, he balanced himself on Otis' desk with one hand while extending his other arm outward, as if pointing to some far away land. "You listen to me… Don't ever let these sons of bitches sleep late! You will never get paid!" he shouted at me with his broken English. Steadfastly, with an expression of deep understanding, I listened like a master was schooling me. "You knock on their door at the crack of loser, and you won't get shit!"

"The crack of loser?" I asked incredulously.

"The crack of loser! The crack of loser, dammit!" Guru shouted, annoyed that I didn't understand his reference.

"Mr. Guru believes that anyone who doesn't get up at the crack of dawn gets up at the crack of loser," Mr. Uhlen explained with a smile from across the room as he took his coffee and headed for his desk.

"Oh, I see."

"You listen to me, and you will learn how to deal with these sons of bitches," he said, pointing in my face before leaping up and returning to his desk. I took a deep breath and rolled my eyes, catching an amused Mr. Uhlen toasting me with his coffee, as if congratulating me on surviving the encounter. Just then, the locks on the main doors leading to the lobby and other offices began creaking and rattling from the other side. A moment later, Roger Hamilton pushed them open and secured them in place with the latch located on the bottom of each door.

"Good morning, gentlemen," he said with a smile before heading for the coffee pot.

"Good morning my ass!" Guru shouted across the room. "I want to talk about these bullshit transfers you sent to me from that horseshit district in Maywood," he blurted out.

"I promise you'll have my complete attention, Mr. Guru. Just let me get some coffee and settled in, okay?" Roger said while pouring his coffee.

"No bullshit, Roger. You got fifteen minutes," Guru continued, sounding a stern warning.

"Hey, Roger, not to pile on or anything, but when you get a chance, I need to talk to you as well," I said somewhat meekly after Guru's demands. Roger seemed pleased that I spoke up, finished stirring his coffee, and strolled over to my desk.

"Why don't you come in right now?" he said in a low tone while pointing towards his office. I was completely caught off guard by his invitation, figuring I had all morning to collect my thoughts and prepare myself for our meeting. My knees felt weak as I pushed away from my desk, stood up, and followed him into his office. Suddenly, a chill went up my spine and fear gripped ahold of my senses. It seemed like every bit of confidence I woke up with that morning had disappeared, and every plan I concocted was idiotic at best. I wasn't just having second thoughts; I was ready to bail out of the fucking ship. Who was I kidding? What was I really going to accomplish? It was like every step I took towards his office was an affirmation of futility.

"Fifteen minutes, Roger! I'll be coming in there in fifteen minutes, goddamn it!" Guru shouted as Hamilton and I exited the room. While the last strains of Guru's voice echoed through the office, my consciousness was begging me to give up this fool's cause of justice for Sandra. Just how the hell was I going to bring Hamilton down by mailing a bunch of letters to myself? This was my big fucking plan? My mouth literally dried up as Roger opened his office door and held it while I walked in and sat down in the chair facing his desk. I clenched my teeth, waiting while Roger took off his suit jacket and laid it carefully over the arm of the couch. He moved a stack of papers from one end of the couch to the other, then walked around his desk and took a sip of coffee before sitting down and rolling forward in his executive chair.

Everything about him was so intimidating. The way he dressed, the way he combed his hair, his impish smile, his chiseled good looks, and, most of all, his ability to size you up and down while controlling every aspect of the conversation. *Why don't I just fucking quit and get the hell out of here,* I thought to myself as it dawned on me just how afraid I was of this guy. I was about to surrender without a fight, figuring my noble quest for justice had just come to an end. Then, I looked into his eyes for a moment and caught a glimpse of superiority that actually felt condescending. I watched as he carefully placed his cup on the desk and leaned back in his chair with the look of a man who had just won a bet and was gloating to himself. This was a game to him, and he was amused by the fact that I had capitulated so easily. Obviously, he spoke to Teddy over the weekend and was completely assured that I'd be here Monday morning, cowering before the great man, quaking in my Beatles boots, grateful for the opportunity. And here I was. The hypocrisy alone was sickening, but the lack of decency and respect towards Sandra and her family was appalling and snapped me back to my senses.

I regained my composure and realized that I didn't have to be smarter than Roger Hamilton. I just had to be completely honest and genuine. He would see through bullshit in a minute. He wasn't looking for me to kiss his ass; he just wanted to know I could be trusted. If I tried to outwit him or challenge anything concerning the offer Teddy put on the table, he'd pull back, take the company line, and shut me out of everything. I'd be left to fend for myself and have no hope of getting Sandra's family anything, even if it was just the cost of putting them into the ground. *If it meant I had to suck up and allow myself to be manipulated for the time being, then so be it,* I thought as a look of feigned concern emerged on his face.

"So, how are you doing?" he asked softly.

"It's been pretty tough, but I'm feeling a little better," I said, slowly trying to control my fear and insecurity of confronting him.

"Are you sure, Ron? Because, from where I'm sitting, I'm looking at a guy who looks pretty beat up," he said with a comforting voice. I could sense that he was looking for something, as if studying my demeanor for some indication as to my state of mind.

"I don't know, Roger," I said, puffing out my cheeks while exhaling. "I have never been through anything like this. It's been unreal. I just feel so guilty about everything," I said while running my fingers through my hair and sliding down into the chair like a beaten little kid in a principal's office. "I wanted to come in and apologize to you for the way I treated you on Friday. There was no excuse for that; I was literally at my wits' end," I said humbly. I watched as a warm glow came across Roger's face, and an all-knowing smile formed at the corners of his mouth.

"You certainly don't have to apologize. You care a lot about your clients, and that's what makes you a good agent," he said with a long sigh.

"I just felt so guilty for lapsing her policy. I didn't know where to turn. I didn't know what to do. I just lost it," I said honestly.

"You did the right thing, Ron," he said.

"It didn't feel like it, Roger," I countered. "It felt awful. It was like I failed these people in every way imaginable. I still can't believe how responsible I feel for this poor family," I said, shaking my head. He leaned forward and placed his elbows on his desk, interlocking his hands while resting his chin on his knuckles.

"You know, it's no secret that we service some of the poorest people in Chicago, Ron. Trying to keep them focused on paying a life insurance premium when they can barely keep their kids fed is no easy task. It's a very hard job. I know. Trust me, I know," he said with a sigh before continuing. "I can tell you from personal experience that it's never easy. Unfortunately, this is our business, and, if you're here long enough, chances are better than not that someone on your ledger is going to be killed," he said. I perked up and nodded my head in agreement, figuring he certainly must have insured people who were killed on his ledger.

"Something like this happened to you?" I asked.

"It happens a lot," he snorted. "We all lose clients, but we never expect them to be murdered, and from what I read in the newspapers, this was pretty bad," he said.

"It was in the paper?" I asked with surprise.

"You didn't see it?"

"No."

"Oh yeah, Saturday's *Sun-Times*," he said.

"Shit, I missed it!" I blurted out in dismay as my back stiffened, and I began peppering him with questions. "What did it say? Did they catch the guys who killed her? Did they say why she was killed?"

"No, nothing really. It just talked about the murder and that she had some sort of cream all over her face," he said quickly and dismissively, not wanting to talk about the details of her death.

"Jesus Christ!" I exclaimed out loud, as if the shock of Sandra's murder had stung me again for the first time. I looked up at him with watery eyes, wanting so desperately to talk about Sandra that, momentarily, I didn't even care about his role in manipulating the claim for profit. "I still can't fucking believe this," I bemoaned, trying to shake it off.

"So, tell me what happened. Did you try to collect her money? When was the last time you saw her?" he asked, as if sensing I was about to break down.

"I talked to Sandra Wednesday afternoon," I said automatically.

"How was she?"

"Fine, I mean… she was alive and walking down her stairs towards me," I said in disbelief how a seemingly meaningless moment in time would forever be etched in my memory.

"…And you talked to her, I assume?"

"Yes, of course," I said, somewhat annoyed at the question. "She was about to get in a car with a couple of guys, and I told her that her insurance was going to lapse and asked if she could give me something to hold it," I continued.

"What did she say?" he asked innocently. I paused and stared deep into his eyes without recognition. The memory of her speaking to me for the last time momentarily drew me into a hypnotic trance and then faded as quickly as it came. I looked away and shook it off, barely able to remember his question. I swallowed hard before saying, "I don't remember exactly, Roger. She told me to see her the next day, or on the weekend, or something." I took a deep breath and tried to compose myself, realizing how raw and fragile my emotions really were. I glanced back and saw Hamilton looking down at his desk. I could tell he was at a loss for words himself. "…And then she was dead," I said as my eyes began to well up. Without a word, Roger turned in his chair and grabbed a box of tissues from his cabinet, then quickly turned back and handed it to me.

"Here, Ron. Take your time," he said sympathetically.

"Thanks, Roger. I'm okay," I said, pulling some tissue from the box and blowing into it. "So, that's basically it," I said with finality, still patting my nose with the tissue to make sure it was dry. Hamilton drew a deep sigh and, without saying a word, swung his chair around, stood up, and walked over to his glass-enclosed trophy case. He paused in front of it for a moment and studied the contents, as if looking for something of great significance. The case was overflowing with awards and accolades from his career as a ledger agent, staff manager, and district manager. I sat quietly and observed the man as he pondered his decision. A few moments passed before he slid open the glass doors, bent over, and fumbled about, moving things from side to side until he found what he wanted. He turned and walked up to me holding out a green ribbon that read, "2ND PLACE, SALES, 1968." "Do you see what that says?"

"Uh huh."

"That was the first award I ever won with this company, and it was last time I ever came in second place," he said with a furrowed brow, trying to drive home the point.

"Wow, are you serious?"

"I never lost another contest, and I was number one in sales my entire career. This district has never come in second to anyone in the company, and you know why?" he asked, pointing a finger at me. I just shook my head. "Because I'll do whatever it takes to win. I refuse to give up, and I refuse to let someone else out work me," he said while taking a last look at the ribbon before placing it on his desk. "Did you know that Mr. Guru was my staff manager when I was an agent?" he asked while backing up, crossing his arms, and perching himself against the desk.

"Really? No, I didn't know that," I said with surprise.

"Yep, and he was just as rude and defiant and crazed then as he is now," he said with a chuckle. "But that old son of a bitch taught me how to sell and how to keep people on the books. He made me get up and canvass with him at 7:00 a.m. three days a week and wouldn't let me go home until ten at night. We set sales records for weekly insurance that have never been broken. One week, we sold over $300 in weekly premium sales."

"I know! The guys were talking about it a while back. That's truly amazing," I said in astonishment.

"That's the big trophy on the bottom of the cabinet," he said with a smile, pointing to the case.

"Jesus, what is that, like $7,500 in commissions?" I asked, my jaw hanging open just thinking about the amount of money that had to make.

"That's right, and the reason I'm showing you this isn't to get your mind off of what happened last week. I'm showing you this because I know this business can kill you. It can eat you alive when something bad happens to you," he said with a long sigh before walking back around his desk and sitting down. "I decided a long time ago that the only thing making this business worth doing is the ability we have as salesmen to make a lot of money doing it. That's it!" he said with authority. "There is no other reason to risk your life, your health, or rack your brain in guilt because a client dies in a senseless murder that defies common sense. You're a good guy and a good agent. You care about the people you insure, and you also possess the killer instinct every good salesman needs to make a living in this business. I don't want to lose that. Do you understand?" he asked with a tone that demanded an answer.

"Yes, I do," I said with a sigh.

"We are a team," he reinforced. "We stick together as a team, and together we are going to make this right," he said quickly. "Listen, Ron, I'm not going to let you get killed out there because people think you're a bad insurance agent or that our company doesn't pay its claims. I wouldn't let that happen to you," he said convincingly. I stared at him for a long moment, realizing that he had just confessed to rigging these claims, and the scary thing about it was that he sounded almost righteous. For a split second, I actually sympathized with his justification. I marveled at his technique, with half of me wanting to applaud his sales ability and the other half wanting to tell him to fuck off. Of course, I knew better and refrained from doing either, so I just sat there humbly, nodding my head in agreement, as if every word he spoke was gospel.

"That means a lot to me, Roger. You have no idea," I finally said, matching his bullshit with a dose of my own. "Actually, everything you just said makes it easier for me to bring up some stuff I wanted to talk to you about," I continued. He straightened up in his chair and looked at me as if there weren't anything in the world he wouldn't be willing to do. "With everything that happened, I just don't feel comfortable working with Mr. Meadows right now. It's not that I have anything against him or that he did anything wrong. I just feel like I need a change. I would like to transfer over to Mr. Minka's staff if that's possible?" I asked as sincerely as I could.

"Did Meadows make you feel guilty for lapsing that policy?" he asked sympathetically. I looked at him and felt my mouth drop for a quick second as the realization hit me that he had just asked a perfect question. In addition to justifying my move from one staff to another, he insinuated that it was Ray Meadows who caused the problem. Not only did he set the stage - he afforded himself a perfect excuse for making the move. Not that any of it was true, of course, but the implication was pure genius. It allowed him to throw Meadows and the rest of the staff under the bus without impunity or regret, all under the guise of salvaging my feelings. I loved it!

"Ray is a good guy," I said, ready to fuel the fire. "I just feel that he doesn't seem to understand how difficult this job can be for, um, well, you know,"

"A white guy," he interjected on cue.

"You know what I mean," I said, stuttering as if embarrassed to unburden myself. "I was so torn up about everything, you know? He just kept telling me I should have called him before you, and, well, he sort of made it sound like it was my fault, and, Jesus Christ… I mean, you're my boss! If I'm not supposed to confide this stuff in you, who am I supposed to tell, you know?" I pleaded to perfection.

"It's okay, Ron. Don't worry. You did the right thing. Did you discuss any of this with Mr. Meadows?" he asked softly.

"No, sir, um, don't get me wrong or anything, I like Ray a lot, but I just feel like I need a change and some new direction in order to be as successful as I can," I said, following the script that Lobranski laid out to the letter. I could see by the expression on his face that Roger was pleased; after all, he wrote the fucking script. I had accomplished my first task, which was to convince him of my sincerity. Like he once told me, "Everything in life is a sale," and in that moment, I knew I sold his ass.

"I definitely think the change will do you good and needs to happen," he said after a moment of contemplating my request. "As a matter of fact, I have given some thought to the situation, and there

380

are a few things I'd like to do. First of all, I want you to transfer the Wesley case to Teddy. I believe he's had some experience with the family. I want him to deal with this, see what can be done to ease their burden, and get you away from the situation. So, I want you to sign that transfer right now," he said, pulling open the top drawer of his desk and taking out a file jacket.

He opened the file and retrieved a set of transfer forms neatly stapled together and layered with carbon paper to be filled out. He handed me the forms, then returned the file to his drawer before pushing it closed. I studied the papers for a moment, dismayed to see the transfer had been completely filled out by hand and awaiting my signature. It included every member of Sandra's family I had insured on my ledger. That meant someone had to pull the office register from my book to retrieve the information. Transfers were supposed to be filled out in carbon copy triplicate, providing one copy for the home office, one for the district office, and one for the agent. I realized immediately that there were only two pieces of paper stapled together and not three. It was readily apparent that the agent, namely me in this case, was not going to be provided with a copy.

"Everything okay?" he said somewhat impatiently at my examination of the form.

"Oh yeah," I said matter-of-factly while refraining from saying anything about the missing copy. "I just wanted to make sure you had everyone listed," I said without bothering to inquire as to who pulled the information.

"Okay, good," he said, removing a pen from the inside of his jacket pocket and sliding it across his desk, prodding me to sign it. I felt trapped in the moment. I had to sign it or risk blowing everything, but I desperately wanted a copy, knowing in my heart that it wasn't just a transfer - it was evidence. By signing this document, I was on record as participating in this fraud. I needed a copy to prove that I was coerced into these deals, or at least show that by keeping these records, I was preparing to defend myself.

Hamilton could have signed it, he had that authority as district manager, but he wanted my signature on the document. He wanted a record that I was the one who initiated the transfer. I placed the forms on his desk and reached for the pen while he looked on with satisfaction. "There's something else, Ron," he said, inadvertently giving me an opportunity to stall and focus my undivided attention on him. "I think it's important that we do something for you."

"I don't understand what you mean," I said honestly.

"Well, you had a really tough week, and I think you need some time to get your head together, so I don't want you to worry about sales for a while," he said.

"I appreciate that, Roger, but I can't afford to have my pay go down right now," I chimed up.

"I know, that's why I'm going to give you an additional ledger to collect."

"Another ledger?"

"I have a partial that was split off of another agent's territory, and I want you to collect it for a while."

"So, you want me to collect two books?" I asked incredulously.

"Yes, at least until you get back on your feet and things calm down a little. It's a decent-sized collection, mostly mail in, and it will pay you about $150 more per week," he said with a smile.

"Wow! A hundred and fifty per week!" I exclaimed to his delight.

"That should give you some breathing room so you don't have to worry about your pay going down. Does that sound good to you?" he asked with a sly smile. I knew my mouth hung open for a moment before I could respond.

"Seriously, Roger, I'm literally speechless. You're a lifesaver," I said after taking a deep breath.

"Like I said, Ron, I take care of my good agents, and from this day forward, you will make more money than you ever imagined. You're a bright guy and not like some of these others that work around here. Once things calm down, you're going to be a very important part of this office. Now, sign the transfer," he commanded while motioning with his head for me to get to it.

We made eye contact for a long moment. My heart was pounding like crazy. I felt like I slipped into another dimension where movement slowed as I forced a smile to creep across my face in acceptance of his offer. At the same time, a chill went up my back as I realized just how easy it would be to go along with him. Oh, no question, he was going to have my signature on a document that could hang me, but, at the same time, he was giving me a huge raise, in addition to a cut from Sandra's insurance proceeds. My life would improve immediately, and how soon I would begin to look forward to the next scam.

I wasn't tempted in the least, but I now understood how he was able to operate and keep everything together. I leaned over, about to sign the transfer, resigned that I'd have to figure out another way to get a copy when a divine miracle in the form of Mr. Guru interceded on my behalf.

"I told you fifteen minutes, goddamn it!" Guru shouted as he burst into Hamilton's office.

"Vati! I'm in a meeting!" Hamilton shouted back angrily.

"Vati?" I blurted out, realizing that I had never heard anyone speak his first name before. Mr. Guru turned in my direction and lashed out at me.

"Don't you ever call me by that… EVER, you fucking asshole!"

"No, sir, I promise I won't," I replied meekly.

"I'm almost finished with Mr. Pickles. Please give me five more minutes?" Roger pleaded.

"Fuck that! And fuck you! Do you want me to lapse my whole goddamn ledger?! I will lapse the whole fucking thing right now. You can walk up and down the fucking streets trying to pry money from these sons of bitches! Is that what you want, goddamn it?"

"Jesus Christ, you know I'm going to take care of those transfers," Roger said with exasperation. This was my chance, and I didn't hesitate one second. I grabbed the transfer and jumped to my feet, going head-to-head with Mr. Guru.

"Mr. Guru, nobody could ever collect your ledger the way you do! Excuse me for intruding on your time. It's my fault for taking up so much of Roger's time. Please forgive me?" I begged while rushing for the door. I turned back toward Hamilton when I reached the door and waved the transfer. "Roger, I'll take care of this at my desk. I'll bring it right back," I said as Guru erupted into another tirade. I ran away from his office and flew into the agents' room. I bolted over to the supply cabinet, grabbed a handful of blank transfer forms and a few sheets of carbon paper before scurrying back to my desk. Carefully, I lined up a piece of carbon paper and blank transfer to the back of the forms Hamilton gave me and then laid them carefully on my desk. I pulled open my desk drawer and rifled through it until I found a sharpened pencil. I held the pencil tightly at a low angle and pressed it hard against the top of my desk till it snapped. The lead broke away, leaving a sharp piece of wood that was perfect for tracing the information on the front of the transfer.

I was careful to be as exact as possible but really only concerned that my signature matched all the copies. Transfers were extremely easy to fill out and only consisted of names and policy numbers with a transferring address. I was scared I'd run out of time but bolstered by the fact that Guru was doing his part and raging non-stop in a volume that could be heard throughout the office. I finished tracing the information as quickly as possible, grabbed a pen from my drawer, and signed the document as hard as I could to make sure it transferred through to every copy. I had just lifted the pen off the paper when Mr. Guru marched back into the agents' room and sat stoically behind his desk, apparently satisfied that his issues had been addressed. I grabbed the bottom copy and jammed it into my drawer before placing the copies that Hamilton gave me on the corner of my desk with a sigh of relief.

Before I could take another breath, Hamilton popped his head in through the girls' window and asked if I had signed that form. Nonchalantly, I reached over and picked up the form, stood up, and handed it to him as if it meant nothing to me. He smiled and thanked me before taking the transfer from my hand and returning to his office. I sat down and took a deep breath while opening the drawer and retrieving the copy of the transfer I fought so hard to get. I stared at the paper for a long moment, still disillusioned at how completely it had been filled out. If, before this, I had any question as to the extent Hamilton was involved, that piece of paper served notice that he was in charge.

I retrieved a company envelope, scratched out the return address, and wrote my home address in both spots. Calmly, I folded the transfer and slipped it into the envelope when a hand tapped me on the shoulder, giving me quite a start. "Ronnie, my boy, you seem nervous. Is everything okay?" Mr. Uhlen asked with a look of concern.

"Oh, Mr. Uhlen, I didn't see you there. You scared me," I said, catching my breath.

"Everything all right? I see you running around the office like a chicken with your head cut off," he laughed.

"Yeah, everything is fine," I said with a smile.

"Good. I'm going to make us a fresh batch of coffee. I'll bring you some as soon as it's made."

"You are the best, Mr. Uhlen," I said with gratitude as he walked away. I looked up at the clock, surprised that it was only 7:45 in the morning; it felt like I had been there for hours. I gently pushed the envelope with the transfer in it to one corner of my desk, figuring I'd mail it to myself the minute I left the office. I knew Mrs. Bolger would be opening up the girls' office soon, so I figured on waiting around and making a deposit for the collections I made over the weekend. I finished my deposit and leaned back in my chair, relaxing for a moment while taking a few sips of the hot coffee Mr. Uhlen dropped off moments before. I sat there quietly waiting for Mrs. Bolger while allowing my nerves to settle down from the earlier meeting with Hamilton. My brain was trying to process so many things at the same time. I couldn't concentrate on anything and found myself easily distracted anytime someone came in or out of the office.

I rarely came into the office on Monday morning and was surprised at how many agents stopped in to drop off deposits or finish up paperwork from the weekend. Most of the agents were from Mr. Singh's staff and included Mr. Wicks and Henry Weinstein, as well as Guru and Mr. Uhlen. Vinnie and Chucky from the stoner staff came in together and plopped down at their desks as if dreading the tedium of work they needed to finish. Other than an obligatory greeting, no one spoke, unless it was to address business concerns.

As I glanced around the office for the umpteenth time, I was amazed how everything seemed so incredibly normal when I knew that nothing was normal about this place. It changed me. My transformation from the wide-eyed kid, bouncing from place to place with unbridled optimism and a Beatles song on my lips, had given way to a sarcastic, suspicious adult who looked at everyone as if they had a hidden agenda. I lost the ability to trust people, or maybe I just didn't want to give that power away. This job taught me something terrible about human nature. It taught me that trusting others was akin to surrendering your own will in hopes that someone else would keep your best interests at heart.

Looking around the room at this motley collection of men attempting to earn a living by selling people on dying only solidified my cynicism. For some reason, my eyes locked on Mr. Wicks. I watched intently as he casually went about his business, filling out forms with a long cigarette dangling from his lips. I was intrigued by his technique of sucking long drags of smoke, then lifting and turning his head to exhale the clouds away from his face, while working feverishly at his task.

It was Mr. Wicks that had tried to tell me about the black ledger and the power it possessed, as if it had a life of its own and was hell-bent on doing evil. I couldn't help but wonder if he got caught up in one of these scams and decided to place the blame on an evil entity instead of accepting responsibility for going along with the program. It was then that Sandra popped into my head, and I could feel one of those moments of sadness and loss beginning to boil up. I braced hard and fought it off, clenching my teeth while trying to focus and think about something else. In my entire life, I never felt a loss to the point where it crippled my entire being. I knew the only thing saving me from breaking down and losing control was the deep-seated anger I had for the entire system.

Mrs. Bolger came in at 8:00 a.m. on the dot, and Irene strolled in a few minutes later. I figured I'd give Mrs. Bolger a few minutes to settle down before turning in my deposit, so I flipped through my ledger and filled out a route card for the day, all the while thinking about my next move. The problem, of course, was that I didn't have a next move. Convinced that Mrs. Bolger had ample time to settle in and begin her day, I pushed away from my desk, about to get up, when Vinnie jumped from his seat and beat me to it. I sat back down with exasperation and waited patiently until he finished with Mrs. Bolger, then jumped up to catch her before she walked away from the window and sat down at her desk. "Unusual to see you here on a Monday morning," she growled while adding up the checks and cash I handed her.

"Yeah, I know," I mumbled.

"Got any mail you want to go out?" she asked.

"Mail?" I asked defensively, thinking about the letter I was going to mail to myself.

"Yeah, you know, office pays or anything?"

"Oh, yeah, right," I replied, glancing over at the envelope on my desk and contemplating whether or not I should just give it to her to mail.

"Well, bring it over," she said at my hesitation. "The mailman gets here early on Monday mornings."

"I'm not quite ready. I might have a few more things," I said, thinking I should just mail the letter myself.

"Suit yourself. Hey, I hear you're switching staffs?" she asked with a quick tilt of her head to make sure no one was standing behind her.

"Yeah, it looks that way," I said, assuming that Hamilton told her to start preparing whatever office correspondence might be necessary to facilitate the move.

"Alright, you're recorded, but you should think about that move," she said while pushing a receipt in my direction. She looked me dead in the eye before turning and sitting down at her desk, but the raised eyebrow and skeptical expression on her face left no doubt that she felt I was making a mistake. I picked up the receipts and returned to my desk, wondering about Mrs. Bolger's subtle warning. In two years of dropping money at that window, she never offered an opinion on anything, but now, she goes out of her way to subtly warn me about changing staffs. What possible difference would it make to Mrs. Bolger if I changed staffs? Why would she even care? It didn't escape me that she looked over her shoulder to make sure no one was in earshot of our discussion, but why? Could it really be for fear of losing her job? *Jesus, is everyone in this place beholden to Hamilton and scared to cross him?* I thought to myself as I started clearing my desk to leave.

Just then, Irene came sauntering into the agents' room like a swinger strolling through a nightclub on a Saturday night. This particular Monday morning, she chose to wear a short, burnt orange dress, so incredibly tight that it begged you to peel it off her hourglass figure. Her legs glistened in the nude shade of pantyhose she wore as they contoured perfectly into her black pumps while she glided across the floor. She made her way around the office slapping down "while you were out" notes on everyone's desks while ignoring the ripple effect she had on almost every man in the room. As if Irene were silently directing an orchestra of men to perform at her slightest movement, heads would lift from their desks and turn in a hypnotic-like state, commanded by the aura of desire she projected while passing.

Irene's voluptuousness was so demonstrative that it hobbled your senses. Your heart craved her attention, if even to retrieve a note. If she came to the window after the meeting and called out your name to get a message, you jumped to your feet to retrieve it in person. You knew that every agent in the room was watching your interaction with jealousy, as if she validated your importance. She was a sexual goddess. Looking at her put you into a different frame of mine. You just ached with wonder at the thought of making love to a seductress who unabashedly flaunted her sexual prowess in your face without caring one bit about your feelings. She would leave the room or fade away behind the glass, and, just like that, you awoke from the fantasy, staring aimlessly around a smoky room filled with men all trying desperately too hard to quell their thoughts and desires.

I fell in line with the pack and serenely gazed upon her magnificence as she floated about before coming to a stop beside Mr. Guru, who kept his head firmly planted in his ledger book. "Is this your client, Mr. Guru?" she asked while placing the message directly under his nose. He pushed himself away from the desk, annoyed at the interruption, then grabbed the note while adjusting his glasses down his nose to read it from his outstretched hand.

"No!" he said firmly before resetting his glasses then flicking the note to the side of his desk and returning to his original position. You had to be blind, crazed, or completely out of your mind not to be affected by her presence, which may have explained the lack of interest from Mr. Guru. Undaunted by his callousness, she rolled her eyes with exasperation, snatched the discarded message from his desk, and then turned abruptly and headed towards my group of desks. I almost fell off my chair trying to look preoccupied, flipping through my ledger book and shuffling through my briefcase, as if frantically looking for a misplaced item. I actually began to wonder if there wasn't something wrong with me that I couldn't function when she was in the room. It was demoralizing to think that a woman in a dress could have such an effect on your state of mind, and I began to get angry with myself for feeling that way. She stopped in front of Otis' desk, which butted up against mine, and stood fanning out the messages like a bridge player stacking her hand. Methodically, she grouped the messages for delivery, then slowly walked around the desks, dropping them as she passed. I kept my head down, pretending to ignore her until she walked up next to me and held out a stack of notes.

"Thanks, Irene. I appreciate it," I said, taking the notes from her hand while glancing up at her with a smile.

"No problem," she deadpanned without expression before heading back into her office. As usual, I couldn't stop myself from turning and watching as she walked away, but suddenly, something popped into my head and hit me like a slap in the face. *Who the fuck wears that?!* I thought to myself with a healthy dose of skepticism as she disappeared behind the doors.

Although Irene and Mrs. Bolger were the only women working in our office, the bank building was loaded with beautiful women, and none of them dressed that way. As a matter of fact, most of the women at the bank were dressed very professionally in either pencil skirts with jackets or slack suits. These ladies were here to conduct business and wanted to project that image to their male counterparts, in stark contrast to Irene, who seemed as if she relished every opportunity to promote the power of her overt sexuality.

I began to wonder why Hamilton never asked her to dress more office appropriate, obviously aware of the effect she had on his agents. I tried to shake it off and get focused on my situation again, but something kept nagging at me. I took one last look over my shoulder and caught a glimpse of her in the window as she disappeared into Hamilton's office, carrying a stack of paperwork. I turned back and just sighed, when it occurred to me how much time she spent in Hamilton's office. *Good Lord, was I just looking for ways to disparage Hamilton's character?* I lamented to myself. For a moment, I seemed to forget that the Hamilton I now knew wasn't the Hamilton I knew last week. I tried to stop thinking about it for fear of being too irrational, but it began to occur to me just how many times I had seen them together. *It had to be dozens. Oh my God!* I thought in disbelief as one particular memory hit me like a thunderbolt. I leaned back in my seat and tossed the stack of messages into my opened briefcase, flabbergasted that I didn't put this together earlier.

"Shit! How could I have forgot that?" I muttered to myself, then quickly looked around to make sure no one heard me. "Jesus Christ, I was so naive," I scolded myself as a couple of more agents walked into the office. I had totally forgotten about the time I came into the office one Saturday afternoon. I had been collecting all morning and realized that I forgot someone's policy and detoured back to the office to pick it up. I didn't even think about going in through the office and just let myself in through the agents' doors. I was really rushed for time and began tearing open and slamming shut my desk drawers in search of the policy. Within seconds, Hamilton threw open the big oak doors and burst into the room, startling me. Immediately, I turned towards him, but out of the corner of my eye I caught a glimpse of Irene through the office window, as she ran out of Hamilton's office and back to her desk. I remembered at the time thinking she looked a little disheveled and surprised that she actually wore jeans to the office instead of some gala ball gown. Hamilton seemed out of breath and nervous as well, but laughed and seemed relieved when he saw who it was and not an intruder. We joked for a second while I continued shuffling through my drawers, looking for the policy. Once I found it, I quickly excused myself, explaining that I didn't want to be collecting my ledger too late on a Saturday night. He heartily agreed, and I ran out of the office and down to my car as fast as possible.

At the time, I didn't give it a second thought. It never crossed my mind that Roger might be having an affair with Irene, much less cheating on his wife. The thought of him screwing her in the office on Saturday afternoons never even occurred to me until this very moment. But now, it all began to make sense. I caught them in the act, and I was too damn stupid and naive to even realize it. She wasn't dressing like a French whore to impress or tantalize the agents; she belonged to Hamilton, and he wanted her to dress that way. He got off knowing that every man in that office desired her and admired him for being so "suave and sophisticated" that he could work side by side with this woman and not be tempted in the least to succumb to her charms.

He had everyone in the office, not to mention the entire company, believing that his integrity could not be impugned. Even his motto, printed out on the huge banner above the blackboard, summed up his philosophy perfectly: "Do It, And Do It Clean!" He would never hold a lapse, he would never forge a signature, and he would never take a dime of company money that didn't belong to him. "As an insurance agent for Unified Insurance Company, you are a professional and need to carry yourself in a professional manner at all times. Don't ever forget that," he would preach. *Unless, of course, you were fucking clients out of their death benefits or fucking Irene in the office on a Saturday afternoon,* I snickered to myself.

My briefcase was a mess, so I sat down and slid it across the desk and up to my chest to evaluate what I needed and what I could throw out. The pink "while you were out" messages that I casually tossed inside had scattered all over, and I had to pick each one up individually and shuffle them into a stack before reading them. Most of the notes were from Friday, when everyone was trying to get ahold of me, but one caught my eye and made me pause before dismissing it as trash. There was a message from Ruppert, addressed to both Otis and me, that we should collect his money on Monday instead of next week, when he'll be out of town. I stared at the message for a second before jumping up from my seat and bolting over to the girls' window. I knocked on the window and held the note up to catch Irene's attention, thankful that she was back at her seat. "Hey, Irene. This is Otis' client. Why do you have my name on it?" I asked.

"I don't know. Let me see," she said, obviously miffed that she was forced to get up from her desk and walk over to the window. She took the note from my hand and studied it for a moment. "Oh yeah, this guy said Otis collected the money but that both of you were his agents. He said something about forgetting to leave the money with his grandma and wanted to make sure one of you stopped by his house today," she said, handing the message back to me.

"Shit," I muttered under my breath.

"What's the problem?" she asked.

"Oh, nothing. I doubt I can get ahold of Otis to pick this up today, that's all," I said with a sigh.

"So, you just go get it," she said with a condescending tone before turning and strolling back to her desk. Again, I found myself watching as she walked away but not with admiration and desire, but contempt. First, I didn't like her tone implying that I was pissing and moaning about collecting Ruppert's money when, in fact, she didn't have a clue as to the dangers of dealing with Ruppert and his gang. Secondly, my little epiphany earlier made me realize that, whether I was right or wrong about her and Hamilton, one fact couldn't be denied: she was just a bitch.

I swiped the message off the counter and returned to my desk, staring down at the phone number and address the whole time. *Fuck me, could my life get any fucking worse?* I thought before plopping down in my chair and reaching over to another desk for a phone. As usual, the phone wire snagged between the desks, so I had to stand up, reach over, and pull the desk apart to release the stuck wire. After a few tugs on the cord, I was able to get enough slack to move the phone to my desk. Reluctantly, I banged out Ruppert's number, half hoping he wouldn't answer, while leaning on the desk with both elbows resting my head.

"May I help you?" said a voice I immediately recognized as Ruppert's.

"Hi, Ruppert. It's Ron Pickles from Unified Insurance Company. I popped into the office and got your message. Otis is unavailable, but if it's still okay with you, I can come by and collect today?" I asked, hoping he'd say no.

"My man, Mr. Pickles, absolutely! Your presence is welcomed. Do you know my address?"

"Yes, it's here on the message. This is just west of Racine, right?"

"Correct, first floor. Can you arrive by noon?"

"Sure, no problem, I'll see you then," I said, hanging up the phone. I sat there for a minute, feeling as if my life truly wasn't my own. I wasn't afraid that Ruppert would cause me any harm. It was more the fact that I knew he could if he wanted to. He was a dangerous guy with a street army and the means to eliminate you if the cause suited him.

I've been scared to death ever since Otis and I wrote him that bogus insurance, knowing that if for any reason he filed a claim that didn't get paid, we were as good as dead.

Despondently, I folded up the message with Ruppert's address on it and stuck it in my shirt pocket, then tossed out some garbage and closed up my briefcase. I stood up to leave when I noticed the corner of the envelope peeking out from under my briefcase. *Holy shit!* I thought to myself before grabbing the envelope and scurrying back up to the girls' window. "Mrs. Bolger, is it too late to get this in this morning's mail pick up?" I asked with concern.

"You're good. Give it here," she commanded.

"Thanks," I said, sliding the envelope under the window. I was in a near panic realizing how careless I had been with that envelope and wanted it mailed as soon as possible. At this point, I didn't give a shit who put it in the mail, as long as it got mailed. I went back to my desk, shaking my head in disbelief at my own stupidity. I couldn't fucking believe that I almost lost the first actual piece of evidence I worked so hard to get. Quickly, I gathered up my ledger book in one hand and briefcase in the other and headed out of the office, still berating myself for being that stupid.

CHAPTER 27

After leaving the office, I stopped at the Lake Street Diner and got some much-needed breakfast before heading out to work my ledger. I walked out of the air-conditioned restaurant and took a deep breath of warm, humid, city-tainted summer air, just as an L train rumbled overhead with a near-deafening assault on my eardrums.

It was a bright and sunny day, with that Chicago summery feel you can only understand if you've lived in the city. Summer in Chicago is like a complex mosaic of intertwined sounds, smells, and sights that envelope your senses and make you feel alive. I wanted to take in that mosaic and enjoy every breath, but I couldn't. The pall of sadness hanging over my head left me feeling selfish and guilty for enjoying something as simple as a breath of fresh air.

I hopped in my car and followed Lake Street east, then turned right on Racine until I found Ruppert's address. I pulled up in front of his building, parked my car, and took a deep breath before turning off the ignition and preparing to go inside. I straightened myself and glanced in the mirror to make sure I looked presentable. *God, I hate this fucking job,* I thought to myself as I grabbed my portfolio off the front seat, got out of the car, and walked up to Ruppert's front door. I was pleasantly surprised at the outside appearance and general upkeep of all the buildings in the area. His was a three-flat red brick building with a concrete stairway to the right of center leading to the entranceway. An array of colorfully potted plants sat on the tiered slabs of stone that encased the stairs and doubled as banisters when you walked up to the entrance. I didn't see a doorbell to ring and was about to start knocking when I heard the inside door open. Just then, my old friend, Mosley, the bandito, appeared and opened the front door, motioning for me to enter.

"Mosley, how are you doing?" I asked politely.

"Alright," he mumbled without much indication that he was interested in striking up a conversation. I walked past him then waited inside the vestibule while he closed the front door. Once he closed and locked the bottom door, he turned and escorted me up a few more stairs and through another door into Ruppert's apartment. I walked in and waited for him to shut that door, amazed at the majestically decorated living area that began in the front room of Ruppert's apartment.

The floor was covered in a snow white, shag carpet that was absolutely spotless. It served as the foundation for a room that looked as if it belonged in a castle on a French countryside. All the furniture in the room was French Provincial and upholstered in red velvet, with a distressed white finish along the wood trim. I recognized the style immediately because Jessica and I once walked into a high-end furniture store on Michigan Avenue, and we were amazed at the style but couldn't believe the amount of money it would cost to actually have it in your home. It was covered in clear plastic protectors, perfectly fitted for each individual piece. The couch was enormous and butted up to a beautiful set of white drapes that were pulled opened and hung across an expansive window to the left as you entered the apartment. The end tables on each side of the couch were remarkable pieces, perfectly matched in the distressed white, adorned with a reddish marble inlay and a small, raised cabinet in the rear. Each table held an ornate lamp with a set of cherub angels dancing around the stem, as if the designer hadn't a care in the world when he created his vision. Sloping white lampshades that tiered down several layers rimmed around each lamp and created a perfect covering for the figurines as they danced away.

"This place is awesome," I said as the big guy walked past and gestured for me to follow behind.

"Stay on the plastic," he said, referring to the runner leading through the front room into the dining area. A large archway separated the two rooms where the French revolutionary décor stopped and a fifteenth-century medieval dining room began. It was complete with a dark wood floor and large slatted table with heavy, high-backed chairs surrounding it. Apparently, Ruppert had a penchant for red velvet, as the upholstered chairs were the same color as those in the French side of the house. Great big pictures of knights and castles adorned the walls, and, as gaudy as the whole place seemed at first, I really started to like the motif he was trying to create. There were two hallways in the rear of the dining area, one leading to the kitchen and another leading to some other rooms in the apartment. Mosley took us down the hall to the right and stood by the opening of what appeared to be a study where Ruppert was sitting on a lounge chair with his feet perched on an ottoman, talking on the phone. He held up a finger and made some small talk into the phone before apologizing to his caller, saying that his insurance man had just arrived, and he needed to go. I was disappointed that the room seemed normal, and no particular time period of human history was represented.

"Mr. Pickles," he said with a smile and a flare for the dramatic as he swung his feet off the ottoman, stood up, and shook my hand.

"How you doing, Ruppert? It's been a while," I said as if we were old friends.

"Doing well, my man, doing well," he said before walking past me and motioning to follow him back into the dining room.

"So, tell me, what is that big nigga's excuse for not coming to see me himself?" he joked as he led me into the dining room.

"Oh, I don't think Otis got the message. It sounded like you missed Granny Jones or something, so I figured I better come over, otherwise I'm sure he would have been here. By the way, I love the way you have the place decorated. The apartment is beautiful," I said honestly.

"An upgrade from those projects you met us in," he quipped. I'm sure my expression contorted, because he started laughing, then called out to Mosley who had sat down at one end of the dining room table, reading a newspaper. "Mosley, I think Mr. Pickles thought we all lived in those projects," he said with a smile.

"That right," Mosley snorted without looking up from the paper. I actually chuckled with them and just shook my head at their good-natured ribbing.

"Have a seat, Mr. Pickles," Ruppert said, pointing to a chair at the opposite end of where Mosley was sitting. I obeyed his direction and pulled the chair out from the table and sat down, noticing that he was looking at me with a perplexed look on his face.

"Is there something wrong?" I inquired while placing my portfolio on the table and removing a pen from my pocket.

"I just remembered that I was going to ask Otis a question about fire insurance on my belongings. You probably can't help me if this isn't your territory."

"Sure, I can! Otis and I are both listed as your agents, so either one of us can write you some fire insurance," I replied.

"Does your company have a good policy?"

"Absolutely not. This fire insurance is total shit," I shot back without hesitation.

"Really?" he laughed. "You are a shit salesman, Mr. Pickles."

"No, I'm a realist, Ruppert, and the last thing I'm going to do is piss you guys off by selling you a bunch of crap," I said half joking. "Seriously though, it's just a contents policy. Truth be told, they depreciate the shit out of everything you claim, and without a receipt, you get a basis cost from some outdated book on what things cost in 1955 or something. It's really bad," I said.

"I appreciate your honesty, Mr. Pickles, but let me ask you something. Do they pay even if you have other insurance?" he asked.

"Well, in fact, they do, which is probably the only reason to buy it, but don't have a claim for at least six months, or they will investigate and want every last match in the house accounted for," I said seriously.

"Haha, I'm not looking to burn down my crib. I just want to recoup if something should happen. Niggas around here have no respect for a man's castle. Believe it or not, there are even some people around here that find me somewhat undesirable and would like nothing more than to see my house burn down. Now ain't that a damn shame, Mr. Pickles?" I just shook my head at his obvious sarcasm. "Oh damn, I forgot you need that receipt book. Figure out what kind of fire insurance I can get; I'll be back in a minute," he said before disappearing into another room.

I took a deep breath before opening my portfolio and searching for some fire insurance applications, as if preparing to do business, when in fact, I was just trying to look busy and not disturb Mosley. I realized quickly that my presence didn't seem to concern him in the least, especially when he held up the paper and blocked me from his view while leaning comfortably back in his chair. He was completely engrossed with some article and ignored me completely, which was both comforting and disturbing at the same time. I glanced at him quickly, then looked away before turning back and staring intently at the paper he held in his hands. He must have sensed my peering eyes because he slowly lowered the paper and stared right back at me, "You want something?" he asked with annoyance. "Hey! I'm talking to you!" he said, breaking my momentary trance.

"Oh God! I'm sorry, Mosley, I just noticed you were reading Saturday's paper," I said.

"So?"

"So, um, yeah, right. I'm sorry; I think I'm losing my mind. It's just that something bad happened over in my area, and I was told it got reported in Saturday's paper," I said, stuttering and stammering, desperate to read that paper, yet cognizant enough to be as polite as possible. "I was wondering if you'd mind if I took a look at it when you were finished? I asked.

"You talking about that woman and her kid that got killed, ain't you?"

"Um, yeah, did you read about it?" I asked calmly while trying to keep things in perspective.

"Yeah, it's right here," he said while folding the paper to the right page and tossing it across the table. I grabbed the paper as quickly as I could and zeroed in on the article, trying to absorb every word as if it had been written specifically for me. Just then, Ruppert came strolling back in the room and plopped a bunch of twenties and the receipt book on the table before sitting down across from me. I was so engrossed in the article that I didn't even lift my head to acknowledge he came back. I assume he must have raised an eyebrow or looked into Mosley's direction because the bandito chimed up a moment later. "Pickles said that shit happened in his area," he said.

"What shit would that be, Mosley?"

"That woman and her kid," Mosley replied.

"I see. Did you know these people?" Ruppert asked while tapping at the article, trying to get my attention. I pulled my head away from the paper slowly and straightened up in the chair.

"I did," I said, looking at Ruppert with a blank expression on my face.

"Hmm, you're not as white as you were a moment ago, Mr. Pickles. Apparently, you knew these people well."

"The woman was my client, and I knew her and her family really well. I've sort of been in shock since this happened," I said, looking away and shaking my head.

"The ghetto is a dangerous place," he said without emotion.

"I knew her," Mosley spoke up. "Went to school with her."

"That so?" Ruppert inquired.

"Yeah, that shit's fucked up. She was all right," Mosley said as if reminiscing fondly.

"Let me see that paper," Ruppert said, taking it out of my hands and looking over the article. I just sat there quietly, looking down at the table with what seemed like a million things racing through my brain. After a moment, Ruppert tossed the paper back onto the table, leaned back in his chair, and stared a hole through me.

"So, this woman was your client?" he asked.

"She was."

"How long did you know her?"

"A little over a year."

"How did you meet her?" he asked. I shrugged my shoulders and turned my head, somewhat agitated at the question. "I'm not trying to pry, Mr. Pickles, but I am genuinely curious as to how you came to meet this girl," he said, following up on my reluctance to answer. I stared at him for a moment and then figured it really didn't do any harm to answer his questions. In a way, it felt good to talk about Sandra to someone. I let out a heavy sigh and smiled slightly while leaning back in my chair, recalling the first time I had ever met her.

"Kind of a funny story, actually," I said.

"How's that?"

"Well, if you haven't already noticed, I'm a white guy."

"Damn, no shit!" Ruppert shot back before I could finish. "Hey, Mosley, did you know this was a motherfuckin' cracker when you let him in my crib?"

"Yeah, thought he was here to fix something," Mosley replied dryly.

"If you're both finished fucking with me, I'll continue the story," I said with a smile.

"Yeah, I'm finished. Mosley, you finished fucking with this guy?" Ruppert asked in jest, knowing that Mosley wasn't going to reply. "I'm sorry, Mr. Pickles. Please continue with your story. But yes, to answer your question, we are all fully aware that you are a honky," he said flatly.

"Thank you," I acknowledged with a nod. "Well then, I got the bright idea to bring my dog out with me for protection when I had to make some nighttime collections."

"Whach you got?" Mosley asked with a demanding tone that caught me off guard.

"Got?"

"You got a shepherd, pit, Dobie, Rotter? Whach you got?"

"Oh, well that was the problem: I have a collie," I said, turning towards the big man, figuring I'd have to explain why the breed made a difference.

"You brought motherfucking Lassie out to the ghetto to protect you?!" Mosley said with as much emotion as I'd ever seen from him.

"Well, yeah, I know now that wasn't such a great idea," I admitted.

"Fuck no, that ain't no good idea! Lassie is like the patron saint of dogs around here. Motherfuckers sit home all day and watch reruns of Lassie. Black people love Lassie!" Mosley said with a scowl, crossing his arms and staring at me like I was an idiot. Then, as if struck by a bolt of enlightenment, the expression on his face changed from one of angst to almost zen-like clarity as he unfolded his arms, leaned back in his chair, and placed his hands upon the table. "However, no one in the black community would ever own a motherfucking Lassie dog," he said with all-knowing raised eyebrows. I glanced at Ruppert, who just shrugged at the big man's logic.

"...And why wouldn't anyone in the black community own a collie?" I regretfully inquired.

"Because motherfuckers would get their motherfucking dog stealed off their porches every other day. You ain't going to steal no motherfucking pit bull off someone's porch, but you'll steal a motherfucking Lassie dog. Motherfucking dog would get stolen so much, it'd become community property!" Mosley shouted out in a fit of laughter. "It be like, 'Who got the motherfucking Lassie dog this week?' Shit, it be like, 'Damn, bro, it's my turn to steal that shit...'" Mosley shouted with uproarious laughter while slapping the table. Ruppert and I couldn't help but laugh along at the obvious joy

Mosley took from thinking about a fictitious dog being stolen from house to house on a regular basis.

"Please continue, Mr. Pickles," Ruppert finally said as Mosley's temporary lapse subsided and his stoic demeanor once again took hold.

"Well, Mosley is right, actually," I said, pausing for a moment to look at Mosley for any reaction, then continued when there was none. "I damn near caused a riot by bringing my collie out here one night. It was hot outside, and we got spotted by a bunch of kids playing in a fire hydrant when I drove down the street. They all came running up to the car in order to look at the dog, and, of course, that got everyone on the block's attention. That's how I met Sandra. She was talking to her neighbor, who happened to be an existing client of mine, when I pulled up looking like the Pied Piper with kids running after my car screaming for the dog."

"You do know how to make an entrance," Ruppert quipped. I just shook my head and laughed, recalling the craziness of the situation.

"Trust me, that was not my intention," I lamented. "Anyway, they came to the car to see the dog, and after talking with her a bit, we realized that I had both her mom and dad insured and that she was looking to buy some insurance for herself. So, I became her agent."

"...And so now you have to pay her mom and dad for their dead daughter and granddaughter," Ruppert said with more than a little empathy in his voice at the situation.

"I wish it was that easy," I muttered under my breath.

"I didn't mean to imply that your task was an easy one, Mr. Pickles," Ruppert corrected.

"No, no, I didn't mean you, Ruppert," I said apologetically. "She missed a payment and her policy lapsed. ...And it really sucks because they're not going to pay the claim, and I have to deal with her mom and dad," I continued with a long sigh. Ruppert leaned back and peered into my eyes for a long moment. I stared right back to let him know just how deeply affected I was by her death.

"Did you see her often?" he asked with a sensitivity that caught me off guard.

"Yes, I collected from her every month. You know, like I do with everyone," I replied cautiously. "Why do you ask?" I watched as he slowly straightened up in his chair and leaned forward, placing both elbows on the table and pointing his fingers at me like guns.

"Because you were you fucking this girl, weren't you, Mr. Pickles?" he asked point-blank. I could feel my mouth drop open at his deduction, both amazed at his perception and horrified at how easily he came to that conclusion. My first thought was to dismiss him with some laughter or some other deflection and blow off his contention as ridiculous, but there was something about Ruppert that made me feel like he was genuinely concerned and wanted me to confirm what he already knew. In that moment, I forgot who he was or what he represented and just felt grateful for an opportunity to tell someone how I felt. I took a deep breath and looked down for a moment before raising my eyes to meet his. "We weren't intimate, but we were close," I said softly.

He looked at me and nodded his head as if to acknowledge my meaning, and I could tell that he was pleased with my honesty.

"That's a sad story, and I'm sorry for you, Mr. Pickles. You seem like a decent man, and I can tell you are truly upset at the loss of this lady," he said with genuine kindness. From his expression, I got the feeling that, somewhere in his past, he too suffered some horrific loss and knew what I was going through. I just nodded back, satisfied that he was well aware of my feelings for Sandra.

"Thanks, Ruppert. I still can't fathom why someone would want to do something like this to a woman and her child," I added.

"Paper says motherfuckers covered her face with all that shit. That shit's fucked up," Mosley spoke up.

"It certainly is, Mo. It certainly is," Ruppert replied as if in deep contemplation.

"Mosley, let me ask you something. Why do you suppose they painted her face?" Ruppert asked somewhat rhetorically.

"Oh, they was sending someone a message, boss. No doubt they was sending someone a message," he replied. Ruppert turned and looked at me with raised eyebrows.

"Did you hear what Mosley said, Mr. Pickles?" he said, leaning closer and tilting his head to the side while focusing his eyes on mine. "Whoever did this was trying to send someone a very disturbing message," he said with an ominous tone. He knew as well as I did that the message was meant for me, but neither of us spoke of it or the consequences. I looked down at the article one last time, folded up the paper, and pushed it back towards Mosley, who took it as if nothing had happened and picked up reading where he left off.

"Well, let me get this recorded for you," I said, reaching for the receipt book and pulling the money towards me. "Were you serious about the fire insurance?" I asked while counting up his money and recording the payments in his receipt book.

"Yeah, write that shit up," he said.

"How much do you think the contents of your apartment is worth?" I asked, quite businesslike.

"I don't know exactly. Twenty or thirty thousand," he replied casually.

"Well, technically, I'm only allowed to write you $7,500, but if Otis and I both sign an application, I can get you $15,000."

"That'll work. What's it going to cost me?"

"It's all a standard fee. About $36 per month," I said. He reached into his pocket and withdrew a wad of bills, peeling back a bunch of twenties and tossing them across the table to me. I gathered up the money and counted it out. "So, I got $120. You want to pay three months?" I asked.

"Three months is good," he replied. I dug into my pocket and counted out $12 in change and slid it back across the table, along with two applications for him to sign.

He quickly signed them and slid them back across the table. I filled in a couple of boxes, then returned them to my portfolio, figuring I'd fill out the rest of the information at the office. Ruppert didn't say anything while I was conducting his business, but I sensed he had something on his mind and was waiting for me to finish.

"Did you talk to the Man?" he questioned the moment I closed up my portfolio.

"The police? Oh yeah, that was fun," I snorted in disgust.

"Let me guess," he said with exuberance. "Not too interested in another welfare nigga coming off the public dime," he quipped.

"Pretty much," I said with a sigh. "I told them what I saw the day she was killed, and they said they already knew everything and weren't too interested in anything I had to say."

"Hell no. They already buried the file on that shit," he said before stretching his arms above his head and dismissing the police as a waste of taxpayer money. "Honestly, Mr. Pickles, the fact that someone got killed in the ghetto doesn't really bother me, especially in my business," he mused. "What intrigues me is the intent of this message. It would seem to me that an individual who would strangle a mother and her child wouldn't blink twice at capping an insurance man if indeed the message was intended for you. Perhaps you should look for another line of business," he said with a tone that I took seriously.

"I hear you, Ruppert, and trust me, I just have a few things to clean up before I take that advice," I said, standing up and preparing to leave.

"Don't wait too long, Mr. Pickles," Ruppert said, slapping the table and standing up. I took the lead as we walked to the door in silence, then stepped aside to allow him access to the series of locks to undo. After a moment, he pulled the door open and held it while we shook hands and I stepped into the hallway. I turned around and was about to ask the forbidden question when Ruppert instinctively cut me off before a word could escape my lips.

"Not our job, Mr. Pickles. The Man frowns on gangsters doing police work," he said with a forced smile. The guy blew me away with his powers of perception, forcing me to chuckle at his mind-reading abilities.

"Okay, I get it, but if you should hear anything, I could use the help," I said half jokingly.

"I already gave you great advice," he retorted. I shook my head, not catching his drift. "Get the fuck out of the ghetto!"

CHAPTER 28

Tuesday, July 7th, 1981

I stood poised and ready that Tuesday morning, clenching my briefcase in one hand and clutching my ledger book with the other, patiently waiting for the elevator to deposit me on the fifth floor. I knew full well that I would have to confront Ray Meadows and explain why I felt the need to transfer off his staff. I knew he would be upset and try to talk me out of it, and I knew I was determined to stay the course. What I did not anticipate was Ray Meadows waiting for me at the elevator, forcefully grabbing me under the arm, and ordering me to follow the moment the elevator door opened.

"What are you doing, Ray?" I shouted out as his claw-like hands dug into my bicep.

"Shut up and come with me!" he snarled under his breath as we raced side by side down the hallway. Before I knew it, he kicked open the bathroom door and threw me inside. I stumbled, barely able to keep my balance as he marched in behind me. I wobbled to my feet, turning to face him in a defensive posture, half looking for a punch to be thrown my way.

"What the fuck is wrong with you, boy?!" he screamed at me with a face full of rage as he cornered me against the bathroom stall. In that moment, I was terrified of the man I had come to trust and look up to in so many ways.

"Ray, I know you're upset, but you have to listen to me," I said, trying to calm him down, though I knew he wouldn't understand.

"Bullshit, Ron! I told you those motherfuckers were crooks, and now you're going to be one of them! What the fuck is the matter with you? Doing this behind my back... I walk in here and get blindsided by that greasy motherfucker Lobranski. Son of a bitch telling me that you quit my staff because I don't have your back." The look in his eyes cut me to the core, knowing how betrayed he felt by my actions.

He backed off and stared at me in disbelief. "…But that's not even the worst of it!" he cried out. "Not five minutes later, Hamilton calls me into his office and tells me that you transferred to that cocksucker's staff… You know what, boy? Fuck you! You're one of them. Fuck you… Fuck you!" He seethed with anger. "You go do that crooked shit, and watch me laugh at your sorry ass when the police come for you like they did T.J. Fucking stupid!" he shouted in my face. As bad as I felt for Ray, I just couldn't take it anymore, and that pent-up anger burst out of my mouth.

"Fuck you, Ray!" I screamed at him. "I'm doing this for a fucking reason. I have no choice but to do this! It's the only way I can make things right for Sandra's family!" I shouted back. His face contorted for a moment as he backed up and stared at me with his mouth wide open.

"I don't fucking believe this," he said, as if stunned.

"What don't you believe?" I asked incredulously.

"I don't believe that you sold out!" he screamed back.

"I told you, I didn't sell out. I'm doing what I got to do, goddamn it."

"You fucking sold out! You sold out our staff, yourself, and me. Guess what, motherfucker? You sold out Sandra too just to soothe your conscience and get her family a few bucks they don't even deserve," he said with disgust.

"You know about these scams and the shit Hamilton does?" I asked in disbelief.

"Everyone knows what they do, boy! Do I look stupid to you? Does Wahl look stupid to you? What, because we're the nigger staff we're not smart enough to know what those crooked motherfuckers do? Is that what you think, boy?" he asked, stepping up and pointing in my face. "They have scams set up all over the place. But I don't let them do that shit on my staff! I told you that when you started," he said.

"So, you know Hamilton's involved?" I asked, wanting to make sure we were both on the same page.

"You are fucking stupid! Those assholes couldn't do shit if Hamilton didn't allow it," he said. I could feel my mouth drop open, shocked at how much he knew. I hung my head for a moment, then slowly looked up and stared into his eyes.

"This is wrong, Ray. This whole business is wrong, and you're just as fucked up as they are if you have known about it the whole goddamn time and didn't call the police or something."

"...And lose my fucking job?! I give a shit if these motherfuckers get busted, but if they do, I want the home office to know that I did everything the right way. I'm a fifty-five-year-old black man with no education and no retirement. What am I supposed to do? Get this place shut down because of these crooked motherfuckers?" he said with a long sigh. He closed his eyes and dropped his head for a moment, as if contemplating his next words. When he looked back up, the anger in his face had been replaced with a genuine expression of fatherly concern. "All weekend long, I've been thinking about Sandra and her family. You forget that I've known these folks for ten years. I knew Sandra when she was just a teenager, and I've been in their home hundreds of times. I can't even imagine what they are going through, and I've racked my brain trying to figure out any way possible to help them. You know that I take care of my agents and the people on my ledgers. I wouldn't have thought twice about covering a deposit to pay her claim, but cooking the books for a couple of thousand dollars ain't worth it to no one. Ron, I run a clean staff and do things the way they are supposed to be done, but I'll be goddamn if I'd sell out to those bastards!" he stressed.

"It's not like I'm selling out for myself," I said.

"The reason doesn't matter. They see you as a way of making money for themselves. They want to own you. That's what they do..." he emphasized with a long drawl. "I told you, Hamilton don't want to lose me because he can't get people to work the projects.

That's why he leaves us niggas alone, but he's been gunning for you since you started here, goddamn it. Don't you see that, Ron?"

"Ray, I needed to do this for Sandra. I loved that girl so much, and I feel like it's my fault she's dead," I said grinding my teeth.

"You're right. She's dead, boy. She's dead, and there ain't a goddamn thing you can do to bring her back. ...And knowing Sandra, I'm quite sure she'd tell you to stop acting like a goddamn fool, 'cause all you're doing is putting money in those motherfuckers' pocket." I threw my back against the stall and looked up at the ceiling as Meadows backed off and paced around for a moment. Then, he stopped and faced me with outstretched arms, begging me to reconsider. "Have some integrity, Ron?" he begged. "You're not like them! You're not some greedy, ignorant, white-ass motherfucking drug addict looking to kill yourself. Those motherfuckers on that staff aren't alive. They're dead as shit, and all they do is suck the shit Hamilton gives them to stay alive. That's not you, boy. Don't let them do this to you!" he pleaded with a tear forming in the corner of his eye.

"It's too late," I said, shaking my head and wishing he would have had this conversation with me when we met last Friday.

"It's not too late!" he argued.

"I already agreed to go along with everything," I said with despair.

"It's not too late. All you have to do is tell them you changed your mind. I'll go in and back you," he said forcefully. He would never know how badly I wanted to do it his way, nor would he ever know how much I loved the man for trying so hard to keep me anchored to the right path, but I couldn't.

"No, I'm sorry, Ray. I can't do it. I got a plan, and I'm going to see it through," I said with a deep breath.

"You ain't got shit, motherfucker, and let me tell you why," he pleaded. "Roger Hamilton had your fucking number the minute you called and begged him to pay that claim. He's going to own you,

Ronnie, lock, stock, and fucking barrel, don't you get that?!" he said with determination to make me understand his point of view.

"Not if I get him first," I said coolly, staring deep into his eyes. Ray looked at me for a moment, then shook his head with disgust. He turned and headed for the door, stopping just short before turning back toward me and pointing in the direction of the office.

"You're never going to outsmart Roger Hamilton. He's going to bury you," he said before pushing the door open and leaving. A sigh of relief came over me when he left the room. I walked over to the sink and turned on the cold water while staring at my haggard reflection in the mirror. With cupped hands, I bent over the sink and scooped up as much water as possible, drenching my tired face and repeating the process over and over. I had just finished pat drying my face with paper towels when the door to the bathroom swung open and the intimidating presence of Otis Wahl appeared in the doorway. Without hesitation, he stepped up and towered over me with a terrifying scowl cemented to his face. "What the fuck, Pickles?!" he shouted down at me.

"Jesus Christ, Otis! I just went through all this with Meadows. I'm not about to do it again with you!" I shouted back. I tried to step around his massive frame, but he cut me off and pushed me backwards against the bathroom stall again in what now seemed to be my whipping-boy position.

"Listen up, motherfucker! I don't give a shit what you do, but this shit is wrong! You dig? This shit is going to fuck you up, you dig?"

"Otis, I got to do this. What do you want me to say? I have to get something for this girl's family. I owe it to her," I explained.

"You don't owe anyone shit, including the dead girl. I don't care if you were fucking her, Pickles! She knew that shit was due, and for whatever reason she didn't pay it. Fuck that shit, Pickles. You did what you were supposed to do. You did the right thing. You lapsed her fucking policy."

"What… Does everyone in the office think I fucked her, for Christ's sake?"

"Nobody does the shit you're doing if they hadn't," he shot back.

"Well, I didn't, goddamn it! I truly loved this girl and want to get something for her family," I said with exasperation.

"But that don't make this shit right," he scolded.

"What do you mean?" I asked in confusion.

"I mean that loving her, or fucking her, doesn't make what you're doing now right. Goddamn it, Pickles! You're so far out of your motherfucking league with these dudes. You ain't got a clue. I know what those motherfuckers do, and if you don't do exactly what they tell you to do, they will fuck you up," he continued.

"That's the same thing Meadows said, but I don't get you guys. If they're all that bad, why hasn't anyone stepped up to do something about it?" I asked.

"You remember T.J.?" he asked out of the blue.

"Yeah. What the fuck does he got to do with anything?" I said, annoyed at the reference.

"Because he's dead, motherfucker!" he scowled.

"Jesus Christ! What on earth does that have to do with me?" I yelled out.

"He ended up in the bottom of that lake because these boys thought he was going to blow on them," he said with wide eyes, raised eyebrows, and extended arms.

"Oh bullshit. He was drugged up and killed himself," I retorted.

"Goddamn, Pickles, you been here for two motherfucking years, and you believe that shit? Fuck that shit, Pickles! He got his motherfucking ass killed because he was told to take care of some business for them boys and backed out at the last minute," he said. I looked at him for a long moment, confused by what he was saying. I remembered talking to several people about T.J., and the story was always the same.

"Otis, you're wrong. He didn't even work here anymore," I said dismissively.

"Not selling insurance, but he was still doing their deeds," he stated with conviction. I looked at him like he was crazy then flashed back to the time T.J. threw the hot dogs at me. He was completely strung out but also scared to death. I remembered T.J. saying something about his book being short, and that he shouldn't have let somebody talk him into something, but I never thought he was talking about Hamilton.

"So, you're saying Hamilton had him killed?" I asked in disbelief.

"I'm saying he fucked up and paid the price. ...And I'm saying you're fucking up and going to pay a price if you go through with this shit," he said sternly. I could tell by the look on his face that he was concerned and sincerely trying to warn me against transferring to the stoner staff for my own good.

"Look, I'm not stupid, and I know what I'm doing, okay? I just want to help out the family of this girl and wrap up some loose ends before I quit this place for good," I said.

"You should just quit now," he replied. He stared at me without expression, as if resigned to the fact that nothing he could say would change my mind.

"I can't do that, Otis. I got to get my paperwork started," I said, stepping past him and exiting the bathroom. Once outside the bathroom, I took a deep breath and headed for the office, knowing how stupid I was for not heeding his advice. I wanted to. I truly wanted to run away from that place with every fiber of my being, but somewhere deep down inside, I felt as if Sandra were begging me to stay the course and make things right. All the same, I marched down the hallway towards the office with a sinking feeling in my stomach. I stopped just short of the agents' door and wiped away beads of sweat that had formed on my brow before entering. I opened the door and walked into the noisy, smoke-filled room and strolled over to my desk on Meadows' staff as if nothing were wrong. Mr. Meadows was sitting in his usual spot at the end desk with his head buried in a ledger book, sucking on his pipe. He knew I sat down but wouldn't even raise his head to acknowledge me. Terrell and Meriwether were busy at their desks, and a few moments later, Otis came strolling in and sat across from me at his desk. Everyone went about their business without saying a word, and I felt very uncomfortable, as if I truly did betray the whole staff. I wanted to say something but changed my mind and decided to let things be for the time being. I picked up my briefcase and placed it on my desk just as Teddy came pacing into the room from Hamilton's office. Immediately, he spotted me and came strutting up to our staff like a rooster looking for a cockfight, positioning himself behind Otis.

"Pickles! What the fuck are you doing sitting over here on the dark side of town?" he said sarcastically. I cringed the moment he spoke, knowing he had just thrown gasoline on a smoldering fire. I was right, of course, but to my surprise, it wasn't Mr. Meadows who responded but Otis who jumped up, turned, and shoved his finger deep into Teddy's chest. The expression on Teddy's face changed instantly from one of "bold belligerence" to that of "petrified pissed pants" in a matter of seconds. No one ever saw Otis lose his cool, and everyone in the office got quiet when the big man stood up and towered over Lobranski.

"Fuck that shit, Lobranski! You want to see the dark side, motherfucker? Say another punk-ass word and watch me drop you like a bad habit."

"Shit, Otis. I was seriously just fucking around," Teddy said while cowering away from the big man. "You know me, man. I was messing with Pickles. Ain't that right, Ron?" he pleaded, hoping that I'd intervene.

"Teddy, you're an asshole, and one of these days you're going to get your ass handed to you because you're an asshole," I scolded.

"…And you're goddamn lucky Meadows ain't got bail money, or I'd go to jail for fucking you up right now," Otis interjected. Just then, Meadows got up and pulled a massive wad of collection money out of his pocket and threw it on the desk.

"Whatever the fuck you need, Wahl!" he shouted out as the whole office burst into laughter, diffusing the situation. A nervous laugh spilled out of Teddy's mouth as he backed away from Otis and drifted closer to his staff.

"Come on, Pickles, get your stuff. You're moving over to the WHITE SIDE! Is that okay?!" he shouted with a stupid-looking grin in Otis' direction.

"Pickles, this shit is fucked up," Otis said, peering into my eyes before returning to his seat and resuming his paperwork. Terrell and Meriwether were just staring at me with raised eyebrows as I stood up and gathered my things to leave. Mr. Meadows ignored me completely as he went about picking up the money that splashed across the desks when he threw it down. I wanted to say something but just kept to myself as I slunk away and moved to the other staff.

Even though the stoner staff was just a few feet away, it may as well have been in another room. Each staff had its own distinct character and ambiance unique to the group of individuals interacting with each other. The stoners were a raunchy group of guys with a sarcastic view of life and a penchant for self-indulgent, deviate behavior. With the obvious exception of Roger Hamilton, the stoners didn't associate with anyone outside of their staff and were pretty much despised by everyone else in the office. No one could figure out how this group of bigoted, racist, obnoxious white guys could manage to produce the incredible sales figures they did in a place they hated to work. Obviously, I was beginning to understand the process since it included scamming the company and clients out of proceeds from death benefits, but I knew there was more to this scam thing, and I was more determined than ever to find out how they operated and close it down.

"Ronnie, my boy, let me officially welcome you to Mr. Minka's staff," Lobranski called out while standing up to greet me and ushering me over to the staff manager, Tom Minka. In unison, the guys on the staff started clapping as I approached.

"Good to have you on staff," Minka said while jumping up and grabbing my hand. After some chitchat with Mr. Minka, I walked around the staff, shaking everyone's hand as they welcomed me aboard and congratulated me on the move. With the exception of Teddy and Vinnie, it dawned on me that I had rarely spoken to any of these guys in all the time I've worked here. The brothers, Frank and Bobby Tomicina, were always arguing with each other, and it seemed pointless to get involved in any of their conversations. Wojo was a sports fanatic and crazed gambler that I avoided like the plague, and Chucky Laduke kept to himself and rarely held a conversation with anyone. Once the greetings were over, everyone pretty much buried their heads in their paperwork, trying to get their deposits and new business into the window.

"Boys, we got a superstar in this guy," Teddy said to no one in particular while guiding me over to an empty desk between himself and Vinnie. "This will be your desk, next to me," he said, motioning me to sit before taking a seat himself. I placed my ledger book and briefcase on the desk, then sat down next to him, all the while looking over at my old staff and wondering what in the hell I was doing. I opened up my briefcase and pulled out the fire insurance applications I wrote for Ruppert the day before. Once I finished filling out both applications, I counted out the money I collected and looked over to see what Otis was doing. Ruppert's accounts were on Otis' ledger, so he was going to have to deposit the money and turn in the fire applications with his account. I figured he'd be happy, or at least cordial, that I put $75 of commission in his pocket, as well as making a rather substantial collection for his book. The office had finally calmed down from the earlier confrontation between Otis and Teddy. The last thing I wanted to do was kindle that fire again by calling out to Otis, so I stuck the wad of cash in my pants, stood up, and walked to the far end of the office by the storage cabinets. I mulled around for a moment, shuffling through the cabinet, as if looking for supplies, before doubling back and tapping Otis on the shoulder.

"What's this?" he grumbled as I placed the applications on his desk.

"With all this bullshit, I didn't get a chance to tell you that Ruppert called the office yesterday and wanted one of us to pick up his money," I said. He looked up at me with a twisted look on his face.

"He called looking for you?"

"No, he called and left a message with Irene, who gave it to me," I corrected.

"Why did she give the message to you?"

"Because he told her that you and I were his agents, and he wanted someone to come out yesterday. I called him as a courtesy, and he asked me to stop by, so I did, alright?" I said with exasperation.

"You went over to Granny Jones' place in the projects and picked this up?" he asked incredulously.

"Hell no! Are you crazy? Ruppert asked me to stop by his apartment because he forgot to leave the money with Granny Jones on Saturday, and he wanted some fire insurance on his place," I said.

"You went to the man's crib?" he asked in disbelief.

"Yeah, why?"

"It's all good," he said, shaking his head. Otis picked up the applications and read them over before looking up at me. "You wrote two contracts?"

"Yeah, one from me and one from you, that's cool right?" I confirmed while digging in my pocket for the money Ruppert paid. "Here, he paid three months on the life insurance and three months on the new fire insurance," I said, handing him the cash.

"Alright, that's cool," he said with a sigh while taking the money and placing it on his desk. Without saying anything else, he picked up a pen and started filling out some paperwork, as if I didn't exist.

"Hey, Otis, I, um…"

"I got to get this shit in the window, Pickles," he said, cutting me off before I got started.

"Yeah, I better finish up," I said, walking back to my desk with a sinking feeling in my heart. A few minutes later, Hamilton marched into the agents' room with a serious look on his face and stood between Mr. Meadows' staff and my new home, the stoner staff. He placed a hand on Ray's back to get his attention while facing us.

"Gentlemen, listen up for one moment, please. I'd like to see Mr. Meadows, Mr. Minka, and Mr. Pickles in my office before the meeting. If you need more time to make your deposits, I am going to tell Mrs. Bolger to keep the window open for an additional fifteen minutes after the meeting." With military-like obedience and precision, the three of us dropped what we were doing, stood up, and marched into Hamilton's office as ordered. Hamilton led the way, leaving a wake of musky cologne for us to walk through as we followed behind. He then stood outside the door of his office and waited for the three of us to enter before closing the door and following behind. Mr. Minka helped himself to the chair right in front of Hamilton's desk, which forced Ray and me to sit uncomfortably close to one another on the couch.

"This will only take a moment, gentlemen," Hamilton said while hurrying behind his desk and pulling up his chair to sit down. He leaned over and took a quick sip of coffee from his mug before moving it to the side of his desk. "Okay then," he said with a sigh while folding his hands on his desk. His expression was serious, but his tone came across sympathetically as he spoke.

"We all know what happened on Ron's ledger last week. A woman by the name of Sandra Wesley and her little girl, Lucy, were brutally murdered in their home last week. They were clients of Mr.

Pickles." I watched with interest as he paused for a moment, taking a breath and chewing on his lower lip before continuing. "Unfortunately," he said with a deep sigh, "as all of us have experienced, she didn't pay her premium on time, and her policy lapsed. Mr. Pickles did everything humanly possible to keep her insurance in force, including trying to collect her money the day she was killed," he said with a nod in my direction. "Of course, almost everyone on his ledger blames Ron for lapsing the policy and thinks that Unified is a shit company for not paying the claim," he said as if disgusted by the notion. I sat there with a blank expression on my face but noticed that both Meadows and Minka were shaking their heads, as if disgusted by the thought as well. Satisfied with their reactions, he continued, "It's a stressful situation for anyone to be in, especially a young guy like Ron." He looked at me with concern. "I don't want to lose Ron as an agent. Do you two gentlemen understand what I'm saying?" he directed at Meadows and Minka, as if angry that anyone would even suggest such a thing. Of course, they hadn't and felt compelled to agree wholeheartedly with Roger's admonition. "Ron Pickles has been an incredible asset to our district and to the company as a whole. With the right guidance, I see Ron in a management position in no time at all," he said with a smile in my direction. I practically choked back a little vomit, trying to return the smile, feeling nauseous at the heap of dung that was flowing out of his mouth. "So," he continued, "what I'm going to do is transfer Ron and his ledger book to Mr. Minka's staff. Is that understood?" he directed at everyone. Collectively, we all nodded our heads as in perfect agreement with his reasoning. "In addition, I'm going to give him a partial ledger to start working this weekend. I'll have that for you Thursday," he said with a wink towards me. I nodded my approval, and he continued. "Tom, I want you to help Ron with any collections he might feel uncomfortable with on the old book. Is that okay with you?"

"No problem, Roger," Minka said automatically.

"Good. Ray, obviously this means that your staff will be short a book for the time being. So, what I think is fair is to give you credit for Ron's sales and collections for the next sixty days. You know, until this situation calms down and we put another book together for your staff."

"I don't understand," I spoke up. "How do you put another book together?" I asked.

"It's easy. We take bordering streets or even some territory from other districts that aren't producing and form a new ledger. If I'm not mistaken, your current book was actually chopped in half before we gave it to you. Isn't that right, Ray?"

"Yep, I had that book big and fat at one time," Ray chuckled before lowering his head and looking at the floor, as if mourning the loss of the book from his staff. We all sat in silence for a moment as if a courtesy for Ray's loss.

"Anyways," Roger finally spoke up, "I wanted to bring you gentlemen in here so there was no animosity between anyone. Ray, I spoke to Ron about this yesterday, and he truly didn't want to leave your staff. However, in light of the situation, I thought it was the best thing for everyone," he said, daring Meadows to object.

"Whatever you think is best, Roger," Ray said before clearing his throat and swallowing hard, knowing he just ate Hamilton's shit.

"I understand that you knew this family pretty well, is that right?" he asked Ray.

"Yes, I did. I mean I do, and it's a terrible thing, Roger, a terrible thing," Ray said with a deep sigh.

"That's another reason I'm taking this ledger off your staff. I don't want you to have any contact with these folks. Is that understood?" he asked with a serious tone and raised eyebrows. Meadows straightened his back and pursed his lips while shaking his head slightly, attempting to disagree with Hamilton's directive.

"They're good people, Roger. I don't think there will be a problem," he responded.

"Ray, when it comes to money, there is always a problem. I don't care how good these people are; I don't want you having any contact with them. Is that understood?"

"Yes, sir, but…"

"Ray, I'm not trying to be an asshole. If they choose to get an attorney, they could drag both you and Ron into this and may even insinuate that you guys promised to pay for the insurance or something. Regardless, we don't want a situation where the company has to spend thousands of dollars defending allegations that aren't true. Do you agree?" he asked in a tone that only expected one answer.

"Absolutely, I understand," Meadows responded sheepishly. Roger turned his attention towards Minka, who just shrugged his shoulders in agreement, and then towards me.

"I'm fine with everything Roger," I said as a matter of fact.

"Good. Okay, unless there's any other questions, this meeting is over," Hamilton said with a slap on his desk like an auctioneer ending a sale. The three of us stood up together and marched out of the room as we came in, single file. No one said a word, and it took all the willpower I could muster to stop from screaming "BULLSHIT" at the top of my lungs. I headed back to the stoner staff and passed Ray Meadows as he took his seat at the head of his staff. I took a couple of steps past him, then stopped and turned around. I couldn't just go back to my seat without saying anything to Meadows, who had just gotten through tongue-lashing the hell out of me in the bathroom.

"Seriously, Ray?" I said, creeping up on him from behind while keeping my voice as low as possible. He tilted his head in my direction then turned back, resuming his paperwork without saying a word.

"Defend allegations that aren't true? Jesus Christ, Ray, you sat there and ate shit out of the man's hand like you were starving. What were you telling me twenty minutes ago? That I should stop what I was doing, and you'd have my back? That I was a traitor for jumping staffs? That I should give up this idea of doing something for this family?" I asked, seething under my breath.

"You're not helping anyone, Ron," he said stoically.

"But you fucking are?" I whispered.

"Listen, boy," he said with a growl as he turned to face me. "I know what kind of shit I have to eat in order to keep my job. I also know when I'm being told to mind my own fucking business and stay away from a situation. Hamilton just told all of us that you belong to him now, and there ain't a goddamn thing anyone can do about it. You're just too goddamn young and dumb to realize what's going on around here. I tried to warn you, Ron, but you know everything. You're smarter than everyone, and you think you're doing the right thing. But these guys have been playing this game before you were even born, and they are going to eat you up and spit you out if you go against them. Remember who told you that," he said, turning his back on me.

CHAPTER 29

Thursday, July 9th, 1981

Forty-eight hours later, I was riding the elevator back up to the fifth floor, half wondering who would be waiting to drag me off when I arrived. To my relief, the door opened without incident, and I lumbered into the office as usual, weighed down by my ledger book and briefcase. Instinctively, I took a step towards my old desk, stopped, turned around, then headed for my new home on the stoner staff.

It was a little after 8:00 a.m., and the office was already buzzing with the usual group of agents wanting to beat the 10:00 a.m. rush to the window and get their deposits in early. I had just dropped my stuff on the desk and eyed the coffee pot when Teddy Lobranski came gliding into the agents' room from the outer office.

"Pickles, you're here. Excellent!" he said, walking up and dropping a small ledger book next to my stuff on the desk. "This is it, as promised," he said with a wide grin.

"The partial, huh?" I said unenthusiastically.

"Cool, right? Like dropping 150 bucks in your pocket every week, buddy," he said, moving closer and slapping me on the back.

"Is this close to my area?" I asked, picking up the book and thumbing through some of the accounts.

"It's a little further south, right around the jail. You know, 26th and California," he said before leaning in and whispering in my ear. "Shit, Pickles, it is all the fucking ghetto. Who cares as long as you make some money? You know what I mean?"

"Yeah, whatever," I sighed. "Hey, Teddy, how are we doing with the other stuff?" I asked. He straightened up, shrugged slightly, and

425

dropped his mouth open, feigning disbelief that I would dare to inquire about our scam in the office. "I'm not in the mood for bullshit, Teddy. All I want to know is if we're on track," I said, dismissing his dramatics. He shook his head, took a deep breath, and motioned for me to follow him into the hallway. Mr. Uhlen got to the agents' door a moment before us and held it open for Teddy and me to walk through. "Thank you, sir," I said as I passed.

"You sirs are most welcome," Mr. Uhlen replied. "Apparently, nature has tapped the three of us on the shoulder at the same time," he said with a smile.

"No, Teddy and I have grown close and need our private time," I said with a nod and a wink.

"Jesus, Pickles, if I would have known you were such a fag, I'd have let the niggers keep you," Teddy quipped back.

"Really, one of those guys hear you call them a nigger again, and your asshole is going to look like an airplane hangar," I answered, more serious than joking.

"Well, you boys try not to hurt each other," Uhlen retorted to our amusement as he turned and meandered down the hallway to the restroom. I turned to face Teddy and caught him staring intently over my shoulder in the direction of Mr. Uhlen. I turned just in time to see Mr. Uhlen tapping his watch before continuing on his way to the bathroom.

"What was all that about?" I asked, looking back at Lobranski with a frown.

"Oh, nothing. He wanted me to send him over a transfer before the meeting started," he said somewhat hesitantly.

"Speaking of which, I'm not going to bust your ass on this shit or harass you every minute of the day, but I want to know that everything we talked about is going to happen," I said with authority. He moved closer, then stopped and looked up and down the hallway before answering me in a hushed, angry voice while illustrating with his hands.

"I understand, Pickles, but I fucking told you we never discuss this shit in the office. Not in the office! Not in the hallway! Not even in the fucking shithouse. That's the fucking rule, and you agreed to it," he insisted.

"This is important to me, Teddy," I growled back.

"…And it's important to us, Pickles. Look at what's happened in the last week," he said, counting off the accomplishments on his fingers. "First, you switched staffs. Second, we got the case transferred to me. Third, we got you that partial, and fourth, you got a $150 raise. None of this would have happened if we weren't working to get this thing resolved," he said with a forced smile.

"Alright," I said, looking away with an unconvinced sigh.

"Everything is in play, Ronnie. That's all I can tell you. Everything is going to be taken care of just the way we talked about, okay?"

"That's all I wanted to know, Teddy. Just keep me in the loop," I replied as we heard the elevator door open from around the corner. Instinctively, we backed away from each other and took up the posture of two guys chewing the fat before heading back into the office. Just then, Craig Branson came strolling around the corner, looking quite sharp in a three-piece, blue-striped suit.

"Gentlemen," Craig greeted.

"Damn, dude! Look at you. Someone has a hot date after the meeting," I said, articulating with outstretched hands.

"Looking good, Branson," Lobranski spoke up.

"Thank you, good sirs. I thought I'd bring a little class to the office today," he chuckled.

"Oh, I see. No sales this week," I shot back to an instant grin.

"Exactly!" he said, pointing at me like I won a prize. "I haven't sold a fucking thing in two weeks and thought the suit might help Hamilton appreciate my dedication," he said with a wide grin.

"Hamilton's a numbers guy, Branson. Pickles here is the fag who appreciates a sharp suit," Teddy remarked. It was funny, and even I chuckled along at the quip. Craig walked around us and opened the door to the agents' room, then paused and looked back at me before he entered.

"Hey, Ronnie, let me know when you got a few minutes? I wanted to tell you something about my kid," Craig said.

"Hold up, I think we're done here, right, Teddy?" I asked dismissively, not wanting to listen to any more of his bullshit than I had to.

"Yeah, we're cool," he said, exchanging places with Craig, who backed away from the door at the same time. "But hey," he called out before going inside. "That partial has a collection that needs to be picked up at 10:00 a.m. on the dot tomorrow. Don't leave the office until I give you that address, alright?"

"No problem, man. Just leave the address on my desk," I replied.

"Okay, cool, but you got to be there at ten, or this broad will blow the dough," he stopped and reiterated before continuing into the office.

"I'll be there," I said as the door shut behind him. "What's up with your kid?" I turned and asked the moment Lobranski disappeared. Craig stepped back and perched himself against the wall.

"My kid is fine," he brushed off. "I didn't want to talk to you in front of that scumbag, Lobranski. The buzz in the office is that you went through some serious shit, but transferring to the stoner staff? What the fuck is going on, Ronnie?" he asked with concern.

"It's a long story, Craig," I said with a sigh, shaking my head and looking down at the floor. "Jesus Christ, so much has happened over the past week, it's been unbelievable."

"I know about the girl. She was the one you really liked, wasn't she?" he asked.

"Yeah, it was Sandra," I said, looking into his eyes.

"I don't know what to say, Ron. I'm so sorry," he said with genuine sympathy in his voice.

"I can't believe it's already been a week," I lamented.

"Wow!" he sighed. "I had no idea any of this was happening until Otis threatened to kill Lobranski on Tuesday," he said with astonishment.

"It's been crazy. You have no idea," I said.

"I got to take a leak. Walk with me down to the can," he said.

"You're not planning to kick my ass, are you?" I chortled as we walked down the hall.

"What?"

"Yeah, Meadows dragged me into the shitter on Tuesday and reamed my ass for switching staffs, and then Otis took his turn," I snorted.

"Honestly, I don't blame them. I was going to ask you the same thing. You know those guys are bad fucking news," he said with concern.

"You think I would have done it if I had a choice?" I asked.

"I don't understand."

"It was the only way I could try to make things right with Sandra's family," I said as we reached the bathroom and went inside.

"What do you mean?"

"I lapsed the fucking policy last week, Craig."

"So, they don't get shit," he said.

"Well, this is between us, but I took a deal to get them some money," I said softly.

"Oh man, they're blackmailing you into one of those funeral home scams, aren't they?" he said with disgust.

"They are, but they aren't. I don't have to do it, but I don't really have a choice," I said, heading up to the sink and washing my hands while Craig hit the urinal.

"Wow, that's fucked up. What about the girl and her daughter? Did they find who killed them?" he questioned.

"No, and honestly, I doubt they ever will," I said with a sigh. "God, you have no idea how much I hate this place. Fucking books shouldn't be called the black ledger; they should be called the death ledgers," I said while pulling some paper towels from the dispenser as Craig headed over to the sink to wash his hands. "All they are is a record of people who are going to die," I lamented while drying my hands. I tossed the wet towels in the garbage, then turned to find Craig staring blindly at his reflection in the mirror. "Hey, you okay?" I asked.

"Yeah, I'm fine, but you just made me think of something I never considered," he said, looking into my eyes through the mirror. I shook my head slightly, confused at his epiphany, but more so by the intense look of dismay that crept across his face. It was almost as if he had changed into a different person right before my eyes. "Ron, it never even crossed my mind before, but that's what the Nazis used to call them," he said as if thinking out loud.

"What are you talking about, Nazis? What did the Nazis call what?" I asked, baffled at his sudden interest in World War II.

"Death ledgers, Ron. Death ledgers!" he exclaimed as if he had just discovered the theory of relativity. "The concentration camps kept accounting books of everyone they killed. They called them 'The Death Ledgers,'" he said, seeming to snap back to his old self. "I'm sorry, dude, it just struck me as bizarre that the Nazis used 'death ledgers,' and we use 'black ledgers' to record basically the same thing. You know?"

"What do you mean, 'same thing'?" I asked.

"You know, dead people," he summed up.

"How the fuck do you know all this shit about death ledgers?" I joked at such a random bit of trivia. Craig looked at me for a moment, then shrugged his shoulders and rolled his eyes in amusement before offering an answer.

"Well, um, I did some college, you know, and I wrote a paper on the different concentration camps. Most people think there were only a few camps, like Auschwitz and Dachau, but there were actually hundreds all over occupied Europe, and they all kept death ledgers of some kind. Once the Nazis figured out they were going to lose the war, they destroyed all the records. But there was this one camp in Austria called Mauthausen, and they actually found the death ledgers still intact." Just then, we heard the toilet flush and looked at each other with surprise that someone else had been in there with us. I let out a sigh of relief when the stall door opened and Mr. Uhlen popped out and stepped up to the sink.

"That was the camp Mr. Guru and I escaped from, Mr. Branson. You know your history," Uhlen drawled in his broken English as he leaned over the sink and turned on the water. Craig didn't say anything and backed away with a blank expression on his face.

"Mr. Uhlen, I'm sorry, we had no idea you were here. We were just bullshitting about the crazy shit that goes on around here," I said, glancing down at the number tattooed into his arm by the Nazis.

"Don't be sorry, Ronnie. It's just history now," Uhlen said. "Isn't that right, Mr. Branson?" he directed towards Craig, who stood silent.

"It was definitely fucked up," I interjected, trying to break the tension that Craig was creating by not answering. Mr. Uhlen seemed hell-bent on pushing the subject that obviously got under Craig's skin.

"You are right, Craig. Death ledgers *were* kept by the Germans," he said slowly. "They were used to record everything belonging to the Jews and other victims who entered the concentration camps. The Germans told everyone to bring their belongings because they were being relocated for the war effort," he said without emotion. "Those belongings were then confiscated..."

"You mean stolen," Craig added somewhat snottily.

"Yes, stolen. And recorded in the death ledgers that you fellows are talking about," he said while shuffling away from the sink and extracting some paper towels to dry his hands."

"The Nazis destroyed most of the ledgers before Germany was liberated," Craig said.

"That's correct. They didn't want to be held accountable for their crimes, Mr. Branson. But what criminal does?" he added rhetorically.

"No offense, Mr. Uhlen," Craig said with folded arms. "You almost sound like you're defending the Nazis," he insinuated with a disrespectful tone.

"Craig, come on, dude!" I said, angered at his remark.

"It's okay, Ronnie," Uhlen said, wiping the water from his hands. "Craig is a good boy. He certainly knows I'm not defending Nazis, and I know he didn't mean anything by it. Did you?" he asked, staring directly into Craig's eyes.

"No, nothing at all," Craig deadpanned.

"You can't change history, Mr. Branson. It was what it was," Uhlen said with raised eyebrows and puckered lips before leaving the bathroom. Craig just stood there frozen, as if his thoughts were a million miles away.

"Hey, what the fuck was that?" I asked at his caustic behavior while snapping my fingers to break his hypnotic state.

"Nothing, Ronnie. It was nothing," he said, shaking his head back to reality.

"Well, something bothered you," I said seriously.

"It was just that one thing he said... I'm probably wrong," Craig said dismissively.

"Said about what?" I wanted to know.

"He said they escaped from Mauthausen," Craig shrugged.

"So, what's the big deal?" I asked.

"I told you, I did that paper in college. No one ever escaped from Mauthausen."

CHAPTER 30

Friday, July 10th, 1981

I'll admit it bothered me that the partial ledger was located in the neighborhood that wrapped around the Cook County jail, but, for a moment, I thought that might be a good thing. After all, it was a secure facility and loaded with a police presence that would put Fort Knox to shame. "It has to be a fairly safe and secure area," I mumbled to myself. Of course, that illusion was shattered all of fifteen minutes into my arrival while stuck at a red light.

An unfortunate older colored lady made the rather careless mistake of leaving her purse on the front passenger seat of her car instead of placing it on the floor outside of window view. Some kid crossed the street with the light, as if minding his own business, then took a sharp turn and pitched a huge metal ball through the woman's passenger-side window. He grabbed her purse and flew down an adjoining alley before the light turned green. The poor lady just sat there in shock, unaware of the cars behind her and people laying on their horns for her to get out of the way. I pulled my car to the right of hers, got out, and stuck my head in the smashed-out window of her car to ask if she was okay. She was crying, but said she was fine. I asked if she could pull in front of me and let the other cars go by, and that I would stay with her until the police came. Once she pulled over, I ran into a nearby liquor store and asked the clerk to call the cops, then ran back outside to make sure she was still okay.

"I knows better, I knows better," she kept saying over and over as I stood by and helped her out of the car. She was a heavy-set woman, all dressed up in a Sunday-go-to-church, flower-patterned dress, complete with black patent leather shoes. I felt bad for this little old grandma, knowing that she'd never get her purse back and now had to deal with the added expense and aggravation of getting her window smashed out. To their credit, the police showed up right away and calmed the poor lady down, even offering to take her to a mechanic who would fix her window. I gave them my phone number and a quick description of what I saw before continuing my task of exploring the latest addition to my black ledger.

I had become so desensitized to traumatic events since working the ledger, I barely considered this robbery more than a nuisance, like getting stuck at a train. I wanted to drive around the new ledger and see what I had gotten myself into but was running out of time. Teddy insisted that I collect from a lady named Debra Samson at 10:00 a.m. sharp, or she would blow the money and lapse her policy, so I just headed right over to the address he gave me after dealing with the cops.

Debra Samson lived in a large brick apartment building that was shaped like a horseshoe with a courtyard entrance. I hated these kinds of buildings because the entrances were always recessed deep into the courtyard, and you had to walk all the way to the back to get inside. There were three entrances to this building, one on each side facing the courtyard and one all the way in back.

Of course, this lady lived in the rear, so I had to march past two entrances where anyone could be watching and then all the way back, where I was basically trapped if something bad was to happen. It was still early in the morning, so I just took a deep breath and walked quickly, figuring I'd get in and out of there as fast as possible. I was happy that the outside door to the building was locked and that I had to ring a buzzer to be let in because that meant people couldn't just hang out inside the vestibules. I quickly scanned the doorbells and found Samson, immediately pressing it a couple of times to make absolutely sure it would ring, if it even worked. After a few seconds, a scratchy intercom fired up and a female voice asked who was there.

"It's Ron Pickles from Unified Insurance Company," I shouted into the intercom.

"'Surance man?"

"Yes, ma'am," I replied.

"Alright, come up," she said as the door buzzer rang out. I pulled open the heavy door and walked inside the hallway just as I heard the sound of locks being unlatched from a door on another floor somewhere above me. I walked up two flights of stairs before coming face to face with a rather stunning lady, dressed like an office professional, with black slacks, heels, and a white, button-down blouse. Although she seemed rather terse, her coffee-creamed face was angelic and smooth with make-up applied to perfection. Her long, black hair was curled and bouncy, as if she had just walked out of a salon, and I was shocked to find such a lovely woman waiting to pay her insurance.

"Debra Samson?" I asked.

"That's right."

"Nice to meet you," I said, extending a hand to shake. "My name is Ron Pickles, and I'll be your new insurance agent," I said as she dropped her hand in mine like a wet fish that just slipped away. She looked at me rather cynically, without much of an expression.

"You got some identification?" she asked abruptly.

"Um, yes, I do, actually," I said, digging into my pocket protector for a business card. "Here you go," I said, handing her the card. "Didn't Teddy Lobranski call and tell you I was coming?" I asked as she studied the card.

"Yeah," she sighed, still staring at my card.

"Alright, come in," she finally said, motioning me inside. I didn't take more than two steps into her living room before getting one of those gut feelings Meadows always talked about that something wasn't right. There wasn't a picture on the wall, a laundry basket on the floor, or even an extra pair of shoes scattered about the place. Instead, there was an old couch centered in the middle of the room, with an end table lamp on one side and a raunchy-looking coffee table in front of the couch. It all looked as if it had just been pulled from the garbage. A couple of Coke cans and a crumpled-up bag of

Cheetos were scattered about the coffee table, and I knew instantly that her apartment wasn't a home. The place smelled stale, and it was quite warm without so much as a table fan running to circulate the air. If that wasn't enough, I knew she was too cautious about letting me inside and way too well dressed and attractive to live here.

She didn't say anything as she shut and locked the door and then just walked past me, as if terribly annoyed by the entire ordeal. I followed as she led me up to a doorway leading into the kitchen. I stopped just inside while she walked all the way to the back door before turning around to face me. With the exception of an old, green Formica table and a couple of chairs, the kitchen was empty of belongings, including appliances.

"Did you just move in?" I inquired, wondering if perhaps I wasn't misreading the situation. She folded her arms and shook her head without looking me in the eye.

"Is everything okay?" I asked when she didn't answer.

"I don't like this," she snapped back without reason.

"I'm sorry, Debra. Did I catch you at a bad time?" I asked, thinking I needed to get out of here as soon as I could.

"It ain't that. Every damn month, I'm getting a new 'surance agent knocking at my door, looking to collect my money, and I'm getting damn sick and tired of letting strangers into my house," she said, looking past me with disgust. I knew right then and there that I was in trouble. I quickly glanced behind me, and then back at her, knowing that she was stalling.

"Oh, I know what you mean, Mrs. Samson. I hear that from a lot of folks, and to be honest with you, I'm sick of it too. I'm going to make a special report to the home office and have a manager come out and see you right away," I said, matching her anger as I backed out of the kitchen. Not a moment later, I heard footsteps approaching from behind me and turned smack into a tall black man that pushed me back into the kitchen. Another guy came in behind him and stood blocking the doorway while the tall guy backed me further into the kitchen.

"You ain't going anywhere, motherfucker!" he said with a deep lisp. "Sit your ass down," he said, pointing at the kitchen chair. Without taking my eyes off him, I pulled out the chair and sat down, petrified with fear.

"What the fuck took you so long, goddamn it?!" Debra yelled out with anger from behind me. "How much longer did you think I was going keep this motherfucker standing around listening to me bitch about some goddamn insurance policy?" she said, walking past both men into the front room.

"Shit, Debra, Bobby downstairs bleeding like a motherfucker from the first two cocksuckers we took care of," he said.

"That one dude fought like a motherfucker," the smaller of the two said.

"I don't give a shit about that. Ain't this the motherfucker we suppose to get?" she snapped back while pointing at me. In that moment, I panicked, knowing I was set up, and bolted from the chair in a frantic attempt to get out the back door.

"Son of a bitch, get that motherfucker!" she yelled out as both guys lunged for me at the same time. The door was locked shut, and I didn't have a prayer of escaping, so I started screaming at the top of my lungs, "HELP! SOMEBODY CALL THE POLICE! HELP ME PLEASE!" I shouted over and over, hoping someone might hear.

"SHUT THE FUCK UP," the smaller guy said as he grabbed me from behind and threw me down to the floor. The big guy jumped on top of me and grabbed my throat so hard I thought I was going to pass out right there. My arms were pinned under his legs, and I was totally at his mercy, gasping for each breath.

"Don't kill that motherfucker here," Debra yelled out from the doorway.

"I'LL RIP OUT YOUR FUCKING VOICE BOX IF YOU MAKE ANOTHER SOUND!" he screamed into my face. "You fucking understand me?" he asked, loosening his grip somewhat from my throat.

"Yes," I said, trying to swallow.

"I don't trust this dude! Debra, get me something to put in this man's mouth," he commanded.

"I promise, I won't say anything else," I begged. He looked into my eyes and nodded his head as if he believed me.

"That right, you promise?" he asked.

"Yes, I promise," I answered. Debra's hand came into view, holding a dried-up washrag. "I promise, I won't say anything," I pleaded again.

"Alright, dude, calm down," he said, loosening his grip on my throat a little more. "I can see you're a man of your word, right?"

"Yes, I promise, please," I said again.

"Okay, good. Then we got an understanding, you and I, correct?"

"Yes, sir," I said obediently.

"Good," he smiled before gripping my throat tighter with a jerk that pushed my head backwards. "FUCK YOU AND THAT MOTHERFUCKIN' BULLSHIT!" he hollered in my face while snatching the rag from Debra and forcing the rancid thing into my mouth. Within moments, the two stood me up, clutching my arms in a death grip while Debra ran around us and unlocked the back door. The moment she pulled it open, they rushed me out and down the stairs to a waiting car with the trunk lid popped open. Without hesitation, they positioned me in front of the trunk, kicked my legs out from underneath me, and dropped me to the ground. Before I knew what was happening, the two picked me up by the legs and arms and hurled me into the trunk, slamming the lid shut a moment later. I ripped the rag out of my mouth the moment the trunk closed and almost threw up at the taste it left behind. Seconds later, the vehicle rumbled to life and accelerated without warning, spinning me backwards until I hit the back wall. I was reeling in pain and dizzy, almost car sick, from being bounced around. I couldn't understand what was happening, who to blame, or what to think. I wasn't panicked or hysterical but incredibly disoriented and confused, paralyzed by the situation.

I had no concept of time and only knew we had reached our destination when the car came to a stop and the engine was turned off. I heard the doors open and felt them slam shut as the occupants got out of the car. My hearing was amazingly acute, as well as my sense of touch, feeling every vibration or movement someone made. My breathing grew heavy in anticipation of the trunk opening. I desperately felt around for something, anything, I could use as a weapon and started to panic when I found nothing. Out of nowhere came the muffled shouts of angry voices growing louder and louder as they approached the car. I knew they were coming to get me, and I started gasping for air and sweating profusely as they got closer. Suddenly, I heard the strains of what I thought was a familiar voice standing right outside the car. "What the fuck possessed you to put this man in the motherfucking trunk of your car?!" I heard that voice scream.

"All you said was bring the motherfucker to you. How was we suppose to know you friends with this honky?" another man said.

"Ruppert, is that you?" I called out from inside the trunk.

"Hold on, Mr. Pickles! Stop fucking around and open this goddamn trunk now!" I heard Ruppert shout.

"I'm trying to find the key," the other voice said nervously as the sound of keys jingled right outside the lock. After a moment, I heard the key being inserted into the lock and clicking the trunk lid open with a thud. An instant later, the trunk popped open, and I was blinded by the sunshine that slashed across my eyes like a knife. I tried to lift myself out of the trunk, only to fall backwards before feeling a couple of sets of hands grab me by the arms and lift me out of the vehicle.

"I told you to bring this man to me," Ruppert directed angrily at the two guys that threw me into the trunk. "I never said anything about fucking him up or locking him up in your trunk. You alright, Mr. Pickles?" Ruppert asked, still holding me up while I got my bearings.

"Yeah, I guess. What the fuck is going on?" I asked, finally standing on my own while the other two guys moved to the front of the car.

"Sorry about this shit and these dumb motherfuckers," he said, pointing to the trunk before waving the other guys off in disgust. "I had to get your ass over here as soon as possible, and this was about my only option," he said apologetically.

"What's going on, Ruppert?" I pleaded with a serious look and outstretched arms.

"We need to go inside and talk some things over," he said with a long sigh before motioning me to follow.

"What do you want us to do?" the taller of the guys called out as we walked away.

"Y'all wait out here by the car. There's going to be some more people coming in a few minutes. Don't shoot them, ya hear?!" Ruppert commanded more seriously than not.

"Yes, sir," the taller one replied.

"I ain't finished. Come down and let me know the moment they get here," Ruppert continued.

"What's going on, Ruppert?" I asked again.

"Come on, we're going to go downstairs and talk about it," he said, motioning for me to follow. I looked up and realized for the first time that we were at that abandoned building Ruppert used to administer justice to those guys who mugged Otis almost a year ago. A sinking feeling began to come over me as I walked behind him, still groggy from being bounced around in the back of the trunk. We walked down the side of the building and around the corner to the stairs leading to the basement. He waited for me to catch up, then motioned for me to go down the stairs and in the door. I walked inside and stepped away from the door to allow Ruppert room to enter. The dark, musty-smelling basement was exactly the same as it was the last time I was there, except that the only one sitting at the old wooden table this time was Mosley, who acted as if he were waiting for us to arrive.

"Good to see you, Mr. Pickles," he said, standing up and offering his hand in an uncharacteristic sign of humility.

"Good to see you, Mosley," I said, walking over and giving up a seasoned soul shake that I learned from two years of working the black ledger.

"Sit down over there, Mr. Pickles," Ruppert directed to the left of Mosley. "What did you do with the packages, Mo?" he asked.

"I put them in the closet," Mosley said, still standing and pointing to a storage door in the corner of the basement.

"That works," Ruppert said, glancing in the direction of the storage closet before looking back at me and shaking his head. "Motherfuckers damn near killed Mr. Pickles by sticking him in the back of the fucking trunk," he said with a grimace on his face.

"Why did they put him in the trunk?" Mosley asked with concern.

"Because the two of them they ain't got a goddamn brain cell," Ruppert replied.

"What's in the closet?" I asked.

"We'll be getting to that in a couple of minutes," Ruppert casually dismissed. "Mosley, did you bring that water?"

"Yeah, I got that cooler and some cups out in the car."

"Do me a favor and run out and bring this man a cup of water," he commanded. Before I could say anything, Mosley took off like a good soldier and marched out the door as ordered.

"I appreciate it, Ruppert, but I'm fine, really," I said, taking my seat. Ruppert pulled out the chair across from mine and sat down with a look of concern on his face. He inched the chair forward and placed his elbows on the table before leaning towards me, as if searching for the right thing to say.

"Ruppert, you gonna tell me what's going on?" I finally asked after a few moments of silence.

"I'm working on it, Mr. Pickles," he said with a deep breath.

"Working on what? This is insane!" I exclaimed with shrugged shoulders and open hands resting on the table.

"I know," he said, reaching up to rub his forehead. "Okay, listen up. You're involved in some complicated shit, and you inadvertently got me involved in some complicated shit, and I'm trying to figure out the best way to explain this complicated shit so it makes sense," he said with purpose.

"Why didn't you just ask me to come by and talk about it instead of having these guys drag me here?" I asked, knowing something extraordinary had taken place and that my life was about to change forever.

"That was not an option, and this is not a social call. I don't invite people over to rat-infested, piss-stained basements to talk about the meaning of life. But when you understand the situation better, you'll be extremely thankful that you're in this rat-infested, piss-stained basement and not dead," he said forcefully.

"Dead! What do you mean dead?" I asked incredulously as Mosley came lumbering through the door carrying a thermos bottle and cups. He walked up to the table and put the thermos down before separating one cup from the rest and placing it in front of me.

"You didn't tell him yet?" Mosley asked Ruppert as he unscrewed the top of the bottle and poured me a cup of water.

"Just getting started," Ruppert replied.

"Boss?"

"No thanks," Ruppert said, waving off the water.

"You should start with me," Mosley said as he replaced the top on the bottle before making his way back to his seat. Ruppert waited for him to sit down, then looked at the big guy and nodded his head in agreement.

"Mosley is right. If it wasn't for this big nigga, you'd be dead as shit right now," Ruppert said point-blank.

"I don't understand what you're talking about. I didn't do anything. Who would want to kill me?" I questioned angrily.

"You were targeted for assassination this morning, Mr. Pickles. …And if Mosley hadn't talked my ear off after you left Monday, you'd be as dead as your girlfriend last week," he said coldly.

I was confused and looked at him, trying to comprehend what he meant. "Are you saying that whoever killed Sandra wanted to kill me?"

"That's exactly what I'm saying. The thing is, Mosley over here was the one who figured it out," he said in praise of his assistant.

"No, man, I didn't figure out shit. It was you that did all the thinking, boss," Mosley said, returning the compliment as they reached across the table and fist bumped each other.

"Hey, look, I'm really grateful to whoever figured out whatever, but I just got hit in the head, strangled, thrown in the back of a fucking trunk, and still don't know what the fuck either one of you are talking about," I said with exasperation.

"Well, that's what we're trying to explain to you," Ruppert snickered at my remark. "See, normally I wouldn't give a shit since motherfuckers are getting their ass killed out here all the time."

"I remember. You told me it wasn't any of your business," I quipped.

"Right, except that Mosley was convinced that your girl's murder was something different and that it might be more than a crime of passion," he said.

"I don't follow you," I said honestly.

"The white cream," Mosley spoke up.

"Exactly! The white cream," Ruppert said, nodding at Mosley before turning his attention to me. "See, it's like this, Mr. Pickles; niggas that kill their bitches do it with lots of anger and a whole bunch of justification that don't mean shit to anybody but the nigga doing the killing, you dig?

"I guess," I shrugged.

"Well, that's the thing! You see, a black man ain't going to kill a kid and some bitch that he don't know just for the sake of killing them. This is the motherfucking ghetto! This isn't some crazy-ass rich white community where you got a bunch of sick motherfuckers cooped up in a laboratory plotting the end of humanity. Niggas ain't got time for statement killings. We get in, do the deed, and get the fuck out, the way you're suppose to kill a motherfucker. You dig?" he asked seriously. I looked away for a moment, understanding what he was implying, but totally confused at his logic.

"So... you think she was killed by a white guy?" I asked hesitantly.

"We know she was killed by a white guy!" Mosley stated flatly.

"What? How could you possibly know something like that?" I asked Mosley in a demanding tone.

"Let me explain," Ruppert said, holding his hands out to calm me down. "You know this area belongs to me and I got people all over the place, right?"

"Yeah, of course," I said, nodding my head.

"Well, when I put word out on the street that I need some answers, you can bet your ass I'll get those answers before the day is out. So, Mosley and I made some phone calls. We put the word out looking for dope about who, what, and why this happened to the woman and her child. You're with me, right?" he paused to ask.

"Yeah."

"Good, now you really need to pay attention. 'Cause, you see, people around here know that when I ask for something, it means somebody fucked up, and nobody wants to get involved in that shit, you dig?"

"Because they'd pay the price if you found out they knew and didn't tell you," I said, remembering the lessons that Otis told me long ago. "So, obviously you found out something, or I wouldn't be here," I concluded with a sigh. He stared at me for a moment before pursing his lips and shaking his head in disagreement.

"That's just it, Mr. Pickles. We didn't find out anything that made sense."

"I don't understand," I said, glancing at both Ruppert and Mosley.

"Let me put it this way. You know who I am, correct?"

"I know who you are, Ruppert," I said, tilting my head with respect. He nodded slightly and cracked a small smile of appreciation at my response. A moment later, his eyes turned cold, and the smile evaporated from his face. I was taken aback by the instant change in his demeanor and leaned forward to absorb everything he was about to say.

"You know I'm a serious man and I don't fuck around?"

"I know that."

"My people know I'm a serious man and don't fuck around. When I ask a question, I want an answer. I don't want excuses. I don't want tomorrows. I don't want maybes or bullshit speculation. I want a fucking answer," he said, tapping the table with his finger. "...And if I don't get a satisfactory answer, I'll come down on a motherfucker faster than a twenty-dollar whore giving a fifty-dollar blow, you dig?" he demanded in a rhetorical sense. I knew that Ruppert was the leader of a dangerous street gang, and I knew he wouldn't think twice of killing me if he felt the need. But I also knew that he was a complicated man. He demanded respect and prized honesty above all else, which seemed like a horrible paradox for a Chicago street gangster. Nonetheless, I could tell by the look in his eyes that he wanted to help. Somehow, I think he empathized with my loss and was even more perplexed by the deaths of Sandra and Lucy because it didn't fit his knowledge of the streets.

"I understand what you're saying, Ruppert," I replied with a nod. He dropped his eyes and leaned back in his chair before bringing them back to meet mine. They were softer than the moment before, almost sympathetic.

"I'm taking the time to explain this to you in this manner because we got nothing!" he snarled. "Do you understand what I'm saying? Not one nigga in this fucking city knows what happened to your girls. NOT ONE!" he shouted in anger. I leaned back with a blank stare and an empty feeling, trying to grasp his words. I understood, but it truly didn't make sense, unless...

"...And that's why you think she was killed by a white guy?" I wondered out loud.

He looked at me with a blank expression, pushed his chair back, stood up, and crossed his arms for a moment, before scratching his cheek and pointing a finger in my direction.

"Well now, that's where it gets interesting," he said with that sly smile returning to his face. "Tell him, Mo?" he directed at the big man.

"The white dudes," Mosley piped up.

"The white dudes?" I questioned. "More than one?"

"That's right, Mr. Pickles, the white dudes," Ruppert said as he began to pace the floor. "Let me ask you something. Do you know what a candy man is?"

"Yeah, a street dealer, drug runner, whatever," I answered.

"That's partially right," he nodded while he paced. "...But a candy man is a lot more than just a drug dealer. It's true he's a street salesman for my crew, but they also serve as lookouts, spies, and opportunists for both themselves and our operation. A candy man has to be vigilant and know everything about their hood. You dig where I'm coming from?" he asked.

"Sure," I replied.

"A candy man has to know what time people leave for work, when they got home, and pretty much who lives or visits each house or apartment in their area. They hustle for a living, and my best guys know when someone forgets to lock a car door, leaves a bike unattended, or simply gets careless and leaves a bag of groceries outside on a stoop too long. More than anything else, they pay particular attention to white men cruising their streets who might be undercover cops looking to put an end to a candy man's business."

"I hear you."

"…And I got candy men all over the West Side, including one that lives a few doors down from your girl. He got the word that I called but didn't know or see anything and told that to Mosley. Right, Mo?"

"That's what he said," Mosley confirmed.

"But then he started thinking about something and called Mosley back a couple of hours later. Go ahead and tell him, Mo," Ruppert directed.

"Dude calls back and says he did see something but didn't think it was what we was looking for. My man said a couple of white dudes went into your girl's house sometime the evening she was killed. He thought they might be cops and figured he'd keep an eye out," he said.

"Like I said, the last thing a candy man wants to see is a couple of detectives checking out their hood. You dig?" Ruppert asked.

"Yeah, I get that part, Ruppert, but, if I understand you correctly, you think two white cops killed Sandra?"

"No, no, no," he said, waving me off with his hands. "I'm not saying that at all. Don't get ahead of me. This shit is fucked up, and I'm trying to lay it out so you understand," he said seriously.

"I'm sorry, Ruppert. Please continue."

"…As I was saying, this candy man saw these two white dudes walk up the street and into your girl's house through the front door, but they never came out."

"What do you mean they never came out?" I asked.

"…They didn't come out the way they went in," Mosley added.

"Which means they went out a back door and limited their exposure on the girl's street," Ruppert concluded.

"And you're positive the candy man didn't step away and miss them come out?" I asked.

"I'm positive they didn't come out the front door," he said with confidence.

"What happened next?" I asked.

"That was it," he said with raised eyebrows. "The next day her place was swarming with cops. They found the little kid, then came back again and found your girl, BUT you didn't pay attention to what I said earlier," he reprimanded.

"I heard you. They went in the front door and never came out," I said to both as they glared at me intently.

"But you missed something," Ruppert sighed as I shook my head slightly, trying to understand what he wanted from me. "Vehicles draw attention," he continued. "Honkies getting in and out of vehicles draw even more attention," he said impatiently. Suddenly, Mosley took a deep breath and slammed his hand down on the table in exasperation.

"They WALKED up the street, motherfucker!" Mosley exclaimed at my lack of comprehension. His outburst was the smack I needed to understand exactly what they meant. I fell back in my chair and looked up at the ceiling, shaking my head.

"Jesus Christ! They didn't drive up, they walked up," I said in disbelief.

"I believe you just woke up, Mr. Pickles," Ruppert quipped.

"'Bout goddamn time," Mosley chuckled.

"Mr. Pickles, there are only two types of honkies that walk up and down the streets of the ghetto: cops and…"

"SALESMEN!" I interrupted to a nod of approval from both men. "It had to be someone I know," I said, looking back at him with a chill going up my spine.

"Exactly, because other than you, this woman didn't have any white men in her life," he said, pursing his lips tight. "Give me a cigarette, Mosley," Ruppert commanded before strolling back to his chair and twirling it around to straddle it from behind like he did the first time we met. Mosley handed him a cigarette, then struck a match and cupped the flame for Ruppert to light up. He took a long drag, blew it towards the ceiling, then leaned over the back of the chair and looked into my eyes. "And that is the question you have to ask: WHY would two white salesmen want to kill a black woman and her little girl?"

"Not just salesmen, but pros," Mosley added.

"Pros?" I questioned.

"He means professionals. People with experience who know how to get shit done without getting caught, you dig?"

"Jesus Christ!" I gasped while sinking low into my chair. "The fucking claim?! But, but that doesn't make sense?" I questioned out loud.

"Well, it's going to make a lot of sense in just a minute because we got the two motherfuckers that killed your girl locked up in that closet," he said, pointing to a storage door on the other side of the basement.

"WHAT?! Lobranski and Hamilton?!" I screamed at the top of my lungs as I leaped from my chair and bolted for the closet door, seething with anger.

"Wait!" Ruppert shouted as he lunged across the table and tried to stop me. "Mosley!" he called out when he missed.

"WAIT, MOTHERFUCKER!" Mosley screamed as I bolted for the door. I was like a mad dog, foaming at the mouth and baring my teeth with a rage that wanted to kill either one of those bastards. I beat him by half a second, grabbed the door handle, and yanked it open before he could stop me. I was ready to pounce on both of those murderers, only to stop dead in my tracks, shocked at the sight of the two men hunched in a fetal position on the floor.

"What the fuck?!" I shouted at the top of my lungs when I recognized Mr. Uhlen and Mr. Guru bound and gagged with duct tape, gasping for air. Without hesitation, I side-stepped into the closet and kneeled down to offer assistance before the giant hands of Mosley grabbed me from behind and hurled me back into the basement. I became hysterical at the injustice and ran back to Ruppert to plead my case. "No, no, no! You got this wrong. I know these guys. This is a huge mistake. Ruppert, I don't know what your drug dealer or candy man saw, but it wasn't these guys! I know these guys! JESUS FUCKING CHRIST! These are the nicest guys in the world. They didn't have anything to do with Sandra. IT'S A MISTAKE! It's such a mistake; it's a huge mistake! My God, Ruppert, these guys are survivors! They're Jewish refugees. They escaped from a concentration camp. They wouldn't hurt a fly."

"MR. PICKLES! You need to calm down," he said sternly while grabbing me by the shoulders. He guided me back to my chair and forced me down, all the while maintaining his grip on my shoulders. "Now, listen up…"

"But Ruppert…"

"SHUT THE FUCK UP!" he shouted to my face while taking a hand off my shoulder and pushing a finger into my chest. "Before you say another fucking word, you're going to listen to me and how this shit went down. You understand? Now, are you going to be cool, or is Mosley going to tape your ass up like he did those guys?" he asked with a serious tone. I looked into his eyes and nodded before taking a deep breath, trying to collect myself. The emotional swing from absolute rage to sympathetic hopelessness drained me to the point of near collapse. I wanted to cry. I wanted to go home. I wanted to get out of that basement, and, for a brief moment, I just wanted to die.

"Are you going to be all right?" Ruppert asked after a moment or two. I nodded my head and took a few deep breaths, wiping some spittle away from my mouth before answering.

"Can we get them some water or something?" I asked softly while trying to snort a gob of mucus back down my throat.

"Fuck those guys," he said, releasing his grip on me and standing up. "Bring them motherfuckers in here," he directed towards Mosley while still looking at me. Confident I could be trusted, he walked around the table and dragged two chairs to the middle of the basement. Ruppert stepped back and propped himself on the table as Mosley reached into the closet and tugged Mr. Uhlen to his feet before nudging him to move. In addition to covering his mouth, the duct tape was wrapped around his body like a straitjacket, securing his arms and hands in what looked like a torturous position.

"This has to be a mistake," I kept muttering to myself as Mosley walked Mr. Uhlen in front of one of the chairs and pushed him down.

"Watch this motherfucker. He fights like a fucking alley cat," Mosley directed before heading back to repeat the procedure with Mr. Guru. I didn't know what happened, but Mr. Uhlen looked as if he had been dragged behind a car, and my heart sank when I saw him clearly for the first time. He was missing a shoe, and his black pants were tattered and torn, covered in white scuffmarks. Most of his short-sleeved shirt was hanging out of his pants and looked as if it were hastily retrieved from a laundry bin. Its blue background set the landscape for swaths of dirt and blood that swirled around the shirt like a tie-dye pattern. His face and arms were streaked with fresh scratches and blisters still oozing droplets of blood and appeared to be extremely painful. His lifeless eyes glanced at me briefly, then focused straight ahead as a look of resignation crept across his face.

Mosley dropped Mr. Guru in the other chair before taking up a defensive position behind his two captives. Other than the duct tape plastered across his mouth and binding his arms and hands, Guru looked relatively unscathed compared to Mr. Uhlen. Ruppert and I exchanged glances before he slid off the table and stepped forward to remove the duct tape from their mouths. I watched with interest as Ruppert used a fingernail to loosen a corner of the tape from each man's cheek before clenching it tight between his thumb and forefinger and ripping it away from their flesh. Both winced in pain, as did I at the sound of the tape separating from their skin. Ruppert balled up the tape and threw it into a corner before stepping back and resuming his position on the table. Then, he scratched his cheek before folding his arms, pursing his lips, and snorting a grin as if something struck him funny.

"You wouldn't know it to look at them, but these are two mass-murdering motherfuckers right here, Mr. Pickles," he said cynically. "Ain't that right, boys?" he directed towards Uhlen and Guru, who sat motionless, staring straight ahead. Ruppert took a deep breath and shook his head at the old men before turning to face me. "Now, let's get back to what I was trying to tell you before you went off and attacked the motherfucking closet," he said to a chuckle from Mosley.

"Tell me what?" I asked while ignoring Mosley.

"That whoever killed your girls had to be connected to you and had to have something to do with your business, remember?" he asked with raised eyebrows.

"I agree, it made sense, but…"

"Listen up," he said, cutting me off. "It didn't make sense, and this is where it gets confusing," he mused out loud.

"What do you mean?"

"I mean, dipshits like you and all the rest of those pansy-ass salesmen that work with you ain't got the balls to walk into some woman's house and strangle her and her child to death. That meant we were looking for pros. People with experience, who know how to get shit done without getting caught, you dig?" he asked, catching me off guard with a question I never even considered.

"I guess, ah, I don't really know," I said, looking at Guru and Uhlen with growing disdain.

"Well, the thing is, most pros have some kind of written history, and the librarians in the case are the police. Now, as the leader of a fairly notorious street gang, you can probably assume that I've had some involvement with the law enforcement community," he said

452

with a shrug. "Occasionally, it is wise to offer a token of value to that community in exchange for allowing a business such as mine to operate unencumbered by needless bureaucracy. Do you understand?" he asked sarcastically.

"You buy protection," I stated flatly.

"I nurture beneficial relationships," he corrected. "…And one of those relationships happens to be with a member of the Federal Bureau of Investigation," he continued.

"You know someone in the FBI?"

"I do, and I called this individual on Tuesday morning explaining the situation and providing some basic information as to the name of the insurance company and our theory of what happened to your girl. I figured he'd get back to me in a few weeks since researching gang requests for information are not very high on the FBI's list of things to do," he said, somewhat amused at himself. "Anyways, I received a phone call less than two hours later from an individual at the Department of Justice wanting to see me immediately."

"The Department of Justice? That's different than the FBI, right?" I asked without a clue.

"Much different, Mr. Pickles. Turns out the Department of Justice has been investigating these motherfuckers for a couple of years," he said, shocking me to the core.

"Ruppert, I hear what you're saying," I said, trying to plead my case. "But there has to be a mistake. I know for a fact that it's Teddy Lobranski and my boss Roger Hamilton who are running scams and fucking people out of their insurance benefits. They have a whole network of agents and funeral homes that steer death benefits away from beneficiaries and into their own pockets. These guys are innocent. They're Jewish survivors!" I said, throwing up my hands in disbelief before turning towards the old men.

"WE'RE NOT FUCKING JEWS!" Guru choked out with resentment and a hunk of phlegm he spit on the floor.

"REINHARDT!" Uhlen exclaimed.

"They're fucking Nazis, Mr. Pickles. That's why the Department of Justice is after them," Ruppert said.

"Fuck you and your Department of Justice!" Guru shot back.

"Reinhardt! You're not thinking!" Uhlen said condescendingly.

"SHUT YOUR MOUTH!" Guru slammed back at the slight. "It makes no difference now. Everything I've built has been destroyed. Listen to me, you sons of bitches. I came to this country with nothing, and I built this business. No one else! Roger doesn't run shit! It's me. It's always been mine," he yelled out.

"You're a scary motherfucker, you know that?" Ruppert said, somewhat taken aback by Guru's outburst.

"Is that true, Mr. Uhlen?" I asked, ignoring Ruppert's comment.

"Quite true, Ronnie," Uhlen replied, dropping his eyes to the floor.

"I can't believe this... Who are you people?" I asked in dismay.

"We are the people that offered you a chance to join us and make something of yourself," Uhlen said almost fatherly.

"By blackmailing me into screwing a family out of their money?" I asked incredulously.

"BINGO!" Ruppert exclaimed while pointing a finger in my direction. "...And now you know the reason you were dragged into this rat-infested, piss-stained basement."

"They had to kill you fast," Mosley added.

"WHAT?" I yelled out in astonishment.

"BLACKMAIL!" Ruppert proclaimed. "They had to kill you before you amassed enough evidence of that blackmail to take to the police. Isn't that right, gentlemen?" he asked the old men rhetorically before turning and looking at me with a serious expression. "They were going to kill you this morning, Mr. Pickles," he said coolly.

"Kill me? But how did you know - how did they know - I was collecting evidence?" I asked Ruppert in confusion before turning my head slowly and looking at the cold, blank expressions on the Nazis' faces.

"Teddy Lobranski," he mocked, causing the rock-chiseled expressions on both men's faces to crumble before my eyes.

"THAT FUCKING POLLOCK MUTT," Guru snarled with contempt. I could see by the twitching of his temple that he was livid at Lobranski's betrayal.

"How did you know I was collecting evidence, Mr. Uhlen?" I asked.

"We were watching you. I knew what you were doing," he said with a shrug. "Hamilton offered you an amazing opportunity, and you were going to try and fuck us. You ran out of his office like a madman trying to copy that transfer Monday morning. When you left the office, I pulled the letter out of the mailbag..."

"...That's fucking illegal!" I shouted at him.

"Shit, Mr. Pickles, the motherfucker's killed thousands of people, and you think he gives a fuck about stealing a piece of mail?" Ruppert quipped.

"The transfer wasn't that big of a deal, but we knew you were a problem that needed to be eliminated as soon as possible," Uhlen said dryly. My mouth dropped open when he finished speaking. I was completely disillusioned and so bewildered by everything that my mind went blank trying to process the unbelievable.

"Yep, old Teddy ratted your asses out nasty style," Ruppert said with a grin.

"Do you have Teddy here too?" I asked with exasperation.

"Naw, right now he's in police custody. He's trying to save his own ass from doing life in prison for being associated with these assholes," he snickered.

"Ruppert, are you guys some sort of undercover cops?" I asked seriously.

"Oh, hell no!" he started laughing. "We're the same old badass gangster motherfuckers that we always were. Ain't that right, Mosley?"

"Sure the fuck is," the big man replied.

"I can't fucking believe this. When did Lobranski tell you all this stuff?" I probed with a healthy dose of skepticism.

"He didn't tell me shit. He told Debra, and Debra told me," he said.

"Debra from the apartment?" I asked.

"Yes, indeed. The lovely Debra," he drawled slowly. "See, Mr. Pickles, in my business, it's important to employ a wide range of people in order to satisfy all types of clients. Now, Debra is sharp, sophisticated, and smart as a fucking whip. She's not a hooker, but I'll be damned if she couldn't use that body and charm to coax a flea off a dog's ass if she had a mind to do so," he chuckled. "She's also my top earner and has lots of business-type people as her clients. It just so happens that one of her best clients is a cocaine-snorting motherfucker named Teddy Lobranski, you dig?"

"That's the first thing that's made sense so far," I answered.

"Well, old Teddy had orders to get you someplace where the Nazis could kill you right away, so he recruited Debra to help set you up. It's my understanding he used her services in the past," he said calmly.

"Just like that?" I asked caustically.

"Don't take it personally," he said, sensing my resentment.

"I'm sorry, Ruppert, but I take it very personally that all these people were setting me up to kill me," I said angrily.

"Yeah, I guess I would too," he snorted at my reaction. "You have to understand something, Mr. Pickles. Most of my employees are independent contractors. As long as they pay their dues, I don't give a shit what they do on their own time," Ruppert tried to explain. "...But the good news is that Debra got the word earlier in the week and called to tell me what was going down, so I decided to put an end to this shit," he said.

"Why didn't you just call the cops?" I asked.

"...And tell them what, exactly?" he asked sarcastically while putting his hands together like he was praying. "Officer Friendly, I'm the leader of a street gang that deals in some pretty nasty shit. You know, all the basics, like guns, drugs, whores, but occasionally, I do believe in the rule of law, and I would like to inform you of a situation that needs your attention. One of my drug dealers works for some escaped Nazis that kill niggas on a regular basis for profit, and I think they are planning to set up an insurance guy who is being blackmailed by them, and I was wondering if you could do something to stop the situation," he finished, barely able to contain himself.

"I'd pay to hear that conversation," Mosley said, grinning from ear to ear. I shook my head, realizing the idiocy of my question, but in no mood to laugh about anything.

"I'm sorry, Mr. Pickles. I don't mean to make light of this situation, but you're not living in the real right now. You're living in my world, and you're still alive because I call the shots in my world," he said seriously. "If it makes you feel any better, I did drop a dime on Teddy Lobranski yesterday, which is why he's waist-deep in shit at the Department of Justice, ratting out the whole crew," he said, and, as if on cue, someone started banging on the basement door. A moment later, the door opened, and one of the guys who threw me in the trunk poked his head inside. "Boss, we got some serious police just pulled up outside," he said nervously.

"Shit," Ruppert said, jumping off the table and heading towards the door. "Everything is cool. They're expected," he said, gesturing with his hands for the guy to relax. "Find the Justice guy, his name is Aaronson, and tell him I need five minutes, you dig? Don't let anyone down here for five minutes," he commanded.

"...but boss?"

"WHAT THE FUCK DID I JUST SAY?!" Ruppert screamed at his reluctance.

"Yes, sir," the guy said. Ruppert slammed the door in his face, then locked it by sliding an old latch into place before hurrying back to us.

"So, listen up. Y'all know this shit has come to an end, right?" he asked rhetorically of Uhlen and Guru. "In just a few minutes, there will be some serious law enforcement coming here to collect your asses for hanging, and I think you owe Mr. Pickles some explanations," he said with a nod in my direction. I looked at him hesitantly before coming to grips with the thought of interrogating Sandra and Lucy's murderers. My chest tightened, immediately making it difficult to breathe as the realization fell on me like a ton of bricks. For the first time that morning, I felt weak-kneed and sick to my stomach, trying to grasp the thought of these two men, who I knew and respected, brutally killing two people I loved so much. I laughed and joked with these guys. I went on vacation with both men and always considered them with the highest regard. Yet now, in less than an hour, I had to accept the fact that they killed Sandra and Lucy, tried to kill me, and quite likely took part in one of the greatest atrocities ever committed. In that moment, I realized just how sick and demented these two individuals must have been their whole lives, and my blood began to boil, wondering how they got away with this shit for so long.

"Jesus Christ," I said, running my hand through my hair and exhaling deeply. "I still can't believe these fucking guys did this," I sighed.

"The thing is, Mr. Pickles, no one thought Richard Speck was capable of murdering eight student nurses until he got caught killing them girls," Mosley said seriously.

"It's up to you, but you don't have much time," Ruppert said, pointing to the basement door.

"I know, um, yeah, I do want to ask some questions," I said, swallowing hard while turning and glaring at the old men.

"We're not telling you a goddamn thing!" Guru said with contempt. The words barely left his mouth when, to everyone's surprise, Mosley struck Guru with a hard slap to the back of his head, almost knocking him out of the chair.

"Now that we understand each other, I believe Mr. Pickles has some things he'd like to ask you gentlemen," Ruppert said calmly. I looked at Ruppert anxiously, who nodded back as if encouraging me to begin. I straightened up in my chair and looked at the old men before reaching back across the table and grabbing the cup of water Mosley brought me earlier. My lips had dried up so badly, I could barely open my mouth to drink, much less speak. I felt better after taking a couple of huge gulps of water and placed the cup back on the table before beginning to speak.

"Mr. Uhlen, what role did you play in those girls' deaths?" I asked, grinding my teeth and trying to remain calm. He turned his head to face me with a look of indifference and a slight shrug, as if dismissing my question as a trivial matter.

"Ronnie, I'm sure this is difficult for you," he said with a patronizing tone that cut me like a knife. I lunged out of my chair and went face to face with him while putting my hand in the air to let Ruppert know I was in control.

"Did you fucking kill them?!" I yelled. Neither he nor Guru said a word, but the looks on their faces were smug, almost proud, as if they had taken some sort of pleasure in the act. "Jesus Christ," I muttered in horror at their emotionless expressions as I backed away in a state of shock. I kept walking backwards until I bumped into my chair and collapsed in the seat, drained by a betrayal that seemed unfathomable. I felt myself becoming nauseous and quickly turned my body away from everyone and dry heaved a couple of times before bringing up some of the water I had swallowed. I lumbered off the chair and slumped against the wall of the basement where I heaved a few more times before settling down. No one said a word while I threw up, and no one looked at me until I returned to my chair and sat down.

"You alright?" Ruppert asked with a quick glance in my direction.

"No, I'm not alright," I seethed while staring intently at both Guru and Uhlen. "Why?" I gasped before crying out again, "Why, goddamn it?! Why?!"

"Because there was a lot of money involved, Ronnie. And..."

"SHUT UP, YOU FUCKING MUTT!" Guru screamed in anger when Uhlen spoke.

"It's OVER!" Uhlen shouted back.

"It's over because you're an ignorant MUTT like these niggers," Guru grimaced with anger. Immediately, Ruppert pointed at Mosley who clocked Guru twice as hard as before, knocking him semi-conscious with his head bobbing from side to side.

"Neither Mosley or I appreciate white people calling us niggers," Ruppert quipped.

"It's over, Reinhardt," Uhlen surrendered.

"What are you fucking telling them?" Guru slurred incoherently, still reeling from the punch.

"Please, he's an old man, don't strike him anymore. I will tell you everything you want to know," Uhlen requested almost casually.

"Start talking," Ruppert said in acceptance of the offer. Uhlen nodded at Ruppert, then looked at me and smiled like he had done countless times before.

"Ronnie, my boy," Mr. Uhlen said with a sigh. "We thought you'd want to take advantage of the opportunities we could offer you. "We thought you were one of us," he said with an accent that teetered between German and Yiddish.

"What do you mean, 'one of us'?" I asked with disdain.

"Not a nigger, but a white!" Guru spoke up. Immediately, Ruppert put up his hand to stop Mosley from clocking Guru in the head again.

"What Guru means is that we wanted to trust you. We wanted to bring you into our family and help you succeed," he said like a mentor.

"Not me. It was you!" Guru growled at Uhlen. "I told you not to trust this son of a bitch. I told you! I didn't like the way he buddies up to all the niggers on his staff, like he was one of them. I fucking told you!" he ranted.

"You told me, you told me. What difference does it make now?" Uhlen said dismissively before looking back at me. "Ronnie, we didn't know…"

"Didn't know what?" I begged the question.

"We didn't know that you were a nigger lover. That is all," Guru blurted out for what was to be the last time. Having enough of Guru's interruptions, Ruppert jumped off the table and retrieved an old rag that was lying in a corner. He strolled back and grabbed a handful of Guru's hair, yanking his head backward while forcing the rag in his mouth at the same time. Guru tried to shake the rag out of his mouth, then gave up after a moment or two. Mosley and I gave each other a look of approval, and even Uhlen seemed relieved to shut him up. Ruppert returned to the table and propped himself up while giving Uhlen a nod of his head to continue.

"Ronnie, you have to understand, we didn't know that you were romantically connected to the girl," Uhlen said with disappointment in his voice.

"Nobody knew that. How did you know that?" I demanded.

"She told us," he said.

"What did she tell you? When did she tell you?!" I yelled out jumping from my chair.

"The night we saw her."

"You mean the night you killed her?! I want to know every fucking word she said, or that man is going to beat this fucker to death in front of your eyes!" I stepped up and hollered into his face. At the same time, Mosley grabbed the back of Guru's head and pulled it back while balling up his hand, as if to land another blow.

"I said I'd tell you everything you want to know. This isn't necessary," he said calmly while tilting his head in Guru's direction.

461

"I want to know everything. Why you targeted her and what happened from the time you walked in that house to the time you left," I said coldly.

"You really want to know? I will tell you, but you should know it won't be pleasant," he began. "We have a system, and we work as a team," he said meekly. "The moment your girl called the office, we knew an opportunity existed, and we moved to take advantage of that opportunity," he said calmly.

"When did she call the office? What are you talking about?" I demanded.

"Irene took the phone call. The day you tried to collect from your girl."

"Sandra called?" I asked with dismay.

"Yes, and she wanted to pay the premium on her policy. She left a message for you to pick up a check at her father's house," he said.

"Irene never gave me that message," I fired back.

"Irene works for us. It's her job to cross check potential opportunities."

"Oh my God! I don't fucking believe this," I said, burying my head in my hands. "The check her father showed me was actually written by Sandra," I lamented to myself. I was so incredibly sick to my stomach, I could barely function, much less process his words, but somehow, I found the strength to press him for answers. Slowly, I lifted my eyes to meet his, revolted by the sight of the man. "So, just like that, you decided to go kill her?" I asked incredulously.

"We had a meeting…"

"Who?"

"Guru, myself, and Roger, of course," he said.

"Fucking Hamilton was in on it all the time," I said in disbelief at how they played me.

"Roger Hamilton is Mr. Guru's son and my nephew," Uhlen said, looking down at the floor. Immediately, Guru started shaking his head and stomping on the floor. At one point, he tried to stand up, only to be hammered back into his seat by Mosley from behind.

"They would have found out eventually," Uhlen said to Guru who was seething with anger.

"So, it's a family affair," Ruppert said with a smile.

"Jesus Christ! Guru is your brother? …And this is what you people do? Sit around and figure out who to murder on any given day?" I asked, feeling as if my head were about to explode.

"Shit's fucked up," Mosley added. Guru began to calm down, and Uhlen took a deep breath, as if relieved to unburden himself of the secret.

"So, you had this meeting," I said, prompting him to continue and ignoring his revelation.

"Yes, we discussed the possibilities and made sure we cross checked the opportunities before making a final decision."

"Cross check opportunities?" I asked.

"Yes, there are situations where a death claim can be very profitable if it meets certain criteria."

"What criteria?"

"Well, it's important that the policy has no cash value. Obviously, we can't intervene if a policy has value and a claim is paid directly from the home office. We also have to be able to control the lapse card and make sure the agent doesn't hold it an extra week.

"You took that lapse card out of my hand, you son of a bitch," I said as the memory came back to me clear as day.

"I was watching you carefully that day."

"Go on."

"Well, you have to understand, most importantly, we don't take intervention lightly…"

"Intervention?"

"He means killing someone," Ruppert quipped.

"Well, it has to be worth it," Uhlen responded as if talking shop with a fellow businessman.

"But it isn't worth it, goddamn it! You destroy a family for a $20,000 claim. It doesn't make sense. After paying the funeral home, Teddy, the office girls, and the cut you forced down my throat, you're talking about less than $3,000 a piece... That's insane! It's total bullshit, Uhlen!" I screamed at the idiocy of such a plan.

"Ronnie, do you really think that poorly of us to believe that we would execute someone for a paltry $3,000?" he said dismissively.

"Then how the fuck did you figure on profiting by killing these two people? It doesn't make sense. You didn't know when the policy was going to lapse, and you sure as shit didn't know if I was going to hold it and pay a month out of my pocket. For that matter, you had no idea if the woman could have already mailed the money into the office. So, cut the bullshit, and tell me exactly how you planned to profit from killing Sandra and Lucy," I commanded. He looked away and took a deep breath, dropping his eyes and raising his eyebrows, as if embarrassed by what he was about to say.

"We don't pocket the money from the claim for ourselves. We use that money to generate more sales. Do you understand? More sales and fantastic commissions," he said as if exhilarated by the thought.

"You're fucking kidding me, right?" I asked with disgust.

"No, Ronnie, you have to remember this stupid fucking insurance company pays us a multiplier. Twenty-five times every dollar of premium you write.

"They also take it away if you lapse it," I interjected.

"Correct, but they also have exceptions to that rule."

"You mean death claims, because you don't get charged for death claims."

"I mean transfers to other districts... You don't get charged a lapse if your client moves to another district. As long as the policy is paid for three months, you can transfer the fucking thing wherever you want, and it's up to some other poor son of a bitch to try and keep it from lapsing," he said, sounding like a madman.

"So, you use the money from the death claim to write bogus contracts?"

"Not bogus contracts. We insure real people. We just don't do this on our own ledgers; we go to areas operated by other districts. The key to our operation is that we have two dozen addresses on our own black ledgers to use as a client's original address, even though they live somewhere else," he said proudly.

"So, these are the addresses you use to originate the sale before transferring the case out of the district," I said, trying to follow the process.

"Now you're starting to understand. All we do is promise three months of free insurance to anyone who has an address and is willing to sign the contract," he said.

"Then, you pay the premium for three months and transfer the case to another district, knowing full well the receiving agent will never be able to collect the case," I concluded.

"Exactly, and that is why we decided to intervene with your girl. After expenses, a $20,000 death claim would have left us $12,000 of operating cash. Divide that by three, and you have $4,000 to purchase new weekly insurance on anyone you want. The commission will pay $100,000, Ronnie. Think about that! $100,000! That's why we killed your girlfriend..."

"I'm in the wrong fucking business," Ruppert muttered to himself.

"So, you just decided to kill her and hope everyone would go along with a scheme?" I asked out loud, not really expecting an answer.

"I'm sure this won't make a difference, Ronnie, but I knew we made a mistake. By then, it was too late, and we had to continue," he said with a hint of regret in his voice.

"I'm sure that makes Mr. Pickles feel a whole lot better knowing that you felt remorse for killing his girlfriend," Ruppert spoke up at the ridiculousness of his comment.

"I never feel remorse," Uhlen replied coldly. "I said it was a mistake."

"Explain!" Ruppert demanded.

"The girl let us in her house because she recognized Mr. Guru as the agent of a friend of hers. The moment we got inside, she started talking about Ronnie and how mad he was that she didn't pay the insurance. She figured that Ron sent us there to pick up the check, which she had already left at her father's house. I could tell by the tone of her voice that she really liked him, but it wasn't until I began the process that she started crying about how much she loved him and that she was sorry," he said without emotion. I couldn't take it. I buried my head into my lap and started crying uncontrollably.

"Why did you kill her kid?" Ruppert asked.

"The child was asleep. The noise woke her up, and she became a witness," Uhlen said, figuring that Ruppert would understand.

"Why did y'all rub that cream all over her face?" Mosley asked with disgust. Again, Guru started shaking his head from side to side, trying to get the gag out of his mouth.

"Take it out. Let's hear what this Nazi motherfucker has to say," Ruppert directed Mosley, who promptly tugged Guru by the hair, reached around, and plucked the gag from his mouth.

"I put the cream on that bitch's face," he said hoarsely, trying to talk with a dry mouth.

"Don't do this!" Uhlen begged.

"Fuck you. What the fuck do I care about some nigger bitch?" he fumed back. "You want to know why I rubbed that cream all over her face? I'll tell you why, goddamn it! I did it because as he strangled her, she kept crying about this faggot son of a bitch and how much she loved him," he directed at me. "She wanted to be a white woman, so I granted her wish and made her a white woman right before she died," he said in a heavy accent while laughing all the time.

"You are one sick motherfucker," Mosley growled with disgust.

"If I didn't know for a fact that both of you are going somewhere to die, I'd kill you right here," Ruppert said without blinking an eye. Just then, someone started banging on the door again. I looked at Ruppert, who nodded for me to continue. I stood up and calmly walked up to the old men, kneeling down and looking them both in the eyes. Uhlen wouldn't look at me, but Guru turned his head in my direction, like the little girl from *The Exorcist* who was possessed by the devil.

"Mr. Pickles, trust me, I think I want to kill these bastards worse than you do," Ruppert admonished slightly.

"I'm cool," I said, twisting slightly to address his concern. Of course, I thought about beating them both to a pulp, but Guru was completely insane. I wasn't so sure about Uhlen, who seemed like he was in control yet somehow subservient to every beck and call that Guru made.

"Sandra didn't want to be white, Mr. Guru," I said, staring back into his crazed eyes. "She wanted to live, and she wanted to love, and she wanted to be loved. She was an amazingly warm and beautiful girl with a heart of gold and passion for life that neither of you could ever understand. It's true that you took her life, but her spirit will live long after both of you are forgotten and rotting in some unmarked grave reserved for Nazi war criminals. But know this: you didn't kill Sandra - she killed you. She gave her life to stop your insanity and put an end to this fucked-up business. You're both going straight to hell, and the best part is that it was a little ol' nigga gal from the South Side of Chicago that sent you there," I said, standing up and walking back towards the table.

"Well said, Mr. Pickles," Ruppert commented with an outstretched hand to greet me. "I got to let those guys inside now," he said, patting me on the back before walking away and unlocking the latch. He pulled the door open and stepped outside, gesturing to someone before coming back in the basement and standing to the side.

Within seconds, a parade of people came marching into the basement, including the familiar faces of Craig Branson, Otis Wahl, and Ray Meadows, as well as two Chicago police officers and two other gentlemen dressed in suits and ties. The Chicago cops made a beeline for Guru and Uhlen, taking up positions on each side, while Mosley continued to stand behind them.

"Gentlemen, welcome to our little get together," Ruppert said, shaking everyone's hands as they came in and formed a circle around the table.

"What are you guys doing here?" I asked with surprise at the presence of Otis, Ray, and Craig.

"Shit's fucked up, Pickles," Otis growled while stroking his beard.

"I'm really sorry, Ron. We didn't know it was like this," Meadows said, motioning at Uhlen and Guru who sat quietly staring into space.

"I wanted your friends here," Craig said, pointing at Otis and Ray. "Nobody knew about this shit," he continued, throwing Guru and Uhlen a scornful look as he passed in front of them and walked up beside me. "You're doing okay, right?" he asked thoughtfully.

"Yeah, I'm good, and I'm glad to see you, bud, but how did you get hooked up in this shit?" I asked as we shook hands. His face sort of contorted into a grimace as he shook his head and looked at me with apologetic eyes.

"I'll get to that in a minute. Let me introduce you to these guys first," he said, pointing at the two gentlemen I didn't know. "This is Special Agent Sam Johnson with the FBI," Craig said, directing my attention to the rather stern-faced gentleman standing on the other side of the table.

"We go way back a long way, don't we, Sammy?" Ruppert laughed as the agent stepped forward to shake my hand.

"Mr. Pickles, it's a pleasure," he said.

"Agent Johnson."

"…And this gentleman is Ralph Waters," Craig said, motioning to the other well-dressed man. He was older and vaguely familiar, though I couldn't place him.

"Mr. Pickles," he said, offering a sweaty, trembling hand to shake.

"Mr. Waters."

"Mr. Waters is the director of operations with Unified Insurance Company," Craig said, jogging my memory.

"I think we met at one of the company outings," I said, releasing his hand and wiping mine on my pants.

"Quite possibly," he said in a quivering voice.

"Okay, wait a minute," I said in confusion as I turned to face Craig. "How do you know all these people? What are you even doing here?" I asked, realizing that Craig was running the show.

"Ronnie, you got caught in the middle of a criminal operation that is literally mind-boggling," he said while reaching into his jacket and retrieving a leather wallet with his identification and badge. "My real name is Craig Aaronson, not Branson," he said, holding out his identification.

"OSI?" I asked, looking at his badge while offering a limp handshake.

"That's right, Office of Special Investigations," he said while I stared intently at the badge. I looked up at him, then instinctively glanced over at Otis and Meadows to see their reaction. Both nodded back as to confirm what Craig was saying.

"Jesus Christ, is that like the secret service or something?" I asked with confusion.

"No, I belong to a unit that was created by the Department of Justice to investigate Nazi war criminals who came into the country illegally. I've been working undercover as a ledger agent trying to build a case against these guys," he said, looking at Guru and Uhlen with disgust. "Officers, cut those two out of that tape and cuff them," Craig directed at the uniformed cops.

"Aren't you going to read us our rights, you fucking Jew?" Guru seethed as the officers began tearing and cutting the tape off their bodies.

"You're not a citizen. You have no fucking rights," Craig shot back.

"So, they really are Nazis?" Meadows asked in disbelief.

"Oh yeah, fucking scourge of humanity," he scowled at the old men before turning back towards us. "But it wasn't until yesterday that I was able to confirm our suspicions and prove who they really were. Do you remember what Uhlen said in the bathroom?" Craig asked me.

"Yeah, he said they escaped from that concentration camp, um…"

"Mauthausen," Craig finished for me.

"That's it, Mauthausen," I concurred.

"What the fuck did you tell him, you fucking mutt?!" Guru turned and screamed in Uhlen's face while thrashing about wildly "YOU TOLD THEM ABOUT MAUTHAUSEN?!" Guru hollered while jamming his tattooed arm under Uhlen's nose.

"HEY, KNOCK IT OFF!" the cop yelled, trying to keep Guru in his chair. Agent Johnson bolted over to help, and together they were able to remove the last of the duct tape while managing to get Guru's arms behind his back and hands cuffed tight.

"It doesn't matter what they know, Reinhardt. Calm down!" Uhlen pleaded while shaking his head dismissively.

"Oh, but it did, Mr. Uhlen. It was better than a confession," Craig said with a smirk.

"A confession?" Mr. Meadows asked with curiosity.

"Not exactly a confession, Ray, but a slip of the tongue in front of me and Ron yesterday. First of all, there isn't one recorded escape from Mauthausen. Secondly, he said they escaped from Mauthausen instead of being liberated, or rescued, or even left to die at the hands of the Nazis, which is how most Holocaust survivors would have phrased their survival, so it was just a matter of searching a database to see if their names popped up. ...And for Mr. Guru and Mr. Uhlen, that presents a quandary, since, according to the death ledgers from Mauthausen, they apparently died on April 17th, 1945," Craig said as we all stood captivated by his words.

"Jesus Christ" I sighed.

"But most important are the tattoos burned into their skin. That's when I knew he was a lying Nazi son of a bitch," Craig said with a scowl.

"I don't understand. I thought all the Jews were tattooed for identification?" Meadows asked.

"That's what most people think, but in fact only one camp branded their prisoners, and that was Auschwitz. Which meant these two burned the numbers into their own skin to avoid detection and make anyone believe they were in fact Jewish survivors.

"Damn!" Meadows gasped.

"Wait a minute, you said the death ledgers!" I exclaimed.

"Ring a bell?" Craig smiled at me.

"So, they did exist," I said.

"You're damn right they did," he confirmed.

"What are death ledgers?" Otis inquired.

"Well, Otis, what you have to understand is that concentration camps were run like a business, and records had to be kept in order for the business to succeed. The Nazis kept meticulous records of everything, including the exact date a person would enter the camp and the exact day and time a person died or was executed in the camp. They called these records the death ledgers."

"So, you're saying these two stole the dead men's identity?" Ruppert chimed.

"Exactly, then burned the tattoos, figuring no one would question their authenticity. But in order to do that, you had to be pretty well connected," Craig nodded in Ruppert's direction. "Interestingly enough, there were two Nazi officers that couldn't be accounted for after the liberation of Mauthausen on May 5th, 1945. They were known as the Brunner Brothers, and they simply disappeared. Now, these brothers were stationed at the Mauthausen complex as part of an elite Nazi accounting group that reported to none other than Heinrich Himmler. Himmler was batshit crazy, and the only people he trusted were the criminally insane: people who worshiped Hitler as a God."

"Holy shit! They're the Brunner Brothers," I concluded quickly.

"Mr. Guru's real name is Reinhardt Brunner; he was the captain in charge of the death ledgers at the Mauthausen concentration camp. His brother, Mr. Uhlen, was a lieutenant and his chief of staff. According to survivors' accounts, the Brunner Brothers were more than just ruthless; they were sadistic," Craig said.

"What do you mean, 'sadistic'?" Otis asked.

"The shit was fucked up, Otis," Craig lamented as if he didn't want to think about it. "These pricks would have new prisoners stripped naked in front of them while recording their belongings in the ledgers. They pried open people's mouths with crowbars to count gold and silver fillings for extraction when they died and would cut off fingers when rings wouldn't slide off easily," he said quickly, as if reading it off a report.

"Damn, Meadows, they would have cut all your fingers off," Otis quipped at a very inappropriate moment.

"Fuck you, Wahl. No one asked you shit!" Meadows slammed back angrily while Craig just took the exchange in stride.

"Anyways, in addition to recording the belongings of new prisoners, they were tasked with recording the deaths of those who died from the intense work, sleep deprivation, disease, or starvation. Occasionally, the camp became overcrowded, and room was needed to accommodate new arrivals, so the Brunner Brothers would stroll through the camp, shooting those who weren't producing to their standards. Together, they accounted and recorded thousands upon thousands of deaths at Mauthausen," he said with disgust.

"Hey, Craig, we all knew this one was fucked up in the head," Otis said, pointing to Guru. "But what made you think they were Nazis in the first place?" Otis asked, straight to the point.

"It all started with T.J.," Craig said with a long sigh.

"T.J.?" I asked with dismay.

"About six months before I started working for the company, T.J. wrote a long, rambling letter to the FBI about Uhlen and Guru, claiming they were Nazis who stole Jewish identities and immigrated to the United States. The FBI forwarded the letter to the Justice Department, which is how we got involved. By the time we interviewed T.J., he was so strung out on shit that he didn't even remember writing the letter, but our team at the OSI thought we should investigate further, so I applied for the job," he said with a smile. We all went silent and watched for a few moments, as the officers worked on restraining Guru's legs, when a thought occurred to me that didn't make sense.

"What about Hamilton and Lobranski? They're part of this, and no one has said a word about them," I said with concern.

"Teddy Lobranski is in FBI custody and cooperating fully, but Roger Hamilton and his mistress, Irene, are on the run. We'll get them soon," Agent Johnson spoke up.

"That fucking drug-addicted Pollock!" Guru shouted from his chair while kicking at the officers trying to restrain him. "I told you to kill that son of a bitch months ago, you fucking mutt!" he screamed at Uhlen. "Forty-five years I've been doing this because I don't put up with losers!" he ranted.

"Shut the fuck up, Guru!" Otis shouted at the old man with annoyance, as he did countless times in the office.

"I don't understand something, Craig. If you had all this, why didn't you just arrest these assholes?" I asked incredulously.

"We didn't have proof of anything, Ronnie. Remember, I wasn't investigating murders or even the funeral home scams. I was trying to gather evidence as to these guys' history and true identities. I couldn't just ask them if they were Nazi war criminals posing as Jewish survivors," he said sarcastically.

"This is unreal," I muttered.

"It's fucking crazy, and honestly, these two are in custody and you're alive today because of that man over there," Craig said, pointing at Ruppert. "If he hadn't called the FBI and put word on the street, Teddy Lobranski would have set you up at Debra's house so these guys could kill you like they did T.J.," Craig said.

"But T.J. killed himself," Meadows piped up.

"Did he, Ray?" Craig asked with a frown. "Let me ask you guys something. Do you remember all the bullshit about Uhlen carrying a bunch of money and getting robbed and beat up?"

"Like it was yesterday," I replied.

"You know Ruppert's girl, Debra, right?" he asked.

"Oh yeah, we met this morning," I said, throwing Ruppert a look.

"Well, she was supplying T.J. with dope, so he didn't suspect a thing when she invited him over to get high with her. These guys waited till he got shit faced and passed out, then tried to smother him. Teddy woke up and fought like hell, but in the end, they killed him and dumped his body in the lake. They had to come up with a story about Uhlen's injuries in the fight, so they said he got robbed. Collection money is insured, so the Nazis pocketed Uhlen's weekend collections and charged the company for killing T.J.," Craig explained.

"Holy shit!" I said, looking at both Ray and Otis, who just shook their heads and shrugged along with me. "Can I ask you something?"

"Sure, Ron. What?"

"Why isn't Debra sitting next to these guys?" I questioned.

"Because there are bad guys, and there are worse guys, Ronnie," he said plainly as I turned and looked at Ruppert with suspicion.

"Don't look at me all warm and fuzzy, Mr. Pickles," Ruppert quipped at my glare. "I told you this shit was none of my business. It was this big, ol' soft-hearted nigga," he said, pointing at Mosley. "He got all sentimental when you told him that story about Lassie and wanted to save your ass like Timmy," he said to a chorus of laughter.

"Why you got to do me like that, boss?" Mosley scuffed.

"No sir, I'm still the badass gangster who doesn't give a shit what honky-ass motherfucker gets himself killed in the ghetto. I don't do shit unless there's something in it for me, which brings me to my piece of paper. I'm assuming you have it?" Ruppert asked Craig.

"Do you have something for me?" Craig asked with raised eyebrows.

"Oh yeah, I almost forgot. Mosley, can you retrieve the man's property?" he asked.

"Sure thing, boss, but y'all got to move away from the table," The big guy asked courteously. We all glanced at each other in confusion as we stepped away and watched Mosley get down on his hands and knees and rip at something from under the table. A moment later, he stood up and handed a tape recorder to Craig, who then reached into his jacket and produced an envelope, handing it to Ruppert.

"A complete pardon for Debra's role in all of this and a get out of jail free card for you involving some previous involvement with the law," Craig said with a smile.

"It's good to have friends in high places," Ruppert said with a wink.

"We're ready, Agent Aaronson," one of the officers called out as the group assisted Uhlen and Guru to their feet. With the exception of Craig, the rest of us backed away to make room for them to leave.

Craig took a step closer and put up a hand, motioning for the policemen to wait a moment.

"There is something I'm curious about," he directed at the old men. "All the companies that sell burial insurance call their accounts 'debit books.' Which one of you sick fuckers convinced the office to start calling debit books 'black ledgers'?" Uhlen glanced at his brother, then shook his head and dropped his eyes to the floor as if knowing Guru was going to take some sadistic pleasure in answering Craig's question.

"In my mind, I called them 'Vernichtung Durch Arbeit,'" Guru enunciated with a perfect German accent. "You ignorant bastards can barely speak English, much less understand another language, so when we started making money from the dead niggers, I called them the black ledgers," he snarled. In that moment, everyone in the room knew they were looking into the face of a demon. A beast that thrives when humanity segregates itself from those deemed unworthy or too burdensome to be helped along. Guru was the evil entity Ol' Man Wicks knew existed.

"Do you believe this fucking guy?" Ruppert pondered with amazement.

"Believe him!" Craig shot back. "Get them the fuck out of here," he commanded. Without hesitation, the officers, followed by Agent Johnson, grabbed Uhlen and Guru and marched them out of the basement. As soon as they disappeared, Mr. Waters walked up to me and held out his hand.

"I just want you to know, Mr. Pickles, that the Unified Insurance Company will be paying Sandra and Lucy's claim in full," he said.

"Well, that's damn generous of you, Mr. Waters, since it was Unified Insurance Company's agents that killed them," I said, ignoring his handshake. "My guess is that Unified will be paying quite a bit more than twenty grand," I said as condescendingly as I could.

"Well, yes, um, of course, you're right. I'm going to go outside now," he said, fumbling for words before turning and running for the door.

"Ruppert!" Craig called out, walking over and shaking the gangster's hand.

"A pleasure doing business with you, Mr. Aaronson," Ruppert replied while accepting the handshake.

"You saved a lot of people's lives today," Craig said seriously.

"…And I was compensated nicely," Ruppert said, holding up the papers Craig had given him.

"Yeah, I guess. Stay out of trouble, all right?" Craig laughed as the two men smiled at each other, as if acknowledging a job well done.

"Always my priority, Mr. Aaronson," Ruppert replied before Craig turned away to address the rest of us.

"Gentlemen, I have to accompany the Nazis downtown, but I'll need to get statements from everyone, especially you, Ron," he said, handing each of us a business card. Once he finished, he turned towards me to shake my hand before pulling me in for a hug. "I know you've been through hell this past week, but you were the one who brought this to an end."

"I'm just glad it's over," I said as we backed away from each other.

"I know Ron. Trust me, I know," he said with sympathetic eyes.

"I wish I would have known you were this big-time undercover agent, you asshole," I griped.

"You didn't think it was more fun this way?" he asked with feigned disbelief.

"Oh yeah, this was fucking a riot," I snorted.

"Maybe you should come work for us and see how fun it really is," he said with a hint of seriousness in his voice.

"I couldn't even get in the electrician's union. I doubt anyone in the government would be interested in hiring me," I laughed.

"Well, I spoke to my director about you, and he thought you might be a nice fit for our department. Something you should consider. Hey, I gotta get those guys processed, but you and I will get a chance to talk about all of this later," he said with a wink before turning and heading for the door.

"For sure," I said, surprised at the offer as he walked away. "Hey, Craig, when do you need me downtown?" I called out as an afterthought.

"I'll be in touch," he said with a wave as he hurried out the door.

"Hey, Ron, Otis and I will wait for you outside," Meadows said as they shook hands with Ruppert and Mosley and followed Craig out the door.

"Hey, don't go nowhere. I need a ride back to my car," I called out as they left. It felt strange being left alone with Ruppert and Mosley now that everything was over, and I took a deep breath before getting ready to leave.

"So, how are you doing, Mr. Pickles?" Ruppert asked as I walked up to say goodbye. I looked down at the floor and shook my head, taking a deep breath before looking up at him with a forced smile. He shook his head, as if admonishing me before speaking.

"It wasn't your fault. There wasn't a damn thing you could have done," he said, as if reading my mind.

"She'd still be alive today if I hadn't come into her life," I said with a deep sigh and contemplative expression on my face.

"The only people responsible for killing those girls are the people who killed those girls. That's just the way it works," he said.

"Boss is right, Mr. Pickles," Mosley interjected.

"The boss is always right," I said, turning to humor him.

"Naw, I ain't fucking around," Mosley said seriously. "These two motherfuckers were certifiable. I know you lost your girl, but these cats were crazy. They killed people by the thousands forty years ago and thought nothing of murdering moms and kids today. That shit needed to stop, and you stopped it," he concluded.

"*We* stopped it, Mosley," I corrected before turning back towards Ruppert. "This dude is amazing," I said, tossing Mosley some kudos.

"Yeah, Mosley will put it together every now and then, but he still fucks up my McDonald's order every goddamn time," Ruppert chuckled.

"Why you got to do me like that, boss?" Mosley snorted as we all laughed at the quip.

"Seriously, guys, I could never thank you enough for what you've done here. I owe you my life," I said, extending a hand. Ruppert grabbed my hand with a firm soul shake and pulled me in for a chest bump before putting a hand on my shoulder.

"You are welcome, Mr. Pickles. You're a good man. You don't see color; you see people. I knew that the first time we met back there in the projects," Ruppert said with a smile.

"Seems like a lifetime ago," I lamented before cracking a smile.

"What are you thinking?" he asked at my change of demeanor.

"Ruppert, I think you missed your calling."

"How's that, Mr. Pickles?"

"Instead of running a street gang, you should run for Congress," I said with a smile.

"Oh man, that's a dirty business," he laughed.

"You'd be great at it," I laughed.

"Gang leader turned congressman, huh? Hell, anything's possible in Chicago," he said with a sigh as I walked over to shake hands with the bandito.

"What the fuck is that?" Mosley asked with a frown.

"What do you mean?" I asked with apprehension while looking at the hand I was offering.

"He gets a hug because he's the boss, and I don't get shit," Mosley moaned.

"I didn't hug him," I laughed while looking over at Ruppert.

"That big motherfucker wants a hug, Mr. Pickles. You better give him a hug," Ruppert insisted with a hearty laugh.

"You guys kill me," I said, wrapping my arms around Mosley, then getting a soul shake before heading for the door.

"Take care of that collie, Mr. Pickles," Mosley called out as I turned around and smiled at them one last time.

"…And stay the fuck out of the ghetto," Ruppert chortled.

"Take care, gentlemen," I said, choking back a tear as I walked out the door. Slowly, I walked up the stairs and turned down the gangway leading to the front of the building, completely drained by the enormity of what had just taken place. In contrast, Ray and Otis were waiting on the sidewalk as if nothing had happened. Ray was puffing mightily on his pipe while Otis stood there stroking his beard as I walked up to greet them.

"I don't know about you guys, but catching Nazis makes me hungry," I said, taking a deep breath of the mid-day air.

"Shit, Pickles, I could eat something," Otis growled.

"Tell me this ain't the perfect time to get some liver and onions," Meadows said with a puff of smoke and a healthy dose of enthusiasm. Otis and I looked at each other with blank expressions before busting out in laughter.

"Fuck that shit, Pickles. Let's get some liver and onions!" Otis bellowed.

"Anything but buffalo," I howled as we headed for the car.

THE END

Made in the USA
Columbia, SC
25 July 2024